Studies in European Culture and History

edited by

Eric D. Weitz and Jack Zipes
University of Minnesota

Since the fall of the Berlin Wall and the collapse of communism, the very meaning of Europe has been opened up and is in the process of being redefined. European states and societies are wrestling with the expansion of NATO and the European Union and with new streams of immigration, while a renewed and reinvigorated cultural interaction has emerged between East and West. But the fast-paced transformations of the last fifteen years also have deeper historical roots. The reconfiguring of contemporary Europe is entwined with the cataclysmic events of the twentieth century, two world wars and the Holocaust, and with the processes of modernity that, since the eighteenth century, have shaped Europe and its engagement with the rest of the world.

Studies in European Culture and History is dedicated to publishing books that explore major issues in Europe's past and present from a wide variety of disciplinary perspectives. The works in the series are interdisciplinary; they focus on culture and society and deal with significant developments in Western and Eastern Europe from the eighteenth century to the present within a social historical context. With its broad span of topics, geography, and chronology, the series aims to publish the most interesting and innovative work on modern Europe.

Series titles

Fascism and Neofascism: Critical Writings on the Radical Right in Europe
Edited by Angelica Fenner and Eric D. Weitz

Fictive Theories: Towards a Deconstructive and Utopian Political Imagination
Susan McManus

German-Jewish Literature in the Wake of the Holocaust: Grete Weil, Ruth Klüger, and the Politics of Address
Pascale R. Bos

Exile, Science, and Bildung: The Contested Legacies of German Intellectual Figures
Edited by David Kettler and Gerhard Lauer

Transformations of the New Germany
Edited by Ruth Starkman

The Turkish Turn in Contemporary German Literature: Towards a New Critical Grammar of Migration
Leslie A. Adelson

Terror and the Sublime in Art and Critical Theory: From Auschwitz to Hiroshima to September 11
Gene Ray

German-Jewish Literature in the Wake of the Holocaust

Grete Weil, Ruth Klüger, and the Politics of Address

Pascale R. Bos

palgrave
macmillan

GERMAN–JEWISH LITERATURE IN THE WAKE OF THE HOLOCAUST
© Pascale R. Bos, 2005.

First published in 2005 by
PALGRAVE MACMILLAN™
175 Fifth Avenue, New York, N.Y. 10010 and
Houndmills, Basingstoke, Hampshire, England RG21 6XS
Companies and representatives throughout the world.

PALGRAVE MACMILLAN is the global academic imprint of the Palgrave Macmillan division of St. Martin's Press, LLC and of Palgrave Macmillan Ltd. Macmillan® is a registered trademark in the United States, United Kingdom and other countries. Palgrave is a registered trademark in the European Union and other countries.

ISBN 1–4039–6657–5

Library of Congress Cataloging-in-Publication Data

Bos, Pascale R.
    German-Jewish literature in the wake of the Holocaust : Grete Weil, Ruth Klüger, and the politics of address / Pascale R. Bos.
        p. cm.— (Studies in European culture and history)
    Includes bibliographical references and index.
    ISBN 1–4039–6657–5 (alk. paper)
        1. Weil, Grete, 1906—Criticism and interpretation. 2. Klüger, Ruth, 1931—Criticism and interpretation. 3. German literature—Jewish authors—History and criticism. I. Title. II. Series.

PT2647.E4157Z57 2005
830.9'8924—dc22   2004043197

A catalogue record for this book is available from the British Library.

Design by Newgen Imaging Systems (P) Ltd., Chennai, India.

First edition: June 2005

10 9 8 7 6 5 4 3 2 1

Printed in the United States of America.

Ter nagedachtenis aan mijn opa
Jules (Juda) Isaac Erwteman (1911–1943) Auschwitz-Birkenau
en oma
Jetty (Henriëtte) Rozenberg (1912–1998) Amsterdam

CONTENTS

ACKNOWLEDGMENTS

This book could not have been written without the help of many dear friends and without several forms of institutional support. I thank the Hadassah International Research Institute on Jewish Women at Brandeis for their Senior Research Grant, the University of Texas at Austin, which awarded me a Summer Research Assignment Grant early on in my working on this book, and two Dean's Fellowships at a later stage, all of which allowed me invaluable time off from teaching. Thanks go out to my wonderful University of Texas colleagues Lisa Moore and Katie Arens and former DAAD visiting professor Barbara Wolbert for their constant encouragement, thoughtful reading of several chapters, and insightful comments. Many thanks also to Maria Brewer, Naomi Scheman, Ruth Ellen Joeres, Arlene Teraoka, and especially Jack Zipes for their advice during a much earlier phase of this project, as well as to my friend Rebecca Raham.

I further wish to express my gratitude to a number of colleagues whom I have had the pleasure of getting to know in the past few years and who have deepened or changed my understanding of the field of Holocaust Studies and whose work has inspired me: Marianne Hirsch, Leslie Morris, Sara Horowitz, Irene Kacandes, Gary Weissman, Michael Rothberg, Susan Rubin Suleiman, and Ken Jacobson. I also thank the participants and the faculty of the 2003 Faculty Summer seminar on Holocaust literature organized by the USHMM's Center for Advanced Holocaust Studies as their discussions and readings were enlightening to me in quite unexpected ways. Thanks to my parents, Eelco and Anita Bos, in whose home my love for literature and for critical debate was first instilled and honed, to my sister Jacqueline, to my friends Neena Husid and Hillary Miller for readings of my work and support, and to my students who challenge me with their questions and who make my life as an academic feel meaningful. Finally, thanks go out to Aliza for so many years of love and support, and to my little *boefjes* Eytan and Matan for being such a wonderful distraction.

PREFACE

It is rarely noted how astounding it is that some Holocaust survivors came to write about their wartime experiences at all. Very few survivors who did write would publish their writing, yet, it is often overlooked how exceptional the existence of these publications is. How were these survivors able to tell their stories, to write about them, and to open themselves up in this fashion to the public? What did it take to be able do so? How did they find an opening for themselves and their audience to be able to narrate this story? At the same time, we rarely acknowledge how strongly indebted those of us who were not there are to this literature in coming to any kind of understanding of what it was like then, there, in hell on earth. It has been sixty years, both the length of a lifetime and the blink of an eye removed from the present, but it is the reading of this literature that still provides one of the most profound confrontations with this reality, a brief glimpse of what it was like to encounter this kind of violence and to have to endure this kind of suffering.

The question of how and why survivors wrote, and what impact their literature had, for themselves, and within the cultures in which they published their narratives in not a common one. It is the kind of question that does not sound theoretically sophisticated, it is *messy*, seemingly, and somewhat taboo. It is the kind of question that does not get asked within literary studies because author's intent and the writing process are not supposed to matter, they are not relevant to our literary inquiry. What matters is *our* reading of this literature, and what we write on is precisely that: how *we* read this or that particular text. I have always found this premise somewhat disturbing, first while working within feminist studies, and more strongly even while working within Holocaust studies. How could we argue that it *never* matters who or what an author is, how and when they wrote their texts, in what circumstances, and with what aim? How can we argue that the literature is only relevant as text, and not as statements that serve social, political, and cultural functions out in the world as well?

In my years of working on Holocaust literature, I came to realize that these questions are always relevant to me, and perhaps more so because of my own background. This background, as it turns out, matters more than I was willing to explore for myself or admit to others. Yet, I have had to. As Kalí Tal suggests, cultural criticism is a self-conscious act, "one in which the critic acknowledges that her choice of subject has meaning, and that a choice of subject is itself open to interpretation."[1] That is, as cultural critics we "seek to establish a mode of discourse in which each person can first uncover and acknowledge his or her beliefs, and then test them, compare them to the beliefs of others, understand their implications, and modify them to reflect a changing understanding of the world" (5). In putting myself out there as a critic it is necessary to be clear as to who I am, and how this background may matter.

As someone born in the mid-1960s who grew up in a family in Amsterdam, the Netherlands in which on my mother's side almost everyone was hunted down and murdered by the Nazis, and in which there was such an overabundance of what I call "impossible" memories among the survivors, creating a palpable presence of absence, of what could not be said, thought, or otherwise touched upon, Holocaust literature provided for me an important window unto a historical reality that was at the same time also a family story that I did not otherwise have access to. Although I came to puzzle together the story of my family bit by bit over the years through pieces of conversation with my grandmother with whom I was quite close, much of what I wondered about constituted impossible questions, that is: questions with impossibly revolting answers. Instead, I sought to put some of my questions to rest by voraciously reading memoirs and autobiographical literature by survivors. Without being aware of it as a teenager, I gravitated to survivor stories that filled in the particular blanks of my family history. I read much on the experiences of Auschwitz (where my grandfather worked as a doctor in the sick barracks of Birkenau before being killed at age thirty-one), I read much on Dutch Jews, and on living in hiding.

Many of the family stories were too overwhelming, too painful to deal with and I waited a long time to explore the specifics. What I did not dare imagine was my grandfather's life and death in Birkenau (of illness, starvation, gas?), the train ride and arrival of both sets of great-grandparents to Birkenau and Sobibor respectively, and what awaited them there (swift industrial-style killing), the separation from her husband that my mother's aunt endured in Auschwitz and her death together with her ten-year-old son in the gas chambers. I know of their last moments only because of Primo Levi, Gerhard Durlacher, Tadeusz Borowski, Ruth Klüger: other inmates who were selected to live (as slaves, briefly, the very few who made it through) and who witnessed these events, and were able and compelled to bear witness afterwards. Their literature does more than function as testimony in a historical sense for me: it confronts a reality that remained unspeakable in my family.

Then there were my other questions, less extreme, but equally impossible nevertheless: how did my mother and grandmother rebuild their postwar lives after such enormous losses? What psychological mechanisms did they and the Jewish community in which they returned devise to ward off or deny the reality of this all-encompassing loss? Were silence and (attempts at) forgetting the only possible way to move on? What had it meant for them to be "made into" a Jew as mostly strongly assimilated middle-class Jews? Was their ambivalent, complex sense of Jewishness after the war a direct result of this persecution?

The speech acts these Holocaust memoirs and novels represent for me are so significant as they embody the exact opposite of the silence in the family and culture in which I grew up. Not only did this literature give me some sense of what the answers to these questions would look like (if only I dared to ask them, and if only they could be answered), as an act that asserts survivors' sense of self, their survival, and that addresses those who had stood by (or even aided in) their persecution, I found this writing an incredibly powerful statement about agency.

Because I read this literature not primarily with the eyes of a scholar but as someone who comes from a family and a community of survivors in which silence rather than speech has been the norm, I have been particularly intrigued by this ability of some to speak of the Holocaust. Even if my questions would remain unanswered, I felt that they needed to be asked: what were the mechanisms through which these authors were able to write about what they had seen, what they had experienced? Why could they speak while so few others did? What compelled them to bear witness, to write, and to publish for a European audience that approached this history in general and Holocaust survivors specifically at best in a neutral and more often in an antagonistic fashion? From where did they find the strength to speak back to this world that had sought to annihilate them, and now wished to silence this story? What does it mean to speak up, to demand an audience, to appeal to an audience to engage with the most wrenching moral failure of recent Western history?

In part, I came to see these kinds of publications as reflecting the need for survivors' reintegration: a desire to find a bridge between what has happened to them during the years of persecution, the prewar past, and the present. For assimilated Jews in particular, the need to reconnect to a national community from which they had been excluded by force was important, for it was not the Jewish collective to which they felt most strongly tied and to which they could return to make sense of their experiences. In some cases, this literature indeed seemed to function precisely this way: the author's words were heeded, the literature was widely read within their national culture, remained in print over the years, and sometimes the survivor even continued to write and became a celebrated author in his or her own right. These cases, however, were rare. More often, this literature was not received enthusiastically, was not reprinted (or was never even published), and only became part of a more widely read genre when the Holocaust had finally transformed politically and culturally from a source of private Jewish grief to a foundation for new national and European self-understanding.[2] That is, not until the late 1980s, profoundly belated, four decades after the fact.

Considering these serious difficulties for survivors to find an audience in Europe more broadly, it were the cases of German and Austrian Holocaust literature that intrigued me especially. Seeking a kind of return and psychological and cultural reintegration and finding an audience was even more complicated for assimilated Jews in countries where the Nazis had come to power and found full support in the national community, such as Germany and Austria. To what kind of a community were German- or Austrian-Jewish survivors appealing with their works? What did such an appeal mean? It is this peculiar literature in which survivors address not just an audience of compatriots, but of compatriots who were also their persecutors, which for me has come to serve as the most complex yet paradigmatic case for coming to understand survivor literature's near impossible attempt at address more broadly. The possibility of speaking at all in a situation in which survivor authors needed to anticipate their audience's antagonism is quite astonishing. What did it take to come to appeal to such an audience? What did it mean to come to speak of this experience? How did the audience respond, and what did this response mean to these authors? It is questions like these, which stem in part directly from my own experience of growing up in a family and a Jewish community of postwar Western European Jews dominated by silence, that led me to investigate the authors and the cultural history with which this study deals.

This book does not answer all these questions, and in the many years of working on it, I came to realize that one of the answers I initially had deemed most urgent turned out to be less relevant later on. Rather than the psychological explanation that I had been looking for, it were the texts themselves which came to compel me. Their richness, their forceful response to the particular cultural climate in which they were written, the complex strategies they employed in trying to engage and interpellate their audience intrigued me. I thus came to seek a fuller confrontation with what this literature is telling us, what kind of (speech) acts it represents, and the cultural impact it has had.

I wanted to explore what it means to "return" in writing, to assert one self after the annihilation of the Holocaust. What does the response of the German audience and the critics to this literature suggest about their willingness or their ability to confront this past throughout the past decades, from the mid-1940s to the mid-1990s? Were the 1980s, which are often seen as a pivotal moment in the cultural recognition of Jewish survivors' trauma in Western Europe (and which I certainly personally experienced as an important break in terms of the public discourse on the Holocaust in the Netherlands), truly the decade that generated significant change upon which the debates of the 1990s simply expanded? This study represents a search for these answers.

CHAPTER ONE

INTRODUCTION

In 1980, the German-Jewish author Grete Weil published the autobiographical novel *Meine Schwester Antigone*. Through an innovative rewriting of Sophocles' Antigone myth, the novel both deals with the protagonist's wartime experiences under the Nazis (exile in Amsterdam, her husband's deportation and death at the Mauthausen concentration camp, her survival in hiding) and also presents a critique of late-1970s German culture and its failed attempt at *Vergangenheitsbewältigung* (confronting the past). The novel won great acclaim in Germany, and Weil was awarded several literary prizes for this and a subsequent novel, *Der Brautpreis* (1988). A few years later, in 1992, Ruth Klüger, an American of Austrian-Jewish descent, published the German-language memoir *weiter leben: Eine Jugend*, which recounts a childhood under Hitler in Austria, deportation and survival in several concentration camps, subsequent postwar life in the United States, and the complex relationship of Jews to present-day Germans and things German. The book became a bestseller in Germany and was hailed by one critic as a "Miracle of Language" with which Klüger achieved a "return" to Germany.[1]

These two Jewish survivor authors' considerable critical success in Germany in the 1980s and 1990s at once marks the radically changed reception that literature by Austrian- and German-Jewish authors received at this time (which in turn seems indicative of the cultural changes in Germany that had created a greater willingness to confront the Holocaust)[2] and the *belated* and even *displaced* nature of this success.[3] For in Weil's case, her achievement had been many decades in the making. After returning from exile in the Netherlands she published three literary works (in 1949 in East Berlin, as no publisher in the Western zone was interested, and in West Germany in 1962 and 1968), all of which found little resonance with a German audience. Profoundly disappointed with this lack of response, when Weil published her Antigone novel many years later, she did so with a Swiss press, not a German publisher. She was already in her mid-seventies when her work finally won critical acclaim. In the case of Klüger, her work had to literally cross thousands of miles to reach its audience, as the author had resided in the United States and not Germany for nearly forty years. Furthermore, she chose to publish the memoir in Germany, not in her native Austria, and dedicated it explicitly to a German audience. Her success, then, was both displaced and belated, and in more than one way less self-evidently a "return" than the German critic in his review of her work suggested.

This study examines both the cultural moment that marked the literary success of Jewish authors such as Weil and Klüger in the 1980s and the (early) 1990s in Germany (and the decades of marginalization of Jewish voices that preceded this success), and the particular "return" their textual address to the German audience represents. After all, because both authors stem from assimilated bourgeois Jewish homes, their "return" to Germany in the form of their work is anything but self-evident. For this group of Jews, the Nazi persecution had brought about a traumatic shift in identity. Not only were they assigned a particularly problematic kind of racial Jewish identity through legislation enacted by their own governments, but they also became isolated from their national culture with which they had strongly identified, for as Jews they could no longer be German or Austrian.

For Weil and Klüger and other (upper-)middle-class, highly acculturated Jewish *Bildungsbürger*, the question of what German and Jewish identity were and meant went through a particularly dramatic transition.[4] For whereas they had previously identified only marginally with a Jewish religious tradition, to become identified through Nazi legal discourse as a "racial" Jew, and to become persecuted as such, constituted a major caesura in their self-perception. Once the war was over and the scale of the destruction of European Jewry became known, the political and legal failure of German-Jewishness as a viable national identity seemed underscored.

As a result, the majority of German and Austrian Jews in the first decades after 1945 saw themselves as having to make a choice. They would either live as Jews, but no longer in Germany or Austria (or even Europe altogether), or have to renounce Jewishness and live as Germans or Austrians only.[5] Nevertheless, for a small group of German and Austrian Jews, often those who had been most assimilated and who had considered themselves to be as German as the Germans (and for Austrian Jews, this meant being strongly German-identified, culturally), this question of identity remained unresolved and of central importance. What then could they be, if they could no longer be German or Austrian? Jean Améry, an assimilated Jewish-Viennese intellectual who fled to Belgium after the *Anschluß* of Austria in 1938 and who survived both torture at the hands of the Gestapo and imprisonment at Auschwitz, would two decades after the war formulate this sense of estrangement as follows:

> Suddenly, the past was buried and one no longer knew who one was. . . . My identity was bound to a plain German name and to the dialect of my immediate place of origin. But since the day when an official decree forbade me to wear the folk costume that I had worn almost exclusively from early childhood on, I no longer permitted myself the dialect. Then the name . . . no longer made sense either. . . . And my friends, too . . . were obliterated . . . everything that had filled my consciousness—from the history of my country, which was no longer mine, to the landscape images . . . —had become intolerable to me . . . I was a person who could no longer say "we" and who therefore said "I" merely out of habit, but not with the feeling of full possession of my self.[6]

Améry, who had been called Hans Maier before 1938, never returned to Austria, for after seven years in exile and imprisonment, he no longer felt it was his home: "When my country lost its national independence on March 12, 1938 . . . it became totally alien to me" (55). It is not just that he lost his sense of national belonging, but rather, that German-Jewish and Austrian-Jewish identity had been made retroactively unimaginable: "We . . . had to realize that it had never been ours. For us, whatever was linked with this land and its people was an existential misunderstanding" (50). Although the longing for his native country, its landscape, its language, would remain strong for Améry, after his liberation he returned not to Austria but to Belgium, where he committed suicide in 1978.

Just as for Améry, the reconciliation of identity remained elusive for most assimilated German and Austrian Jews, and few would in fact return "home." Those few German and Austrian survivors who did decide to return soon realized that the attempt to reconcile the different aspects of their identity would prove difficult. Their sense of self was no longer shaped by a merger of two clearly and positively defined cultural poles (Germanness and Jewishness); instead, the Holocaust had become the defining factor in their identity. Dan Diner has called this kind of relationship, in which the postwar life of German Jews is determined in a thoroughly negative fashion by their relationship with non-Jewish Germans and by the Holocaust, a "negative symbiosis."[7] This form of German-Jewish symbiosis is not based on a mutual and fruitful exchange, but refers to the fact that the self-conception of both Germans and Jews became interdependent because of the shared history of the Holocaust. The same can be seen among Austrian Jews.

German-Jewish Literature as Address and "Return"

Yet, it is also possible to conceive of a different form of Jewish "return" to Germany. This study argues through the cases of Grete Weil and Ruth Klüger that some German and Austrian Jews would indeed come back to Germany, not in order to try to return to "what was lost," that is, as an act of mourning or nostalgia, but to publicly call Germans into a dialogue about the Nazi past.[8] Through the creation of a provocative literary discourse, they brought to the public attention the continued presence of this tainted past and the complexities of postwar German-Jewish relations. Thus, although Weil's and Klüger's work seeks to actively engage with questions of postwar German and Jewish identity and belonging, it does so both to describe the alienating effects of racial persecution and to try to call their German compatriots into some sort of a (new) relationship. This literature *creates an address*: a German audience is appealed to explicitly and invited into a dialogue about the role of the Holocaust and of (German) Jews in contemporary German culture, discourse, and national identity.

I take Weil and Klüger as paradigmatic cases for what really presents itself as a cluster of novels and autobiographical works by (Austro-)German Jews published in Germany in the 1980s and early 1990s. Although one could look at different periods in which Jewish literature was published in Germany after 1945, and at the works of a range of different Jewish authors, the literature published during the particularly culturally and politically volatile era from the late 1970s to the early 1990s (which saw a resurgence of political conservatism and a dramatic reconfiguration of German national history, identity, and memory after reunification) represents the emergence of a new kind of critical public Jewish discourse. Unlike the occasional breakthrough of a Jewish author writing in German about the Holocaust, for instance in the late 1940s, (Ilse Aichinger's successful childhood fable of a half-Jew under the Nazis in *Die größere Hoffnung* from 1948), in the 1950s (the poetry of exile author Paul Celan, stories by Aichinger), in the 1960s (Hilde Domin's and Rose Ausländer's poetry, Peter Weiss's plays, Jean Améry's essays), and in the 1970s (the prose of Jurek Becker, Jakov Lind, and Edgar Hilserath), the amount of work published from 1980 on, and the acclaim it garnered throughout the next decade, needs to be seen as a significant change from earlier periods.

The authors of most of this Jewish literature published during the 1980s and 1990s were, however, German and Austrian Jews of a younger generation, born after the war. They include such authors as Maxim Biller, Rafael Seligmann, Ronnith Neumann, Barbara Honigmann, Esther Discherheit, Lea Fleischmann, Ruth Beckermann, Irene Dische, and Robert Schindel.[9] Klüger and Weil are indeed quite exceptional as successful survivor authors, as few German and Austrian Jews of this survivor generation wrote literary works addressed to a German audience. The majority of survivors had settled elsewhere after the war, and if they wrote at all, very few did so in German. That is, whereas aging survivors in the United States in particular started to publish memoirs in large numbers in the late 1980s and 1990s, this was not the case in Germany. Furthermore, the small number of authors who did so rarely produced work of the quality of either Weil or Klüger.[10] What therefore makes Weil's and Klüger's address so remarkable is that unlike the postwar Jewish authors in Germany for whom Nazi persecution was a national and a familial legacy but not a personal experience, Klüger and Weil do write from this personal experience of exclusion, isolation, and genocidal persecution. Consequently, their work represents a particularly powerful and difficult kind of voice to deal with for a German audience.

The fact that they found success in spite of this reluctant audience is significant, and seems to suggest that these two authors employed a particular set of strategies in their literature that made it possible for a German public to engage with it. A careful reading of these authors' works furthermore reveals how important a statement it is to write as a former victim and address a nation of perpetrators and descendants of perpetrators. Such an act has political, cultural, and considerable personal implications, all of which are considered here.

What makes Weil's and Klüger's work of this period exemplary and stand out from the (few) other memoirs by German-Jewish Holocaust survivors published during this period (and what accounts at least in part for their success), moreover, is their effort to rise above the documentary impulse of the eyewitness testimony. Unlike many survivor memoirs that attempt to eliminate all obvious signs of "style" for a semblance of objectivity,[11] Klüger and Weil show an acute awareness of the constructed nature of their narratives, and neither author's works recount the actual events of (respectively) escape, exile, hiding, or imprisonment in a straightforward documentary fashion. Instead, their works are sophisticated, semiautobiographical narratives that explicitly problematize memory and the limits of language and of imagination in the face of the Holocaust. This self-awareness makes them particularly relevant to this study, which investigates the Jewish attempt to engage the Germans in an exchange about the Nazi past and the German-Jewish present, and also examines how the literature describes the effects of Nazi persecution on (upper-)middle-class, highly assimilated Jews when it first occurred, how this reification was dealt with, and the role that autobiographical writing plays in this process.

Moreover, not only does the work of Grete Weil and Ruth Klüger display an unusual array of compelling new strategies in engaging a German public and reflect the changed nature of this literature with its explicit *address* to a German audience, but their respective lives and careers also intersect in interesting ways with broader cultural and political currents in the Germany of this period. Hence, a discussion of Weil's and Klüger's lives and literature allows for a view of this particular period and its transformation of German-Jewish relations, as well as the decades of exclusion and near silence that preceded it. Weil and Klüger also have a similar kind of assimilated Jewish background that is unique to the particular history of German and Austrian Jews in the early twentieth century. Born in 1906 in Southern Germany and 1930 in Vienna, respectively, Weil came from an upper-middle-class family and Klüger from a middle-class home, and their sense of ethnic identity represents the most common variety of German-Jewishness of this period: although Klüger is Austrian and Weil is German, as assimilated Jews they both identify with German culture and *Bildung* (a typical middle-class German notion of personal cultivation in High culture and of personal improvement with strong moral overtones that emerged in the nineteenth century). As I investigate the notion of (assimilated Jewish) identity and how a sense of both Germanness and Jewishness could (or could not) be sustained during and after the war, their divergent stories open up a window into the significance of these different kinds of experiences and their impact on identity.

Weil fled to the Netherlands in the mid-1930s and lived in hiding in Amsterdam for the last eighteen months of the war; Klüger was deported from Vienna and survived several concentration camps, including Auschwitz. Both Weil and Klüger write on what it meant to those who felt "more German than the Germans" to lose German citizenship, and on the other side of this "loss," what the imposed "gain" of racial Jewish identity meant. Their work suggests what the possibilities and limits of writing are in terms of sorting through this kind of sustained crisis of identity.

What consequently connects these two authors' literary projects (and at the same time distinguishes them from other survivor literature and second-generation literature in German) is that they both published in the 1980s and 1990s autobiographical texts in the German language that sought to intervene in a German public discourse on the Nazi past through a form of explicit address, and that their texts succeeded in finding an unprecedented large German audience and critical response. In so doing, they changed the literary landscape in Germany as they mustered in the return of the critical German-Jewish voice.

Even though both authors wrote autobiographical literature in German and published these texts in Germany, their address nevertheless represents different kinds of projects that received different kinds of public response. Whereas Weil (at age forty) returned to Germany from Amsterdam soon after the war ended and (unsuccessfully) attempted to get her literary career off the ground (i.e., find a German audience for her work), Klüger left Europe for the United States as a teenager in 1949 and, apart from brief professional visits, returned to Germany (and not Austria) in the 1990s only in the form of her publications. (Klüger publishes texts in the German language in Germany, but she maintains her residence in California.) Thus, whereas a discussion of Weil's early publication history reveals the profound difficulties of engaging a German audience of the 1950s and 1960s in any form of dialogue with living Jews, and her work in the 1980s suggests the effects of certain cultural shifts that allowed for a different reception, Klüger's work in the 1990s not only problematizes this dialogue, but also questions the possibility of an *actual* Jewish return to Germany, or Austria.

Public Address/Personal Closure

In the following study, the particular "return" Weil's and Klüger's textual address represents is read in two ways. First, I show how one may read these works as forms of testimony by survivor-witnesses that carry an emancipating potential for the authors. As autobiographical texts written by subjects who were discriminated against and marginalized, these texts can provide a space to reformulate identity, renegotiate agency, and make sense of a life story fragmented by persecution and trauma.[12] The notion of reading Holocaust literature this way—both as public address and as highly personal and complex attempts at witnessing that bridge the then and the now, the traumatic and the everyday (i.e., as a form of testimony)—has not yet been fully explored within German-Jewish literature. In Holocaust and trauma studies, however, much recent work on testimony suggests that the articulation of one's own story can be a powerful act that reasserts a former victim's sense of agency. Being able to articulate one's memories is significant in that it may provide a measure of psychic control, as Dominick LaCapra suggests:

> When the past becomes accessible to recall in memory, and when language functions to provide some measure of conscious control, critical distance, and perspective, one has begun the arduous process of working over and through trauma in a fashion that may never bring full transcendence. . . . but which may enable processes of judgment and at least limited liability and ethically responsibility agency. These processes are crucial for laying ghosts to rest, distancing oneself from haunting revenants, renewing interest in life . . .[13]

For survivors of severe trauma, finding words for what they went through while speaking or writing may have an inherently liberating effect, and for Holocaust survivors perhaps especially so, as their experiences are considered to be so far outside of the realm of the "normal" that they are difficult to communicate to those who were not present.[14]

In my reading of the German-Jewish works of Weil and Klüger as testimony of trauma, I not only employ a nonspecific, generalized notion of Holocaust trauma, but I argue that what is an understanding of the (Austro-)German-Jewish experience is a very *specific* trauma: the process of reification, or of objectification, which was experienced both *during* and *after* the war.[15] First, the self-perception and self-definition of German Jews as full members of the German nation changed dramatically when a new legally imposed racial definition went into effect under the Nazis. Even though the Nazi conception of Jewishness could not "scientifically" be tied to race and still rested on institutional ties rather than blood, the effects of the racial laws were no less destructive as they relegated, as Ken Jacobson suggests, "a whole range of people—irrespective of how they lived, what they believed, or who or what they took themselves to be—to a single group, whose limits were created by the Nazis themselves."[16] Being singled out for persecution purely on the basis of a racial construct altered both the meaning of Jewish and of German identity, and it became increasingly difficult for German Jews to retain a sense of dignity, of creating, "out of this sense of imposed difference a meaningful sense of one's own identity."[17] Jews became increasingly socially isolated, an isolation that was in many cases experienced as psychologically deadly.[18] This process by which Jewishness was imposed and by which Germanness was lost, was psychologically highly problematic as it competed with other forms of

self-definition that were more essential. This objectification proved difficult to overcome, even after the war. What was left of one's identity if it could no longer be German?

Second, not only were (Austro-)German Jews reified through the *discursive* racialization of the Nuremberg race laws and through the experience of *actual* racial
persecution, but after the war this process of reification continued through the use
of a discourse of medical–pathological difference. Traumatized survivors were seen as
"damaged goods," or as having "regressed" to an "infantile state," as their trauma was
interpreted as the expression of an earlier neurosis, as pathogenic. This discourse stems
in part from the inability of the medical community to grasp the full psychological or
cultural implications of the Holocaust in the first years after the war. Furthermore,
mental health specialists worked from within a Freudian psychoanalytic paradigm
that proved wholly inadequate,[19] and that led to misdiagnoses of profound trauma as
rooted in childhood, instead of in the experiences of Nazi persecution.[20] Although
within two decades the tide had turned, as new research was now conducted specifically
on what would come to be known as the "KZ" or "survivor's syndrome,"[21] these diag-
noses were experienced by survivors as value judgments, and as a further attack on their
integrity. To make matters worse, much of the early findings were reflected in published
studies, which over time led to a number of pervasive misconceptions about survivors
and survivor trauma.[22] Thus, after reification by the Nazis, (Austro-)German-Jewish
survivors now saw themselves faced with more reification, this time in the name of
science, and in the terminology of psychopathology. As Jack Terry suggests, within the
medical community "The survivor has been avoided, blamed, 'syndromized,' exploited,
and rarely understood, even by those who profess to support his best interests."[23]

Both of these forms of reification greatly complicated survivors' ability to articulate
for themselves who and what they were both during and after the war, and what their
experiences meant to them. This process of estrangement through internalization of
racial objectification and the different forms of postwar reification is articulated repeatedly in both authors' works. Grete Weil, for instance, comments on the effects of Nazi
racialization as follows: "We are no longer what we were until only recently. At least not
in the eyes of the others. But you cannot undergo a change in the eyes of others without
your own sense of self changing as well."[24] Klüger describes the experience of postwar
reification in the encounter with a Jewish-Viennese psychiatrist in New York shortly after
the war. "It was as if, in the person of this Jewish doctor, the Nazis obtained a spiritual
authority they had never had for me in Germany, in the sense that here was a man who
didn't let me be what I was (and that implies, does it not, a denial of the right to live and
is a kind of death sentence)...."[25]

This study shows how Weil's and Klüger's autobiographical texts can be read as
attempts at overcoming these kinds of reification that lead to estrangement from the
self. As the writing of the life story into fiction or into (complex) memoir discursively
repositions survivor authors in a post-Holocaust world, it allows them to formulate
their experiences differently for themselves and assign their own meaning to them.

Besides tracing the emancipating potential of these textual returns, the second way
in which these literary texts are read in this study is as products of a specific political
and cultural discourse in the 1970s and 1980s in West Germany in which this literature at the same time attempts to intervene. For their appeal to the German public at
this particular moment in which it seemed more eager to move away from a serious

consideration of the implications of that past is striking. By publishing this work in the German language in the country in which they were formerly persecuted, and inter-pellating this national discussion about the Nazi past at a moment that proved to be a critical juncture, Weil and Klüger moved their private, emotional, and psychological battle of exclusion from, and persecution by, the national community of their forebears to the public realm. They reinserted themselves into the German language and culture from which they had been removed during the Nazi years. In so doing, they created an "address" for their stories, a step that can be seen as not only psychologically crucial for survivors, but important culturally and politically as well. Through their literature, they reclaimed a space for themselves as (Austro-)German Jews within this national community at a moment that Germans no longer considered their relationship to Jews or to the past of importance for their own national self-definition and displayed considerable impatience in wanting to move on.

How one should interpret this kind of Jewish "reentry" into the German national consciousness at this particular historical juncture, however, remains open to debate. In part the effect of these texts depends on how one interprets the cultural and political developments of this particular period, and how one reads the reception of these authors and their literature and their degree of success at an "intervention" into this 1980s debate about the past that excluded (living) German Jews. One could, for instance, consider the literature and its reception to be a continuation of a German-Jewish symbiosis, or con-versely, of a negative symbiosis, as Dan Diner has characterized the postwar relationship between German Jews and other Germans.[26] Or one could instead conceive of the literature of Weil and Klüger as a form of "minor literature" as defined by Deleuze and Guattari in their reading of Kafka as a literature that self-consciously positions itself outside a mainstream to which it belongs.[27] This kind of writing "understands itself as peripheral and yet constantly relates itself to an imagined center from which it sees itself excluded."[28] Yet, using the term minor literature risks marginalizing this literature unnecessarily (because by definition it can only be seen as residing at the margins). As bestsellers that became central in discussions about the Nazi legacy in the 1980s and 1990s, these texts certainly did not remain outside of the mainstream.

Reading Against the Disputed German-Jewish Symbiosis

My analysis of Jewish writing in postwar German culture by assimilated (Austro-)German Jews takes as its implicit point of departure the dramatic changes German and Austrian Jews underwent during 1933 and 1939, and the effects these changes had on self-perception and on German-Jewish relations. I thus write explicitly against the inter-pretation—common since 1945 in works that deal with (Austro-)German Jews, Jewish life in Germany, and Jewish art and literature in Germany (and to a lesser extend Austria)—that judges the century-long Jewish integration into German society to be a "failed symbiosis," or a symbiosis that never really existed at all, that is, a merger of identity and culture that only existed in the imagination of highly assimilated Jews. According to this view, the German (and Austrian) host society was either far less hospitable than Jews cared to see, or symbiosis always meant giving up too much of one's own culture.[29]

I consider the kind of history that takes the events of 1933–1945 in Germany and Austria, World War II, and specifically the Nazi extermination of European Jewry as its retrospective point of reference, to be highly problematic. Constituting a historical narrative move that Michael Bernstein calls "backshadowing," which is, as he suggests, "the most pervasive, but also the most pernicious variant of foreshadowing," this form of historical approach chooses to reinterpret that past, in particular as experienced by (Austro-)German Jews, through a post-1945 lens.[30] The question about Jewish identity, history, and culture and its relation to German identity, history, and culture is then decided and "solved" historically. There is no more *Deutschtum und Judentum*, no more symbiosis, as if there had never been such a possibility. In such a view, Auschwitz determined everything that came later, as well as retrospectively, everything that had come earlier. Auschwitz has made it impossible to think of German-Jewish existence in the past as a reality.[31]

What is problematic about this version of history is that the past unavoidably leads to certain facts or events in a later future, which in fact means that later events are now refigured as logical, inevitable, and thus as predictable for the actors at an earlier stage.[32] What often results from this process of backshadowing is a reification of German Jews, as they can only be seen as victims, as people who did not have (or did not exert) agency. Their extensive history of living in Germany and Austria as independent, autonomous subjects is erased.[33]

In analyzing the prewar (Austro-)German-Jewish culture that Weil's and Klüger's work refers to, I instead make use of a different process that Bernstein calls "sideshadowing." Sideshadowing, in contrast to backshadowing, gestures "to the side, to a present dense with multiple, and mutually exclusive, possibilities for what is to come" (1). What this move allows one to do is pay attention to "the unfulfilled or unrealized possibilities of the past" as a way of "disrupting the affirmations of a triumphalist, unidirectional view of history in which whatever has perished is condemned because it has been found wanting by some irresistible historico-logical dynamic" (3). Instead of arguing that the Nazi genocide of the Jews was somehow inevitable, and that therefore the sense of German-Jewish symbiosis was at least naive and at worst a lie, it is thus important to look at what was once the present and acknowledge what this looked like for the people who lived then.

Prior to the onslaught of the Nazis, the identity of Jews living in Germany and Austria had always been closely linked to the possibilities offered to them in their environment, but was also to a certain degree self-determined.[34] Which of these two forces, environment and self, played a greater role depended in turn on the circumstances. When German Jews' surroundings were extremely hostile, there was less room for self-determination. When social and political circumstances were more favorable, the development of certain identifications and subcultures flourished. In fact, from the nineteenth century on, Jews in Germany had sought, and were to varying degrees allowed to seek, both integration and Jewish identity, both *Verschmelzung* and *Eigenart*.[35] That is, although most German Jews sought integration in the form of equality under the law, they also wished to preserve identity, as they remained faithful to their cultural and religious heritage.[36]

Jewish acculturation had been made possible by both the legal emancipation after German unification in 1871, and by the Jewish Enlightenment (the *Haskalah*), which had led to a loosening of the ties of Jewish religious law since the nineteenth century.[37] These changes had in turn led to a change in Jewish identity, reflected in the Jewish community's self-definition. No longer primarily defined as Jews, as "German Jews," or "Jews residing in Germany" (*Deutsche Juden*), but rather as German citizens, they now saw themselves as "Germans of Jewish Faith" (*deutscher Staatsbürger jüdischen Glaubens*).[38] Soon after legal emancipation, the majority of Jews attempted at least to a certain degree to integrate into German society in return for citizenship, and in the hope that it would protect them from antisemitism.

What this meant in practical terms is that most Jews acculturated; that is, on the one hand, they accepted the behavior and standards of the dominant, German (Christian) culture, they moved out of Jewish neighborhoods and became middle-class German nationalists. On the other hand, their perceptions and sentiments, their career patterns and holidays, and their attitude toward intermarriage and conversion, were still Jewish-identified, still separate. Most German-Jewish men and women had thus acculturated by the 1930s, but only a small minority had assimilated. Although in some families there was a complete adoption of Christian culture, this was relatively rare.

What took place instead was the formation of a new kind of private, *domestic* Judaism in which Jewish women played a central role. As Marion Kaplan has argued, women became "agents of class formation and acculturation on the one hand," but "determined upholders of [Jewish] tradition on the other."[39] This became possible, as middle-class Jewish women had assimilated more slowly, as their opportunities for education and "participation in the public realm of economy and civic life" had been restricted.[40] In their upbringing of the children and the cultivation of a family life, Jewish women were thus inhibitors of complete assimilation. On the other hand, Jewish mothers were also responsible for acculturation, which took place through an immersion in German bourgeois practice, in *Bildung*.[41] *Bildung* entailed "the development of character, the establishment of morality, and the creation of culture,"[42] and amounted to an education of predominantly "high culture" combined with "character formation" and "moral education," resulting in individual cultivation. *Bildung* was especially important for Jewish integration, because it could be attained by everyone through self-development and education.[43]

Thus, up to the 1930s at least, Jewishness defined the identity of the vast majority of German Jews more than has generally been acknowledged.[44] Most Jews chose to remain Jewish, even if conversion, secession, or intermarriage would have been the easier route to take, at least economically. Jews participated in the majority culture and formed a part of it, but they formed a minority culture nevertheless, which in turn transformed what they appropriated from German culture, a transformation that proved extremely successful.

The integration of the Jews in Austria (or Vienna, the city where the majority of Austrian Jews lived),[45] parallels in many respects that of German Jews. Jews in Austria underwent a project of cultural assimilation that mirrored German *Bildung*; they acquainted themselves with German Enlightenment culture, in particular its literature and philosophy, instead of "the culture of any specifically Austrian tradition."[46] Overall, this meant that Austrian Jews were more German-identified than the non-Jewish population.

Similar to German Jews, they were both highly acculturated as well as immersed in a Jewish subculture. Living in predominantly Jewish neighborhoods and associating mainly with each other, "Jews in Vienna prevented the kind of assimilation which might have led to the dissolution of the Jewish group."[47] In other aspects, such as their middle-class status, their occupational, educational, and demographic patterns, and their success in Austria's cultural and intellectual life, Austrian Jews also mirrored the social and cultural patterns of German Jewry. The cultural elite in turn-of-the-century Vienna (the educated liberal bourgeoisie) was, as in Germany, a Jewish bourgeoisie. Because of their tremendous accomplishments in Viennese cultural and intellectual life, the *Jüdisch-österreichischer Symbiose* seemed at least as real to Austrian Jews as German-Jewish symbiosis was to Jews in Germany.[48]

Up to 1933, then, the German and Austrian environment indeed offered many possibilities for a flourishing Jewish culture. German-Jewish life, despite its seeming contradictions, provided for many decades a strong and viable sense of national identity, as Jews were neither separated rigidly from German culture (as outsiders), nor assimilated completely into Germanness (as insiders). This, then, was the prewar sense of self-definition from within which much German-Jewish and Austrian-Jewish literature, including Weil's and Klüger's autobiographical works, are situated. Not only had Jews for centuries progressively integrated into the German and Austrian nations and their culture, Germany and Austria adopted much of what its Jewish authors, composers, journalists, politicians, industrialists, and scientists had to offer. Both Weil and Klüger grew up in Jewish families and a subculture that were proud of this integration, and trusted it to continue. German-Jewish symbiosis, at least for that moment, seemed a real possibility.

Analyzing Female Experience

The focus in this study on the writing of Grete Weil and Ruth Klüger as *female* German-Jewish and Austrian-Jewish authors is deliberate. First off, their literature's remarkable success in the 1980s and 1990s has to be understood in light of a broader interest in literature written by female authors that problematizes the position of (Jewish) women. But second, and no less important, there is still very little known about the experiences of Jewish women[49] generally, and within the context of the study of the Holocaust in particular, female experience and the work of women is still too often subsumed under that of male authors. This has left an analysis of gender out of the picture entirely.[50]

Furthermore, as Shulamit Magnus has suggested, looking in more depth at the experience of Jewish women may lead to "a fundamental revamping of the categories with which we conceptualize the past" (28) as the criteria used thus far, "derived from the history of men [and] may be inadequate or inappropriate to the history of women" (30). Introducing the question of gender (difference), then, challenges the culturally dominant ways of categorizing what is historically important and what is not.[51] The need for such a review of categories is relevant here in two ways, in regard to the subject of assimilation and Jewish identity in (Austro-)German Jews, and that of the history and the literature of the Holocaust.

As Marion Kaplan and Paula Hyman show in their respective studies,[52] since it is the experience of assimilation of German-Jewish *men* that has formed the material for countless works on German-Jewish identity and culture, these particular studies have subsumed all German Jews under the rubric "highly assimilated."[53] If one takes female experience into account, however, this picture becomes much more complex and diverse, as Jewish women displayed fewer signs of radical assimilation.[54] Kaplan suggests that "historians have inadvertently overestimated both the desire of Jews to assimilate and even their capacity to do so."[55] Since Jewish self-definition is a central aspect of this study, the different degrees of assimilation are of importance. If women were in fact less assimilated and more Jewish identified than men in the decades before the war, one could hypothesize that the transition to being defined as racially Jewish might have been different for women than for men, and affected the possibilities to assert or reclaim Jewishness in a positive manner after the war. I discuss this possibility in relation to Weil's and Klüger's work.

Furthermore, gender analysis is important in the study of Holocaust, as feminist research conducted since the mid-1980s suggests that there are recurring patterns of difference in the way male and female survivors describe their experiences in hiding and concentration camps.[56] As I have discussed elsewhere, some of this scholarship is problematic as it essentializes male/female difference, glorifies a so-called women's culture, or uses survivor testimony indiscriminately as a basis for historical conclusions. (There is often little analysis of how Holocaust narratives may relate to a historical reality, and testimony is read or interpreted as a reflection of the truth.) Other research is thought provoking, however, and proves useful in an analysis of this literature, as it locates the gendered nature of survivor narratives in men's and women's different prewar socialization and their ensuing ways of acting in, looking at, describing and experiencing the world.[57] Gender socialization may affect how men and women experienced the war, how they remember it (women and men tend to emphasize different kinds of experiences in their process of remembering)[58] and how they each write about the memory of the experience.

As the autobiographical work written by Weil and by Klüger does not naively deal with history but explicitly draws into question the processes at work in memory and narrative that make it possible to speak of this history after the fact, and as both authors problematize the perspective of the female protagonist and her right to speak of this experience and history without having her version or her memory challenged, the issues of gendered memory and narrative prove quite relevant. Ruth Klüger's work, in particular, forms a running commentary on this kind or research as she engages with many aspects of it in provocative ways.

Theoretical Intersections

A study of Jewish literature by women authors, and in particular one that focuses on authors who are Holocaust survivors and who wrote about this particular experience *in German*, is by necessity a study of crossroads, of intersections of cultures, disciplines, and of different disciplinary approaches. One cannot write a literary study on German-Jewish Holocaust literature without the perspective of the German cultural, historical, and literary landscape, of course, but this alone is not sufficient. In turn, a Jewish angle, although important, cannot be examined without the particular national German context, and finally, neither aspect can be understood without taking into consideration the Holocaust and its cultural impact over the last six decades.

While this study's analysis relies on research and tools from all of these fields, the ways in which German-Jewish survivor literature has been approached up to this point signals precisely the tendency to isolate and exclude it in peculiar ways. This work is part of a German literature, for instance, for it is written in this language and published in Germany, but at the same time, German- and Austrian-Jewish authors had a difficult time getting their texts published in Germany, because of their subject matter, especially as they sought to problematize the Holocaust in the present, rather than to merely memorialize it. At other times, these authors or their works were not considered properly or fully "German." Weil and Klüger are good examples of such exclusion: despite her considerable oeuvre, Weil was not included in standard reference works on German literature until recently,[59] and in terms of categorization within the German literary establishment, Klüger as an American citizen is deemed even more problematic.

Literary scholars in Germany actually came exceedingly late to studying literature by German Jews in any systematic fashion. In part, this oversight can be explained by the fact that there was no category in which to think of this literature. A term such as the "Holocaust" (denoting the German genocide of the Jews of Europe) did not come to be used in Germany until the late 1970s. While there were plenty of studies on Nazism, and of literature on Nazism, the perspective of the victims in the form of survivor literature was not an object of study at all. Furthermore, the long prominent *Tekstimmanente* approach in German literary scholarship, which sought to isolate a close reading of the text from an analysis of the author's biography and the text's historical context, was not conducive to an analysis of survivor literature. Even in one area of German literature scholarship in which this would have been self-explanatory, that of literary exiles (*Exilforschung*), the analysis of Jewish authors remained unexplored until recently.[60] If Jewish issues were looked at at all, it took the form of an analysis of the portrayal of Jews in German literature by non-Jews.

While American scholars initiated the analysis of Holocaust literature as a genre in the mid-1970s, in their work the literature was approached primarily in a comparative, international framework, according to what Alan Mintz has called an "exceptionalist model," which "is rooted in a conviction of the Holocaust as a radical rupture in human history. . . . Hewn out of the same void. . . . works of art, no matter their different origins or languages of composition, make up a canon of Holocaust literature with a shared poetics" (39). These American scholars did not look at this literature specifically as different *national* literatures, thus not further elucidating the unique German case, or for that matter, *any* other national literature.[61] Only very recently have German scholars adopted a more sophisticated perspective on Holocaust literature borrowed from these American studies and paired it with a reading of this literature within its German context.[62] This German work still remains heavily indebted to the studies by American scholars of Germanistics.[63]

Not only was Jewish or Holocaust subject matter long deemed problematic for German critics and scholars, but works written by female authors received even less attention. The influence of feminist theory on the academic field of German Studies was very late in comparison to the United States, and "women's literature" was often marginalized and excluded from any serious discussion. Only from the late 1980s on were more efforts made to add women to the German canon. The exploration of specifically Jewish *women's* writing and women's exile writing in German academia and in literary criticism took still longer, as Jewish women suffered from a double invisibility within the German context.[64] On the one hand, they were invisible as women in the few works that thematized Jewish life or literature in Germany as men's experiences were assumed to be representative.[65] On the other hand, these authors were also invisible as *Jews* in most work on women authors written by German feminists. This latter oversight was the result of a tendency to focus only on the victimization of women in patriarchal society, while excluding considerations of racism (even at times equating the victimization of women under patriarchy with that of Jews under the Nazis), which left no room to acknowledge the specific oppression of Jewish women.[66]

Most recently within the field of German Studies in the United States, several feminist researchers have made attempts to analyze these texts more interdisciplinarily, from within a German or American feminist literary perspective. These studies tend to fall short on either one of two accounts, however: they are either not actual readings of the literary texts as texts (as in the case when the works are described instead as cultural moments in a larger literary history of Germany or of German Jews), or if they are indeed close readings, the texts are discussed without any of the broader framework and insights gained from Holocaust studies.[67]

Finally, within literary Holocaust studies, a field of study with a decidedly international perspective, but which has long been performed almost exclusively within U.S. academic institutions, many German-Jewish (women) authors and their works are again marginal at best because they write in German, and because their literature deals (in great part, but certainly not exclusively) with things German. As much of this German work is not translated (or translated well, or only in translations that are out of print), they are not widely read in the United States and thus not included in a larger (international) canon of Jewish literature, even though such inclusion would be appropriate, based on the subject matter. Furthermore, as a *German*-Jewish literature, the cultural context as well as the address of these texts generally tends to be seen as odd by American critics: they deem German-Jewish culture an oxymoron, and question why survivors of the Nazi regime would want to write for a German audience. Consequently, even when these texts are translated, as in the case of Weil and Klüger, neither the critics nor the audience are entirely sure how to approach them.

As a result, in neither German nor U.S. scholarship much work is done on authors such as Klüger and Weil.[68] These women's projects, their lives, and the reception of their work has thus remained outside of the scholarly approaches, which have attempted to integrate this kind of literature more fully into cultural studies of the Holocaust. This study, which attempts to do justice to this literature within all of these approaches and disciplines, is consequently a project that highlights these intersections, and it tries to bridge their exclusion, isolation, or marginality. As such, it forms part of a new kind of cultural studies of the Holocaust that has emerged in the past decades, but it also seeks to question the focus and premise of some of these new analyses.

Theorizing Holocaust Representation

This study was conceived of during a period that marked a remarkable activity in the new field of cultural studies of the Holocaust. A wealth of new critical discourse has been published in the past fifteen years that in particular focuses on the representation of the Holocaust in monuments, memorials, museums, film, art, and popular culture. These publications reflect a great recent interest in how both individual and public memory of the Holocaust is constituted over time and in different political, cultural, and national contexts.[69] Sophisticated readings of these arenas of culture production have become the norm, as critics examine political agendas, dominant ideologies, and discourses that reveal themselves in these representations of cultural memory. At about the same time that this theoretically complex cultural analysis of Holocaust representations emerged, a new interest in oral Holocaust testimony (in particular in video format) became apparent as well.[70] At least in part, the newfound curiosity for eyewitness testimony seems to have been symptomatic of a broader cultural anxiety over the loss of immediacy as survivors started to die in greater numbers.[71] The work on videotaped survivor testimony may have seemed like a way to preserve an "empirical presence" of the event in the form of the image of the survivor's body and voice, in contrast to literature, whereby this link may have seemed more tenuous. One scholar suggests for instance (somewhat naively) that these spoken "versions of survival" found on videotape produce "language as physical substance, the thing itself." This means that unlike literature, he argues, these testimonies are "unedited" and therefore closer to the truth.[72]

I believe that one can view these two approaches to the Holocaust as representative of a fundamental split in Holocaust studies today. One focuses on how Holocaust "discourse" manifests itself in different artistic and political arenas and is strongly indebted to postmodern theory and the study of representation. The other argues that it focuses on "the event itself," and on ways to gather all possible historical evidence as long as some eyewitnesses are still alive. This approach relies more heavily on the tools of the historian. The split is more complex than merely reflecting a disciplinary difference between scholars of literature and of history, however, as in the case of Holocaust literature, long-held views on both isles have had to be revised.

At this point, a consensus has emerged in the field of Holocaust studies that it is not one particular medium or another that makes one form of "evidence" more reliable or valuable than others as a source of "true memory," or of "history" of the Holocaust (although some historians would disagree).[73] As the different kinds of representations that bear witness to the Holocaust (historical documents, photographs, eyewitness testimony, art, museum exhibits, films, autobiographical and fictional literature, and so forth) are examined in a more sophisticated fashion, Holocaust studies has started to move on to a more complex understanding of the very particular issues that are brought up by work on this subject. It has moved on to become *cultural studies* of the Holocaust. I would characterize this new discourse as thoroughly aware of its "*post*" Holocaust nature. That is, aware of the culturally mediated, incomplete, and delayed nature of both these representations and our understanding of the events of the Holocaust and its impact. This aspect of mediation and delay is progressively becoming part of the scholarly inquiry, and in some cases, even of the literature itself.[74]

Fundamental to this shift, I believe, is a broader understanding of the phenomenon of trauma (and how trauma affects memory) that has emerged from within cultural studies since the early 1990s. Trauma seems to complicate an exhaustive individual and collective understanding of the Holocaust. The notion of trauma as articulated by Cathy Caruth as "an overwhelming experience of sudden or catastrophic events in which the response to the event occurs in the often delayed, uncontrolled repetitive appearance of hallucinations and other intrusive phenomena,"[75] has become widely used within Holocaust studies to denote a loss of control, the limits of language, and of agency. To be traumatized is "to be possessed by an image or an event."[76] If one accepts Caruth's suggestion that the greatest confrontation with reality in trauma occurs as an absolute *numbing*, then one needs to conclude that there can be no simple access to the truth of trauma, as it is indirect and incomplete, deriving from a memory over which the survivor does not have complete mastery. Coming to understand the effects of trauma, both individual (in survivors and even their children) and collectively as a fundamental inability to fully grasp the experience as it occurred, leading to a delayed response to the experience, and seeing this trauma as central to an understanding of the Holocaust and its cultural memory, one comes to speak instead of the *delayed, mediated, transferred, second-hand* nature of witnessing and of testimony, or of "postmemory," as Marianne Hirsch has coined the term.[77]

Caruth's work on trauma (as well as that of Shoshana Felman and Dori Laub) has come under attack recently by critics such Ruth Leys, as it seems to apportion too much importance to the role of the listener/scholar/analysant, and to suggest that the role of scholars in the production of the "true" story of trauma is indispensable.[78] One need not necessarily agree fully with Caruth's reading of Freud or with the more controversial aspects of her analysis (which may indeed lead to disturbing forms of appropriation if one fails to distinguish between the trauma experienced by the survivor and the trauma "witnessed" by the scholar),[79] to still see that a more complex and different understanding of the nature of memory and memoir due to traumatic memory is important. Among others, it has led to a shift within Holocaust studies away from a primarily historical paradigm, to a broader cultural studies model. This different approach has in turn led to a new (or renewed) appreciation of the role and function of Holocaust literature.

For nearly four decades after the war, literature on the Holocaust was considered one of the more problematic modes of witnessing within Holocaust studies, due to the still unresolved tension between art and atrocity. Literature was deemed to be either unreliable, or morally ambiguous, as it presumed aesthetic beauty,[80] and little sophisticated theoretical work was published on literary testimony. Paralyzed perhaps by Adorno's oft-cited (and even more often misinterpreted) dictum that "to write poetry after Auschwitz is barbaric," which seemed to articulate so powerfully the postwar cultural climate in which language (especially German) had become suspect, scholars were not sure how to consider this literature. (In other cases, Adorno's supposed admonishment was simply skillfully used to justify avoiding the topic altogether.)[81] Not only did concerns about the tainted nature of rhetoric fuel the concerns of authors and critics alike, but the sense that language itself was simply incapable of conveying the sheer scale and severity of the events and the individual and cultural psychic trauma it left in its wake played a part as well.

Although the theoretical approaches to Holocaust literature have undergone significant changes over the past two decades, the overriding concerns have remained remarkably similar and constant. Instead of a literary analysis of these texts, the kind of cultural commentary they presented, or of how they function within a larger public discourse on the Holocaust, many studies instead took up the issue of what this literature *should* be like.[82] In her reading of this earlier critical discourse on Holocaust literature, Sara Horowitz observes that the fear that literature might trivialize and betray the events dominates the discussion.[83] In Holocaust literature, the assumption is that bearing witness, producing testimony, is the central function. This literature needs to be the bearer of historical truth. Fiction, on the other hand, is per definition imagined, and thus perceived as containing lies or untruths. The medium therefore seems mismatched with the aims of the survivor (and Holocaust critic). Critics would see the more documentary style memoirs as legitimate texts, but were not sure how to treat their (lack of) literary quality, yet would dismiss fiction off hand as suspect.

Horowitz has responded to this criticism by defending this literature (especially fiction) as a mode of narration that is truthful and valuable both as document and as art. Literature is a "serious vehicle for thinking about the Holocaust" she argues, which, although it does not adhere to the kind of exactitude that is expected of historical narratives, can attain "a different kind of exactitude" (1–2). She articulates the point of Holocaust literature to be not so much about learning facts, but about breaking "down the cognitive and emotional barriers that keep the past safely in the past for listeners, readers, and viewers" (7). Indeed, literature can do what other forms of testimony may not, Horowitz argues, as it claims "the space of what remains unuttered in other modes of narrative, offering a vehicle to express, think through, and sometimes resolve complexities that underlie the critical discourse" (24). What makes literature unique in her view, ironically, is precisely what makes it so suspect in the eyes of many critics, namely the fact that "literature foregrounds its own rhetoricity. In fiction and poetry, language is acknowledged and explored not as a transparent medium through which one comes to see reality but as implicated in the reality we see, as shaping our limited and fragile knowledge" (17). Literature foregrounds precisely that which is true for *all* forms of language, and which makes many Holocaust critics uneasy, namely that "literary narrative substitutes language for world" (17).

Texts are not, and cannot be, "material fragments of lived experience."[84] Language itself cannot serve as proof, as evidence of a reality no longer present. James Young takes this as his point of departure for his study on narrative form in Holocaust literature. Not in the least anxious about the problem of reference, he addresses the issue in depth, and argues that since all our knowledge (historical, documentary, or literary) on the Holocaust is dependent on how—in what kind of presentations—events are passed on to us, our focus should be precisely on these representations, not on questions of veracity.[85] That is, literary and historical truths may not be entirely separable, as "reality" cannot be understood separate from language itself. Young is aware of the fact that this is an uncomfortable conclusion to reach, not only for (some) Holocaust scholars, but also in particular for survivor authors themselves who fear that the empirical link between their experiences and their narrative might be lost in its literary construction. Survivors may feel that unless they can show "that the current existence of their narrative is causal proof that its objects also existed in historical time" that writing may be useless (23). Thus, in an attempt to establish this semblance of objectivity, of historical truth, many survivor authors display "an almost obsessive tendency . . . to rid their narrative of all signs of style in order to distinguish between factual and fictional works" (8). As Young points out, however, this is nothing more than a rhetorical move, and this "rhetoric of fact" becomes a style in itself.

Yet, as mentioned, we now understand more fully that representation is not only complicated because an empirical link (i.e., a nonlinguistic, nonnarrative link) between the events and their depiction, that is, the historical or artistic representation that establishes the testimony as truthful, cannot be established in literature (or for that matter, in any other kind of medium). We also see that any view of the events themselves has already been profoundly complicated by their traumatic nature. This view is filtered, colored, fragmented, affected by forgetting, repression, and acting out. Thus, whereas linguistic reference is generally problematic, it needs to be recognized that literature is not necessarily more unreliable than other forms of Holocaust testimony; it is merely a kind of language that is more *up front* about its own rhetoricity, as Horowitz emphasizes. The problem of Holocaust testimony therefore, does not reside in literature itself—from which one could then stay away if necessary—but is inherent in all representation, especially that of traumatic events.

This way of reading trauma narratives now allows for a reading of those aspects of survivor literature formerly seen as troublesome as precisely that which makes these texts so rich in possibilities, I suggest. For what survivor literature does, on the one hand (as illustrated by the decades-long controversy over the medium), is to bring the discussion about the dichotomy between historical and fictional truth and the limitations of language and reference to the foreground. On the other hand, it shows that if experience is not transparent and does not translate itself simply and directly into language (especially when it is affected by trauma), then Holocaust literature becomes something *else* than testimony. This literature allows for the creation of a new (subjective) construction of certain experiences and memories into narrative. Such a narrative provides the promise of the rearticulation of agency, and as bearing witness allows the survivor to have a voice out in the world, the promise of some kind of broader cultural impact.

The impact and effects of this kind of writing for the person who produces it, as well as for the reader, can be better understood if it is read with the cultural and historical context of a text's production and publication in mind. In this way, we can see these texts as works that potentially embody *both* the survivors' agency *and* a political purpose. It is the latter, the cultural and political impact of this literature, which regrettably is overlooked too often in the recent studies that focus on the problems of representation and trauma and of the thoroughly mediated nature of our understanding of the Holocaust. These otherwise compelling studies neglect to look at the literature *both* from this theoretical point of view, as a particular form of traumatic language, and from the point of view of the particular cultural and national context in which the literature is produced, published, and received. It thus tends to gloss over the national context in which Holocaust literature emerges and the cultural (or even political) impact it may have (had) on the postwar communities in which it was originally published and which it addresses.

In part, this oversight may be due to the comparative nature of these analyses that underplay national differences and context, and to the fact that the dominant scholars in the field of Holocaust studies are primarily either Americans or located in America at American academic institutions, and are often themselves based in the field of English literature. As a result, the works they discuss tend to be literature that is published in English (or is translated to English) in the United States. If the cultural influence of these works is discussed at all, it is generally limited to their impact on American (Holocaust) consciousness. In turn, this prevalence in these studies of what Alan Mintz calls an "exceptionalist" approach to Holocaust literature may stem from their theoretical underpinnings: variations of a New Critical approach or a more recent poststructuralist literary criticism are visible that resist having literary analysis turn "into writing about history . . ."[86] Here, the position seems to be that a study of authors, their intent, and their writing as political statement do not belong in literary analyses.

I strongly feel that the attempt to remedy the latter kind of analysis through commenting "on art only and not on life," is misplaced here. In analyses of Holocaust literature, art and life are not so easily separated, and I would even argue that such a separation is inappropriate. A fuller understanding of the details of a certain texts' cultural and historical background may be particularly instructive, in two respects. First, different national backgrounds "constitute a different kind of lens that refracts the Holocaust differently and recalls the Jewish past differently because of the different nature of the Jewish community's relationship to modernity and to the particular gentile society that surrounds it."[87] The context will help us understand the text itself better, as it is each survivor's particular cultural identity "that provides the essential lens through which they focus their vision" and by which we may perhaps be better able to gain access to the work.[88] Second, and at least as important: for authors for whom the literary impulse came forth out of the need to bear witness, a separation of the specific context and address of their work from the work itself would seem undesirable as well. As Talí Kal has argued, "bearing witness is an aggressive act," and the speech of survivors can be "highly politicized" (7). To claim for the literature of trauma "that an author's intent is irrelevant" (17) seems therefore highly misplaced. To understand and fully appreciate the political impact of these works, the broader reception of a text (not just our own) as well as the text's genesis is significant. A considerable bonus of reading these texts in this way is that we may avoid adding to the reification of these survivor authors. By not reading their works as "cases" which only we as experts are capable of analyzing fully and definitively, we leave survivor authors with the last word.

Thus, although some of the recent theoretical studies on the complex, mediated, and fragmented nature of Holocaust trauma in these narratives inform my work, I deliberately chose to focus this study on the in-depth examination of precisely the questions of production, audience, and both the personal and cultural impact of Holocaust literature within a specific cultural context. This is an analysis of a *specific* Holocaust literature: that of a number of German-Jewish Holocaust survivors, the historical events and personal dilemmas unique to German Jews that their literature refers to, the circumstances of their literary production, as well as the effects of this literature within the particular national culture and time period it was published from the late 1940s on, and its belated success in the 1980s and 1990s.

Literary Interventions

The works by Grete Weil and Ruth Klüger on which this study concentrates represent a response (and intervention) that is culturally and historically specific, and should be read as such. While I highlight the major departure from earlier decades their literary works and the public discussions that Weil and Klüger were part of in the 1980s and 1990s represent, in order to appreciate the change of this later success, it needs to be read within the context of this earlier period of neglect.

The sociopolitical climate in which this literature emerged, one in which German Jews in West Germany were isolated and silenced for more than three decades, is sketched in chapter two through a discussion of Grete Weil's early career, as the lukewarm response to her work after her return forms in many ways a reflection of the more general waxing and waning interest in Jewish voices in Germany in the first postwar decades, lasting well into the 1960s. For whereas progressive political and cultural changes of the early 1960s seemed to positively affect German-Jewish relations, the climate for critical survivor literature such as Weil's did not improve. This chapter analyzes Weil's publications from 1949, 1963, and 1968, and the broader cultural dynamics that account for their lack of impact.

Chapter three discusses Weil's publications of the 1980s, the success of which is read from within the context of political and cultural changes taking place since the 1970s. These changes consisted of a number of broader contradictory phenomena. On the one hand, there was a new focus on the individual, the growth of the German women's movement, and the emergence of "new subjectivity" in literature (both of which represented outgrowths of the 1960s leftist movements), and a newfound interest in the experience of Jewish victimization and the memory of the Holocaust in both Jews and Germans. On the other hand, there was also a conservative political shift in which a new center-right administration sought to actively formulate a new history for Germany, out from under the "shadow of Hitler." The ensuing conflicting tendencies within German culture at this time, to want to acknowledge Jewish suffering and loss, and the desire to "normalize" German history, are seen as affecting both Weil's sudden acclaim at this time, and her works' still less than successful address. A detailed reading of the three novels she published in the 1980s suggests Weil's anticipation of these difficulties and the still very complex interaction between the views of a survivor author such as Weil and those of her German audience.

This kind of a Jewish intervention seemed even more urgent after reunification, when the public sentiment to leave the past behind and move on with a renewed sense of national pride became stronger than ever in Germany. It is at this historical juncture that Ruth Klüger published her memoir that as a bestseller came to play an important role in this discussion about the past. It functions as a commentary on this discussion, and on the function of memory (and memoir) for Jews and Germans more broadly. Whereas for many Germans reunification symbolized the definitive end of the war's political aftermath, Klüger's work intervened in this German public discourse on the Holocaust as it showed Germany's relationship to its Jewish citizens and exiles still to be highly contentious and of great importance to present-day politics and culture. As a German language memoir by an American author of Austrian-Jewish descent, this work shows the difficult position of Austrian and German Jews in relation to things German as the work calls into question the possibility of an actual return to German(y) and sheds light on the highly complex address the work of Jewish survivors seek.

Chapter five returns to the notions of a Jewish address, return, and intervention in German culture and suggests the different ways in which the impact of Weil's and Klüger's work may be read. Within the context of the (re)emergence of a Jewish literature in the 1990s, should their work be seen as a sign of a renewed German-Jewish symbiosis, or perhaps a negative symbiosis? Or should the (belated) success of authors such as Weil and Klüger and the recent interest in all things Jewish in Germany since the 1990s be seen merely as a nostalgic German attempt at recapturing a culture the Nazis destroyed? Does their work bring forth a genuine interest in living Jews, and does the enthusiasm for the work mark a real shift in mentality?

CHAPTER TWO
THE JEWISH RETURN TO GERMANY

Danach bin ich wieder Mensch: Weil's Return from Exile

In 1947, Grete Weil-Dispeker returned to Germany after a twelve-year absence. Having lived in exile in Amsterdam since December 1935 (spending September 1943 to May 1945 in hiding), now 41 years old and a widow, she was eager to return. For as she saw it, the mood in Germany befit her own. After having briefly visited Sweden and Switzerland immediately after the war, she realized that she could not feel at home there, as people had little awareness of the immense suffering caused by the Nazis: "In both countries, I conclude that I cannot live among people who have experienced nothing or almost nothing."[1] Having been an eyewitness to the deportation of the Dutch Jews, having lost her husband (who was killed in Mauthausen), having lived under the threat of murder herself, she was unable to just return to normalcy: "I couldn't have returned in '45 to an intact country, it would have made me furious . . ."[2] Instead, she felt that the defeated, divided, bombed-out German nation was as destroyed as she was: "The ruins? They suited me, not only the German cities had been ruined by war, I had been, too."[3]

Despite all that had happened, Germany was still the landscape of Weil's memories, her culture, and her language. She *had* to return, as she explained years later, for she was still a German: "Whether I like it or not—and very often I do not like it—I am a German,"[4] and Germany was still her home: "I want to go home, even though I know that everything I loved before no longer exists. I want to go there where I came from. The longing hasn't diminished in all these years, but has grown."[5] She was well aware of the apparent contradiction of declaring Germany still her home after fleeing a murderous regime that declared her German citizenship void, and as such she was criticized by many (Jewish) friends for returning.[6] Yet she argued that although her Jewish identity had taken on a new importance during the war years, it was not sufficient to form the foundation of a new life (e.g., in Palestine or later the state of Israel).[7] Instead, Weil concluded, "I have lost my homeland (*die Heimat*) Germany and not found another in its stead."[8] What thus affected Weil's decision to return, besides the desire to reunite with a close friend, Walter Jockisch, the man she later remarried,[9] was her profound sense of Germanness, her connection to the German language and culture, and the (Southern) German landscape.

This was not unusual among her class of German Jews. Born Margarete Elisabeth Dispeker in Rottach-Egern (Southern Germany) in 1906 into a highly assimilated, well-to-do family of Jewish lawyers, Weil describes in much of her work a privileged, upper-class childhood in which *Bildung*, a "so-called good upbringing,"[10] was of far greater importance than a formal Jewish education.[11] This *Bildung*, "the development of character, the establishment of morality, and the creation of culture,"[12] amounted to a secular, humanist education of predominantly "high culture." In Weil's family, German-Jewish assimilation was an accomplished fact, no longer a project that had to be realized. *Deutschtum*, German culture, was where Weil felt most at home.[13] In contrast, there was little in the way of Jewish traditions growing up, Weil suggests. Whereas Jewish holidays were observed little, her family celebrated some of the traditional German (Christian) holidays.[14] Weil's literary alter egos describe their relationship to Judaism as "lukewarm and lax, without clear contours."[15] Before Hitler, she could only conceive of Jewish identity as religious, and as an atheist, she felt herself to stand outside of the Jewish tradition.[16] Although Weil would in her later work articulate her identity as stemming from a "dual set of roots," German and Jewish, and a bit sarcastically point out how this may serve as an advantage for her career as a writer, "Access to both. . . . The triumphant rationality of the Enlightenment and the transcendental magical formula for the sole, invisible, omnipotent God,"[17] it was still the former, the German tradition of *Bildung*, with which her narrators express most affinity. "I feel closer to Antigone than to Ruth."[18]

Although the events of 1933–1945 had certainly changed that what German culture and history seemed to stand for, and on a more personal level, the experience of persecution had profoundly altered German-Jewish identity and German-Jewish relations in ways that Weil was only just beginning to sense and would go on to explore for the next five decades, she hoped and trusted that there would be enough common ground with surviving Germans to rebuild her life, and to help rebuild the "true" Germany, that of a liberal, humanist tradition. As such, Weil proved to be an exception, as most German and Austrian Jews would not return to their native country, as they no longer considered it safe, considered their sense of German-Jewish identity a failure, or no longer felt at home.

As thoroughly German-identified, however, Weil accepted neither the thesis of collective German guilt nor of a German *Sonderweg*, the notion that the Third Reich had been the result of unique historical developments in Germany (in particular a delayed process of modernization and liberalization), which had resulted in a "special German path." She returned from exile in the Netherlands because she felt that she could make a difference in the rebuilding of a new democratic Germany. She intended to do so in the form of writing, in an address to a German audience. Not only was German her language—"I want to write, write in German, in another language this is impossible for me, and I need an environment in which people speak German"[19]—it was the dialogue with left-leaning German intellectuals and artists that she sought. This did not represent treason on her part, Weil argued, but rather the opposite: "To be there and perhaps to dig up that which is buried is not a betrayal of the dead, but the careful attempt to not let their beloved and sacred lives be forgotten, as long as one is alive oneself."[20] Writing, for Weil, was framed as an act of remembrance and resistance, as well as a justification to return to German and Germany.

Writing, furthermore, was no new endeavor: Weil hoped that her return to Germany could get her literary career off the ground that had been prematurely halted by the Nazis coming to power. For in 1932, while working on her doctorate in German, she had started writing her first novel. She would finish *Erlebnis einer Reise* (*Reise*, The Trip) (a triangulated love story of a twenty-something, well-educated well-to-do sexually liberated couple, disillusioned by the political and cultural climate of their time) in January of 1933, when it became impossible to publish the book under the new Nazi regime.[21] Within months, her husband Edgar Weil who worked as a dramaturge for the progressive München Kammerspiele was arrested with a number of his colleagues. Although the others were soon released, as the only Jew, he was kept in jail for over two weeks. Thus realizing the severity of the Nazi threat, the couple emigrated, fleeing into exile in Amsterdam. Edgar set up a branch of his father's pharmaceutical factory there in 1934, and Grete followed a year later after having been trained in Germany as a photographer. She had realized that it would be next to impossible for them to survive in exile as a German theater-maker and a writer.

In exile in Amsterdam, deeply unhappy and fearful, Weil saw no chance to write. Without the German cultural context to which they felt so strongly tied, Edgar and she felt as if their lives had ended. What followed were the "eight years of decline, during which we lose almost everything we called our own: country, language, security, and finally our own identity."[22] Emigration for Weil meant "not merely falling out of one's own social class into a lower one; emigration is plummeting into a bottomless chasm."[23] By 1938, Weil's father had passed away due to illness, her brother had fled to England, and her mother had escaped from Germany and made her way to Amsterdam as well. All ties to Germany were severed, and there was no telling for how long. Instead of writing, Weil now worked as a portrait photographer of Amsterdam Jewry, which she continued after the Nazis invaded Holland in May 1940.[24] The couple made a failed attempt to escape soon after the invasion, but found themselves trapped. In March 1941, Edgar was arrested by chance on the street during a Nazi round up (an unexpected Nazi *razzia* in retaliation for Dutch-Jewish resistance), sent to Mauthausen, where he was murdered within months. Deeply despondent at Edgar's death and at her failure to free him while still in the Netherlands, Weil contemplated suicide, but her sense of responsibility for the care of her mother kept her from following through. For a brief period Weil worked for the Dutch resistance, falsifying photographs on identity papers. By July 1942, when the deportations of the Jews started and Weil was called up, she obtained a position with the Jewish Council of Amsterdam. As such, Weil ended up doing administrative work at *de Joodsche Schouwburg*, a Jewish theater that had been turned into a collection point for Amsterdam Jews from which they were deported to the Dutch transit camp Westerbork and then to concentration camps in Poland. In this function, Weil became an eyewitness to the unprecedented Nazi deportations in the Netherlands (nearly 83% of the Jewish population was deported, resulting in an astonishing 75% Jewish death rate).[25] She worked for the Council until September 1943, after which it was dissolved and its remaining members deported. Weil was able to escape this final round up and went into hiding with a friend in Amsterdam until the end of the war, May 1945.

While in hiding, Weil returned to writing after a nearly decade-long hiatus, as she found that it was the only thing she could do to preserve her sanity. Locked inside for over a year, confined at times of danger and at night to a makeshift room between a wall and a concealed bookshelf, nearly completely isolated from friends and her mother, she wrote two works: a puppet play, *Weihnachtslegende* (*Legende*, Christmas Legend) in late 1943, which she performed for a couple of friends in her hiding place on Christmas eve, and a novel in 1944, a love story, *Der Weg zur Grenze* (*Der Weg*, The Road to the Border),[26] dealing with the experience of Nazi persecution. Both were quite different from her prewar work.

Whereas in her early work, literary influences such as that of Thomas Mann were apparent, and *Legende* and *Der Weg* also borrow from prewar German literary modernist models, the subject matter in these latter works makes for a very different tenor. For instance, the puppet play, which as its name suggests is loosely based on the Christmas story, reads in its formal characteristics—a brief (thirty-two page) set of dialogues that are partly set in rhyme—as an expressionist experimental play. In terms of content, however, the piece is acutely historical. It opens with a variation on the nativity scene (a woman is giving birth to a baby boy in the presence of three men), but the scene does not take place in a stable, but in an attic, the date is Christmas eve 1943, and the woman who is giving birth is a Jewish woman in hiding who has been smuggled by the resistance out of a theater that serves as a deportation center for the Nazis. The woman's husband has been left behind in the theater so that her escape will not be detected, and he is about to be deported. The scenes in the attic are interspersed with those in the theater where an absurd cabaret is performed (complete with a Greek chorus), which recounts in satirical fashion the position of the Nazis and the prisoners. The characters are Death, the *Sicherheitsdienst*, the *Führer*, and the "*Verschleppte Juden.*" The play ends as the woman in the attic dies after giving birth. Her (Jewish) baby will be hidden with a farmer.

In contrast to the puppet play *Legende*, the novel *Der Weg* is closer in form to Weil's prewar manuscript *Der Reise*. It is a novel with a (strongly autobiographical) story embedded within the main narrative, but here, too, the content makes it a very different kind of text. Although it contains a similar love story and a critique of the political situation in Germany, it also questions the kind of aesthetic norms and ideals *Der Reise* still seemed to espouse. *Der Weg* plays in 1936, the main narrative is the story of Monika Merton, a thirty-something German-Jewish woman who is being sought by the Gestapo and who hopes to be able to cross the German border illegally. During her trip she meets Andreas von Cornides, a young, well-educated but apolitical German poet who has been clueless up to this point about the true intentions and violence of the Nazi regime. They travel together, and Monika decides that Andreas needs to know her story, for "everything is about knowledge, now more than ever before . . ." she wants to make him less complacent, as isolating himself from the political reality of the day has become unacceptable: ". . . you imagine you know the world, because you can feel it with your artists' sensibility, but my dear, that will not do, it is not enough, it is a deadly luxury. . . . Haven't you heard of Dachau yet? . . . You are deaf to the cries of agony, just as deaf as all those others."[27] Monika thus comes to tell Andreas the story of her marriage, a tale of two Jewish German intellectuals against the backdrop of the changing political climate of the 1920s and 1930s, and of her husband's death at Mauthausen. Andreas, shocked by Monika's story and now fully aware of the Nazi threat, decides that he wants to flee together with her. Monika does not want him to, and when she crosses the border, he stays behind. Andreas is later killed by an SA border patrol.

Der Weg is a text that is much more explicitly political than Weil's prewar work as it specifically seems to invite non-Jewish Germans to engage with the issue of Nazism. Here, a German is confronted with the reality of a murderous Nazi regime through his encounter with a persecuted German Jew and then comes to struggle with his lack of involvement and adequate response. It hints at some of Weil's later work in which the narrative structure is set up so as to find ways to engage a German audience with the issue of Nazism. Rather than meant for publication, however, both *Legende* and *Der Weg* seem to have been to a significant extent personal writing projects that functioned for Weil as *Trauerarbeit* to work through the loss of her husband, and to deal with the uncertainty of her existence while still in hiding. Even after Weil's eventual return to Germany, neither text would be published. Weil considered them formally flawed. These texts, she believed, would not work for a German audience.[28]

Right after her liberation in May 1945, while still in Amsterdam, Weil finished a new manuscript *Ans Ende der Welt* (*Ans Ende*, At the End of the World), a novella that she was indeed eager to get published in Germany. This text gives a good idea of what Weil believed was now her task as an author. No longer focused on finding success as a belletrist, her literary aspirations had turned to the task of bearing witness. *Ans Ende* is based on the horrors Weil had experienced first-hand during the war years in Amsterdam, specifically her experiences in working for the Jewish Council. The text presents itself as a stylized, controlled form of literary testimony: the story is told in an emotionally understated, tightly structured short narrative (less than ninety-pages long) with an auctorial narrator who knows more than the Jewish protagonists whose drama unfolds in the text. This leads to an uncomfortable tension between reader and protagonist. We, too, know what will eventually happen to these men and women, and their end seems as senseless as it seems inevitable.

The novella does not focus on the Germans and their crimes, but instead puts a magnifying glass to the complex set of responses Jewish victims devised toward their persecution. In this case, the persecution of the Nazis gets enacted by fellow Jews, through the Jewish Council. The council was put in place by the Nazis to represent the Dutch Jews and was made complicit in the deportations of fellow Jews as they were in charge of deportation lists and exemptions. A perverse Jewish hierarchy was created, as the members of the Council were exempt from deportation for as long as they helped with the deportations of others.

Ans Ende tells of this institution and its devastating effects on the Dutch Jews caught in it through the story of Dr. Salomon Waterdrager, professor of law, his wife, and daughter Annabeth, who have been taken from their home in the middle of the night to the *Joodsche Schouwburg* to await deportation. On the basis of his professional status, Salomon believes that his family should have been exempted from deportation and argues that some mistake must have been made. During the same night, another family also named Waterdrager, Sam (a cousin of Salomon, an impoverished working-class Jew), his wife, and his son Ben have been hauled in as well, and Salomon assumes that they meant to take this family in and not his own, and thus demands that the "error" be rectified. Both families are told to stay in the theater until matters are sorted out. During this time, Salomon's formerly spoiled daughter Annabeth and Sam's son Ben, the young socialist resistance fighter, fall in love with each other. Their connection is so profound that Annabeth will twice decline a chance to be smuggled out of the theater.

The story turns into a bitter farce when Salomon discovers, much to his disbelief, that for the Nazis his social class and professional prestige make absolutely no difference, and that it is in fact his poor cousin Sam and his family who prove to be valuable to the Nazis (Sam has important connections as union leader of the diamond workers) and who will be sent home again, not he and his family. In his anger about this "injustice," Salomon betrays Sam's son: he reveals to the Nazis that Ben is a member of the resistance. As a result, Ben is tortured and sent to a concentration camp, but so are Salomon, his wife, and Annabeth. Ben's parents stay behind. The story ends at the concentration camp where Annabeth and Ben are selected for labor, while Salomon and his wife are last seen walking toward the gas chamber.

The novella highlights both the naiveté and helplessness of previously well-integrated, trusting Dutch Jews (and shows their selfishness, and their holding on to absurd class distinctions in moments of profound distress), and the cruelty of the Nazis and their policies, always designed to mislead, confuse, and provide false hope. While both sides are portrayed critically, it is nevertheless clear that the reader's sympathy should lie with the desperate deportees, in spite of their egotism. More complex is the story's judgment of the third group of actors in this drama: the Jews who work for the Germans in the Jewish Council. The Council members are discussed in highly ambivalent terms: while some would use their position to help deportees, even risking their own lives to free some of them, others seem to care only for their own survival, even as it means collaborating with the Nazis and sending other Jews to their death.

This ambivalence becomes explicit in a scene in *Ans Ende* that seems to contain a thinly veiled self-portrait of Weil in the form of a German-Jewish typist of the Council with whom Salomon has a conversation. Upset about his family's deportation and annoyed at the lackluster response of this typist to his demand that his case be reconsidered, Salomon confronts her with the fact that despite being German, she, too, is a Jew. The typist answers: "Only for the duration of the war." To this, Salomon responds: "And afterwards you will perhaps no longer be?" She answers: "Afterwards, I will be (a) human again" (*Danach bin ich wieder Mensch*). Upset, Salomon replies: "That is easy for you to say, Miss, here from your good post. When the Jewish Council has sent all other Jews to Poland, their employees might have the chance to experience those fortunate times again in which one is allowed to be just human. For us ordinary mortals, the prospects are considerably less favorable."[29]

While Weil's portrayal of the typist and the interaction are set off by irony (we find out next that Salomon had up to that moment been exempt from deportation on the basis of his own membership in the Jewish Council), it certainly reveals the dubious position members of the Council such as Weil were in. As Weil would later write: "Members of the Jewish Council are not required to leave. They are performing their work detail in Holland, the Germans explain cynically. Helping the Germans deport other Jews."[30] As such, the text not only bears witness to the suffering of Jewish victims, but also to one of the most perverse aspects of the "Final Solution": the way in which the Nazis forced Jews to implicate themselves in their crimes.

What this scene furthermore hints at is the complex position of many thoroughly assimilated (upper) middle-class Jews under the Nazis who still wished to see themselves primarily as citizens of their respective nations and not as Jews, something that had become impossible, for German Jews in particular. Although the comments of the typist seem hopelessly naive (the reader is all too aware that the desire to survive the war and to be seen as simply "human" again would prove futile for nearly six million European Jews, regardless of how assimilated they had been), it was in part this desire to undo the racial stigma, and the belief that she could indeed be "human," be just German again, part of a German cultural dialogue, that made Weil return to Germany, with this manuscript ready for publication.

Weil visited occupied Germany briefly (illegally) in 1946, returned permanently in 1947,[31] after which she entered into a relationship with Walter Jockisch, an old friend who worked as opera director in Darmstadt. Soon after, she tried to find a publisher for *Ans Ende*. This proved to be extremely difficult, however. Her work was offered to publishers in Germany, the United States, Palestine, and Switzerland,[32] but the text was rejected and shuttled back and forth for years until it finally was accepted by the publisher *Volk und Welt* in East Berlin in 1949. As it turns out, no publisher could be found for this sober novella-length work in the West, as it was far too problematic for a West German audience. Not only because it dealt in a realistic style with the actual historical experience of Jewish persecution, thereby recounting events which were fresh in people's memory but which most Germans were loathe to confront, but also because it did so in a self-critical way, painting a complex portrait of persecuted Jews. It was this unflattering depiction of Jewish characters that now clashed with the philosemitic policies imposed by the Allied victors.[33]

Although *And Ende* was well received in East Berlin (there were several positive reviews),[34] the lack of response to the work in the West was devastating for Weil.[35] She had returned to Germany to play a part in the process of democratization in which she believed that the memory of the Nazi crimes and in particular the murder of the Jews would play an important role. Instead, her testimony fell on deaf ears as Germans shied away from this past and focused their energies on the present. Disillusioned by the lack of audience for *Ans Ende* and unsure of her ability to serve as a (literary) witness and of her literary talents now that she was already in her forties and her first published book found no resonance, Weil retreated. "The first postwar years in Germany were exciting. But later I got the sense that everything had been for naught. I wanted to speak, but no one wanted to listen."[36] She did not yet realize that this lack of interest was in many respects typical for this period,[37] and that it had little to do with the book's quality (or lack thereof).[38] This larger political–historical context would only over time become clear to her, and she would come to criticize it in her later work.

Informationsverweigerung

The opportunities for radical democratic renewal that had brought Weil back to Germany initially looked promising, as the successor states of the Third Reich, Germany (soon to be divided in the *Bundesrepublik Deutschland* in the West and the *Deutsche Demokratische Republik* in the East) as well as the former German "province" Austria had a pronounced need to legitimize their new constitutions in their relationship to Nazi Fascism.[39] Yet Austria, although formerly an integral part of the Third Reich, quickly managed to claim victim status, and *externalized* National Socialism as a German "export product." In Germany, the chances for a confrontation with the past seemed better: the 1945–1946 Nuremberg Trials, which left almost none of the members of the top of the Nazi hierarchy unpunished, and the promise by commanders in each of the occupied zones to deal with the lesser Nazi officials, suggested that Germany would deal with the legacy of the Third Reich more effectively.

This optimistic mood with which Weil and other Jews had returned would nonetheless soon be crushed by the reality of a political crisis between the two opposing political and ideological blocks in the West and the East, based on very differing interpretations of and proposed solutions for Germany's disastrous course. The Soviets used Marxist analysis to explain fascism, and thus saw capitalism as the root cause for Germany's failed past, and socialism as the only solution. The Americans took the opposite view: the lack of economic liberalism had been the problem, they suggested, and restoring a market economy would automatically lead to democratization. The U.S.-led currency reform and economic aid in the form of the Marshall plan, while indeed crucial in aiding Germany's economic recovery, quickly exacerbated these tensions between the United States and the Soviet Union. The result was an escalation that led to the creation of two separate German states with their own constitutions in 1949.

This ideological split led to very different attitudes toward the past in the two German nations that would affect Jewish returnees. East Germany *universalized* fascism, viewing it as intricately connected to capitalism. As the DDR had rejected the capitalist state, Nazi fascism was argued to be the exclusive inheritance of West Germany.[40] West Germany, however, could neither universalize its National Socialist past nor externalize it (as Austria had done), and instead had to *internalize* it, making its success in moving "through" and away from it the measure of the new state's success, for better or for worse.[41] It was thus the West German state where the need to acknowledge responsibility for the crimes of the Third Reich and to make up for these past Nazi failures was most strongly felt and articulated, and it was the Federal Republic, rather than the Communist "Democratic" Republic where most of the (small number of) Jewish returnees resettled.

Even in the West, however, this need to work through the past was immediately complicated as a result of the escalating Cold War tension. Denazification, deindustrialization, de-cartelization, and demilitarization put into place in West Germany just years earlier was soon suspended or phased out as the Western Allies' perceived need to rebuild the country as a buffer in their struggle against Soviet dominance in Europe became the new priority. West Germany's strategic appeal as an additional Western ally took precedence over a thorough reckoning with the Nazi past.[42] In its new role as a Western antisocialist partner in the Cold War, West Germany would be encouraged to form a government that consisted of a coalition of conservative (antisocialist and anticommunist) parties. In this process, a large number of ex-Nazis were rehabilitated and reinstated into positions of political power, while former anti-Fascist resistance fighters, mostly member of the socialist and communist parties were locked out. This conservative coalition in turn fostered an active denial about the recent past, a climate of cultural conformity, order, and repression.

The initial phase of what Chancellor Adenauer considered a project of German "restoration" was, as Ernestine Schlant and others have argued, marked "by consistent efforts to ignore, repress, deny, and/or circumvent acknowledgment of the atrocities committed during the Holocaust."[43] Only Hitler or "the system" was deemed guilty or responsible, while the German people were seen as victims, both of the Nazi dictatorship and of denazification. There was no interest on the part of most Germans to consider the implications of the Nazi past, and instead, the new German state intended to move on from its problematic recent history to focus on the reintegration of all of its citizens (which included ex-Nazis but not necessarily Jews or other victims of the Nazi regime) and to rebuild a sense of national identity and cohesion. Meanwhile, the dramatic impact the Nazi years had had both on its victims and on German political, legal, and cultural institutions was underplayed. This new government in fact argued that the amnesty of Nazi prisoners was necessary for a sense of (West) German "unity."[44]

The profound anticommunism of these days in the disguise of "antitotalitarianism" reinforced such denial, for not only did it allow Germans to avow their now radical rejection of the Nazi legacy, but it also provided a chance to change the focus away from this past and on the "still present" forms of totalitarianism, that is, Stalinist communism in the East. As anticommunism had been an integral part of German ideology both during and after Hitler, this allowed for an interesting twisting of historical reality: "The Germans had already been part of the Western Alliance while they supported Hitler's fight against Russia."[45] The new regime relativized the Nazi crimes with a focus on the (ongoing) crimes of Stalin, the separation of Germany, and the victimization of the East Germans. Such views were one of several ways in which this past was made harmless.

On another level, this process of circumvention can be seen in German public attitudes toward Jews. While Allied denazification policies had made antisemitic sentiments officially taboo, they were now replaced by philosemitic attitudes. These proved very much to be continuous with antisemitism, however, as they provided Germans with a ready-made, instrumental way of dealing with Jews along accepted lines, but left deeper unresolved feelings of antisemitism, guilt and shame toward the past and resentment toward the Jews (for being part of that past and for reminding Germans of it) untouched.[46] As a result of this proforma change, much in the relationship between Jews and Germans remained as problematic as during the twelve Nazi years, even though publicly, philosemitism was the norm.

This continuum is reflected in public opinion polls of the early 1950s, which show that exposure to the atrocities perpetrated by the Nazis (through news reports, or the ongoing war trials) did not create empathy for Jewish victims among West Germans, but instead led to attempts to distance oneself from the Nazi crimes by holding only Hitler and the Nazi bureaucracy responsible. Such views ran deep, allowing even politicians who could hardly be accused of harboring apologetic tendencies such as the social democrat Kurt Schumacher to view the Nazi era in rather abstract terms. He would thus remark in 1949 without any hint of irony that "Hitler-barbarism has dishonored the German people through the destruction of six million Jewish people."[47] It was the Nazi *system* (seen as an almost mythical, impenetrable entity) that was considered to have "dishonored" the German people by murdering the Jews. As if no one German individual had driven the trains, had guarded the ghettoes, had built the camps, or had opened the Zyklon B gas.

Confronting the German people with the unpleasant details of the Nazi crimes could even backfire into antisemitism. The need to deny a sense of guilt brought on by the full awareness of the German treatment of the Jews led to so-called *schuldreflexiver Antisemitismus* (antisemitism in response to guilt).[48] This could take on rather extreme forms, as some Germans came to view their defeat, the continued postwar occupation, the loss of territory, and the expulsion from Eastern-Central Europe (in a vision that reveals a dubious historical reversal of cause and effect) "as a form of revenge for the millions of murdered Jews."[49] Thus, they argued, "the Jews must somehow be responsible for that which had befallen [the Germans]."[50] This guilt complicated the postwar relationship between Germans and Jews possibly even more profoundly than antisemitism had before Hitler.

Still, on a symbolic level, the German state's relationship to the Jews and the new state of Israel were deemed of central importance. This led to Adenauer's 1951–1953 negotiations over financial reparations, *Wiedergutmachung* to both the state of Israel as a whole and Holocaust victims and their descendants (and these reparations were meant to be moral, legal, and political, as much as financial).[51] The repayments were also politically pragmatic: West Germany showed itself a full partner in a community of Western nations. In the end, however, these payments would function to exculpate the majority of Germans, rather than lead to a moral reckoning, as no one had to admit personal responsibility.[52] In areas other than financial reparations, however, the question of the lasting legacy of the Nazi regime and its crimes was nearly entirely silenced. For the Jewish community, then, reparations were a double-edged sword, as settling matters with the Adenauer administration implied "the acceptance, without major protest, of Adenauer's course of reconciliation with Nazi sympathizers and accomplices."[53]

This "dual dynamic," of, on the one hand, a reckoning with the past, and on the other, a redefinition of an "untainted republican culture" can be seen as characterizing the first fifteen years of the West German Republic.[54] Within this context, the position of the small Jewish minority that had returned or stayed in Germany after 1945 was a complex one. Although Jews outside of Germany argued that Germany had become uninhabitable for Jews,[55] many non-Jewish Germans and Austrians did not expect Jews to return to or stay in their respective countries, either.[56] (In Austria, the situation was possibly even worse, I return to this situation in chapter four.) Returning or surviving German Jews sensed that they could return to live in West Germany but only as Germans, and not as Jews.

This complex West German political and cultural climate of denied culpability and continued (silent) antisemitism was apparent as well in the literary world. Grete Weil's failure to find a German publisher for her work in the West serves as only one example of the difficulties most returning German-Jewish authors (or aspiring authors) encountered.[57] This lack of publication opportunities, of audience, and of critical interest for German-Jewish and exile authors' works in the immediate postwar years in West Germany was caused first of all by the continuing dominance of certain groups of politically conservative authors and literary critics who had stayed in Germany during the Nazi years. Their "competing memories" now effectively shut out most exile or survivor authors from their publishing houses, periodicals, and reviews.[58]

This dominance of conservative authors and critics was at first strongly contested in 1945/1946, as two groups of authors (prominent), exile authors (Jews and non-Jews), and authors who had stayed in Germany, the so-called inner emigration, each battled to claim Germany's "true" cultural legacy.[59] Despite accusations of collaboration, the "inner exile" authors were able to suggest that the exiles who had left during the Nazi era had "abandoned" Germany in its darkest hour, and that therefore the literature they published was out of touch with German reality.[60] Due in part to the overall cultural–political climate that favored a reliance on apolitical, conservative postwar

forms of idealism and ideology, and that rejected socialist or otherwise left-leaning literature, these authors who had stayed in Germany ended up taking charge of literary periodicals and the literary critique, and would determine the tone of literary production.[61]
As a result, the politically conservative Germans who had been unable to understand the
dangers of National Socialism as a *political* movement in 1933 and who still had not
come to grips with it in 1945 dominated the postwar literary scene. Aesthetic forms
such as Magic Realism (seen as concerned "with the inner world of the spirit") were
applauded, whereas the concrete social and political reality of the recent Nazi past was
ignored.[62] One thus sees in the literary production of Germany post-1945 more continuity with the Nazi period than a change or a real break, befitting the trope of a true
Stunde Null, or for that matter a *Kahlschlag.*[63]

As a result, it was difficult to find publishers for survivor or exile authors, even if they
had been established authors before 1933. Books that had been burned under the Nazis
were not reprinted, and for authors such as Weil who had not yet previously published
and whose experience under the Nazis (in exile, hiding, or in concentration camps) now
gave them the impetus to write, the situation was even more difficult.[64] While these
German-Jewish survivors produced a good number of manuscripts, little of this literature
would actually get published, or only in very small printings. It was effectively silenced.

This conservative cultural climate that sought to deny the importance and influence
of the recent events affected the literary critique as well. Well into the 1950s, a formalist,
Text-immanent critical approach to literature was prevalent in West Germany. Within
this form of analysis, the context of the creation of literature and its critical implications
were ignored. This profoundly affected the reception of Jewish literature and in particular
survivor narratives, as they could not be read without a clear reference to, and analysis of,
their political–historical context.[65] Survivor literature did not fit the aesthetic norms
of the day, and German critics were unable to acknowledge the existence of a genre of
literature that had as its only common denominator its basis in the particular historical
reality of Nazi persecution. As the Holocaust itself was not yet recognized for the cultural
watershed event it represented, "Holocaust literature" as a genre could not be recognized,
either.[66] These literary-formalist concerns, of course, also conveniently served to mask
political motivations. This literature was not only rejected because these authors' styles
did not fit into a certain category, but because it would lead to a too painful confrontation
with the recent past and its implications for the German present.[67] The experiences
of Jewish survivors and exiles were seen as "competing memories," a *Konkurrenz der
Erinnerung*, which needed to be excluded.[68]

In the first postwar decade, many Jewish and exile authors were in fact more likely
to get their work published through presses in the *SbZ*, the Soviet occupied zone of
Germany, and the later DDR, as authors in the East were challenged to engage with
the new (socialist) political and social agenda.[69] As the socialist state did not feel the
burden of the Nazi past (they argued that it was not their legacy, but that of the Federal
Republic), writers were in fact encouraged (as an explicit cultural and educational task) to
face both the present and the past, and the retreat into "neutral themes" (such as nature)
as seen in Western literary circles was explicitly critiqued.[70] As the socialist regime liked
to see itself as the legitimate heir to the culture of a *democratic* Weimar Germany, presses
in the occupied zone and the later DDR were the first (and for many years the only)
ones to reprint many formerly banned works from exiled authors and new work by

former Nazi victims.[71] When the work of German Jews was published in the DDR, it was generally received positively, as can be seen with the publication of Grete Weil's manuscript of *Ans Ende* in East Berlin, which turned out to fit the bill of this new socialist literature quite well, as it critiqued both the Nazi system and the class divisions among the Jewish community.

Then again, for an upper-middle-class author without formal socialist ties, this (small-scale) recognition in East Berlin meant little to Weil, as she had hoped that her literature would make a difference in West Germany where she lived. Most West Germans, however, seemed to have little interest in the literature of surviving Jews, and preferred to focus on the rebuilding of Germany economically, a mentality that served so effectively to ward off any analysis of the recent past that it proved difficult for Weil to bear. Many years later, Weil would remark of this period: "I found this rebuilding-generation horrible."[72]

Like many survivor authors who in vain tried to find an audience for their work the first decade after the war, when Weil's first book proved so difficult to publish and it failed to elicit the kind of response and dialogue she had hoped for, she moved on. Weil would focus instead on her relationship, her new partner's career, and their social circle. As Jockisch had stayed in Germany throughout the war while working for different theaters, his contacts and group of friends had remained intact to a certain extent, which allowed Weil to resettle in Germany without the profound sense of alienation that often accompanied returning exiles who found their community decimated, their friends dead or remaining in exile.[73] Weil's circle of friends, just as before the war, consisted primarily of non-Jews, well-educated intellectuals and artists with whom in the late 1920s and early 1930s she had shared cultural and political affinities. Most of these Germans had opposed Hitler but had nevertheless been unable to actively resist the regime, and most of the men had served in the *Wehrmacht*. (Jockisch, too, had served in the German army during the last months of the war.) Her strong connection to these friends would, in important ways, affect her later writing and sense of audience.

During this period, Weil moved with Jockisch from Darmstadt to Stuttgart, to West Berlin, to Hannover, and finally, to Frankfurt. She supported his career as an opera director, and adjusted her literary aspirations to the situation: she wrote within her husband's theater circles, rarely touching in her work on her wartime experiences. Weil would write two librettos for operas,[74] and she wrote articles for *das neue forum*, a theater periodical. By the mid-1950s, she had started working on a modern story version of Sophocles' *Antigone* plays. This project, on which she would work continue to work in different forms on and off for the next two decades, was initially conceived as a faithful rewriting of Sophocles' original works. Asked years later why she decided to rewrite Antigone this way, Weil suggested that it was likely precisely the distance from the "recent events" of the war years, the *jüngste Vergangenheit* that working on the Greek myth allowed her that had appealed to her.[75] Weil, too, had adapted to the cultural climate of silence reigning in 1950s West Germany.

Competing Memories

By 1960, Jockisch and Weil were officially married and doing better financially, as Weil had managed to sell the pharmaceutical factory of the parents of her murdered first husband. She would spend the next few years writing essays for radio and translating English language literature for Limes Verlag. It was this work and the sense that the political and cultural climate was starting to change that brought her back to writing prose. While working at Limes, her publisher read *Ans Ende* and decided to reprint the volume in 1962, hoping that on the heels of the success in Germany of the play adaptation of the *The Diary of Anne Frank*, this book would find an audience, too.[76] This reprint of the 1949 East Berlin edition in effect represented Weil's literary debut in West Germany, at age fifty-six. Encouraged by the publisher's interest, Weil finished a new novel, which would be ready for publication in 1963, *Tramhalte Beethovenstraat* (*Tramhalte*, Last Trolley from Beethovenstraat) and a collection of stories, *Happy sagte der Onke* (*Happy*, "Happy," the Uncle Said) which was published by Limes in 1968.

In these works, Weil again wrote autobiographically themed prose, whereby in particular *Tramhalte* shows Weil's effort to find an adequate literary form in which to bear witness, in a now less-distanced, more personal tone, and to try to engage a German audience with the Jewish experience under Nazi persecution after the initial failure of *Ans Ende*. *Tramhalte* recounts once more parts of Weil's wartime experiences in Amsterdam, but it does so this time in a complex narrative, which, besides containing a critique of the evasive West German cultural and literary climate of the late 1940s and 1950s, also seems to deliberately create an opening for a dialogue on the Jewish past with a (young) German, non-Jewish audience.

Tramhalte does so by presenting a protagonist with which a German audience could identify more easily than the Jewish families in *Ans Ende*. For whereas *Tramhalte* is based on Weil's personal experience of witnessing from the window of her apartment in the Beethovenstraat in Amsterdam (the mostly Jewish neighborhood where she lived from 1937 to 1943) the secret nightly Nazi deportations of the Jews by trolley car, the novel tells of these events from the perspective of Andreas, a young, male, German (non-Jewish) poet turned war correspondent who is stationed in Amsterdam. The use of the German Andreas as the novel's main protagonist can be read as an attempt to bridge the two very different war pasts and memories of German Jews and non-Jews, and to make the story of a female Jewish survivor more universal.

The text describes approximately three days in the life of Andreas in present-day (1962)[77] West Germany in which he has just walked out on a fight with his wife, a Dutch-Jewish camp survivor named Susanne. She is the cousin of Daniel, a young man Andreas helped hide during the war but who was caught and killed in Mauthausen. Andreas drives off from his native München where he lives with his wife, to return by himself to Amsterdam. In Amsterdam he seeks to relive his wartime experiences, visiting people and sights that remind him of this past, in order to find a way to return to writing, something he has been unable to do since the war. The text moves back and forth between the present and Andreas's memories of wartime Amsterdam.

Andreas's present-day story articulates a detailed critique of the West German literary establishment of the day that had no interest in writers (Jewish or not) who wrote critically of the recent past and focused all its attention on the "new," on literature that was in full flight of this past. Central to the novel are the questions of the meaning of writing literature after the Holocaust, in particular in the German context, and the possibility of bearing witness. The dilemma of bearing witness seems to have two components: how to find the right language in which to do so, and how to find a way to connect to a German audience so that they would be capable of receiving a testimony that deals with Jewish victimization.

Andreas is depicted as having been an ambitious and successful poet before the war, and he therefore initially likes his post as a war correspondent in Amsterdam as he assumes that it will give him time to write his novel. He has isolated himself until that moment from the political realities of his day, as "Writing was the most important thing, more important than the war, which had never penetrated completely into his consciousness" (17). When confronted in Amsterdam with the reality of the Jewish persecution, taking place literally outside of his own window, everything changes. Especially after taking into hiding Daniel, a young Jewish man with whom he feels a strong bond (with homoerotic overtones on his part) who is later caught and deported, the Nazi persecution of the Jews comes to affect him deeply. In turn, Andreas finds that the story he is writing seems to have become irrelevant: "He began to sense the difficulties of writing a novel based on certain norms of social coexistence at a time when the norms had been suspended" (46–47). He can no longer write in the same highly aestheticized, apolitical vein as before, and instead feels an urgency to bear witness in his writing: "For him, the time for telling stories was past. He had an accusation to lodge against his fellow men. Those murderers" (39). He dreams of being able to make a difference with his writing after the war: "No more aestheticism, no formalism: language was a tool for digging into the depths, in order to finally bring out into the light that which has been buried, lost to history" (109).

Despite this desire, Andreas finds that he is unable to articulate what he has seen, as he cannot find the right words to describe the events, as there is no frame of reference, nothing to compare it with. The events he witnessed and about which he seeks to testify are unfathomable, unacceptable: "He had a wildly exaggerated desire to be true, was a fanatic for precision. But he didn't acknowledge any truth that did not begin with four hundred human beings deported in trolley cars. To write about any other subject was impossible. But for this one, there was no word, no symbol, no simile that covered it" (38). The alienation from writing symbolizes his growing personal alienation.

After returning to Germany after the war, his urge to bear witness is profound, but Andreas finds that he is still incapable of writing and that, furthermore, no one wants to hear his kind of story: "To be silent now would be cowardice and he's not a coward. He must give an account of what he'd seen. He should tell what he's witnessed. If he were asked, he'd speak. No one would ask him" (154). Andreas's difficulty in writing is exacerbated by the climate of profound denial in Germany, which is evident in publishing as well. When he meets with his former publisher, her message is that no wants to hear his kind of story of loss, victimization, and injustice. Germans want to forget and move on, but he is just too sensitive a soul: "You just don't have it any more—that's the real story, my boy. People like you just broke apart against that pack of Nazis. Not I. . . . It's a splendid time. So much talent. Youth, inconsiderate youth, doesn't give a damn about the past. The things you cried over aren't even worth kicking aside. They're right. The future belongs to them" (119).

The novel ends when Andreas leaves Amsterdam, still unable to write: "Nothing had come to light that he hadn't already known. He just went on drifting between that which could not be told and the urge to tell it anyway" (157). In a last attempt to get over his writer's block, he decides to visit Mauthausen, the camp where Daniel died, in the hope of capturing some kind of a concrete trace of history. While there, he realizes that there is nothing for him to find, certainly not "an answer to the question of how it had been possible" (160). Walking away from the site, he worries about it having been left standing, still "Ready to be used" (160). For Andreas, the continuities of the present with the past are too great, and German denial too effective.

The novel's unusual structure has the narrator jump back and forth between Andreas's present, a life in West Germany where people are intent on forgetting the Hitler years and on moving on, for "They were paying for something that they had indeed coveted, but had never actually gotten, and that was more than they could comprehend" (114), and the war years in Amsterdam living among the Nazi deportations of the Jews. This structure reinforces the impression that for Andreas the past is still very much present, a presence that in his case is caused by his very different German perspective,[78] in which, unlike for other Germans, there is no radical separation between a German and a Jewish war experience.

It is indeed *Tramhalte*'s unusual focus on a German non-Jew bearing witness to the Holocaust that makes the novel reveal (while leaving unresolved) the continued fissure between Germans and Jews, still present two decades after 1945. This unusual choice of a German non-Jewish protagonist can be read in different ways. Some critics read it as Weil's attempt to facilitate a German audience's identification.[79] By those standards this text actually fails, I would argue, as it reveals instead precisely the incommensurability of German and Jewish viewpoints. That is, while *Tramhalte* presents itself as the actual eyewitness testimony of the Nazi deportation of Dutch Jewry by a German who then attempts to relate these events to other Germans after the war (who prove unwilling to listen), the story is clearly based on the experiences of a persecuted Jew, and this perspective shows itself. Whereas Andreas is faithfully sketched as a kind of non-Jewish, apolitical double (whereby we get elaborate insight into his thoughts, motives, excuses and denial,[80] as well as his background as a German who, not unlike Weil herself, came from a "good home" of *Bildungsbürger*), this complex project of creating a composite out of a German who tells a "German" story that happens to contain "Jewish" memory, does not succeed entirely, and the resulting tension remains visible in the text. For instance, in the passages that deal with the question of how much Andreas (i.e., any German) knew or could have known of what was happening to the Jews, there is ambivalence: it is not clear whether the narrator wants us to believe Andreas, or whether we need to see his answers as evasions and excuses. This suggests that the narrator's perspective is actually more closely aligned to that of a critical victim than that of an apolitical German like Andreas. Another example is the contradiction visible in the passages that describe the deportations. While we hear about them from the perspective of a German who recounts it as a story that *should matter* to Germans, that is: as a *German* story, at the same time, this past as witnessed by Andreas is marked by excruciating historical detail, making it precisely a *particular* (Jewish) history, not a universal story.[81] If *Tramhalte* is read as an attempt to take this history out of its context of Jewish particularity so that Germans could identify with it, the text reveals a pronounced conflict that precisely belies this possibility, as the experiences and memories prove quite distinct.

Stephan Braese suggests on the basis of this unresolved conflict within the novel that Weil's choice to tell her own story by means of a (only half-sympathetic) German protagonist instead of a more autobiographical Jewish figure represents not a concession to facilitate the German audience's identification with Jewish victims, but something she chose because she was not able to convey the story any other way. Braese compares *Tramhalte* to *Der Weg* (the unpublished manuscript written in hiding in 1944), and suggests that the Andreas figure in *Tramhalte* is a kind of composite of both the Jewish character Monika and the German Andreas in *Der Weg*.[82] Braese thus argues that in *Der Weg* Weil was still able to imagine a dialogue between Jews (Monika) and non-Jewish Germans (Andreas), whereby the German Andreas who does not *know* but is willing to listen can hear from the Jewish Monika what the Nazis are doing to the Jews. By the time of Weil's writing of *Tramhalte* in the early 1960s, however, such an open exchange could no longer be imagined, and as a result, the dialogue between the two characters, Jew and German, has been silenced into a monologue by just the German Andreas. Braese concludes that the only way for Weil to imagine telling this Jewish story to a German audience was to have the Andreas figure in *Tramhalte* transform into a German who is the carrier of Jewish memory. He henceforth reads this transformation by Weil not as an opening for Weil's German audience (i.e., as a gesture of goodwill) but as a necessity, as Weil at that moment could no longer conceive that a German-Jewish dialogue was possible.

Because Weil's autobiography constituted an absolute clash of Jewish and of German memory, it could not be recounted as a dialogue between a Jew and a German, as it would only be seen as a *Jewish* story and would not be acknowledged by the German audience. Braese suggests that the figure of Andreas in *Tramhalte* thus functions to make the story more "universal," as a German protagonist bearing witness to these (historical, "Jewish") events in effect seems to make it a *German* story. By making her story less "Jewish," Weil thus hoped to find a *Zwischenraum*, a space between these absolutely conflicting memories that left no room for a Jewish history that was also that of a German.[83]

Taking on a German perspective in *Tramhalte* can be interpreted in still other ways, however. I read the act of "doubling" as a German protagonist as allowing a thoroughly assimilated German-Jewish author like Weil to explore her own position as a German who still felt a strong common bond with other Germans of a similar class and background, but who was cut off from this shared experience under the Nazis. As a German Jew she would have great difficulty reconnecting with Germans afterwards, as they were separated precisely by this very different war experience. The figure of Andreas allows for an examination of what separates Jewish from German war experience through what amounts to a Jewish "impersonation" of a non-Jewish German who tells what is, in effect, a Jewish story. It is significant here that Andreas is a bystander, not a hero. This suggests that if people such as Weil and other (non-Jewish) Germans of similar class and educational background would attempt to come to terms with this past, it is precisely this bystander position, their unwillingness to protest and fight the regime when it first came to power and their later (passive) collaboration with the regime that they would have to analyze, both as Germans and as German Jews. What could, or should they have done? By writing about these questions as a *German* (who in actuality is also a Jew) instead of from an exclusively Jewish (survivor) perspective, Weil not only addressed the Germans from "within," to connect with them for *their* sake, but also for her *own*.

Finally, imagining herself in the present as Andreas meant the freedom to imagine herself as an outsider witness to these horrible events, not as its Jewish victim. This may have created some much-needed emotional distance, while also freeing her for a dialogue with the postwar Germans among whom she lived.

It is this dialogue that *Tramhalte* complicates, however, both *within* the novel, and through the novel's publication history itself. That is, within the story Andreas cannot get beyond his writer's block even after he visits Amsterdam, and he stands little chance of getting his work published even if he finishes it, as the publishers have no interest in his kind of story. The novel suggests that for Germans, the experiences on which Andreas's memories are based are completely foreign, and that there is (as of yet) no communal language to talk about them within a West German context. The encounter between different memories is doomed to fail, even if a German testifies to Jewish experience. As a publication that functioned as an appeal for such a German-Jewish discourse, *Tramhalte* would ultimately fail, too. In contrast to *Ans Ende*,[84] this novel received quite a number of reviews (several in influential periodicals), but most of them suggest that the text could not be read for what it was trying to say, and that the reviewers were quite unfamiliar with books that discussed the Nazi past in the way *Tramhalte* does.[85] The novel was generally considered well written, but was deemed flawed in part because the theme (the literary crisis of the author, which is also a crisis of witnessing of the Holocaust) was considered so unusual for a novel.[86] Reviewers suggested that if a text brings up difficult subjects such as the Nazi past, it should ultimately carry a redeeming message, a moral lesson, something *Tramhalte* does not provide. Most reviewers completely skipped over the central theme of the problematic of representation after the Holocaust, or of the failure of the German literary establishment to respond to literature that does try to bear witness. None of the reviewers actually recommended the book to their readers, as they argued that readers would find that its subject matter was "too difficult," thereby creating as it were a self-fulfilling prophecy. Consequently, even though there were plenty of reviews, this novel that deals with the history of the murdered Jews and with the moral implications of writing "after" could not be read as the complex appeal for dialogue that it was, and failed to find an audience in the critics or the wider public.[87]

Although this kind of reception Weil received was rather typical of the kind of evasive critical response that literature with Jewish themes by German-Jewish authors had received up to this time, still, by 1963, this response seems somewhat surprising. At this point in the early 1960s, after all, had the cultural and political climate in Germany not began to change in ways that suggested the possibility for a greater openness to a discussion of the Nazi past and its legacy for present-day Germans and Jews? A closer look at this period reveals a more complicated picture.

The (Futile) Search for Engagement

Despite the decade-long avoidance of personal or political introspection among many Germans, exacerbated by the complacency of the unparalleled economic prosperity of the postwar boom, a number of changes became visible among younger Germans and within German-Jewish relations at this time. Within the Jewish community itself, there was some growth in communal life (small numbers of German Jews returned, synagogues were rebuilt), and a new sense of permanence. The German-Jewish community was officially recognized by international organizations, official West German relations with the state of Israel were normalized, and the number of antisemitic incidents and membership in extreme right-wing parties declined considerably, as philosemitism had become the norm. Furthermore, the Third Reich had finally become a mandatory part of German high-school curricula, a long-overdue educational effort that suggested a more genuine effort in the 1960s at facing the problematic German past.[88] Of great significance to the German community more broadly were several well-publicized war trials in the early 1960s, most notably the Eichmann trial in Israel in 1961, and the Auschwitz trial that took place from 1963 to 1965 in Frankfurt.[89] These trials created a new awareness in Germany of the nature and extent of the crimes committed by the Nazi regime, and exposed a younger generation of Germans (those who had been children during the war) to their parents' generation's war past in ways like never before.[90]

The Eichmann trial brought to the fore the complex role of the Nazi bureaucracy that allowed high-ranking officers to deny personal responsibility for the Holocaust, and made the issues of authority, obedience and the German denial of guilt topics of discussion, especially among younger, politically left-leaning Germans. Although the crimes the trial dealt with had been known about since the Nuremberg Tribunals, their extent and nature was analyzed anew. It also brought the victims to the center for the first time. The impact of their courtroom testimony was "of an immediacy and directness that left no room for repression, and the historical documentation and the authority of the witnesses allowed for no evasion or subterfuge."[91]

The Frankfurt Auschwitz proceedings in which sixteen SS officers and one Kapo who had worked in the Auschwitz concentration camp stood trial, brought home both issues even more forcefully. As many of the defendants used the *Befehlnotstand* defense with much success as a strategy to escape harsh punishment (the term implied that it had been necessary to follow orders unconditionally, even if one objected on moral terms), the issue of a more general German abdication of personal responsibility became a prime source of contention that polarized the German population. Younger Germans watched the proceedings with deep dismay, and realized that many former ex-Nazis had not been and would still not be prosecuted at all. More conservative Germans argued instead that these kind of trials amounted to a "witch hunt" of productive and law-abiding citizens. They used Germany's present-day phenomenal economic success as a justification for not needing to look at the past. In addition, they argued, financial reparations meant that the past had been acknowledged and dealt with, and that Germans had a right to move on.

At this point, the political tide started turning in favor of this younger generation. The Nazi past indeed did become a more pressing issue to reconsider, which became immediately evident in a phenomenal productivity of new German prose now dealing with the Nazi era by authors who had been children or young men during the Nazi era (e.g. Heinrich Böll, Günther Grass, Martin Walser, and Uwe Johnson).[92] There were also several theater productions based on the Eichmann and Frankfurt court proceedings (most notably Rolf Hochhuth's *The Deputy* from 1963 and Peter Weiss's *The Investigation* from 1965). These productions were significant in that they introduced a new form of play to the German theater: the "documentary drama," that showed an acute concern with an unearthing and depicting of "historical truth."[93] This theater was of great importance as their authors left behind the purely allegorical treatment of the Nazi era that had been so prominent in the late 1940s and 1950s. Yet, the

Holocaust still remained to a certain extent only a "peripheral issue" in most of these texts.[94]

Looking at the literary production of this period, it becomes clear that while facing the Nazi past became more important during the early 1960s, this confrontation took place within a cultural, legal, political, and philosophical framework that still understood Nazism primarily as *a system* that needed to be more thoroughly analyzed, critiqued, and dismantled. What was not yet acknowledged was how the Third Reich had also created a troubling *personal* legacy, which affected present-day Germans in their relationship to the past and to Jews and the Holocaust in the present. That is, the younger generation of Germans born between 1920 and 1930 still saw themselves primarily as victims of the Nazi regime, not as products of it. As their personal responsibility and involvement and that of the parents' generation could not be acknowledged on a more individual level, an open approach to listening to the other side, namely, that of Jewish victims, was as of yet impossible.

Considered in this light, the lack of response to Weil's publications, *Ans Ende* (the reprint) and *Tramhalte* in the mid-1960s is less surprising. Even though Weil's work dealt with the most current of themes, and had been (re-)published right at the moment that, as Dagmar Lorenz points out, one could indeed expect ". . . the actualization of the Holocaust as a topic because of the Eichmann trial,"[95] this renewed interest was not sufficient to get readers to surpass the hurdle of reading literature that focused on the victimization of the Jews by the Nazis, and that laid the legacy of German guilt bare. Texts by German-Jewish survivors such as Weil's were in too many respects ahead of their time, they were too direct, too personal, and too complex in their Jewishness.

By the mid-1960s, Weil had made two trips to the United States and Mexico that inspired her to write on a subject matter a bit more removed from the German present and the Nazi past. It led to the collection of three "travel stories," *Happy, sagte der Onkel*.[96] Finished in 1967, the collection was published in 1968. Although none of the stories in *Happy* are set in present-day Germany, even here this past cannot really be put to rest as Weil shows the question of the problematic legacy of the Holocaust to be ever-present and of relevance to current political and cultural analyses, even in foreign contexts. The stories reflect Weil's strong engagement with the social and political issues of the mid- to late 1960s: inequities between rich and poor, civil rights clashes in the United States, the futility and violence of the Vietnam War, the threat of atomic warfare, and these conflicts are viewed from the vantage point of the continued troubling legacy of the Nazi past. While this kind of engagement would not have stood out among German intellectual writing of the period (a critical stance against the United States had become a staple of the German left), in describing these different injustices, Weil never seeks to minimize the crimes of the Nazis, or compare them in a way that eliminates their specificity, as would happen in much leftist literature. Where Weil's narrators seek comparisons, they lead precisely to a more profound understanding of the uniqueness of each situation of oppression or injustice, and a realization that their own position as victim does not spare them from being seen as oppressors by others. Written in a first-person narrative style, the stories come across as highly personal and to a great extent autobiographical.

The title story starts off with the narrator traveling in Southern California and her skeptical observations of the region, its people, and their views: "One thinks life is good here. Surrounded by the 'keep-smiling people' one would perhaps manage to develop the world view that Russians are bad, the Americans are good, the Negroes certainly capable of improvement, the poor can be helped with donations, and humans are humane" (13).[97] Although the narrator's impressions of the United States are mixed, in particular in regard to the inequalities between rich and poor, and white and black, this criticism stems not from the kind of blatant anti-U.S. sentiment common among German leftist thinkers of the period,[98] but from a sense of solidarity based on her personal experience of persecution. "If I were a Negro in the States, I would rather live in the desert than in the cities, even at the risk that the chance of escape would be very small here. . . . This I knew, I knew how to flee. This I learned during five years on the run and in hiding, long enough to become an expert."[99]

Yet, this experience of persecution does not automatically make Jews better people, as becomes clear from the narrator's visit with an uncle and aunt, German Jews who left Nazi Germany in the 1930s. Now living rather unhappy lives in the Southern Californian desert, the uncle and aunt profess homesickness for the *Heimat* at every turn, even as they are determined to believe that they are better off here than in Germany where they argue the spirit of Hitler still reigns. They exclaim at every turn that they are "happy" and repeat a set of American platitudes: "Everyone is friendly to everyone," "neighbor helps neighbor, the rich help the poor."[100] These platitudes, however, also include racist views. Whereas the uncle first expresses the rhetoric of well-meaning whites (who nevertheless stand by and do nothing in the ongoing civil rights struggle): "A lot has improved, but one cannot solve the Negro question in a day," when the aunt is straightforward in her racism, "The negroes are dirty and stupid. . . . It were best if we sent the Negroes back to Africa," the uncle chimes in: "America for the Americans."[101] The narrator, frustrated by the contradictions with which her uncle and aunt live, confronts them with the loss of their relatives at Auschwitz, after which she is asked to leave. The message is clear: one will not necessarily find common ground merely on the basis of shared oppression.

In the second story, "Gloria Halleluja," this sense of solidarity with African Americans, as well as with Holocaust survivors living in the United States, gets tested again. Surprised to find that Harlem is much like a segregated ghetto in Manhattan, the narrator ventures out on her own to explore it, as she feels that, unlike her liberal white American friends who feel guilt (and fear black revenge), she can understand the situation of the African Americans. As the sole white person walking the streets of Harlem, this sense of shared experience, of commonality, quickly evaporates. She is confronted with her own fear and prejudice, and the people whom she encounters see her as an intruder. Her own experience of oppression is too different, and too unfamiliar to bridge this gap: "But disasters only resemble each other on the surface. . . . Their pain and mine, two continents, two different times . . ."[102]

This message is reinforced twice more within the story. First, as the narrator is invited for dinner at the home of an African American woman tour guide, where she is welcomed until the father of the guide realizes that she is a Jew and she gets thrown out, confronted with most ancient form of antisemitism: "A Jew, a murderer of our Lord. Get out of my house!"[103] Next, she meets the owner of a local pawnshop, a woman camp survivor. The narrator comes to realize that many of the little retail stores in Harlem are owned by poor Jewish immigrants, which causes the relationship between the local Jews and

African Americans to be tenuous. Furthermore, when the narrator reveals to the pawn-shop owner who is of German-Jewish origin that she still lives in Germany, the survivor curses her out, labeling her a traitor. Her stay in Harlem comes to a final and dramatic end in a bar, where she is verbally attacked by male customers who (jokingly?) predict a black revolution in which they, and not white people, will rule the world. She flees.

In the final story of this collection, "B sagen" (if You Say A, You Should Also Say B)[104] an older German-Jewish woman on vacation in Mexico is confronted with memories of her war past that come to color everything she sees, culminating in a (what turns out to be imaginary) dialogue with a tour guide, a man her age in whom she thinks she recognizes a former Nazi camp guard.

What initially triggers these thoughts in the woman is her encounter with the offer altar of the Chichén-Itzá temple ruins. There, she finds herself confronted with the continuity of homicidal cruelty throughout history: "Why had they done this to them? Always the same thing, from human origin on, only the method changes. One learns nothing."[105] At the sight of skulls that are left over from the rituals of human sacrifice, the historical context of centuries of murders becomes blurred: "Men's skulls, women's skulls, no longer distinguishable, in death they are the same, Indians, Negroes, Gypsies, Jews, always the same, at all times, timeless, the end in a mass grave. . . ."[106] Absorbed in these thoughts, she notices the tour guide, in whom she thinks she recognizes a former Nazi soldier who worked in 1943 at the *Joodsche Schouwburg*, the Jewish theater deportation center of Amsterdam Jews.

In the imagined encounter that follows, the ex-Nazi defends himself against the woman's accusations by abdicating his responsibility, "orders are orders," and by suggesting that his guilt would be difficult to prove. He argues furthermore that he joined the Nazis because he was poor, and that she has no right to judge him, as she had more choices as a Jew of privileged background. He then points out that she kept her husband from actively resisting the Nazis in the 1930s, and indicts her for her work for the Jewish Council. He argues that not only he, but she, too, has managed to live on, apparently quite well: "When I see you like that . . . I want to bet that not only have you come to terms with it . . . but you are in great lines okay with this world, which has surely improved for you, but has stayed just as bad for most people. You protest that what you do not like, Atomic bombs, the Vietnam War and Apartheid. . . . But there is nothing left of the young woman who wanted to burn the world down out of desperation."[107]

While the dialogue reveals the unwillingness of the former Nazi guard to face the responsibility for his acts during the war years (and suggests the difficulty of trying to convict such ex-Nazis in current-day Germany), the self-critique of the Jewish narrator is considerable as well. She, too, has failed. She points to the similarities between the two of them, and more broadly between the position of Germans and Jews: for both of them the sense of failure and of guilt is unbearable. As a consequence, both Germans and Jews need to repress it, and thus live on while denying it: "Our past is not one with which one can live, and since we are alive, it could not have been."[108] It is either/or. If this past is true, then you have to draw the consequences (*da müssen Sie auch B sagen*), and live with the guilt. "Draw the consequences, say B, say B . . . have opinions, state opinions . . . always intended to, worked on it, but never fully mastered. . . . The hour of truth, and truth farther removed than ever. Who can tell you the truth? What is your truth?"[109] The imagined exchange shows the narrator's profound discomfort with this past, while at the same time it suggests that it is precisely the inability to fully face it, the desire to repress or deny that creates an uncomfortable bond between Germans and Jews.

In this story, then, the first text in which Weil writes of a direct postwar encounter between a (former) German Nazi and a Jewish survivor, there are no simple answers, no resolutions. While the German is marked by his unwillingness to take responsibility for his actions (blaming his background or "orders" instead), the survivor finds herself in a poor position to accuse him because of what she conceives of as her own failings. This inability of Germans to face the past, the difficulties for Jewish survivors in coming to terms with it, and the inability of German-Jewish relations to normalize as this past always remains present, would remain the central subject matter in Weil's work from here on, as would the use of the intimate autobiographical and fragmentary narrative style which moves back and forth in time from past to present.

Whereas the stories in *Happy* dealt with a range of issues that became extremely current in the charged cultural–political debates of the late 1960s in West Germany, (the Nazi legacy, class and race oppression, a critique of the United States), this work, too, received little thoughtful critical response, nor did it find an audience. Either the political relevance of Weil's stories was overlooked in its entirety, or it was read as a text that only dealt with the Nazi past, not with the continuing problematic political present.

This lack of resonance again seems surprising, as by 1968, the cultural climate in Germany had started to change radically in favor of a more thorough facing of both the past and the present. Why, then, did *Happy* not find a more receptive audience? The answer needs to be sought in the continued complex German relation to the Nazi past that dominated not just those of Weil's generation, but that turned out to have been passed on to their children and to the postwar generation as well.

"Symptoms of German Amnesia"

While the early 1960s had witnessed progressive cultural changes in West Germany, reflecting a move away from denial and repression of the past, a government move to the right in 1966, in which a "Grand Coalition" of the conservative CDU and the social democrats eliminated all political opposition seemed to halt this kind of progress. In response, a younger generation now coming of age was spurred into political action. They no longer felt that they were represented in this conservative, repressive democracy led by a president and a chancellor who both had active Nazi pasts. They protested in particular the German state's emphasis on materialism, as the phenomenal economic growth and prosperity of the so-called *Wirtschaftswunder*[110] of the past decades had seemed to make any critical inquiry into past or present social wrongs unnecessary. Although Germany's new found national pride had been based on this economic success, it was not sufficient for a younger generation to halt a questioning of the past, in particular as within the now reigning (Marxist) analyses of the day, the two, Fascism and capitalism, seemed intricately related.

Growing dissent eventually culminated in massive public protests, organized at first by the German student movement and later by a variety of new grassroots groups who together formed an important part of a growing extra-parliamentary opposition (*APO*) that stirred up the German social, political, and cultural horizon. This popular left protest movement, which politicized an entire generation, developed in West Germany simultaneously with those in France and the United States. In Germany as elsewhere, young people protested the Vietnam War (in which Germany played a part through its Western "capitalist" and "neo-imperialist" alliance with NATO); they sought a democratization of the universities, and the correction of present social injustice. The movement envisioned broad utopian socialist ideals, solidarity with the working class, and a rejection of materialism. Young Germans, however, also very specifically sought a confrontation with their parents and the Nazi past, in the form of an "anti-authoritarian" rebellion.[111]

By 1968, this movement radicalized, as global as well as national political developments seemed to take a turn for the worse (the failure of the Prague Spring, the escalation of the war in Vietnam, the police killing of a German student during a protest, the assassination attempt on Rudi Dutscke, the leader of the socialist league of German students). Protests were staged against these developments, and against the conservative Springer Press that ran tendentious, alarmist, and at times even false news stories about the activities of the movement in their newspapers and magazines. At the same time, a small group of activists, who would later become known as the Baader Meinhof group, or *Rote Armee Fraktion* (RAF) as they preferred to call themselves, disappointed with the lack of progress in the student movement, started developing terrorist activities, such as setting fires in department stores to protest "the burning of children" in Vietnam.

Even as by the late 1960s an important political shift had taken place, in 1969, Willy Brandt became chancellor of a social democratic coalition, followed in 1974 by a similar coalition under Helmut Schmidt, the German government responded to the leftist protests and terrorist acts with increasingly repressive measures. The passing of the *Notgesetze* (emergency laws) in 1968 and the *Radikalenerlaß* (decree against "radicals" that made "disloyalty to the constitution" illegal and that banned anyone declared guilty from civil service jobs such as teaching),[112] seemed to confirm the New Left's accusation of the West German democracy as a protofascist state.

In some respects, the conservative government response that ensued can be interpreted as a sign of a still lingering fundamental insecurity over the strength of the democratic foundations of the new state. When in the late 1960s the status quo became seriously challenged, the new German republic was still less than twenty years old, and democracy as a system still relatively untested. Many conservative politicians still believed that public protest represented a danger to the republic, and using the Weimar Republic's demise as a warning, they interpreted this protest as dangerous, as a sign of a weak democracy.[113]

Conversely, many German Jews initially considered this new "anti-authoritarian" opposition of the younger generation of Germans as a positive development, as it brought about a broader political awareness of the need to reconsider the Nazi past and its legacy. This broader political awareness, for instance, helped to initiate other concentration camp trials and led to intense parliamentary debates over the extension of the statute of limitations for Nazi crimes.[114] It soon became apparent, however, that this new critical analysis of the recent German past also produced new tactics of evasion: the actual present-day relations between Germans and Jews, the continued question of German guilt, and the trauma of the victims remained untouched.

As the analysis of the Nazi dictatorship primarily took place within a Marxist framework, Nazi crimes quickly came to stand in for other state violence, as fascism was seen merely as an extreme outgrowth of capitalism. This kind of critique led to a highlighting of the continuations of a fascist system in present day in Germany in politics and industry, as well as the connections between capitalism, imperialism, and oppression in the West's treatment of people in the Third World. On the one hand, this rather dogmatic Marxist analysis of the ills of the Nazi regime as rooted in capitalism excluded much of the specificity of that regime, in particular the genocide of the Jews. For instance, leftist critiques of Germany's government and economy in which many former Nazis continued to play an important role (many companies had derived major profit from slave labor and stolen assets during the war, but few of their management was replaced or punished), were significant and long overdue, but were quickly broadened into a more general Marxist critique. As such, the Nazi past and the victimization of the Jews would play a role only in the background, whereas the primary focus was on the ills of capitalism and its workings in present-day Germany. On the other hand, this kind of analysis soon came to focus only on broader current political and social issues, only a few of which were specifically German, most of which focused on political inequalities and on war and oppression elsewhere in the world, and none of which concerned Jews or German-Jewish relations. Thus whereas conflicts such as the Cuban missile crisis, the U.S. involvement in the Vietnam War, and the civil rights clashes in the American South were analyzed from within "the shadow of Auschwitz," as it were, it happened in such a way as to precisely deny or underplay the scale and uniqueness of the Nazi crimes and the personal legacy it had left for this generation. Rather than an analysis of the behavior of one's own parents (or the problematic inheritance this represented for this generation), the answer of young leftists to this problematic legacy took the form of a radical critique of capitalism and imperialism.[115]

Consequently, while it seemed that young German students—the first generation who were not themselves implicated in the crimes of the Nazi regime—would be better able to face these crimes and their legacy of guilt, it was precisely their "leftist orientation" that served to "protect . . . them from the need to work through the Nazi past and its legacy" as Schlant suggests.[116] For if the Holocaust was seen as an outgrowth of fascism, and fascism was merely "the most reactionary and most imperialistic development of capitalism," the focus should be to "battle against capitalism."[117] This form of leftist analysis that relegated the Holocaust to the periphery, represents as Andreas Huyssen suggests, another "symptom of German amnesia."[118]

This complex collusion of an undifferentiated leftist rebellion against the parents' generation's legacy and the unexamined Nazi inheritance, as well as latent antisemitism, could be witnessed in its most extreme form in the German left's uncritical support of the Palestinians after the Six-Day War in 1967. While conservative politicians and the media expressed their admiration for Israel's military power, the New Left, seeking to distance itself from the right's militaristic rhetoric, rooted for the Palestinians and became increasingly anti-Zionist and antisemitic. While it was predictable that the left would choose to oppose the government's course, their identification with the Palestinians also functioned to relegate the role of the Germans in the Holocaust to the background: there was no *Aufarbeitung der Endlösung*.[119] Instead, as Jeffrey Herf argues, in their leap "from the German past to the Israeli and Palestinian present," Marxism and the politics of identification with the Third World "served as defense mechanisms preventing a distinct left-wing grasp of the anti-Semitic past."[120]

As it turns out, this younger generation was no better equipped to deal with the Nazi past than their parents, perhaps because as Eric Santner has suggested, "the second generation inherited not only the un-mourned traumas of the parents but also the psychic structures that impeded mourning in the older generation in the first place."[121] Many older Germans had never mourned the loss of Hitler, of *Völkisch* belonging and loyalty, nor the unbelievable loss of life and land. Unable to reconcile their mostly happy memories of the Nazi era with the crushing defeat that ended it all and the belated awareness of the immensity of the regime's crimes, they repressed, forgot, or denied. Their children, in turn, would not (want to) know of their parents' past and the troubling legacy it represented for them, either.

Whereas at first, the younger generation's rebellion against the complacency and denial of the parents' generation had seemed to bode well for a more thorough working through of the Nazi past, and for a start of an actual German-Jewish dialogue, by 1968 there was still such a profound clash of perception (and of need) between the former perpetrators and their descendants who inherited this guilt and the victims of the regime, that a dialogue proved impossible to engage in, even for younger Germans. This explains in part, then, why literary texts that attempted to initiate such an exchange for the most part still fell on deaf ears. As a result, when Weil's 1968 story collection *Happy* launched "two signals into the heated midst of the escalated polit-ical discourse in and around the anti-authoritarian movement," as Braese suggests, those signals were not picked up on.[122] "One radically questioned . . . that Jews, and quite particularly Jewish survivors of the Nazi regime were, by nature, genuine partners to the movement. The second pointed to an acute need for radical [German] self-questioning." This work, too, as *Ans Ende* and *Tramhalte*, was ahead of its time. As Nussbaum and Meyer suggest: "When the book came out in 1968, one clearly couldn't do much with its mercilessness, then again, one had only just started to confront/discuss [*sich auseinandersetzen*] the National Socialist past in West Germany."[123]

Even in the cultural climate of the late 1960s, which on the surface at least had seemed more favorable to an open dialogue about the Nazi past, Weil's new works *Tramhalte* and *Happy* that seemed to provide ample opportunity for such a discussion (as texts that looked at both the present and the past from the perspective of a former Nazi victim), were still far too confrontational to be dealt with effectively by the critics or a broader audience. Both texts employ creative strategies to address the German audience in order to engage it: a German protagonist who represents a German as well as a Jewish story; travel stories that weave a critical reading of present-day American life with the narrator's own experiences of Nazi oppression. Yet these works also offered, respectively, a critical view of 1950s/1960s German cultural amnesia, and a broad cultural analysis of the similarities between present-day forms of violence and oppression and that of the Nazi past and the West German present.

It would ultimately take nearly another decade before the cultural climate in Germany changed to such an extent that Jewish literature such as Weil's could make any kind of a significant impact on the cultural and political debates about the legacy of the Nazi past. For Weil and a good number of other German- and Austrian-Jewish survivor authors who had returned to Germany after 1945 because they were still identified primarily as German and sought a dialogue with the Germans, one thus needs to conclude that they did not find resonance for their work, as for two decades after 1945 their address was still seen as too confrontational. The Holocaust had in profound ways caused a rift in Germany that could not be bridged, even if survivors sought to do so, as most Germans were as yet unable to face their own memories, let alone the encounter with a German-Jewish memory of the Nazi era.

CHAPTER THREE
MYTHICAL INTERVENTIONS

"Hitler's Children": The Legacy of Silence in 1970s Germany

After leftist terrorist violence escalated in the 1970s, with bombings of police and government targets, and kidnappings and murders of major German public figures, West Germans became ever more divided on the direction of the nation's political course. As both camps, a conservative establishment (including government and police) and the terrorists and their (generally younger) left-leaning sympathizers saw the present through the lens of the Nazi past, they seemed incapable of thinking in anything but extremes. On the left, terrorists and their sympathizers argued that the West German liberal democracy was no more than a façade behind which a fascist system lay hidden.[1] They saw the government's repressive response as a greater threat to the democracy than terrorism itself. In this sense, young leftist radicals felt that by resisting the system now, they resisted "fascism" in a manner their parents had failed to do. On the right, the conservative-liberal politicians who tried to repress the radical leftist networks, too, felt that they were making up for the failures of the Nazi past, by resisting a new form of "totalitarian violence." The political right did not see the "generation of 1968" as part of a new democratic process, but as new fascists: these young leftists were "Hitler's children."[2]

In some ways, of course, they were. Not in terms of a similar ideology (as conservative opponents argued), but in the sense that they represented a response to the decades long complete avoidance by the Federal Republic's founding generation of any kind of a discussion about the legacy of National Socialism.[3] The resulting rift between the generations, between left and right, was something akin to a "symbolic civil war," in which the parties fought without mercy about the conclusions that should be drawn from the National Socialism past for the present of the Federal Republic.[4]

While politically the student movement's protest would prove to a great degree futile and quickly fizzled out in the early 1970s, in other ways, young leftists did create cultural and social change. Throughout the 1970s, a greater emphasis on the personal emerged: an examination of the self (in literature this expressed itself in so-called new subjectivity, works that focused on one's inner life, leading to a wave of autobiographical texts), the rights of women, and the role of sexuality. This turn toward the personal would eventually lead to a new assessment by a younger generation of the Nazi past of their parents, and a more individual reckoning with this history that proved genuine and fruitful in some cases, but reactive and evasive in others.

It was this climate of continuing generational discord against the background of governmental repression and terrorist violence and its strong links to the Nazi past, coupled with a retreat into private life and a search for alternative modes of living and finding happiness, to which Weil would respond in two novels that she published in the early 1980s. These novels that became very successful, had a different tone from much of her previous work (with the exception of the story "B sagen" from *Happy*)—they were much more directly autobiographical, used an intimate, personal voice, and showed Weil to be influenced by the new culture of the 1970s, in particular the "new subjectivity" in literature and the women's movement. In her subject matter, however, she remained constant: again, she would write on her wartime experiences, embedding them in the context of the German present, trying to bear witness and have her testimony matter to Germans today. This time, however, the issue of both personal and cultural memory had become more central. How do the memories of the Third Reich play themselves out, how are they shaped and reshaped to fit our present needs?

Antigone: Mythical Resistance Fighter or Terrorist?

Weil spent much of the early 1970s in semiretirement.[5] She took care of her second husband who had fallen critically ill with leukemia, continued to write, but made no effort to get her work published. She in fact gave up her work as translator and severed all ties with Limes Verlag. After Jockisch passed away, she moved back to München, the city of her childhood, and undertook trips to India, Tibet, and Nepal. It was not until the late 1970s that she started writing more seriously again, this time on a novel in which she reworked pieces of her 1950s manuscript on Antigone. Weil finished this novel, originally entitled *Todestreppe* in 1978. While this manuscript, too, proved difficult to get published initially, once an editor at the Swiss press, Nagel & Kimche suggested the new title *Meine Schwester Antigone* for it (*Antigone, My Sister, My Antigone*) and published it in 1980, the novel became a great success. It helped that the publication came about right at the time of a new German wave of Antigone popularity,[6] and during a period of great newfound interest of the German audience in the experiences of Jewish victims under Nazi persecution, due to the recent broadcasting of the American miniseries *Holocaust* on German public television.

On the surface, the success of the novel may seem to imply that Weil finally found a way to bridge the distance between her own experiences (about which she writes in *Antigone* more directly autobiographically than ever before) and that of her German audience, suggesting that, at last, she found "address." Moreover, it seems to indicate that possibly something in the German public itself had changed, due to the generational change that had taken place, or perhaps due to a new, more elaborate exposure to the events of the Holocaust. A reading of both this cultural context and of the novel's complex story and structure complicates this notion of a successful address, however. Not only does the literary establishment's response to this work suggest that it is still misread, but the text itself already hints at the impossibility of such a belated understanding between Germans and Jews. It shows furthermore that this appeal to the German audience to engage with the past is fraught with complications, not only for Jewish survivors and older Germans, but for a younger generation of Germans as well.

Antigone is an account of one day out of the life of an aging German-Jewish writer who is both the main protagonist and the main narrator in this text, who has a personal history that strongly resembles Weil's.[7] The narrator struggles on a daily basis with the difficult memories of her wartime past—the years of persecution, hiding, and loss during the Nazi era—while slowly the mental and emotional defenses that she has built up over many years are starting to crumble under the strain of her aging, and the social and political discord playing itself out in the Federal Republic in the 1970s. She describes a pronounced rift that has become visible between an older generation of Germans and their children who were born during or after the war. The former prefer to continue on a course in which the Nazi past is ignored or forgotten on account of Germany's present-day economic and political accomplishments. The latter seek political, cultural, and personal change, as they experience the present-day republic as hollow, evasive, and oppressive, and try to find a voice through protest and terrorism in which some version of this past can be articulated. Although for several decades after the war, the narrator had "began to think that the Germans were capable of adjusting to democracy. Things went well, very well, in fact," for some time now "little flames have been flickering on the site of a fire that must have been smoldering unnoticed for a long while" (117).

The narrative consists of an almost continual stream of consciousness, an inner monologue of about eighteen hours, which follows the thoughts, memories, and associations of the elderly woman from the moment she wakes up in the morning until late in the evening. As the story moves back and forth from the present (she takes a bath, eats breakfast, reads the paper, works on her writing, goes out for an errand), to memories of the past, the text covers many decades, concentrating on three periods in particular: the woman's protected and privileged childhood as a daughter of a prominent Jewish lawyer in München; her experiences of exile and persecution under Hitler; and her encounter as an aging Jewish woman with present-day (late 1970s) West German culture.

Immediately at the novel's opening, we find that the particular day in the life of the narrator represents a crisis. Recently, she has lost her dog, and this loss, she suggests, has opened up a much older and deeper wound: "It was no animal I was mourning for. In my poor head he grew and grew . . . he battered down all the walls I had painstakingly erected around myself in the course of the past forty years to enable me to live" (32). The wound that is opened is that of the Nazi persecution. "My murder complex. My old wound" (12). This past history is presented in the form of fragments of her memories. We learn that she fled from Germany to the Netherlands during the Nazi years, lost her husband Waiki in Mauthausen after he was caught in a German round up, and that she survived herself in hiding, after working briefly for the Amsterdam Jewish Council. She returned to West Germany soon after the war, rebuilt her life with her new husband Urs. It is Urs's recent death, together with the loss of her dog, the physical deterioration that comes with aging (the woman is in her seventies), and the general German cultural climate that now make her feel increasingly estranged, disconnected from life. Soon it becomes apparent that she is overwhelmed by an array of unsettling feelings of guilt, shame, and fear that are brought up by even the most innocuous thoughts and associations that all lead back to memories with which she cannot come to terms.

Her profound sense of guilt stems from her war experiences, and her feeling that she should have done more, should have saved her husband, or other Jews. She wonders why she survived, an assimilated Jew from the German upper class, who had, up to Hitler's reign, never felt very Jewish: "My relationship to Judaism, lukewarm and lax" (146). She struggles with her position of privilege: her class, her wealth, and her connections. Unlike most other Jews, she had a chance to work for the Jewish Council, delay her own deportation, and find safety in hiding. After the war, she rebuilt her life in West Germany, pretended that continuing on as normal as possible was the solution. Now she wonders how she could have done this: "I regret, profoundly regret that I am still alive, and I do not understand how it is possible. . . . I ask myself time and time again what sort of person I am that I can live with Waiki's murder" (32). This sense of survivor guilt is confounded by the difficult questions asked of her by the younger generation of West Germans: "Whether we never considered resisting. No, the thought never crossed our minds" (9).

In order to find answers for herself and for this younger generation about how it got to this point, and to create a bridge between them, her past and the present, the narrator looks, as she has done throughout her life, at the Greek Antigone myth that played such a central role in the cultural imagination of German *Bildung* and in her upbringing.[8] Antigone, the Greek princess born out of the incestuous marriage between Oedipus and Jocaste, resists the will of King Creon when she attempts to bury her brother Polyneices, who has been killed by his brother Eteocles in rivalry over the rule of the city Thebes. Antigone thereby ignores her sister Ismene's advice to not resist Creon's rule. Her act is discovered, and as a result, she is sentenced to death by being buried alive in a cave. She dies in order to defend her brother's honor.

The rewriting and rethinking of this myth has been an important project for the narrator for years, one that she has struggled with: "I tried to write her story, but all I produced was a pretentious sentimental epic on a heroic maiden. Yet I did not give up; there was always an Antigone notebook on my desk, alongside my other projects" (14). While this describes the basic premise and structure of the text, the narrative is so fragmented in its constant shifts from the protagonist's present, via associations, to memories of her past (childhood and war), to the Antigone story (both the narrator's telling about the writing of this story and an actual version of the story itself), that it is difficult to pin down how all its different parts function, in particular the Antigone story. What makes the structure so complex is the combination of the very fragmented interior monologue with the Antigone story, which is for the most part presented in the text independently of this main interior monologue, with few if any transitions between these two. While this makes it seem as if the Antigone narrative stands on its own, the narrator within the inner monologue mentions repeatedly that she is writing on Antigone, "I sketch out a conversation here, jot down an episode there . . ." (14), suggesting instead that the Antigone passages that are embedded are the result of the writing process the narrator recounts in the main narrative. The Antigone story, then, is embedded in the larger narrative, which in turn tells us about the protagonist's process of writing this story. As it turns out, it is the narrator's transformation in her thinking and writing about the Antigone figure that is central to the development of the main narrative.

The narrator's relationship to the figure of Antigone and her depictions of her have undergone many changes during her life time she suggests, and do so again during the course of this one day, in a way that seems to parallel the woman's existential crisis. As a young woman, Antigone's meaning was pretty clear-cut for the narrator: "I simply accepted her fate, as if it were self-explanatory, a grim story, no more" (13). It was "Not until I was brutally jerked out of my princess like existence, brought face to face with murder and annihilation," that Antigone became "larger, more significant, more luminous, more ambiguous" (13–14). The narrator now found deeper similarities between her own life and that of Antigone: both led lives of privilege but were forced through circumstances to leave their homeland (Antigone, too, spends time in exile), and both had to make life and death decisions that would determine their future.

Initially during this day, the narrator describes her fascination with the Antigone figure as rooted in identification and comparison: "How do I see her? . . . At times she is part of me, at other times my exact opposite. A dream over time, the image of what I wish to be but am not, a king's daughter . . . an unyielding resistance fighter . . . a determined soul who refuses to deviate from her own law" (14). The narrator imagines a strong connection between herself and this mythical resistance figure, but she is aware that Antigone may represent a position that actually differs from hers in important ways.[9] While she sought to survive, sought compromise, Antigone did not. Still, the protagonist wants to use her as a kind of moral touchstone, as a figure to identify with and measure herself against, in light of her sense of failure about her own past. The narrator attempts to make sense of Antigone's act of defiance that gets her killed, in order to come to terms with her own lack of resistance under the Nazis that left her husband and so many others dead, yet kept her alive: "I want to write a book about a girl that does not let herself be written by me, measure my stubbornness against hers, see who will win out in the end."[10]

These dynamics of comparing and trying to measure up become increasingly complicated as the older woman comes face to face with a number of young people who confront her with painful questions that change her precarious equilibrium. First, her godchild Christine comes to visit. The narrator feels close to Christine and her peers: "She is my link to a generation over which most of my contemporaries merely shake their heads. From her I can learn many things I knew nothing of, things I need to know if I am to avoid total despair" (26). She invests her hope in this younger generation as they attempt to break through the silence and complacency of their parents. Nevertheless, the encounter is difficult: "They reject people like me out of hand. . . . And why should they trust us? . . . The Nazi generation. The generation of SS officers, execution squad commanders, concentration camp guards . . ." (8). Still, she believes that from her position as a victim of the Nazi regime it should be possible to reach out to them. When she is faced with the difficult question of why she did not resist, however, her position as a German Jew feels ambiguous. She cannot answer the question. Christine knows the narrator well, and confronts her with the fact that this is why she now writes on Antigone: "And now you are writing a book about a girl who did resist" (34).

Exhausted after Christine's visit, besieged with memories of the war past, in particular her work for the Jewish Council, "A criminal organization, a naive organization . . ." (84), the older woman feels a profound sense of failure: ". . . I become aware of the filth I have waded through, the icy coldness when I found myself confronted with decisions that could not but make me guilty, no matter how I chose" (90). When she returns to work on Antigone, she now comes to question how applicable the parallels between the actions of heroine and her self are: "Obstinate, absolutely certain that she is right. Yet is she really right? . . . What would she have done in my position? . . . I think of her with envy, for all she had to do was bury the dead, not try to save the living" (86).

The image of Antigone shifts even more when in the afternoon (two-thirds into the story), a contemporary Antigone enters the scene, in the form of Marlene, a young girl affiliated with a German leftist terrorist group, a sympathizer, a *Sympathisant*. Christine asks the narrator to hide Marlene from the police, and she does so immediately, even though she herself is not "a sympathizer when it comes to murder," but she does "understand how helplessness can breed violence" (109). She believes that the cause of the discord in this generation of nonconformists who are "no longer reachable . . ." ultimately lies with her own generation, ". . . for when did we ever make a serious attempt to reach out to them?" (112). Now this generation shakes things up, gets "on our nerves . . ." they refuse "to let us assert that all is well in the world . . ." and destroy "our complacency" (111–112), and she cannot fault them for this. A change is much needed, and she sees terrorism in Germany as "A despairing reaction to pervasive inhumanity," and thus conceives of "Antigone and Gudrun Ensslin as ideological bedfellows" (142).[11]

Her sympathy changes as she attempts to reach out to this girl by telling her of her own background, her emigration, persecution, and her husband's murder. Marlene responds in a way that suggests an overly simplistic equation of the past and the present, viewing any German, old or young, as a potential executioner, erasing the very real differences between the Germans who perpetrated mass murder under the Nazis and the (merely) repressive politics of the current German government. It is this confrontation that makes the narrator rethink her admiration for the Antigone figure: "The sudden insight that my princess has much in common with Marlene and would be just as difficult to put up with. The thought is painful. I surmise that the flesh-and-blood Antigone, not the one I can call forth and send back into obscurity at will, would put quite a strain on my nerves" (128–129).

Within the course of a day, Antigone transforms from a "sister" with whom she felt affinity on the basis of parallels between her personal life, her family, and her upbringing, to the wartime resistance fighter whom she would have liked to resemble but never did, to the present-day terrorist who does not hesitate to kill to reach her goals and whom she cannot stand: "I reject your belief that there can be paradise on earth, and I certainly reject your hellish ways of bringing about this paradise. You are playing war games, meaningless, sickening games. And I want peace" (149). Antigone, which seemed to be the bridge for the narrator to link the two experiences, past and present, and the two generations, ultimately fails as a model, too. She no longer functions to alleviate the guilt of the past and turns out to be the model for the kind of violence the narrator does not believe in.

It now becomes apparent that the sisterly relationship to which the title "My sister Antigone" seems to refer is not just a symbolic one, but can also be read as literal: it is not the narrator who speaks of Antigone, but it is Antigone's sister Ismene who narrates. The narrator is in Ismene's position, and resembles her, more so than Antigone. The narrator underplays this resemblance, however. This similarity nevertheless becomes obvious when it turns out that the narrator has not only seemingly deliberately minimized the importance of the Ismene figure in her retelling of the Antigone's story (she speaks of her sporadically and does so in a critical way: she is "blond, pale, characterless" (126), while in Sophocles' plays she is a colorful and important character),[12] but has also concealed the fact that she herself has a sister who is of importance. This sister suddenly shows up toward the end of the text, and it turns out that the narrator harbors strongly ambivalent feelings toward her, as she died young (before the narrator was born), and her mother made her feel like her inferior replacement: "If she hadn't died, you wouldn't be here" (187). She has always felt that she was alive only because of her sister's death, literally in the place of her dead sister. The fact that both this sister and Ismene remain entirely in the background up to this point in the narrative can be read as a sign that both of these sisterly relationships, the real and the symbolic, are complex and potentially fueled with guilt. The narrator bears more resemblance to Ismene's character than to Antigone, but she wishes instead that she had been like Antigone, like the (other) perfect (dead) sister. Such a reading gets stronger if one reads Sophocles, in which the conflict between the sisters Antigone and Ismene in the original represent two different responses to the same dilemma that in fact closely mirrors Antigone and the narrator: both feel they should fight for justice and honor, but they act in opposite ways. Antigone rebels; Ismene is afraid to help her, even tries to stop her. This suggests that the narrator is much more like Ismene, the sister who could not resist and who survived, although both Antigone and the narrator's dead sister are models to whom the narrator (and Ismene) can never live up. They are precisely what she is not.[13]

Surprisingly, what the ending of *Antigone* suggests, is that during this one day, the narrator may in fact, at least temporarily, succeed in coming to terms with needing to live up to the image of this ideal dead sister (Antigone, her own), and find peace with her deep sense of guilt about the past. This change takes place as the result of a dream that the protagonist has when she is laying down to rest at the end of the day, after Marlene has been picked up. In a prolonged state between waking and sleeping, she has an image of Antigone who tells her to let her go and accept herself for who she is. "You keep searching for my secret, yet it is so simple: Feel and think yourself, not me. . . . Do not resist yourself. Accept. Learn to empty yourself, that you may absorb the fullness of life" (185). The dream state also transports Antigone into the narrator's war past, making Antigone now face a far more morally ambiguous situation than her own mythical scenario: a pivotal moment during the war during which the narrator may have had the opportunity to kill the *Hauptscharführer* while working for the Jewish Council[14] (or at least show courage through an act of resistance) and potentially set free thousands of Jews about to be deported. In the dream, Antigone is in the narrator's place, and she, too, is helpless coming face to face with this evil, unable to make a difference. Antigone ends up imprisoned, but after her release, the narrator who has waited for her does not take her home, but runs away instead.

After the dream, the narrator experiences a sense of relief. It seems as if she has indeed let go of the ghost of the perfect (dead) sister(s). She is not Antigone, she is herself, like Ismene, full of compromises, and she finally accepts this: "I feel the ugliness, am one with the ugliness, which swirls around me. I let it wrap itself around me, accept it, accept myself, am happy. And tomorrow?" (201). The ending of *Antigone* reveals a sense of acceptance, while at the same time it also hints at the fact that the struggle may start all over again the next day: there is no true closure.

Weil's autobiographical reworking of her story of persecution under the Nazis in light of the archetypical dilemmas of the Sophocles drama results in a highly original kind of survivor narrative. Through an idiosyncratic process of remembrance and of attempting to rewrite the Antigone figure, it ties together the highly disparate parts of the narrator's life: her idyllic childhood; exile, persecution, and hiding under the Nazis; the rebuilding of a semblance of a normal life after returning to Germany.[15] On the one hand, this use of a figure like Antigone in which Weil anchors her story allows a German audience to engage with the protagonist's dilemmas of living under the Nazis and her lack of resistance, and to see these conflicts to a certain extent as universal, as human, rather than particular, or Jewish. On the other hand, by situating this story, the narrator's crisis, within the context of present-day German culture, the novel also makes a clear appeal to the German audience to engage with their own personal past. As the narrator shows both the older and younger generation of Germans (children during the war and those born after) failing to fully confront the Nazi past, she blames the older generation for having lived on comfortably while repressing or minimizing this past, and the younger generation for ultimately overcompensating in such a way that their protest deteriorates in extremism and more violence.

An example of the way in which Germans are appealed to, but so as to not isolate them in their guilt, is the inclusion and framing of a completely separate narrative by a different author within this text: the eyewitness account of a young German soldier who witnessed (and whose army unit took part in) the liquidation of Petrikau, a Jewish ghetto in Poland in 1943. Reprinted here almost in its entirety (almost twenty-two pages long in the German edition, one-seventh of the entire text), the graphic and horrifying scenes of "ordinary" German soldiers doing the work of deporting and shooting thousands of Jewish men, women, and children is a stunning indictment of the involvement of ordinary Germans in the Holocaust. This text seems to have little relationship to the overall narrative of *Antigone* (apart from the fact that the narrator is reading it in the afternoon while Marlene is asleep on her bed), and the account itself does not give us an indication as to how it fits with the rest of the novel. Still, the framing of the text by the narrator does give us some important clues. First, it presents an elaborate description of a Nazi atrocity, something the narrator has not witnessed herself but to which she does want to testify. Second, the author of the testimony is introduced by the narrator as the brother of a friend, as "an intellectual and a man of the theater," who was, "as we all were in those days, a pacifist and a leftist" (123). The implication for the reader is that this man, this soldier, was much like her. In fact, the narrator suggests, "we belonged to the same circles" (123). In speaking in sympathetic terms of a German *Wehrmacht* soldier and of herself in the same breath, and allowing his traumatic description of the murders he witnessed and in which he was forced to participate to stand next to her narrative of persecution and loss, it may aid German readers in identifying more broadly with her particular story. A note in the back of the book, outside of the frame of the main narrative, reads that the soldier studied history and German literature, and received his doctorate at age twenty-one. This detail suggests that he was well educated (not unlike the narrator and her friends),[16] but that this kind of educational background did not help him to guard himself against the ideological onslaught of the Nazis. The narrator draws the conclusion that this makes them both guilty: "Neither you nor I was trained in obedience, but on the other hand no one has taught us to be wary of slogans, either. And so we allowed ourselves to be destroyed, you as a German soldier, me as one of the persecuted" (123).

In speaking of "we," in comparing her self to this soldier (through the suggestion that they had similar class and educational backgrounds) and not singling out Germans, the narrator suggests that an entire generation of educated Germans had failed, making it easier for a certain German audience to engage with this story. She does so, however, not in order to apologize, but to indict both of them. The Holocaust is not simply a story of German guilt versus Jewish victimization, but one that asks difficult questions about responsibility and (in) action of everyone.

Tactics of Evasion

In contrast to Weil's earlier work, *Antigone* had much success in Germany. It was widely and positively reviewed, received much publicity, and Weil won much acclaim and a prize for it.[17] In response, *Happy*, *Tramhalte*, and *Ans Ende* were reprinted in the early 1980s, and now found a much wider audience. Apparently, Weil's new more autobiographical form and more personal tone with its implied promise of an open dialogue attracted a new (younger) audience interested in autobiographical, "authentic" literature. Yet, as mentioned earlier, the book's success also needs to be understood against the background of a number of other events taking place at that time in West Germany. On the one hand, the recent upsurge in the popularity of the Antigone figure (due to a number of recent Antigone stage adaptations) generated a greater audience for this book, due to its title.[18] On the other hand, the generational shift that had taken place (the German reading audience by this time was primarily the postwar generation), and even more significantly, the impact of the 1979 showing of the American television series *Holocaust* in Germany played a role, too.

The change brought about by the airing of the television series on four evenings between January 22 and 26 was quite dramatic, primarily because the serialized drama that focused on a German (Nazi) family and on a assimilated German-Jewish family (and traces the persecution of the latter), allowed for a prolonged kind of identification that most Germans had never entertained. This led to an unprecedented public outpouring of suppressed sentiments. Regret, guilt, surprise, all showed itself in the weeks and months after the show aired. Anton Kaes suggests that it allowed "Germans to work through their most recent past, this time from the perspective of the victims . . ." and argues that in the broadcast's wake, "a new historical consciousness had emerged . . . the past suddenly seemed very present."[19] The new public debate on the Nazi past and the treatment of Jews that was stirred up led to a renewed interest in the autobiographical accounts of former exiles and survivors. Suddenly, it seemed possible to reconsider the legacy of the Nazi past, and the popularity of Weil's publication of *Antigone* needs to be seen in this context.

Over time, it turns out that German attitudes toward Jews and the war past were not fundamentally altered by the *Holocaust* miniseries, as its intense and unprecedented impact ultimately proved limited and short-lived. It presented more of a momentary shock than a fundamental change in a culture of evasion, thus revealing what Saul Friedländer calls the continuation of a pattern of German response from the late 1940s to the present: "a constant seesaw between learning and forgetting, between becoming briefly aware of the past and turning one's back on it. A near automatic process."[20]

The only partial understanding of the Holocaust as a *German* event, an event that should concern Germans, even those born decades after the war, is evident in the reception of this novel as well. Despite its acclaim, the text was generally read in one-dimensional ways as mainly the wartime story of a German Jew, whereby the critics ignored or misread the significance of the complex way in which *Antigone* weaves past and present, myth and history, which in turn suggests how one's memories *continue* to inform the present. For instance, many reviewers stated how moved they were by the reading (referring to passages that deal with narrator's war experiences), but they neglected to discuss how the novel also comments on the state of present-day West German culture, its failure to face the past, and the generational strife this has brought forth. Thus, *Antigone*'s central theme, the continued presence of the war past (*die Gegenwart der Vergangenheit*), is read as something that primarily reflects on the suffering of the narrator (who is usually equated with Grete Weil, whereby the distance between author and narrator is collapsed), instead of an issue affecting Germans as well as former victims. Along these lines, most reviewers also marginalize the terrorism motif, and if they discuss it at all, then only in terms of how it confronts the narrator with her past, not as a sign of how poorly worked through the Nazi past is in present-day Germany.[21]

Even the difficult to read and to place chapter of the soldier's testimony of the Petrikau ghetto liquidation is read along these lines. It is seen not as a textual indictment of the behavior of "ordinary Germans" that questions German notions about the responsibility for murderous behavior under the Nazi regime, but as a document that illustrates why Weil cannot forget her past. That is, reviewers suggest that the Petrikau chapter shows the trauma from which the narrator suffers, instead of this being a nightmare from which all Germans (should) suffer. In this way, they avoid the difficult questions with which the testimony confronts the reader: how were these crimes possible (how did ordinary people become cold-blooded murderers), and could this happen again? By reading the account as affecting the narrator only (and equating her with Weil) but not necessarily the readers, *Antigone* is read as a survivor's story by which the German readers may feel affected and moved, *betroffen* but a true (German) confrontation with the past is avoided.

The success of *Antigone* should therefore in my opinion not be taken too optimistically as an indication of a radical German change of mentality that now lead to a greater willingness to be confronted with the Nazi past and the Holocaust. Rather, I see it as being merely suggestive of a new ability in German readers of the early 1980s to empathize and identify with Holocaust victims and their plight.

Weil was ultimately disappointed, too, both with the critical interpretation and the audience's response. Whereas she was happy with the book's success (even though she felt that it had come too late in her life and career),[22] she found that Germans used her work (or even the confrontation with the series *Holocaust*) to immediately jump to a *Bewältigung*, a coming to terms with the past, a containment, instead of as an opening for *Trauerarbeit*, for the work of mourning, for analysis, as she had hoped. Not only did Weil believe that *Bewältigung* is impossible, but this jump bypasses any kind of deeper reflection. It was particularly disturbing to Weil that critics sought to avoid a full confrontation with the Petrikau ghetto account: "For me, this is a symptom of how little one is really willing to honestly confront one's own history."[23] There was not, as Weil had hoped, a facing of German guilt, or an opening for dialogue. Instead, it was a one-sided acknowledgment of the perspective of the victim and her past without a consideration of the readers' own accountability as (descendants of) perpetrators and the relevance of this legacy for the present. Weil would critique this kind of response explicitly in her next novel.

Bridging the Generations

As the belated interest in her work and the German war past stimulated Weil to write more, she published another novel soon after: *Generationen* (Generations).[24] This work from 1983 is autobiographical and highly personal as well, but seems even more so than *Antigone*, as most of the narrative plays itself out in the present, and is not as fragmented by associations, memories, or by an imbedded mythical text. In contrast to the *Antigone* novel that plays in a one-day period whereby the constant jumping around in the thoughts of the narrator from different memories to the present to imaginary passages about the Antigone figure show the past and present to flow into each other (revealing memory to be an important force in the present), the structure of *Generationen* is more straightforward. The chapters have separate titles and the text spans a period of several years. Even though here, too, the narrator moves around between the past and present within the story, the degree to which she uses fragmentation and flashbacks seems more conventional since the narrative spans several years instead of just one day.

The novel describes a period of about four years in the life of the narrator (roughly between 1974 and 1978), an elderly Jewish woman who (again) strongly resembles the author Weil (same age, same assimilated German-Jewish childhood, same wartime experiences of persecution, exile, and murder of first husband), who relates how after the untimely death of her second husband from leukemia (this detail mirrors Weil's own circumstances as well) she came to live with Hanna, a close female friend, and Moni, a much younger woman. The narrative consists of seventeen short chapters, each of which has a title identifying the stages in the tumultuous relationship between the three women. ("How life gets suffocated by silence," "Longing for attachment," "Escalation," etc.)[25] Interspersed with the unfolding of the personal dynamics are reminiscences familiar from Weil's earlier work (in particular *Antigone*): the narrator's aging process, the German politics of the period, and once again, her own war past in the form of memories, some of which are brought up by associations in the present, and some of which are presented without this context in separate chapters. Here, as in the Antigone novel, the narrator's personal memories of the past and the fact of living in a nation of perpetrators and their descendants informs in every way her present-day reality.

Generationen turns out to form a kind of prequel and a sequel to *Antigone*: it describes the period during the mid- to late 1970s in which the narrator was writing a novel that seems to have been *Antigone*. The action in *Generationen* thus on the one hand predates the existence of the Antigone novel (the narrator is still in the process of writing it); on the other hand the story describes how this novel was finished up, the success it garnered once it was published, and the narrator's response to its reception. In addition, *Generationen* actually considers an alternative ending to the Antigone novel.

The narrator has some initial concerns about the living arrangement because of the age difference that separates all three (she is in her early seventies, her friend Hanna is in her fifties, while the youngest woman, Moni is in her thirties), and because Moni and Hanna are lovers. She goes ahead because she hopes to get closer to Hanna (with whom she has had a lifelong friendship), and because the idea of moving back to München, the landscape of her idyllic German-Jewish childhood is appealing to her after a forty-year absence. She thus hopes to become a "new person in a new environment."[26]

The narrative describes what ensues as several years of communal living that are complicated by precisely the factors the narrator already feared: the relationship between Moni and Hanna leaves her excluded, and the generational differences, in particular with Moni, prove difficult to overcome. Moni is confrontational and unfriendly to the narrator, and she and Hanna often accuse the narrator of being too conformist, too rich, and too "*bürgerlich.*" Meanwhile, the narrator criticizes Moni for how politically uninformed she is. She is full of opinions, and frustrated with the older generation, but unable or unwilling to take responsibility for her own life or be engaged with the course of present-day West Germany. The narrator reads Moni's critique as an empty gesture: while a large poster of Marx hangs in her room, she reads no serious newspaper, and considers herself apolitical, ". . . even Marxism for her is nothing more than a vague dream, a longing to be a part of something."[27] Moni spends a good deal of her time depressed, exuding a lethargy that both the narrator and Hanna have a difficult time understanding in light of their threatening experiences under Hitler. Their conflicts all turn out to be generational, as the narrator observes "I don't understand her, I cannot jump across the ravine between the generations."[28] It is their different experiences and understanding of the Hitler era that separates all three women: it is their respective attempts at (and especially Moni's avoidance of) a form of *Vergangenheitsbewältigung* that complicates their situation.

The narrator becomes progressively unhappy and regrets her decision to live with the two women, until, completely unexpectedly, Moni seduces her. Encouraged by Hanna, the three women for a while live in a complicated but exhilarating love triangle that eases the generational tension. Soon, this arrangement and the jealousy between all three makes things even more complicated. One night, the narrator takes what she suggests is an accidental overdose of sleeping pills and nearly kills herself. Once recovered, things have changed: grateful to be alive, she no longer expects much from the relationship with the two women. Furthermore, she is finally also able to work on a novel that she has tried to write for years. Both her illness and her return to München have brought back so many memories of her youth and the years leading up to Hitler that is has freed her up for her writing, in which she now immerses herself. This resulting novel turns out to be the 1980 novel *Antigone.*

The story ends as the narrator has submitted her manuscript for publication after which she gains a measure of success, which allows her at long last to speak more publicly about her life as a German Jew and her wartime past. In the epilogue, the narrator comments on the reception of this work and suggests that the Germans are finally interested in hearing about her story because of the American miniseries *Holocaust* having been shown on German television in 1979, but that their interest remains superficial. The belated success indeed makes her uncomfortable, as though attributable only to a media event, and not to a substantive impact on German consciousness.

While the narrator and Hanna ultimately are able to give meaning to their lives through their work (Hanna is working on her writing as well), the younger postwar generation has a poorer prognosis: Moni remains lost. No longer able to find her answers within the relationship, desperate to find a place or a community where she belongs, Moni leaves the two women for India to live with the Baghwan. The narrator has great reservations about Moni's admiration for the charismatic guru, reminiscent as it seems of the Nazi era: "I am repulsed, as I cannot stand people who are under [someone's] command. These here reach ecstasy on orders, and remind me of the Nazi Party Days . . . Do you want the total surrender? With lit up eyes, smiling: 'Yes' . . ."[29] Moni and the members of her generation are lost, unable to come to terms with their parents' past, unable to find their way in a culture in which the older generation still sets the tone.

In the epilogue the narrator comments in more depth on the reception of *Antigone*, by recounting what happens after the book is published. Here, the figure of Antigone stands in for her: she is an aging woman who has survived persecution, and lives among a community of perpetrators that remains silent about the past when suddenly the Thebans want to hear and talk about this history. This change takes place because of a "trivial, kitschy" play about this past that touches them through its directness (a clear reference to the impact of the television drama *Holocaust*). Now that everyone talks of it, Antigone finds that this happens in ways that suggest that the past ultimately does not concern the others, and she cannot help but think that these are the same people who were unwilling to help in her time of need. Instead of feeling better understood, Antigone feels objectified: she has become a "case,"[30] a survivor for whom one should feel sympathy. The narrator suggests that this belated success has made her uncomfortable, as she still is not truly being heard, is not engaged in a dialogue with the Germans, and instead is objectified by them.

Generationen, as its title already suggests, even more than Weil's previous work, focuses on the complex relations of the different German generations, in particular those of the war generation with the generation born after 1945. That is, it shows the after effects of this war for its victims (the narrator), for the young bystanders (Hanna), and for postwar Germans (such as Moni) who were raised into a culture fueled by *Wiederaufbau*, by rebuilding and forgetting. This culture of amnesia is described explicitly as connected to the current political situation, the legacy of (the failure of) the 1968 revolution;[31] German terrorism (Hanna and the narrator hear of the RAF's Mogadishu hijacking and the deaths of the Baader Meinhof core at the Stammheim prison); and the continuing violence in the world, which the narrator finds too overwhelming to deal with.

Not all is negative, however, *Generationen* shows the positive influence of the cultural changes effected by the "generation of 68," as the narrator feels much affinity with their progressive politics and would much rather align herself with this younger generation than with her own, despite her difficulties. This work shows in particular the positive influence of feminism, as this novel is explicitly about the relationships between women, much more so than *Antigone*, for instance. Men hardly play a role in it, which is all the more remarkable considering that Weil's actual living arrangement on which this autobiographical text was based, was not with two women, but with a woman and a man.[32]

Nevertheless, on the whole this generation and its calls for progress and change fails in the eyes of the narrator, as is clear from how she describes both Moni's escape into a cult-like movement, and her ambivalence toward the left-wing terrorism of the RAF. This generation seeks answers, but at the same time does not dare to ask the necessary questions of their own parents. They are afraid of being lied to, "And afraid to hear the truth. Or to receive answers like: Hitler is guilty: of the war, of the destruction of the Jews, the division of our country. Hitler alone."[33] The evasive and possibly reactionary response would prove even harder to bear than not knowing at all. This younger generation, too, proves incapable of facing their history adequately. They know more about the victims now, are interested in the stories of the Holocaust, its survivors, but cannot deal with their own (German) personal and national legacy.

Although not as successful as *Antigone*, *Generationen* was generally well received,[34] among others, Weil was awarded the *Tukan Preis der Stadt München* for it. Yet, a certain template seemed to have been set for the critical reviews of Weil's work. Again, as with *Antigone*, the novel was read for what it tells about Weil's war past, her traumatic memories (as this work fills in some of the details that *Antigone* left open), more than for its commentary on the present. This strikes one as somewhat odd, as this text is so clearly contextualized from within late 1970s West Germany. This work, too, failed to reach its addressee.

Weil in fact analyzed (and foresaw) with great clarity the now surfacing contradictory cultural and political developments of the 1980s. At once a new public recognition of Jewish suffering had emerged, a greater interest in the personal aspects of the Nazi period, greater "*betroffenheit*" (which led to the—belated—recognition of her work at this time), yet there was also a persistent refusal to look at this past as a uniquely *German* history, and even the desire to move away from it in order to normalize German national identity and unburden the postwar generation(s).

Changed Cultural Tides

The 1980s were indeed characterized by a constant tug-of-war between these two contradictory impulses. On the one hand, one witnessed under the influence of 1970s leftist cultural politics the (at times compulsive) need for Germans to reconsider and remember the Holocaust, reinforced in turn by a string of significant memorial dates and events throughout the 1980s (almost yearly commemorations, 1983 the fiftieth anniversary of the Nazi takeover, 1984 the fortieth anniversary of D-day, January 1985 the fortieth anniversary of the liberation of Auschwitz, May 1985 the fortieth anniversary of the end of the war, 1988 the fiftieth anniversary of Kristallnacht, etc.). On the other hand, there was a newly expressed desire to "historicize" or "normalize" the Nazi past, promulgated in particular by the new conservative government of Christian Democrats and Free Democrats, which had come to power in 1983. In part, these two movements also reinforced each other.

An important instigator in the change of cultural climate in the 1980s was precisely the conservative political and *geistig-moralische Wende*. Helmut Kohl's administration, aware that histories can legitimize different sorts of national identity, sought to actively formulate a different history, out from under the "shadow of Hitler." The conservatives agreed that the time had come to draw a line between the present and the past, or at least, to create a more positive perception of this past. Germans needed, as Chancellor Kohl argued, a "stable historical self consciousness."[35] At the same time, as former young student rebels had come of age and entered politics in greater numbers in the political opposition of the Green Party, the past was debated in the *Bundestag* between political left and right more openly than before. As a result, events and projects proposed by Kohl that carried strong overtones of his vision of a "new national pride" (such as the creation of a new German history museum in which the twelve controversial Nazi years would be integrated into an otherwise illustrious German history, and the invitation of President Reagan to the Bitburg cemetery in 1985) generated much debate. Both of these issues proved rather contentious,[36] and Kohl's new course divided German politics even more than before.

Yet what had changed by the early 1980s is that this division was openly articulated on both sides, and that the significance of the Nazi legacy was more intensely debated than before, in politics, academia, and the public realm. An example of this is the Historians' debate fought out publicly in 1986–1987 in German newspapers and periodicals between a number of left-leaning historians and cultural critics and conservative German historians over the tendency to want to "normalize" the German past. Initiated by Jürgen Habermas who reviewed two recent historians' works and deemed their approach to German wartime history to be "apologetic,"[37] he judged these historians' attempts at relativizing the "Final Solution" to be "part of a new nationalist and conservative search for a usable past."[38] The chief trend that Habermas objected to in this work was the attempt to normalize German history by putting into question the uniqueness of the Nazi crimes. For "if Auschwitz is admittedly dreadful, but dreadful as only one specimen of genocide . . . then Germany can still aspire to reclaim a national acceptance that no one denies the perpetrators of other massacres," but if one instead insists that the Final Solution is noncomparable, "the past may never be 'worked through,' the future never normalized."[39] One of the historians who stood accused responded publicly to Habermas and others joined in the public discussion that continued for months. The debate was ultimately decided in favor of the progressive critics (a sign that German academia was now represented by a new generation of left-leaning intellectuals who disagreed openly with the government course), but these issues would be revisited again in the 1990s.

The other ways in which the cultural legacy of the 1970s left proved influential, was in the wave of "new subjective" literature that emerged in which first the self, and soon, the younger generation's relationship to one's parents was analyzed in a way that led to a deeper personal awareness of the personal importance of the Nazi legacy. Influenced by theorists such as Adorno, Horkheimer, and Erich Fromm, who suggested that there might very well be a direct link between "SS murderers, authoritarian patterns of socialisation in the German middle-class family and the use of violence," the realization that nurturing Germany's cultural heritage "provided no safeguard against the exercise of brutality"[40] led to a critical examination of precisely these authoritarian German notions of child rearing (and of sexuality), the role of German High culture, philosophy, and religion. Ultimately this critical analysis led to "self-realization" movements among a number of marginalized groups, such as gays, women, and Jews.

The German women's movement was a response to the German antiauthoritarian movement: the blindness to the position of women among leftist (male) activists and the silence to which they were relegated motivated women to organize separately.[41] The issues which had formed a major stumbling block for the New Left became of central concern for feminists: to maintain a connection between the private and the public, or between one's work and one's politics, and to balance political commitment and personal experience.[42] The outgrowth of this movement was both political (abortion laws were changed, the position of women in the work place improved, daycare facilities were built), and cultural: the 1980s saw a much greater production of literature by women (in great part autobiographical writing),[43] and a much increased public interest in these works.

Another group that had come to feel marginalized and isolated within the student movement were young German Jews. As the movement had turned progressively more anti-Zionist, and also in part in response to the conservative government's call for a new sense of patriotic pride and a normalization of German history in the 1980s, Jewish leftist developed a new group awareness. Mostly themselves sons and daughters of Holocaust survivors, these young German Jews resisted this reactionary desire for "normalization" in Germany's conceptualization of its own past, and this protest resulted "in a new self-consciousness among Jews in the Federal Republic of Germany."[44] Soon, Jews from different backgrounds and even the older generation joined in their critique against this forced reconciliation and normalization, and suggested that it displayed the German government's continued discrimination of and insensitivity toward German Jews. This kind of critical public response was quite different from earlier decades, when "Instead of taking the initiative . . . most Jews who remained in Germany after the Shoah reacted to conditions determined by the German government and their own organizations, or they refused to have anything to do with the Jewish community."[45] As Jack Zipes argues, up to the 1980s, German Jews had not made "their presence felt in either West or East Germany," as there was "an unspoken understanding among Jews and between Jews and Germans that it would be best to keep silent and blend in with the rest of the population."[46] They had been all too aware of the German denial and repression of the Nazi past, the hypocrisy of philosemitism, and renewed antisemitism on the right and anti-Zionism on the left, but felt that they lacked viable venues to express their concern.[47] Now they finally became more vocal, more provocative and visible, suggesting that indeed, "The rise of German nationalism and Jewish consciousness are very much related."[48]

German Jews became more visible through their protest (e.g., in their demonstration against the 1985 performance of Rainer Werner Fassbinder's play *Der Müll, die Stadt und der Tod* (Garbage, the City and Death) because of its antisemitic undertones, and the Bitburg affair), but also through a dramatic increase in Jewish literature.[49] At this point the postwar generation, the children of the Jewish survivors started publishing in greater numbers.[50] Their work questioned the feasibility of a Jewish life in Germany, the way in which the Holocaust is commemorated and appropriated by the German state, and they discussed the difficulty of German-Jewish identity, and relations between Germans and Jews. These were new themes, left untouched by most survivor authors.[51]

It was the emergence of both Jewish activism and literature in West Germany in the mid- to late-1980s, and the women's movement and women's literature (Weil openly admired the new German women's literature),[52] more so than the contradictory political situation that Weil would respond to in her last novel of the 1980s. Here, nearing the end of her life, Weil would come to assess in more depth her position as a German and Jewish woman.

Imagining Michal

In 1988, having recuperated from a period of rather serious illness (a minor heart attack and a small stroke in 1984), Weil published her fifth novel, *Der Brautpreis* (The Brideprice). This, too, is a narrative that relies on a retelling of a preexisting story (an intertext), but this time, in a dramatic move away from her reliance on literary examples that stem from her German *Bildung* background (such as the Greek *Antigone*), the story that is used stems from the Jewish tradition, the *Tanach* (the Old Testament).

The narrator in *Brautpreis* whose name is Grete (which blurs the distinction between the author, the narrator, and the protagonist even more than in Weil's previous work), creates a voice for Michal, the first wife of King David, and allows her to tell her side of the biblical story, a perspective that has never been heard before. The framing is such that Michal narrates her own (past) life story in old age, looking back on her life after David has passed away. Interspersed with this narrative, in alternating chapters but far less prominent in this text than in Weil's other work, Grete tells her own story. This narrative once again resembles that of Weil herself: a story of a happy assimilated Jewish childhood, flight from Hitler to the Netherlands, of loss of home and identity, and a return to Germany. She also recounts her difficulty at the present time in coming to terms with her memories, with her losses, aging (she is eighty), and illness. In this novel, yet again, the narrator tells of the process of writing a book (this time about Michal and David), a text that we get to read in the alternating chapters. Michal's narrative takes up far more space than that of Grete, however (over 180 pages versus 60). Michal's story, then, more so than narrator Grete seems to be the focus of this novel.

In this work, the Michal story is used to explore the roles of women under (Jewish) patriarchy, a somewhat similar kind of feminist project that Weil undertook with *Antigone*, but now much more explicitly. For even though there is a similarity between the texts—Lorenz suggests that Weil "points out the same kind of brutality in this culture as before in Antigone's Greece, the same oppression of the weak, in particular of women"[53]—the differences between the two are more significant than their similarity. Not only does *Brautpreis* prove to be much more explicitly feminist than *Antigone*, but the choice of Jewish subject matter in the figure of Michal is also so unusual for Weil, the thoroughly assimilated German Jew (in contrast to her preoccupation with Antigone that was clearly linked to German culture, and the ability to identify with her), that it suggests a significant new direction.

In the *Tanach*, Michal is a relatively minor figure in Samuel I and Samuel II, known only as the first wife of King David, who receives from him a bride price of two hundred foreskins of murdered (or at least castrated) Philistines.[54] This is double the (already unusual) dowry that was set by her father, King Saul, who had hoped that David would get killed in the process of procuring the price. After this plot has failed, and David marries Michal, Saul still feels threatened by David, as he proves to be an ambitious warrior. Consequently, Saul threatens to kill him, and David flees the city. Now that David is gone, Michal is married off a second time, which is for the *Tanach* a highly unusual decision. (Whereas men could marry more than once, the ancient Jewish law of adultery prohibited intercourse between a man and a married woman, in effect making a second marriage for a woman prohibited if the husband was still alive.)[55] While on the run, David meanwhile marries six more wives.[56] The *Tanach* mentions Michal again when David has just become king of the tribe of Judah, and he demands her back from her second husband in order to establish legitimacy as a leader. They have a falling out after Michal mocks David for dancing half-naked around the Holy Ark that he has brought to Jerusalem (Samuel II 6.16), and Michal's story ends here with the verse "So to her dying day, Michal, daughter of Saul, had no children" (Samuel II 6.23).

This, then, is the story of Michal in the *Tanach*, we know of her only in relation to important men: her father Saul, and her husband David. Adding up all passages in which Michal is mentioned in the *Tanach* in fact makes up barely a full page, as her story is entirely subordinated to David's.[57] In *Brautpreis* we now get Michal's story in full, from her own perspective. We learn what Michal thinks when David brings her the bloody foreskins as a dowry, when her father tries to murder her husband, when she is married off again (in defiance of the Seventh Commandment against adultery), how she responds when David takes her back and her place in this marital hierarchy is changed (she is now just one among his many wives), and, finally, what it means to remain childless, and perhaps more importantly, without love for the rest of her life.

This missing perspective is an outspoken feminist one, as Michal is portrayed in *Brautpreis* as a rebel. Her rebellion is directed not only against the men surrounding her, but also against the role of women in Judaism: they are objects, possessions to be traded and exchanged by men. Women's thoughts and feelings do not count, all that counts is their value as objects of exchange: "A wife must remain silent. Subordinate herself to her husband. Will it ever be otherwise? Will the day come when a woman is not sold by her father, does not have to be one among many in the house of her husband?" (42). Michal's position is shown to be especially problematic as she is used for a complex political intrigue on the part of both her father and her (future) husband. As the daughter of the king, she represents a valued possession, but this leaves her no room to be herself and exert her own desires or opinion: "To be a princess only means to be an especially dear and precious ware" (46). As Jewish law, practice, and faith were closely linked to a Jewish patriarchal tradition in biblical days, Michal's critique of Judaism as expressed in *Brautpreis* is at the same time also a critique of the male dominance and misuse of Judaism. By the same token, Michal's criticism of male privilege is aimed against a Jewish religious practice in which this sense of male entitlement is rooted. Michal's critique of these Jewish practices is nevertheless shown to be ambivalent, more a protest against male dominance than against Jewish tradition itself.

This kind of a project, a novel in which a silent biblical female figure is given a voice, fits in with a broader feminist critique of religious traditions that had emerged since the late 1970s. This specific kind of serious (scholarly) feminist critique on Judaism came primarily from within Jewish circles in the United States and England,[58] however, which makes Weil's engagement with it unusual and remarkable. As a German Jew who felt great ambivalence toward her Jewish background, and who suggested that she was not that familiar with Jewish tradition, this work seems to present a deliberate move away from the earlier (German) material and a concerted effort to explore Jewish themes in a feminist manner. The text suggests an intense engagement with the Jewish tradition that can be seen not only in the Michal chapters, but also in Grete's personal narrative in *Brautpreis*.

What Grete recounts in the chapters alternating with Michal's narrative is her personal story of exile, war, and her return to Germany, but now with a specific emphasis on her sense of Jewishness, which, while this was traced in Weil's other works as well, leads here to a different set of conclusions than before. A more in-depth look and comparison of the passages that deal with such issues in *Brautpreis* with similar passages from *Antigone* and *Generationen* reveals in fact that this meaning not only shifts (it shows a particular development), but also how this kind of writing may function in rearticulating identity in response to the experience of racial objectification that proved difficult to undo.

Reconciling Jewish Identity: *Bin ich Jüdischer geworden?*

Besides as an attempt to bear witness to her experiences under Nazi persecution and to open up a discussion about this past with German readers, and as an astute analysis of the ways in which the Nazi legacy is dealt with (or not) by both the war and postwar generations, Weil's three novels from the 1980s can also be read as remarkably consistent articulations of a very specific crisis of identity and subjectivity in the wake of Nazi oppression and racialization. Although Weil's earlier work touches on this issue briefly, these later texts comment on this crisis in more elaborate, direct, and personal fashion. Each work contains long passages that deal with the transformation undergone during and after the Nazi years and sketch this complex change in identity carefully.

What stands out is that even though the three novels differ in many respects, the narrative voice that recounts the particular memories and observations about identity in *Brautpreis*, *Generationen*, and *Antigone* is remarkably constant, and in fact so similar that the three narrators are nearly indistinguishable from one other, and can easily be read as one and the same figure. Furthermore, they seem indistinguishable from the author Grete Weil herself, in terms of how she articulates these issues in interviews and in a later autobiography.[59] Focusing on the novels only rather than the author, I will show that the same distinct stages can be detected in all three works, with only one important distinction: the final developments in *Brautpreis*, which seem to take the question of post-Holocaust German-Jewish identity in a different direction.

The narrator of all three novels, who from now will be described as one and the same, describes the sense of marginalization as one that was only gradually realized. Initially, as the daughter of a thoroughly assimilated family, the danger of the Nazis was not understood: "We lived as if on an island in a lake that became more and more polluted. . . . We practiced the art of looking away, didn't notice much antisemitism. . . . It happened somewhere far below . . ." (*Generationen* 111–112). Her family was unprepared for what was to come: "Our parents were convinced they had smoothed the path for us. In this modern, progressive world their children's Jewishness would never be used against them. We were rooted in that belief" (*Antigone* 9). Then she gained "The sudden insight that there were people who saw me as different" (*Generationen* 112). This discrimination and marginalization began to take its toll, and it became internalized: "At the entrance to every German town a sign is posted: JEWS ENTER AT THEIR OWN RISK. . . . A discreet invitation to a pogrom: it is open season on us. We are no longer what we were until only recently. At least not in the eyes of the others. But you cannot undergo change in the eyes of others without your own sense of self changing as well" (*Antigone* 146).[60]

Hitler's coming to power is described as changing everything for her, it ". . . made me into a non-person, took my identity" (*Generationen* 94). Now only Jewishness mattered: "Now I knew that I was a Jew. Only a Jew. Day and night, night and day. One to be destroyed, one trying to survive . . . Jew as a status. I had four Jewish grandparents, that counted. My language and culture were German, that didn't count" (*Brideprice* 35–36).[61] Neither the narrator's sense of Germanness nor her previously "lukewarm" sense of Jewishness remains intact. What it means to be "made into" a Jew per racial decree and the profound ambivalence this generates is first truly felt while in exile in Amsterdam:

> I meet a stratum of Jewish society I never encountered before: the petty bourgeoisie and proletariat . . . very Oriental, alien, suspicious toward outsiders . . . difficult to handle, and hard to take for me, who am not one of them, who am one of them, an assimilated Jew without religious ties who shares their fate, a fate that extends back thousands of years and forward into the immediate future. (*Antigone* 74)

The experience of being seen by the Nazis as a Jew only, whereby her previous identity as a German with a certain level of education and an upper-class background no longer mattered, and being lumped in with Jews of very different backgrounds with whom the narrator feels nothing in common, is disturbing and complex. She is now one of them, at least in the eyes of the Nazis, and as a result, "I experience things of which I knew nothing in my old identity: I have no rights, am cast out, a Jew among Jews. The slightest misstep can mean the end" (*Antigone* 148). As her sense of Jewishness remained firmly tied to her Germanness, her social class, and her education (i.e., to assimilated Jewish *Bildungsbürgertum*), and could not be redefined in a more positive way, this dramatic change in her self-understanding as no longer German and as only Jewish creates a conflict, a crisis of identity.

When the war was over, neither this social position (a sense of privilege), nor the sense of belonging was easily restored as Nazi persecution had changed the meaning of both German and of Jewish cultural belonging. Most profoundly, it had changed her sense of home, of safety. Initially after the war, the narrator expresses the hope that this crisis can be overcome by forgetting about the imposed, tainted Jewish identity. While quickly reverting to her primary identity as a German after coming back: "My German identity was already clear to me soon after my return and I have never doubted it since then . . ." (*Brideprice* 127), she sought to forget about her Jewishness: "I don't want to hear the word Jew anymore" (*Brideprice* 37). Yet, soon the realization sets in that Jewishness had become of central importance—both to her self-understanding and to other people's perception of her—. "[I] still very often heard the word 'Jew,' which I had not wanted to hear anymore after the war, used it myself, it had become a compulsion . . . to profess the fact. . . . As a Jew, I had been persecuted, as a Jew . . . my husband, had been murdered. I couldn't put being Jewish aside, like a dress that had become old-fashioned" (*Brideprice* 51). Through the experience of persecution, Jewishness had now become a central factor of her identity, even though it took on a very different kind of significance from that which it had before. Precisely because it was imposed from the outside in such a problematic fashion, however, it remains complicated.

In *Brautpreis*, the narrator Grete suggests that it is difficult to redefine Jewishness. She believes that for a Jewish identity, one either has to believe in God, or feel a connection to the land of Israel, and "Neither the one nor the other is present is me, never was present," and ". . . hence, I never had a Jewish identity" (127). Instead, she argues, her Jewish identity remained tied only to the experience of persecution, a *Leidens- und Schicksalgemeinschaft*: "What remains is that I have experienced, as a Jew, what suffering means. So probably the single rudiment of an identity, shared suffering and fate" (127). Her sense of Jewish self up to this point remains molded, then, not by Jewish faith, or Jewish culture, or Jewish national identity, but by the Jewish genocide. Her identity has become that of "the survivor who has not forgotten, cannot forget, and does not want to forget" (124). All three texts suggest, however, that this position is a difficult one to live with.

It is possible to read the narrators' position in these works as typical of that of many assimilated Jews who struggled with the racialization of the Nazis and for whom, as Sidra De Koven Ezrahi has suggested, "The restoration of identity may prove more difficult . . . deprived of national citizenship yet unattached to the Jewish collective, whose definition of self has no social reference" (73). Survivors who did not return or reconnect to a Jewish community after the war missed out on an opportunity for collective mourning and might have been more susceptible to feelings of guilt about surviving. Eventually, Ezrahi argues, such feelings could lead to a state of "Emotional paralysis in which [the survivor] allows himself to be acted upon, but hardly ever acts. He has, as it were, lost his right to his own biography" (92). It seems that it is this kind of paralysis that is articulated by the narrator in *Antigone*:

> Saying no is the only freedom that cannot be taken from you. . . . I said yes. Yes, I shall leave Germany, yes, I am no longer a German, yes, I shall give up my writing, yes, I shall wear the yellow star. . . . yes, I shall make no effort to spring Waiki from the concentration camp, yes, I shall answer to a name that is not my own. . . . In this way I shall save my life while destroying myself (118). [while doing away with myself][62]

Having no other collective to return to but that of the German nation that had expelled her, and certainly not the Jewish community with which she had felt no real connection, the narrator struggles with profound guilt: she suggests that it is she, not the Nazis who "did away" with herself.

Ezrahi's notion of the survivor's loss of "his right to his own biography" is useful here to interpret the very complex narrative structure of *Antigone*, and the (somewhat less) complex structures of *Generationen* and *Brautpreis*. That is, one may see the highly fragmented structure of these texts as symbolic for the narrator's inability to reclaim her biography as German and as a Jew. Leslie Adelson has described Weil's fragmentary style as underscoring "the tormented quest for solutions that neither she nor her protagonist ever finds."[63] The solutions Weil's narrator may have searched for are tied to issues of wartime guilt and responsibility, certainly, but also to the question of identity. How can she define herself instead of being defined by others (first as the Jewish enemy, later as the Jewish victim with whom to feel empathy)?

The three novels seem to serve as narrative "trials" that allow the narrator to try on different identities, to accept some, and reject others. In this sense, the strategies in Weil's survivor literature show similarities to women's autobiographical writing more broadly.

Sidonie Smith suggests, for instance, that although articulating a subject's position in autobiographical writing can be especially daunting for women, it can also aid in emancipating the marginalized subject by allowing it to articulate and assert a variety of otherwise excluded identities: "Women use autobiography as one prominent ground for cultural critique and resistance. While negotiating various identifications (of gender, race, class, ethnicity, sexuality), they discover points of resistance to the integumentary strains of provided subjectivities."[64] Writing can function as a textual search for a less-reified self, as a way to redefine one's own reality and identity.

For survivor authors, this may be of special significance, for they experienced particularly pernicious forms of reification both during the war (as they were treated as racial objects to be exterminated), and after the war (when they were treated like medical cases). Ezrahi suggests that literature offers a way to resist this kind of reifying discourse: "For . . . those who were close to the events themselves, it may be precisely in its resistance to conceptual abstraction, to psychological reductionism, that art as a version of historical memory can provide form without fixing meaning, insight without explanation" (4). In this sense, writing can be a liberating process through which the survivor can become the subject of her own story again. This may be the case in particular, I would argue, when this writing takes place in the German language, the language of the former oppressors, and when such a text is published for a German audience.[65] Such narratives provide a way to "talk back."

In Weil's later oeuvre there seems to be a development in her narrator's self-definition: whereas in *Antigone* and *Generationen*, the narrator seems to define herself in terms of what she is not (a Jew), *Brautpreis* with its Jewish theme throughout suggests for the first time an interest in what it would look like to live in a Jewish world. Grete suggests that her experiences as a survivor have brought her back to Jewish culture, and that this is why she is now trying to tell a Jewish story, out of ". . . curiosity and the conjecture that not only the myths and the history of the Greeks are worth knowing, but those of the Jews as well" (128). She now becomes interested in Judaism as a culture, as text, and writing on the Michal project, she suggests, eventually makes her more strongly Jewish identified as well: "Have I become more Jewish since I've been involved with David and Michal? Yes, surely, something has started that was not there before" (128). Jewish identity remains nevertheless difficult for the narrator, as evident in both Michal's rebellion and Grete's ambivalence.

What keeps the narrator from identifying with the Jewish people beyond a shared experience of victimization, are her rather limited and somewhat conservative notions of what Jewishness is, or can be. Through a definition that focuses on the need to be actively involved either in Jewish religious practice, or in the state of Israel (be a Zionist), she in effect limits her options to a rather antiquated and conservative (prewar) notion of Judaism. This indicates a strong parallel with Weil's personal background: not having reconnected with a Jewish community after the war, she remained unfamiliar with postwar developments within Jewish culture in America and Europe that present a compromise between complete assimilation and a religious, or nationalistic Jewishness: something more akin to an ethnic identification. As a result, the position of Grete in *Brautpreis* remains a position of all or nothing. It also suggests that the tradition of female domestic religiosity (that characterized Jewish identity for many assimilated middle-class Jewish women at the end of the nineteenth and the beginning of the twentieth century) was not something Weil could fall back on.[66] The scenes from her childhood as recounted throughout her work suggest why: her family is described as so profoundly assimilated that almost all domestic Jewish rituals had already disappeared.

Consequently, Grete never feels a similar degree of affinity to Michal as to Antigone; "For me, she was never a sister, like Antigone, admired and envied for her courage. No deep relationship between me and this woman who was pushed around and often misused by men" (128–129). What she feels instead is: ". . . sympathy and compassion. . . . She and I, bound together by our belonging to a people that is not really one people at all but always wanted to be one: two Jewish women" (129). Imagining Michal formed an exercise for Grete: she places herself as a Jewish survivor within a much larger and older Jewish history and culture. And in the end, the narrator of *Brautpreis* seems to have indeed come to terms with her Jewishness to a greater degree than before. In the final moments of her text, Grete speaks of Michal and David as "our people," that is, as a community of Jews in which she includes herself.

Finale

Despite its significantly different main subject matter, *Brautpreis*, as all Weil's works from the 1980s, received a positive reception in West Germany, it was reprinted four times in the course of just a few months, translated to several languages, and was this time quickly translated to English as well (it was published in the United States in 1991). The work was awarded the *Geschwister Scholl Preis*, a prize that Weil was especially grateful for as it put her in touch with former members of the German resistance, people with whom she felt much affinity, but whom she had never been able to connect with. Just as happened with her previous novels from the 1980s, however, the German reviewers again chose to primarily focus on the autobiographical Grete chapters. They in fact discuss the provocative and elaborate rewriting of the Michal story as a parallel to Weil's prior use of the Antigone figure, thereby missing precisely the significant break the use of this Jewish figure represented from Weil's earlier work.[67]

By 1992, Weil would publish one more collection of short stories that she had written in the 1970s, *Spätfolgen* (After-Effects),[68] and in 1998 she published a shorter version of what she had intended to be a three-part autobiography, *Leb ich denn, wenn andere leben* (I Live When Others Live). Both texts were again reviewed favorably. When Weil died in May of 1999, at the age of ninety-three, she had finally become a celebrated author in Germany. She had received many literary awards and other honors, had given hundreds of interviews, was featured in several documentaries, and had at last become part of a German-Jewish canon.

With the highly autobiographical novels that she published in the 1980s that had a personal, subjective style, and, which had different kinds of openings for a German audience to find access—through the use of the Antigone figure, the explicit engagement with a younger generation, feminist themes—Weil did finally find the German readership that she had sought for nearly forty years. She in effect seems to have succeeded in reinserting herself symbolically, reinsert her (Jewish) voice, into a culture that had expelled her earlier, and that had not been interested in understanding what her return had meant.

The more complex way in which her work sought to intervene into a German discourse from which real living Jews were for the most part excluded, however, was not fully understood. Weil sought to engage her audience, to have them read her stories not only as testimony of a Jewish survivor (for which it was by now too late she felt; she had meant to bear witness soon after the war but no one wanted to hear of it then, while by the 1980s this aspect of her work had become less relevant as so much more information was now available), but as an appeal to now confront one's own (German) past. The reception of her work shows that this confrontation often did not take place. Even though these novels suggest that memories are never just about the past, but instead reflect a particular relationship to the present and the ways in which we shape it (and thus thematize and problematize personal and cultural memory), the audience responded in a way that left these memories as firmly rooted in the past only, rather than seeing them as revealing something about the present. Despite the fact that it seemed that in the wake of the near constant public debate about the legacy of the Third Reich and the Holocaust in the 1980s an open confrontation with survivors' stories and the German legacy of guilt had finally become possible, the particular kind of German reading of Weil's work that she had sought was still evasive.

In part, this evasiveness suggests a cultural process not yet completed: Germans still did not confront the Nazi legacy in a way that allowed for an open dialogue between victim and perpetrator. At the same time, the pendulum had already began to swing the other direction: the rebels of 1968 were now increasingly becoming the leaders of the Federal Republic, leaders that soon would be confronted with the greatest challenge against a cultural forgetting yet: the German reunification of 1990, which seemed to "normalize" Germany's history once and for all.

CHAPTER FOUR
CREATING ADDRESS

Ruth Klüger "Returns" to Germany

The German reunification of 1990 in many ways seemed to indicate a symbolic break with World War II and its continued political significance for the German state. If the division of Germany had served as a symbol for the aftermath of the Nazis' unprecedented destructive war and as an indication of the Allies' fears in 1945 that Germany would continue to pose a military and political threat in Europe (and that a profound punishment was in order), reunification seemed to mean the opposite. It served as the acknowledgment by Germany and the rest of the world that the nation had finally left its *Sonderweg*, and that it had proven itself to be a democratic country like any other in Europe.[1]

The symbolic implications of this reunification for a German understanding of the Nazi legacy—which implied an official approval of a "normalization" that had been hotly contested only a few years earlier—would be significant, and became apparent only a few years later. When asked about the significance of the Holocaust in 1994, 52 percent of Germans polled agreed with the notion that "Today after the German reunification, we shouldn't speak so much of the Holocaust anymore but should close the book on the past" and 37 percent agreed with the statement that "the Holocaust has no significance anymore today, because it took place fifty years ago.[2] A more pronounced German denial, not of the events of the Nazi era per se, but of a continued responsibility for this history and of its significance for the present was evident widely. Increasingly, as Germans pushed their association with Nazism to the background, Jews and their critical point of view of the German nation (as expressed publicly in Jewish literature) lost their symbolic importance. Even politically, there was less of an effort on the part of the German government to assuage Jews living in Germany.[3] Furthermore, reunification dramatically called into question Germany's national identity and in some cases brought about a new sense of nationalism that left little room for voices from the margins. This climate in turn allowed Holocaust revisionism, foreigner hate, and neo-Nazi groups to flourish.

It was at this moment, in 1992, that Ruth Klüger published her memoir *weiter leben. Eine Jugend* (*weiter leben Still Alive: A Holocaust Girlhood Remembered*). The work of a first-time literary author, the book is remarkable for its literary qualities as well as for the scathing critique it contains—of much of the recent German discourse surrounding the Holocaust and its survivors as well as that of earlier decades—and it became an important intervention into a post-reunification discourse that evaded speaking of the Holocaust and of German guilt. *Weiter leben* recounts Klüger's childhood under Hitler in Austria, survival in several concentration camps, subsequent postwar life in the United States, and her relationship to Germans after returning in 1988 for a work visit. In terms of its theme, the memoir stands in clear relationship to work such as Weil's, as it deals with similar questions: the (im)possibility of German-Jewish postwar life; guilt and responsibility among Jews and Germans; the question of German-Jewish female identity; and the importance of writing in undoing the effects of reification. It takes up a similar project of bearing witness, while at the same time investigating the limits of both memory and the genre of memoir and critically interrogating Germans' willingness to engage with this testimony. German critics quickly classified Klüger's work as belonging to this same genre of memoirs and autobiographical literature by German-Jewish survivors.

Yet, unlike Weil and other German-Jewish survivor authors, Klüger did not return to Germany at some point after the war, but rather, emigrated from Germany in 1947 to the United States and never returned to live in Europe. The United States is the country where Klüger holds citizenship and where she has lived her entire adult life. Furthermore, Klüger was born in Vienna, and not in Germany. This suggests that although her work may belong to the same cluster of autobiographical literature by Jewish authors published in Germany from the 1980s on, it is at the same time quite different. Klüger's much belated and displaced textual "return," not to Austria, but to Germany (as she published her work in Germany and addressed it literally to her *German* friends) represents, furthermore, something distinct from Weil's *actual* return. *Weiter leben* precisely complicates the notions of return and of address that already confound a reading of Weil's literature: why does an American Jew of Austrian descent seek to address a German audience, and what does such an address mean? Is this the kind of work that aids its author in reconciling German-Jewish identity? Is this address meant to facilitate a kind of return into Germanness? What does it mean for an Austro-German Jewish survivor to publish a memoir in the German language, in Germany, even though she had emigrated forty-five years earlier? What does it mean for the German literary establishment to categorize such a memoir as representing a "return"?

Most German-Jewish survivors, and certainly those who emigrated, would not write or publish their memoirs in German and publish them *in* Germany. Usually, the relation to the language and to German identity had become too ambivalent and the majority of German Jews chose to do away with both after 1945.[4] In particular those German-speaking Jews who survived the war in concentration camps and who had left for America after the war tended to distance themselves from their German background. If they wrote and published their memoirs at all, they almost always did so in the English language with American publishing houses. Klüger, then, represents an exception. By publishing in Germany and not in the United States where there has been a considerable market for (English-language) Holocaust memoirs since the 1980s, Klüger made a conscious choice to reinsert her voice into the German culture. Her text suggests why she did not choose an American, or even an Austrian audience, and in what ways she did still feel connected to Germans and German culture. This bond is not without problems, however, and Klüger's work, more explicitly than Weil's, can be read as a form of critical intervention: an intervention into (German) discussions and notions about the Holocaust experience, about survivors, about surviving, about writing after the Holocaust, and about German-Jewish and Austrian-Jewish relations since the Holocaust. As the confrontation sought by Klüger is at once characterized by both its belated and its displaced nature, it changes the nature of her confrontation: it provides an opportunity to "talk back" to the readers, the critics, and the elaborate scholarly and popular discourses that surrounds the Holocaust and survivors specifically. This kind of an address makes a powerful public statement as it asserts and intervenes.

Klüger had a difficult time finding a publisher for the memoir initially,[5] but once it was published it became a remarkable bestseller that was widely discussed in the German media and won her many important literary prizes.[6] Klüger's peculiar address has led to an unusual German reception, as some German critics somewhat simplistically declared Klüger to "have returned" in the form of her literature, and heralded her as an important postwar *German* author.[7] Such a reception is rather striking, even in light of the changes that had taken place in the 1980s, and begs for an explanation. Why is she reclaimed as "German?" What makes Klüger's work so appealing to the German audience? What kind of "return" does the text represent? Is this positive reception an indication that significant mentality changes took place that allowed for a fuller German confrontation with such a critical Jewish voice?

The answers to these questions prove complex, as this is not at all a reconciliatory work, a work that is easy for Germans to like. It is also a text full of contradictions, which does not allow for a pinning down of Klüger's position, and the book actually represents a much more complicated and ambivalent form of "reentry" into German culture than is generally acknowledged. It functions both as a speech act that seeks to reclaim agency, and as an act of disruption of a German cultural discourse that assigns a limited space to Jewish survivors to speak of memories of the past, and that questions their continued relevance for the post-reunification present.

Unconventional Memories

Weiter leben is not a conventional memoir by any means whereby from the vantage point of the present the events of the past (the Holocaust) are recounted. More "typical" Holocaust memoirs tend to contain a brief section that describes (positive) memories of life before Hitler (in which family and community life form the focus, though they are generally only sketched), and then narrate the (either gradual or sudden) deterioration of life under the Nazis, leading eventually to a complete family's (or even community's) destruction.[8] The focus is thus on the catastrophe, which tends to either confirm or shatter the protagonist's prior cultural and/or religious views and beliefs. The memoir then ends with the moment of liberation, generally a happy ending.[9] Klüger's text complicates this kind of pattern in several ways, calling into question received notions about how memory works, in what relation memory stands to writing, and how personal recollection functions in a broader cultural sense when it is presented to a public that does not share the same reservoir of memories.

Weiter leben is divided into separate sections and chapters (and chapters that are further divided in sections) that on first sight do seem to conform to the conventional structure of Holocaust memoirs: part I, "Wien" (Vienna) Klüger's early childhood in

Vienna; part II, "Die Lager" (the camps) which is subdivided into three parts that recount her stays in concentration camps Theresienstadt, Auschwitz-Birkenau, and Christianstadt/Groß-Rosen; and part III, divided up in "Flucht" (Flight/Escape) and "Bayern," which covers her escape and postwar life in Germany. The memoir continues, however, and also contains a fourth and quite elaborate chapter on postwar life in New York (part IV, "New York"), and an epilogue (entitled Göttingen), which recounts Klüger's return to Germany in the late 1980s for a work assignment.[10] Furthermore, unlike most Holocaust memoirs, the sections that deal with her prewar and postwar life together take up as many (even slightly more) of the text's pages as her discussion of her camp experiences.[11] This emphasis suggests that though the camp experiences are certainly of central significance to Klüger's memories and to her life, they need to be understood in the context of both what preceded it and what came after.

What this structure reveals (as does the book as a whole) is that who Klüger became as an adult, who she is now in the present (the vantage point from which she recounts her life in this text), is as strongly affected by the particularities of (her memories of) her pre- and postwar life and socialization, as by the Holocaust itself. The "weiter leben" of the title, then, is of central significance to the text, not only in the sense of "surviving," but also in the sense of "living on." It is this continued life, the rest of life, and memories of a childhood during the Holocaust that set the tone for this later existence, that are the subject of this work. Klüger's childhood *is* in part the Holocaust, but her life is more than the sum of this event's parts.

Furthermore, although the text in general lines follows the narrator's life story chronologically, it is a much more complex narrative, as she also delivers a continuous commentary from her present position on this past that breaks up the flow of the auto-biography: she moves back and forth in time, she foreshadows and backshadows. This commentary complicates received notions of memoir itself as it self-consciously deconstructs them through a questioning of memory and as it opens a view on the conflicting accounts and interpretations of the past. This meta-narrative in the text engages with external sources, other authors, and with an imagined audience whom Klüger addresses directly.[12] It also calls attention to the fact that it is being refracted through the eyes of the adult who remembers these events that the author experienced during her childhood. The narrator knows more now than she knew and understood at the time she had the experiences and brings this knowledge to the story.

Finally, it is also a dialogic narrative, in which the narrator anticipates her readers' reactions to the stories and events she recounts. She does so by interpellating imagined responses throughout the text, and by regularly warning the audience not to read and interpret certain passages in a particular way. Klüger's unconventional approach is thus visible at every point and within many different levels of the text, in terms of narrative structure, in terms of tone, and in terms of content. Several examples from the text (following its chronology) illustrate the effects of this narrative structure.

Part I, "Wien," consists of fifteen separate parts, fragments that narrate Klüger's life up to age eleven, her experiences before and after the *Anschluß*, a story that provides an unconventional and wholly unsentimental view of her family before the war. Klüger was born in 1931 in Vienna, and although her upbringing is described as quite typical of well-to-do middle-class assimilated Austrian-Jews (with a mixture of German *Bildung* and domestic Jewishness, and social democratic political leanings), she shows in some depth how this ordinary life was strained by pronounced family dysfunction even before the Nazis took power, a process that then accelerated. She describes her family members and herself as "difficult, neurotic people" (52). Take the response to Ruth's father's arrest, for instance. While her father manages to flee the country, Ruth and her mother are trapped together in Vienna,[13] after which their relationship quickly starts to deteriorate: Klüger's mother becomes increasingly paranoid, and Ruth becomes more isolated. Klüger is all too aware of her rather unconventional recollections and anticipates readers to "act surprised, assume a stance of virtuous indignation, and tell me that, given the hardships we had to endure . . . the victims should have come closer together and formed strong bonds."[14] This, however, is "rubbish," she argues, as it relies "on a false concept of suffering as a source of moral education" (52). In fact, just earlier she has suggested that the notion that one can learn a moral lesson, or for that matter, *any* lesson, from the Holocaust experience is nonsense (36).

Her depictions are furthermore full of fascinating contradictions that circumvent easy generalizations. For example, while Ruth's sense of identity changes under Nazi oppression, as she becomes more strongly Jewish identified, the content of her Jewish identity changes to one in which she feels objectified through the increasingly hostile response from strangers.[15] And whereas her life is described as becoming more and more circumscribed, isolated, and abnormal, as she is increasingly prohibited from being part of Vienna's public life (thereby missing out on normal childhood experiences such as going to school or learning how to ride a bike), her main activity of these years, endlessly reading the German classics on her own, is in hindsight seen as having created a deep and positive connection to the German language and its literature that lasts to this day.

Klüger's depiction of her deportation with her mother to Theresienstadt where they remained from September 1942 until May 1944 is unconventional as well. It is not seen as the beginning of the end, but as a continuation of a persecution process that started much earlier, one that she had already adjusted to, and one that led her now to a life that was in some respects better than that in Vienna. Even though Theresienstadt was extremely harsh (they suffered from hunger, a lack of space, privacy, and hygiene), she also describes her happiness in now having a chance to study, to find out about Zionism, and to make friends: "I somehow loved Theresienstadt, and the nineteen or twenty months that I spent there made me a social being."[16] Klüger breaks taboos and provides a new and different view on the Holocaust.

By May 1944, Klüger and her mother were deported to Auschwitz where they end up in the *Familienlager*. Even Klüger's experience at this most well known of concentration camps is described in a wholly unconventional fashion. Upon her receiving the inmate's tattoo, for instance, Klüger suggests that this event brought on a "new awareness" in her. "I was suddenly so aware of the enormity, the monstrosity, really, of my situation that I felt a kind of glee about it. I was living through something that was worth witnessing" (98). Upon anticipating a reader's response to this statement (too unbelievable, did she really have this much foresight or self-awareness?) she suggests that this realization should not be interpreted as something positive, but that it "tells you something about how beaten down and stripped of a sense of self I already was that I thus invented for myself a future based on the experience of the most abysmal humiliation yet" (98).

While life in Birkenau was almost entirely delimited by her experience of intense deprivation, in order to pass the time, she recites poems by heart, and attempts to compose poems of her own, and memorize them. She understands this self-consciously as an important survival strategy, even at age twelve: "Who only lives, without rhymes or thoughts, is in danger of losing one's mind . . . I didn't lose my mind, I created poems."[17] This, too, strikes one as unusual in the memoirs of a child survivor.

Particularly interesting is how Klüger describes her mother's role throughout these years of persecution. Paranoid, she always anticipates the worst, something that ordinarily is impossible to live with for Ruth, but which ironically in the camp environment results in saving both their lives, as the mother suggests that they volunteer for a transport that may or may not select them for direct extermination. Klüger concludes that: "people suffering from compulsive disorders, such as paranoia, had a better chance to pick their way out of mass destruction, because in Auschwitz they were finally in a place where the social order . . . had caught up with their delusions" (104). Yet, there is no redemptive message to be found here, either: "But isn't the price she paid too high: this madness she carried in her like a sleeping tomcat? . . . I don't want to carry such a predator inside of me, even if he could save my life in the next extermination camp" (104).

The selection for this transport proves to be a remarkable story as well: while Ruth's mother is selected, Ruth is not, as she is too young. On an impulse, she steps back to the end of the selection line, tries again, lies about her age, and comes through with the help of an inmate who convinces a German officer to select her, even though she is small and looks too young. This is an extraordinary moment that Klüger highlights: "What happened next is loosely suspended from memory. . . . It was . . . an incomprehensible act of grace, or put more modestly, a good deed" (106). This one inmate's effort on her behalf was completely selfless, and in hindsight proves to be life saving, as the rest of the inmates of the *Familienlager* would be murdered a few weeks later.

Ruth, her mother, and Ditha, a girl that they "adopt" into their family in Auschwitz, finally end up in Groß-Rosen, a labor camp where they work in an ammunition factory. By the winter of 1944–1945, when the starvation and the cold become nearly unbearable, they are evacuated and ordered to march away from the camp (on what would later become known as one of the notorious "death marches"). At the end of the second day of this march, Ditha, Ruth, and her mother in what constitutes a major act of courage and ingenuity, manage to flee into the German countryside. This grand moment of escape is ironically seen as quite unbelievable by others many decades later, when Klüger recounts her story. Perhaps male prisoners could have freed themselves, but not a woman and two girls, listeners claim.[18] Once again, as Klüger suggests, her story falls outside of the established frameworks of understanding.

It is with their escape that part III of *weiter leben* starts, entitled "Deutschland." Their flight leads to a highly idiosyncratic description of the war's end, because rather than experiencing freedom at the hands of liberators, their escape in the midst of the German military (and civilian) retreat out of Eastern Europe in fact meant that they wandered for several weeks through the Eastern German territories along with German escapees, *Ostflüchtlinge*, who were fleeing from Soviet troops. These troops are seen by Klüger as liberators, but are feared as enemies by the now retreating Germans. Finally free from German imprisonment, she thus comes to witness the victimization of many thousands of German families at the end of the war. This leads to a complex analysis of what commonalities there are with these Germans, and of what remain insurmountable differences. For whereas she was still in some danger of being recognized as an escapee, she has mainly "joyous" memories of this moment, while her "German friends" will only remember walking on these same roads, "mourning their losses . . . grieving for the homeland they wouldn't see again" (137). It is herein that "the source of my precarious bond with Germans of my generation" lies, suggests Klüger, "here where our paths joined" (137). This kind of empathy is quite unusual.

For several weeks, they "pass" as German refugees, and eagerly await liberation. When this moment finally comes, it proves to be profoundly anticlimactic. When Ruth approaches one of the American soldiers and tells him that they escaped from a concentration camp, he covers his ears. Ruth concludes: ". . . I was glad that we had freed ourselves and didn't depend all that much on the victors. . . . One thing, I figured, was certain: this war hadn't been fought for our sake" (149). This part of the narrative, too, differs dramatically from more conventional survivor accounts that emphasize gratitude toward the liberators and a happy ending.

Life after liberation follows an unusual arc in Klüger's narrative as well. Even though Ruth and her mother live for several years in Germany before they are offered a chance to emigrate, Ruth's experiences among the Germans are not described as unpleasant, and she does not see the Germans as her enemies. She starts taking classes at the local university (her mother managed to procure a high school diploma for her), and makes friends. One of these friendships is with a boy slightly older than she is, Christoph, a relationship that is described in terms of a mutual fascination for each other's differences, and of (unsuccessful) attempts to overcome these differences, thus in effect mirroring broader postwar German-Jewish relations. Most intriguing for Ruth is Christoph's secure sense of himself as a German: "He was at home in Germany, rooted in a particular German landscape and he came to typify the German for me."[19] This period of time spent in Germany would later turn out to be of formative importance to Klüger, as she became immersed in German life and culture in a way that she previously had not been in Vienna (as her experiences and education had been so severely limited by the Nazis), and thus developed strong ties to the country and its culture.

In contrast, her arrival and integration in New York after 1948 are depicted as marked by profound difficulties, and by a new kind of oppression as a woman, and present no happy end to the memoir, quite the opposite, in fact. Part IV, "New York," deals with Ruth's and her mother's experience in the early years of emigration (1948–1951), which prove to be some of the most painful in Klüger's life. They were poor, looked down upon by earlier emigrants, told to forget about their past, and therefore Ruth's emotional adjustment was difficult. She started college, but suffered from severe depression: "I felt inferior, saw myself through the eyes of others, and there were times when it seemed that instead of having been liberated, I had crawled away like a cockroach from the exterminator" (185). This sense of depression becomes worse when she starts seeing a psychiatrist.

Her relationship with her mother becomes increasingly complicated as well after their emigration to America. After college, Ruth wants to move out and move on, but when she does so, her mother destroys all of her personal belongings. When she gets married in 1955 and has a child, her mother attempts suicide. This is where the memoir ends. It is only from the passages of fore- and backshadowing throughout the memoir that we know more about the rest of Klüger's life. She went on to have another child, her marriage failed, she worked as a librarian, by chance became a graduate student in German at the University of California, and became a professor of German. It is in this function that she returns to Germany in the 1980s to run an academic foreign exchange program.

The epilogue, entitled "Göttingen," takes us to the most recent present, the two years that led to the composition of this memoir, which started literally by accident when, while in Göttingen to run her study-abroad program, Klüger was hit by a bicyclist and suffered a massive brain injury. She suggests here that it took literally a rearranging of her mental capacities to bring back the memories of the past, not a process she could or would have undertaken voluntarily. During her long recovery period, she is revisited by a barrage of memories from her past that she had not thought about for a long time: ". . . there are those ancient objects you think you discarded long ago, pulled back into the daylight" (207). She is disturbed and disoriented, but also pleasantly surprised to be able to suddenly remember much more from the past than before, and to rediscover parts of herself previously forgotten: "You feel dispossessed, because the house has been damaged badly by this wrenching disturbance and now seems an alien place. By and by you notice that there is more of your own self in the chaos than there used to be in the former tidy corner" (207). She recovers slowly but fully with the help of German friends, and pieces her life back together, now with her past more intact than before. Six months later, she writes her memoir, which she finishes up while back home in the United States.

This memoir represents the kind of meditation on memory and narrative modes that fits the mold of a postmodern autobiography,[20] which is highly unusual in survivor literature. Its effects are therefore especially dramatic. For a survivor to call into question how memories and narratives about one's past are constructed and function—not as trustworthy accounts or reflections of a lived past but as complex reconstructions with which one justifies one's past and present choices and behavior—is to break radically with the genre. In addition, Klüger suggests that generalizations about the Holocaust do not work, and seeks to undo a host of stereotypes, both those that romanticize and those that vilify survivors. It is all the more remarkable, then, that this highly unusual and complicated text became such a bestseller after its publication in Germany. How was this possible?

A (German) Success Story?

Klüger's story as told in *weiter leben* is a problematic one, a story of oppression, isolation, life-threatening situations, German murder, and of a difficult reentry into the postwar world, a world that is furthermore full of judgments and clichés about the Holocaust and survivors. By any definition, then, this memoir recounts an uncomfortable story, without a happy ending. What is deceiving in an analysis of this narrative (as with any survivor's narrative) is that nevertheless the author's survival can easily be misconstrued as such a happy end. Klüger anticipates this kind of a triumphant reading of her memoir and she attempts to preempt it, through her critical commentary. She also knows that this is a nearly impossible task:

> Now comes the problem of this survivor story, as of all such stories: we start writing because we want to tell about the great catastrophe. But since by definition the survivor is

alive, the reader inevitably tends to separate, or deduct, this one life, which she has come to know, from the millions who remain anonymous. You feel, even if you don't think it: well, there is a happy ending after all. Without meaning to, I find that I have written an escape story, not only in the literal but in the pejorative sense of the word. (137–138)

Klüger implores her audience not to read her memoir this way: "So how can I keep my readers from feeling good about the obvious drift of my story away from the gas chambers and the killing fields and towards the postwar period, where prosperity beckons?" (138).[21] Her writing on this issue can be seen as a warning to her readers not to read the work as sending a positive, redeeming message.

This attempt at intervention in the reception of her work completely fails, nevertheless. Instead, most German critics proceeded to interpret the work as a triumph, as a success story, as Stephan Braese and Holger Gehle point out in their comprehensive analysis of this reception.[22] The focus in these analyses falls on Klüger's prewar life as a Jewish girl in Vienna, her miraculous selection that took her out of Auschwitz and saved her life, and on her postwar success as a *Germanistin*. Little mention is made of the profound desperation to which the memoir attests. Instead, Klüger's achievement as a postwar academic is hailed as a sign that she managed to become highly successful professionally, and more importantly, that she has "returned to Germany," after all.

For instance, renowned author and critic Martin Walser (in real life a close friend of Klüger's, after whom the figure of Christoph in *weiter leben* is modeled), suggests that her work is a "miracle of language," a *Sprachwunder*, with which Klüger has achieved a return to Germany. He thereby explicitly ignores that she in fact did *not* return: "regardless of where she now resides . . . it is not the passport which tells where one belongs, but language . . . Ruth Klüger has returned to the German language, and in a masterful way."[23] This kind of German review is common, even though Klüger herself suggests throughout the entire narrative that this return is in fact *not possible*. Indeed, instead of engaging with these problems or responding to the provocative comments Klüger makes about of the (im)possibility of a German-Jewish dialogue, German critics seem to have used this book to appease their guilt. As Irene Heidelberger-Leonard argues "Klüger's highly idiosyncratic discourse on Auschwitz has been generally misheard or misread. One applauds without holding back, there where one recognizes one's self, and skips energetically those passages where difference manifests itself as true difference, there where . . . it really cannot be integrated into one's own imagination."[24]

German critics empathize and identify with Klüger; they imagine themselves in her position, her life, instead of engaging with her text as an invitation to confront their own possible complicity, and their personal responsibility to come to terms with the Nazi past.[25] This kind of a response, in which Germans appropriate her suffering instead of responding to it from their own position as Germans, as descendants of the Nazi generation, ironically, is already anticipated in *weiter leben* itself, and Klüger explicitly warns against it:

You should not identify with me, I would much prefer if you did not; and when I seem completely foreign [*Artfremd*] I will accept that . . . and . . . apologize for it. But at least allow yourself to be agitated, don't hide, don't say beforehand: that has nothing to do with you . . . you already have . . . absolved your task of complicity and compassion. Become militant, seek the dialogue. (141)[26]

Klüger seeks to engage her German readers, seeks to unsettle them with her sharp criticism of the German discourse that surrounds the Holocaust. These critical warnings and comments in the text are nevertheless ignored by most of the German critics, and instead, the memoir is read in such a way as to fit in with other works of this particular genre (as can be seen in the reception of Weil), which serves to make these kinds of texts harmless. It is read as the work of a (Austro-)German author who bears witness to her experience during the Holocaust, who lost her place in German society because of the racial ideology of the Nazis, and who is able to "rediscover" her Germanness after the war by becoming a successful professor of German language and literature. What is sought for in this kind of reading of the narrative is solely a *German* identity. Klüger's Austrian background, and in particular her Jewishness, (and after four decades, her unmistakable Americanness) disappear. In short, her *otherness*, her displacement, is taken for granted, pushed to the background, or ignored and thus deprived of its subversive power. Klüger is defined only by her German identity, and Jewishness is either self-evident or merely "an effect of Nazism," and therefore not considered relevant to postwar identity.

In order to be able to misread or over-read *weiter leben*, however, it is necessary to ignore large parts of Klüger's meta-narrative, her present-day critical commentary with which she intersperses her memory text. This is a structural feature that is hard to miss, as it is so unique and furthermore integral to how *weiter leben* is composed as a narrative.

Discursive Interventions

Weiter leben's unique quality lies precisely in the fact that the narrative turns a critical eye toward itself. It self-consciously deconstructs its own testimony and the psychological, historical, and literary discourses that have surrounded this kind of literature for the last twenty-five years, by commenting on it. In some ways, this text seems to "do it all." It provides testimony while commenting on the impossibility of testimony; it problematizes the recall of memory and the constructed nature of survivor narratives, and the function of writing. It invites a dialogue with its readers while commenting on the difficulty of this dialogue; it uses the insights of many different academic disciplines as well as from works of art and literature as intertexts, only to criticize many of these forms of theoretical and artistic discourse.

The highly self-conscious nature of this memoir reflects several unusual aspects of this text and its production, ways in which it differs from most other Holocaust literature (including that of Weil): the late date of its creation; its displaced nature; and the scholarly-critical background of its author. *Weiter leben* appeared much later than most other memoirs of the Holocaust, and it reflects that its author was familiar with the enormous quantities of historical, sociological, political, philosophical, psychological, and literary-critical studies that have already been published on these events and its actors, and on the theoretical, testimonial, historical, and artistic representations. It was also produced from a location of significant geographical remove: Klüger is the quintessential outsider, the Austrian Jew who left Germany four decades earlier, who works as a professor in the United States. Because of its belated date of creation and displaced status, and because of Klüger's profession as a German literary scholar (and critic of Holocaust literature), the text is able to engage with many of the arguments made in these studies. Klüger indeed suggests that the literary and historical texts that have preceded her own writing of *weiter leben* have affected this Holocaust discourse to such a degree that one can no longer write a work on the Holocaust, autobiographical or not, without implicitly referring to, or being influenced by, or engaging with this earlier material:

> It is exactly the first books written on the subject that no one wanted to read at the time that have changed our thinking, so that I cannot speak of the camps today as if I were the first to do so, as if no one had spoken of them before, as if not everyone who reads this here already knows so much about it that they think that it is enough already, and as if not everything has already been exploited, politically, aesthetically, and as kitsch as well.[27]

It is this very different and complex nature of *weiter leben*'s meta-narrative that German critics often do not acknowledge, or only insofar as it fits their own interpretation. This means that two important discourses that run throughout the text remain overlooked or poorly understood: first, how the memoir tries to both open up and delineate the possibilities and the limits of a Jewish dialogue with present-day Germans, and second, how interventions of the kind in *weiter leben* serve the purpose of undoing a sense of reification.

Reluctant Dialogue

Klüger's book seeks a German audience, as becomes immediately clear from its opening and its dedication: "*Den Göttinger Freunden—ein deutsches Buch*" ("For the friends in Göttingen—a German book"). In the text this is articulated even more clearly: Klüger does not write for a Jewish audience, she suggests, for surely she would not do this in a language that is used today by only a handful of Jews, instead, "I write it for those who find that I exude strangeness that is insurmountable. In other words, I write it for the Germans."[28] This statement is significant, in particular in light of the fact that Klüger did publish an English language edition of the work, which she translated herself, which on the contrary seems to suggest that the text was possibly written not only with a German audience in mind. A comparison of the German *weiter leben* with this English translation *Still Alive* reveals, however, that the latter book is indeed a different book: a thoroughly rewritten memoir that contains significant changes, additions, and cuts, relative to the original.[29] Most of the changes reveal a desire to make the book more relevant to its American cultural context. The elaborate and radical nature of the changes, and in particular the fact that most of the original passages with direct address are cut or now changed to address an American reader, actually reiterates just how invested Klüger projects is in reaching and addressing a particular audience, whether they are Germans in the original, or Americans in the English translation. Because the English translation no longer addresses Germans, it becomes a different book.[30]

In *weiter leben*, Klüger seeks a German audience to engage in a dialogue about the Nazi past, about what the Germans have done to the Jews, in order to bring about the possibility for a conversation between Germans and Jews, in the *present*. For until this dialogue about the past takes place, Germans and Jews do not meet on sufficient common ground to function together in a German present or future, she suggests. *Weiter leben* illustrates such German-Jewish dialogue through Ruth's interaction with two figures in this book: her friend Christoph, and the German wife of a colleague, Gisela, both of whom are of her own generation: children during the Nazi era. This makes them stand less on opposite sides of the divide between Jewish victims and German perpetrators than would normally be the case with Germans of an older generation, and creates an interesting bond, one which Klüger does not feel as strongly with older Germans, or even with those Germans born after the war. The interaction is nevertheless described as very complex and often conflicted.

The roots of the conflict between the "average" Germans and Klüger need to be sought in the difference in experience of Germans and of Jews, suggests Klüger, first consciously registered by her when she left Auschwitz by train for Christianstadt, and saw the landscape surrounding the camp for the first time. She then realized that Germany had not even taken notice of them: "The world hadn't changed. Auschwitz had not been on a foreign planet, but part of what lay before us. . . . Life had gone on without a hiccup. I pondered the incongruity of this apparent carefreeness existing in the same space as our transport. . . . What I had gone through hadn't even touched them" (114).

This is not to suggest, however, that Klüger accepts the excuse of Germans who assert that they did not know during the war what was happening to the Jews. After all, toward the end of the war when she and her mother escaped from the death march, she witnessed a group of concentration camp inmates passing right through the German town where she was staying. She thus knows that Germans cannot deny having seen something of this "strange planet." This argument is confirmed not only by her own observation, but also by the statements of Germans themselves, when they for instance seek an excuse for their lack of resistance: "But you can't claim that you didn't know about the Nazi atrocities and at the same time claim that you didn't do anything to oppose them because of fear or cowardice. Either you didn't know about concentration camps, or you were afraid to land there yourself if you didn't toe the line. You can't have it both ways" (156). Furthermore, she suggests, even if there were a general German lack of knowledge about the Holocaust during the war, this should not excuse them from seeking a confrontation with it now.

With her image of concentration camp life as life on a different planet, Klüger refers to the incommensurability between the points of view of Germans and of Jews, which showed itself as soon as the war was over. In Klüger's relationship to Christoph, they each remain trapped within the limits of their own story and experience, neither being fully able to move beyond it and grasp the other's perspective. Christoph suggests that it was she who would not let him speak: "He was to say later that I gave him no chance to talk about our common, and yet so dissimilar, past, whereas I think it was the other way around" (186). Years later when Christoph ends up writing a book on Auschwitz and she wonders why he did not bother to ask her about her experiences, he tells her that he did not realize that she had been there. "That is improbable, I said. . . . And yet it is believable, too, because our minds forget what our hearts won't remember" (167). Their experiences during their childhood, hers in concentration camps, his in the *Hitler Jugend*, differ so fundamentally that ultimately they experienced different albeit parallel histories, which makes them different people: "Memory connects us, memory separates us."[31]

This gap between Germans and Jews as exemplified by her friendship with Christoph continues to the present day. Klüger finds, during a conversation about experiences of claustrophobia with friends in Göttingen, for instance, that she cannot share her war experiences, as these are too extreme and would only silence her German friends. While her colleagues tell of bomb shelters and other (German) war experiences, she is thinking of her transport from Theresienstadt to Auschwitz, pressed together with hundreds of people in a cattle car without air, food, toilet, or water. She does not speak of this experience as it would reveal a profound discrepancy between their childhood memories, and instead, she tells a different story, "And so my childhood falls into a black hole" (93). If she were to have added her experience to the conversation, this unbridgeable gap of strangeness and of severity between those who experienced the Holocaust as victims, and those who did not, would have put an end to the dialogue. "Now I have silenced you, that was not my intent. There is always a wall between the generations, but here it is barbed wire, rusted barbed wire."[32]

The figure of "Gisela" is the second German conversation partner used throughout the text by Klüger to illustrate the German-Jewish dialogue, but unlike Christoph, she functions as the personification of everything that is problematic about the relationship between Germans and Jews after the war. In part based on a real person (the German wife of an American academic colleague from her days at Princeton) and in part a composite of several different people Klüger has encountered in her postwar life, that is, literally, an "average" or "typical" conversation partner (a *Durchschnittsgesprächspartnerin*), Gisela exudes a strong ambivalence about the past and her parents' generation: she cannot come to terms with the legacy of the Third Reich, which expresses itself in her judgment of Ruth's story and her diminishing of the suffering of Jews, which seems to function to alleviate her guilt. Gisela " . . . was determined to reduce the past until it fit into the box of a clean German conscience . . ." (73).

Gisela's response is not merely a defensive gesture toward a past that is experienced as unmasterable, but her comments are also meant as a provocation, Klüger feels, and are "unmistakably aggressive" (73). Her attitude toward Klüger's past, toward her experiences that have made her who she is today, is one of denial. For instance, Gisela suggests that Theresienstadt really was not too bad, and that although Auschwitz must have been horrible, "From all she has heard it must have been a pretty tough place . . ." Klüger did not spend too much time there, "I wasn't there all that long, was I?" (79). Gisela's interjections are stunning to Klüger: "But where did she get off lecturing me on this place from my past?" (86). Gisela equates her German family's wartime experience with that of Klüger and comes up with absurd and insulting parallels: "I got off lightly . . . for I was able to emigrate to America after the war and was spared the first terrible postwar years in Germany. Compared to her mother who lost her husband on the Russian front, my mother was lucky . . . for she found two more husbands in America while in Germany there weren't enough men to go around" (79).

It is this kind of defensive, and at times even aggressive German stance toward her life, her part of their shared history, and the ensuing silence that *weiter leben* tries to overcome. Klüger suggests that she writes to create a bridge, because, ". . . if there is no bridge between my memories and yours and theirs . . . then what's the good of writing any of this?" (93). She suggests that in order to create this connection one should allow an open dialogue and not mythologize or silence the Holocaust.[33] Precisely in the case of the Holocaust, however, most Germans do not dare to assume that it is possible to communicate about it. Her story makes them so uncomfortable that instead they argue that it is an untouchable, almost sacred experience that is so horrible that it cannot be understood by anyone who has not been there, and in so doing, they render communication about it impossible. Initially after the war, ". . . people didn't want to hear about it, or if they did listen, it was in a certain pose, an attitude assumed for this special occasion; it was not as partners in a conversation, but as if I had imposed on them and they were graciously indulging me" (94). Some respond that they already know everything there is to know. Klüger suggests that neither excuse is sufficient. Auschwitz can be communicated to a certain degree, and should be. On the other hand, by seeking to diminish the "strangeness" they encounter in her, in her story, and seeking to identify with her and her past, they deny that a real, unbridgeable gap of experience remains present between their position and hers.

This is the challenge German critics fail to meet. In their reading of this book, they do not use it as the opportunity to communicate from their own position with the "other" this book represents, but instead, they try to identify with Klüger, erasing their difference and avoiding an exploration of their own position. As a result, what takes place is not an encounter in the present with a Jewish survivor, but the work and its publication in Germany is used to conclude that the gap between Jews and Germans has already been bridged: Klüger is "welcomed back" as a German. Klüger's Jewishness is thereby seen as a thing of the past, as related solely to the Holocaust, not a difference that still exists and in a real and viable form informs her identity.

Impossible Vienna

Even though the German response is inadequate, the fact that many Germans do feel that the Third Reich carries a legacy that they have an obligation to confront somehow is what has pulled Klüger back to Germany. For in Germany at least the criminal legacy of the Nazis carries significance. Unlike Germany, Austria was treated separately from Germany by the Allies as a "conquered" and now "liberated" nation after the war (as a result of the 1943 Moscow declaration of the Allies that determined Austria to be the Nazis' first victim,[34] not a country that had served as an enthusiastic accomplice to Hitler's war effort and to the Jewish genocide), and as a result, the Austrian acknowledgment of responsibility for this past, or the effort to improve the situation for surviving Jews was minimal for many decades. Instead, both Austrians and Jews were proclaimed to be victims equally (as if there were no causal relation between the victimization of the Jews and their persecution perpetrated by Austrian as well as German Nazis), and approval of the *Anschluß* was denied, as was any complicity in the crimes that were committed under Nazi rule. The Austrian government denied its guilt, and simultaneously ignored Jews' unique victimization,[35] and was unwilling to repay Jews for the material and financial losses they had incurred. Austrian Jews had a difficult time getting back their property, and the response to these attempts was often virulently antisemitic.[36] Austria did not "denazify" after 1945, and no one saw the need to analyze the significance of the Nazi past or continued antisemitism.[37] This is especially problematic as opinion polls suggest that Austria was rife with antisemitic prejudice well into the 1950s, and that antisemitism remained stronger in Austria than in West Germany or anywhere else in Western Europe or the United States.[38]

The postwar situation in Austria for Jewish returnees was thus even worse than in West Germany, and this climate continued well into the 1980s. As a result,

"Jewish existence in Austria after 1945 is tied in with a mass of identity problems," Ruth Beckermann argues.[39] The long silence on the Austrian complicity in the Nazi crimes was not broken until the mid-1980s (with the 1986 elections that brought the war past of President Kurt Waldheim to the fore). Yet even though since the late 1980s a reconsideration of the *Opferthese* has taken place, and more dissenting voices can be heard in Austria than before, there has still not been a consideration of Nazism as an "Austrian phenomenon."[40]

Austrians thus avoided dealing with the past for so many decades (and claimed that to do so would be unnecessary), that there is no postwar tradition of Austrian-Jewish dialogue to which Klüger can connect. There is not even a "negative symbiosis" in Austria, as Diner has asserted for (West) Germany. Klüger has cut all her ties to Austria: "Today, I no longer have friends or relatives in Austria, at the most a colleague or an acquaintance who lives there. Only the literature of this country speaks to me more intimately than other works . . ."[41] This literature reminds her of her childhood: the same Viennese accent and flow of the language. Nevertheless, her memories of Vienna are solely those of the war, and they have not been replaced by a more positive image, for instance through possibilities for new postwar Jewish life. Even as Vienna for many serves as a popular tourist destination, for Klüger it remains tied to particularly bitter memories: "The city is for me neither foreign nor familiar, which also means in the reverse that she is both at the same time . . ."[42] The city was for her without joy and particularly hostile to Jewish children, *judenkinderfeindlich* (67). She thus instead returns to seek address in Germany, where, however inadequate, some Germans at least feel a need to respond.

It is not only a dialogue that *weiter leben* seeks, though, the work also seems to serve another purpose. As a Holocaust survivor who wishes to tell her story in a thorough post-Holocaust age, Klüger is faced with a great irony: there is a sense that everything has already been said, making her life story seem redundant. This text fights this kind of objectification by commenting on this other work, by "talking back" to it, in order to have, for once, the last word to herself.

Reifying Discourse

The fact that *weiter leben* is filled with a critical dialogue with (German) literary and historical intertexts and commentary on these texts does not mean that Klüger's work only seeks to demythologize and serve as a correction to postwar popular and academic discourse on the Holocaust, in which case she might have been better off publishing her work in English in the United States, since after all, a great deal of (academic) Holocaust studies discourse is produced in North America. By writing in German and publishing in German, the text reveals the subversive function of its critical discourse as it seeks to undo the repetitive patterns of reification that Klüger experienced as a Jewish woman both during and after the war.

In a rather unusual move, however, these patterns are almost always described in terms of her oppression as both a Jew *and* as a woman. Most often, the two prove to be impossible to separate for Klüger. For instance, while her experience of racialization as an Austrian Jew under Nazi policies is described as profoundly alienating, a process that Ruth tries to fight by taking up a self-conscious Jewishness, she finds that she cannot do so because of her difficult position within Judaism as a girl. As a result of the ambivalence of both experiences with Jewish identity, Klüger calls herself a "bad"

Jew, even decades after the war. She refers here to the fact that she is nonobservant. Interestingly enough, then, Klüger, somewhat similarly to Weil, suggests that Jewishness equals Jewish religious observance, and that she cannot be a "good" Jew, as she does not conform to certain implicit (religious) standards. For Klüger, as with Weil, her difficulty in conforming is related to her inability to find a place for herself within Judaism as a woman: "If it were different,. . . . I'd have a friendlier attitude towards this religion which reduces its daughters to helpmeets of men and circumscribes their spiritual life within the confines of domestic functions" (30). In contrast to Weil, however, these feminist objections to Judaism, and her lack of conformity to Jewish tradition, do not deter Klüger from defining herself as Jewish. Her experiences of shared persecution with other Jews have made this identity hers, even if it never becomes a religious one.

Within her experience of racial persecution, too, Klüger depicts in particular the gender aspect of her experience of reification. For instance, during the war, women were treated as badly as men, she suggests, but were less well protected, because at first, the assumption was that only Jewish men were at risk. As a result, many more women than men remained trapped in Europe when the war started, and thus remained within the reach of deportation. Women, she suggests, were seen as less valuable.[43] Klüger furthermore identifies the Nazis explicitly as men. Often, these oppressive forces, men and Nazis, become one in her eyes, for instance, when she writes of "the uniformed Aryan world of men on the outside" (101).[44] On the other hand, she tends to see women, *all* women as potential victims of (Nazi) men. Thus, when she hears at the end of the war that women liberated from camps, too, were raped during massive sexual assaults by the conquering Soviet soldiers, she concludes that women in particular are always the victims of war: "War belongs to men, even as victims of war they belong to them."[45]

In the passages that deal with Klüger's postwar life, *weiter leben* shows its explicit feminist agenda most clearly. Klüger describes her experience as one of constant exclusion: she finds that as a woman she is consistently written out of history, and denied the opportunity to tell her story, as the war is supposedly a story that belongs to men. "Occasionally I tell a few stories of my own, if someone asks. But that rarely happens. Wars, and hence the memories of wars, are owned by the male of the species. . . . Besides, women have no past, or aren't supposed to have one" (18). Even years later in her marriage, she finds that women's stories and her story as a persecuted Jewish woman, does not count. In fact, she finds that her story has to compete with that of her husband who was an American soldier during the war. He is a history professor, but does not want her to talk to his classroom about the Holocaust.

After coming to the United States in 1947, this process of reification and her consciousness of her subordinate position as a woman becomes even stronger, and she explains how all of these forms of oppression seem connected to her:

> First, in my childhood, there had been the contempt of Aryan children for Jewish children in Vienna, then the condescension of Czech children for German-speakers in Theresienstadt, and now the arrogance of men towards women. These three types of contempt may be considered incommensurable, but I experienced them within a few years in my own person, in the order mentioned . . . and so it has validity for me. (166)

For Klüger, these different forms of discrimination are mentioned together not to relativize Nazi antisemitism or its effects, but to draw attention to the severity and continuity of discrimination, and in particular the damaging effects of sexism.

Klüger's condemnation of the reification that surrounds her as a survivor after the war is damning, and with *weiter leben* she seeks to undo the myths that surround survivors. She strongly objects to the assumption that survivors should have learned something and become better people based on their experience of persecution, in particular their stay in a concentration camp. On the other hand, she also resents the opposite assumption, namely, that "what . . . survivors had to do to stay alive [was that] you walked over dead bodies" (66). She finds this judgment insulting: "Later in life, nothing offended me more than the generalization that the camps turned us all into brutal egotists, and whoever survived them must be morally defective" (77). These myths are brought about by those who were not there, suggests Klüger, in order to establish clear boundaries between survivors and outsiders, and they function as defense mechanisms.

This is the kind of reification that for many German Jews began during the Nazi years, but continued far beyond the end of the war, through the different historical, psychological, and cultural discourses generated about them. As mentioned earlier, particularly damaging in this regard has been the medical profession, which formed a problematic set of generalized theories about the mental state of survivors and their behavior in the camps. In Klüger's elaborate description of the effects of the treatment of the Viennese psychiatrist with whom she visited a few times in New York, as well as in comments throughout the text, she suggests that psychiatrists and psychoanalysts in the immediate postwar years had no idea how to treat survivors, and did much damage to their patients:

> The garden-variety psychiatry which flourished in New York in those days avoided all social criticism and any connection between individual suffering and historical evil—it was in full flight from the excess of history which we had just managed to put behind us. Hence all psychic suffering had to have its origin inside, in the mind of the patient. No cold wind from the outside could affect the hothouse of the psyche. (186)

Problems in survivors were seen as unrelated to their experience of persecution and instead, as inevitably located in childhood trauma.[46] Now, many decades later, in looking back on this kind of treatment, she wonders: "Was it really about the truth or about the intent to inflict hurt?"[47] Of her own disastrous experience with the psychiatrist with whom she visited only a few times after the war, she now writes:

> Today I understand (though still not fully) that these men had their own agenda: the Jewish catastrophe was mainly and merely a resounding humiliation to them, not the tragedy of saints and martyrs that our own propaganda had made of it since. . . . What these male refugees who had spent the war in America—my uncle, [the psychiatrist], all of them—held against us was that we were the mothers whom they had left behind, we were the women and children whom they should have protected. (187)

This doctor, as many other so-called specialists, had his own, very different motivation in treating survivors such as Klüger, and this agenda clashed with their needs.

The effects of this "treatment" are still felt after forty years. "Letting go of these conversations that undid [destroyed] me. He disturbs that which says 'I' in me."[48] In the passages that deal with these sessions (which take up a considerable amount of space, almost eight pages describe the three or four visits), the emotion is still raw. These are among the most painful passages in the book because they so clearly illustrate the incompetence or unwillingness of postwar society (even among those who might have meant well) to deal humanely with those who had survived this disaster and its profoundly disturbing effects.

The response that might have been more helpful Klüger suggests instead, and which was already clear to her during her visits to the psychiatrist, is to have been able to fully express her own experiences and views in her own words. For instance, the poems she composed in her mind in Auschwitz helped her articulate what had occurred to her, and she would have liked to show them to the psychiatrist: "There he could have read the words I had found for my grief. For his part, he had not provided any other words. Not even the word *Trauerarbeit*, which he must have known and I didn't. The labor of mourning, the recognition that it's hard work" (190). It is *weiter leben* itself then, which contains both these poems and her life story, and which offers the opportunity to speak back to this reifying discourse that silenced her.

Whereas having been in Auschwitz would determine the rest of her life, she does not wish to be defined in terms of Auschwitz, Klüger makes clear.[49] She resists being made into a "case." Her resistance takes the form of writing, of taking back ownership of her own past, her experiences, her memories. They might be imperfect, as she refers to the unreliable nature of her memory, the difficulty of testimony, but they are all she has left. She takes ownership of her unusual experiences, and articulates her own vision on the events. She is aware of and discusses the difficulties in writing about her experiences, but writes despite these difficulties. She admits that memory is fallible (and serves the needs of those who remember) but still, she writes in order to integrate this highly unusual childhood into her adult life, in order to "live on," as the title of her work suggests. By writing, by "talking back" she undoes the reification she experienced as a Jew, and which she continues to experience as a survivor and as a woman, while reclaiming her position in a postwar (German) world.

Due to its unique perspective, and its late date of creation, *weiter leben* succeeds in engaging in a dialogue with the multiple discourses that precede it, some scholarly, some political or personal, which seek to appropriate and simplify Klüger's reality of the Holocaust, the concentration camps, and her experience as a survivor. In dialogue with this reifying discourse, Klüger shows that as a survivor, she too, has done her reading and should get to have a say in the discourse that is being produced *about* her. Through her writing, she asserts a subject position in which she can articulate her own sense of self, her own narrative, and redefine herself as a (certain kind of) Jew, as a (certain kind of) German, as a survivor.

With this highly unusual German-language memoir, Klüger found a powerful tool to address a German post-reunification audience, as her positive reception in Germany suggests. My discussion of this reception also shows, however, that a true German-Jewish dialogue is not so easily reestablished, as even by the mid-1990s a German audience could not fully and openly engage with Jewish survivors as partners in dialogue, but remained caught in its inability to deal with its own past. Ultimately, Klüger's address, too, was only in part acknowledged and understood for what it is: a critical and complex intervention into a German discussion about Jews and the Hitler legacy that seemed to exclude living Jews.

CHAPTER FIVE

BELATED INTERVENTIONS

The Holocaust ended the life of European Jews as it had existed for centuries. Jews were segregated, isolated, hunted down, and murdered in unprecedented fashion. Whereas the Shoah is commonly understood as having led to the *physical* destruction of the European Jewish community, what has been acknowledged explicitly only in the past decades is how these events also brought about a traumatic *shift in identity* for surviving West-European Jews, in particular the assimilated, middle-class Jews of Western and Central Europe who had to confront and redefine their sense of belonging to Europe after 1945, as Jews and as citizens of a certain nationality.

This shift in identity and the ensuing process of reconciliation was tortured and complicated in countries such as Austria and Germany where, on the one hand, Jewishness had been defined as a racially inferior trait, and on the other hand, national identity had come to exclude Jewishness explicitly. As a consequence, the majority of Austrian and German Jews in the first decades after 1945 made a choice either to live as *Jews*, but no longer in Germany or Austria, or to live as *Germans*, but not as Jews in West or East Germany. The years 1933–1945 thus effectively ended what has been called the German-Jewish symbiosis in culture and identity. For a small minority of Austrian and German Jews the question of identity remained unresolved and *at the center* of their daily lives, however, and was worked out through a renewed confrontation with Germany and things German. They remained in or returned to Germany, in actuality, or in the form of their texts.

This study traced the works and careers of a German-Jewish and an Austrian-Jewish survivor who sought to return to Germany after the war through an engagement with German language and literature, that is, by reinserting themselves through their publications into the culture that had expelled them. As strongly autobiographical texts, these works circumscribe and reinvent what it means to be a German and a Jew after the Shoah. This entails a complex process of renegotiation with both realities and identities and the different political and cultural discourses that assert the limits of their subjectivity and agency and threatens to reify them. As such, these texts represent a particular kind of subjective discourse that can be described as potentially emancipatory. It is the act of addressing a German audience that furthermore broadens such a project from one that has purely private (therapeutic) implications to one that has a broader cultural significance and impact. In the attempt to find address for their stories, to have Germans listen to what has happened to them as Jews (i.e., to bear witness), these texts serve as interventions into a discourse that sought to forget and ignore both these events and the legacy they represented for Germans not just politically, but personally.

Impossible Legacy, Impossible Dialogue

Finding this address and seeking intervention did not always succeed, however. Reading the response Weil's and Klüger's literature received within the particular changing social, cultural, and political context of the past half century in West Germany, one comes to a sober conclusion. Initially, the ideological split of the Cold War allowed both German states to avoid a true confrontation with the Nazi era and instead, this past was seen only through the lens of either the problematic "system" of authoritarianism or that of capitalist fascism, which left individual responsibility and the most striking feature of the Nazi regime out of the picture: its genocidal antisemitism. In the Federal Republic, this led to a culture of restoration and simultaneous repression, of financial reparation without moral obligation. It was a climate in which Jewish voices could not be heard, and Jewish literature could hardly be published.

This was the context in which Grete Weil first tried to get her work in print. Weil had returned to Germany in order to bear witness to those parts of the "Final Solution" she had witnessed with her own eyes, but for decades no one would respond to her work. When by the early 1960s she tried again to find a German audience willing to listen, it was with a novel in which she constructed a complex narrative: a non-Jewish German bears witness to (and becomes involved in) a Jewish story. This construction revealed both the difficulty for Weil of telling her own story faithfully while needing to create a bridge to the German audience (in which she only in part succeeded) to overcome as it were the competition of (German and Jewish) memories, and her struggle to find a place for herself within the postwar context as a German and a Jew. Furthermore, the text intervened explicitly into a literary discourse that sought to silence all (Jewish) "writing after Auschwitz." A dialogue with Germans about this past still proved impossible to create within the text, however, as well as outside of it, as reviewers found the work too "difficult" to deal with.

Once a new and deeper engagement with the legacy of the Third Reich was initiated among Germans in the late 1960s (due in part to a generational shift, and to several high profile Nazi trials), the analysis of this history still primarily took place in a fashion in which the system was blamed. It was not regarded as a history that had left a deep personal and cultural legacy for present-day Germans that they needed to come to terms with. Even the younger generation's protest against their parents' behavior, as seen through the lens of a dogmatic Marxist analysis, served only as a defense mechanism which prevented a more full confrontation with the antisemitic past. Consequently, whereas Weil in her publications of the late 1960s attempted to find ways to connect her experience of oppression to that of present-day marginalized groups (and in so doing showed a great affinity with and understanding for the issues brought to the table by this younger generation of Germans), this approach still failed. Unlike Weil, who saw the present-day violence and the Nazi legacy as intimately connected while still maintaining the distinctions between the two, the uniqueness of each experience, young German leftists instead could not fully confront what their parents' problematic legacy represented for them. In their response to this legacy, they were at the same time trying to disavow it: they were reacting in a way as to do away with it.

When in the 1980s German-Jewish literature more generally and Weil's new publications specifically did find critical success and a much greater audience, it is tempting to regard this change in reception as an indication of a profound cultural change whereby Germans became willing to face an encounter with the Holocaust and its Jewish victims, and to rethink German postwar attitudes toward this past. What a careful reading of the context of this reception suggests, however, is a much more dubious process. Whereas Germans did become more interested in Jewish victimization, due to a number of broader cultural and political changes in the late 1960s and 1970s, they were still avoiding an investigation of German guilt, both as it manifested itself in their own families, and more broadly as a unique German legacy. There was still no real acknowledgment of the Holocaust as a *German* event, an event that should concern Germans, even those born decades after the war, and that affected German culture and politics today, on both the political left and right. Weil's works thus elicited an empathic response, but not one that led to a fuller German-Jewish dialogue. She was still seen as an outsider, and was still made into a "case."

Klüger's memoir as a form of textual intervention, published soon after reunification, seemed to have a better chance of getting such a dialogue going. Her work very explicitly addresses the German audience and engages with the discourse surrounding this German-Jewish discussion, and her publishing her work in Germany calls attention to the fact that such a dialogue takes place in a manner that is both displaced and belated. The reception of her work, again, suggests otherwise: Klüger's critical intervention was made harmless as it was for the most part read as a successful and unproblematic return instead.

Assessing Change

In this period of dramatic transition in the 1990s, of rearticulation of German national identity within the new German state, and of reassessment of the continued importance of the memory of the Nazi era for present-day politics, critical Jewish voices questioning German motives in fact became less important. Both Klüger's and Weil's works and reception thus points to the contradictions inherent in the cultural and political changes of the 1980s and early 1990s: on the one hand there is indeed a new public recognition of Jewish suffering and a greater interest in the personal aspects of the Nazi period, but on the other hand there remains a persistent refusal to look at this past as a uniquely *German* history. Furthermore, the desire to move away from it in order to normalize German national identity and unburden the postwar generation(s) remains strong.

This is not to say that life for Jews in Germany did not radically transform itself after 1990, as a large group of Soviet and Eastern European Jewish immigrants has come to settle in the German state, which has changed the community's make up, size, and status quo considerably. First off, this immigration has made the community more visible as the number of Jews in Germany has grown quite dramatically[1] (it has ironically made Germany the only European state with a Jewish population that has increased in size).

Whether these changes will actually affect Jewish culture in Germany, perhaps leading to a greater critical voice that will change German-Jewish relations, remains open to considerable debate. Michal Bodemann, for instance, suggests that even though the community has numerically gotten bigger, the likelihood of a renaissance of

Jewish life has not grown accordingly.[2] For such a renaissance to take place, he argues, a community needs to meet at least three conditions: "a repository of common cultural practices and memories," and "a degree of cohesive economic and social networks," and finally, "a critical mass of individuals to form distinct Jewish milieux" (52–53), most of which is still missing in Germany today. In contrast, Gilman and Zipes claim that such renascence of German-Jewish life and culture has taken place since reunification. My assessment lies somewhere in between: the now much larger Jewish community has brought forth new growth in Jewish cultural life, yet their voice and concerns are in many ways less uniquely *German*-Jewish than before.

In either case, the life and work of German Jews shows itself not to resemble that of prewar generations at all, as it is far more complex. It is therefore perhaps easy to concur with Diner that a positive German-Jewish symbiosis, *if* there in fact ever was one, is no longer a possibility. What is left is at the most this *negative symbiosis*, the mutual German and Jewish fascination with each other because of their shared experience in the Holocaust on opposite sides, and their mutual self-conception that is based in this experience. Germans and Jews alone are uniquely marked by this history, and the cultural memories of each thus almost perversely inform the other.

The question then remains as to what the future for Jews in Germany and for a German-Jewish literature will hold, if this literature and German-Jewish relations remain thoroughly determined by the Nazi past. German publishers presently show more interest in a "dead" Jewish culture of the prewar period than in recent work by living Jewish authors, and Lorenz has suggested that under their direction, "the legacy of Germany's Jewish past is transformed into a gentrified museum culture."[3] Gilman argues as well that German literary critics have great difficulty in conceptualizing German Jews as part of the present, and not just the past.[4] Jews are still seen in "the fantasy of a discredited cultural symbiosis," but not "in the role of Jews writing about the common past of German, Christian and Jew," which they do have in the present (275).[5] Thus, contemporary authors are ignored, or in Gilman's words "killed," and their status within their cultural world is underplayed. The result is that living German-Jewish writers are denied identity. They can be seen as German, but not as *both* German *and* Jewish (278).

Yet, even though this literature tends to deal with the problematic aspects of German-Jewish coexistence, it is also possible to conceive of it in more positive terms. Brumlik, for instance, suggests that the fact that this literature has come into being and is received well by non-Jews might be "an indication of a growing cultural pluralism, which, under favorable conditions, may also be followed by political pluralism."[6] Perhaps this suggests the applicability of the term "minor literature" for this kind of writing.

Minor Literature

I have suggested earlier that it is possible to conceive of the literature of Weil and Klüger as a form of "minor literature," as a literature that self-consciously positions itself outside a mainstream to which it belongs, and Zipes, Lorenz, and Gilman have indeed argued that the term works well for German-Jewish literature of the postwar era. While this term is fitting in many ways, describing quite precisely the critical edge of this literature and its quality of being both on the inside and on the outside at the same time, using it within German literary studies may marginalize this literature to an unnecessary extent. For instance, it has taken decades after the publication of her most successful works for Weil to become included in reference books of German-Jewish literature, and she is still not included in most standard German handbooks, nor is she fully part of the literary canon. Only time will tell whether Klüger will be considered to be part of the German literary canon, or as part of at least a German-Jewish canon. Using the term "minor" with its connotation of "less important," may reinforce this marginalization. As literature written by women, and as Jewish literature, it is crucial that it is seen as an integral part of *German* literature by the German literary establishment, so that these works can continue to be published and reprinted, and will be read and taught and interrogated widely by successive generations of Germans. Only that way they can keep functioning as the extremely important *Ruhestörer* ("disturbers of the peace"), as the critical outsider/insider voice.

I would rather see the literary establishment struggle to define modern German literature more broadly in order to be able to encompass these difficult (Jewish) texts than using a term that, however fitting, would in other respects allow precisely for their continued marginalization.

Survivors Speak

Finally, if one looks at this literature from the perspective of the author and not of the publisher, critic, or audience which receives the work, it becomes evident that in the past two decades, German-Jewish survivors have seen opportunities to articulate their experiences in the German language and get their works published in Germany increase greatly. This increase is particularly remarkable in the area of German-Jewish women's literature. This cannot be but a positive development, for as I have suggested, these survivor authors write against a profound double experience of reification. "Auschwitz [had] defined . . . what it meant to be Jewish during a certain period of history," as Gilman and Zipes argue, and these survivor authors now seek to resist this "totalitarian way in which they had been defined," as they explore within their reclaiming of the German language "numerous possibilities for self-realization."[7] The use of the German language and the address to the German audience proves crucial exactly in that it simultaneously allows for an active engagement with the process of redefining what a German-Jewish identity means or could come to mean, intervenes into a reifying German discourse on Holocaust survivors, and may undo a long process of reification.

NOTES

Preface

1. Kalí Tal, *Worlds of Hurt: Reading the Literatures of Trauma* (New York: Cambridge University Press, 1996) 5.
2. Diana, Pinto, "The New Jewish Europe: Challenges and Responsibilities," *European Judaism* 3.1 61 (1998) 3–15.

Chapter One   Introduction

1. Statement by Martin Walser in a radio interview: ". . . egal wo sie ihren Wohnsitz jetzt haben wird. . . . es sei nicht der Ausweis, der sagt, wozu man gehört, sondern die Sprache. . . . Ruth Klüger ist zurückgekehrt in die deutsche Sprache; und die sofort auf meisterhafte Art." "Ruth Klüger zur Begrüßung," *Das Kulturjournal* Bayerischer Rundfunk, presented by Peter Hamm, September 27, 1992. Reprinted in Stephan Braese and Holger Gehle, "Von 'deutschen Freunden': Ruth Klüger's 'weiter leben. Eine Jugend' in der deutschen Rezeption," *Der Deutschunterricht* 47.6 (1995) 84–85. ". . . regardless of where she has her domicile, it is not the passport that tells where one belongs, but the language. . . . Ruth Klüger has returned in the German language; and immediately in a masterful way." My translation.
2. Neither German nor English has an adequate term for the 1933–1945 Nazi policies against the Jews that resulted in genocide. Within the Jewish survivor community the Hebrew terms *Churban* (*churbm* in Yiddish) and *sho'ah* were adopted (previously these had been used to refer to the destruction of the First and Second Temple). Since the 1950s in the United States, the term Holocaust has been in use (from the Greek *holokauston*, meaning "whole burnt" or sacrifice by fire). However, while neither the term Holocaust nor Shoah are quite satisfactory (as they both carry religious connotations), these are the names most commonly used, and I employ them both. On the importance of this naming of the Nazi genocide of the Jews, see James Young, *Writing and Rewriting the Holocaust: Narrative and the Consequences of Interpretation* (Bloomington: University of Indiana Press, 1988) 85–89.
3. I have articulated part of this argument in short form in Pascale Bos, "Return to Germany: German-Jewish Authors Seeking Address," *The Changing German/Jewish Symbiosis, 1945–2000*, ed. Jack Zipes and Leslie Morris (New York: Palgrave/St. Martin's Press, 2002) 203–206.
4. I use the term (Austro-)German Jews to discuss both cultures and identities simultaneously, as Austrian-Jewish culture was in many respects as German-oriented as German-Jewish culture (see my discussion of the German concept of *Bildung* in a later part in this chapter). I speak of Austrian and German Jews separately only when the political and cultural developments in the respective countries are discussed.
5. For the statistics of survivors and returnees, see Y. Michal Bodemann, " 'How can one stand to live here as a Jew . . .': Paradoxes of Jewish Existence in Germany," *Jews, Germans, Memory: Reconstructions of Jewish Life in Germany*, ed. Y. Michal Bodemann (Ann Arbor: The

University of Michigan Press) 20. Before 1933 over half a million Jews lived in Germany. About half of this population escaped, another third was killed by the Nazis, 15,000 Jews survived in Germany in hiding, or were protected through their marriage with non-Jews. A few thousand German Jews had survived imprisonment in camps such as Theresienstadt. These survivors were joined by almost 220,000 Displaced Persons (DPs) (survivors who were living in DP camps in Germany) by the end of 1947. When the majority of these DPs had left by the early 1950s, only about 15,000 Jews were left in West Germany. Of this group, only about 6,000 formed the remnants of the original German-Jewish community of about 500,000 people. Austria had a Jewish population in 1938 of between 185,000 and 200,000 of which about 120,000 Jews managed to flee, and almost one-third was killed. After the war, about 6,000 Jews were left in Austria (mostly intermarried Jews). They were joined by a few thousand Austrian Jewish camp survivors, and by several thousands of Eastern European DPs who settled in Austria after the war. In total, 11,000 Jews were living in Austria at the end of the war.

6. Jean Améry, "How Much Home Does a Person Need?" *At The Mind's Limits: Contemplations by a Survivor on Auschwitz and its Realities*, trans. Sidney Rosenfeld and Stella P. Rosenfeld (New York: Shocken Books, 1990) 43–44.

7. Dan Diner, "Negative Symbiose: Deutsche und Juden nach Auschwitz," *Jüdisches Leben in Deutschland seit 1945*, ed. Micha Brumlik, Doron Kiesel, Cilly Kugelmann, and Julius H. Schoeps (Frankfurt: Jüdischer Verlag bei Athenäum, 1986). "Since Auschwitz—what a sad joke—one can truly speak of a German-Jewish symbiosis, a negative one, however. For both Germans and Jews the fact of the mass murder has become the starting point of one's self-understanding, a kind of contradictory union—whether they want it or not" (243). My translation.

8. It is noteworthy that rather than return to Austria, many Austrian-Jewish survivors chose to live and publish in Germany rather than in Austria after the war. (For instance, Ilse Aichinger and Jean Améry. And of course with a forty-year delay, Klüger published her literature in Germany rather than Austria.) This phenomenon is a reflection of the problematic postwar response to Jewish survivors in Austria that made their return impossible, and of a long tradition of a strong German identification of many Austrian Jews. Yet, it also suggests that in some ways, the cultural climate in Germany after 1945 was perceived to be more receptive to Jewish input than that of Austria. For an elaborate discussion of the Austrian situation, see chapter four.

9. Katja Behrens could be added to this list, too, as her work debuted in 1983, but as she was born in 1943 she, technically speaking, belongs to the war generation.

10. Interesting publications of this period by female survivors: Inge Deutschkron (1978), Hanna Lévy-Hass (1979), Ingeborg Hecht (1984), Ruth Elias (1988), Anja Lundholm (1988), and Ruth Liepman (1993). A number of survivor authors who had written of their experiences shortly after the war in prose or poetry would now publish their memoirs: Lotte Paepcke (1979), Gerty Spies (1984), Hilde Spiel (1989–1992). None of these works has the quality of that of Weil or Klüger, however, and many of the memoirs have a relatively simple structure that does not question the genre or complicate the notion of a German audience. An author such as Cordelia Edvardson should be included here as well, but as Edvardson published in Swedish originally (in 1984, translated in 1990 to German), and thus, in terms of an address to the German audience she is more difficult to place.

11. See Young, *Writing* 17. "The Holocaust has compelled writers to assume the role of witness to criminal events, actually rehabilitating the mimetic impulse in these writers rather than burying it altogether. Holocaust writers . . . have assumed that the more realistic a representation, the more adequate it becomes as testimonial evidence. . . . For the survivor's witness to be credible, it must seem natural and unconstructed."

12. I first developed this notion based on feminist theory of autobiography, see among others: Sidonie Smith, *Subjectivity, Identity, and the Body: Women's Autobiographical Practices in the Twentieth Century* (Bloomington: Indiana University Press, 1993). Smith considers

autobiographical writing as an opportunity for women to actively negotiate with oppressive discourses. She thereby asserts that women can gain agency through writing, as language has the ability to allot the subject any position it desires. Shari Benstock suggests that writing autobiography can serve a specific, almost therapeutic function for women and other marginalized groups. Writing is "A means by which to create images of self through the writing act, a way by which to find a voice . . . through which to express that which can not be expressed in other forms" (5–6). Shari Benstock, *The Private Self. Theory and Practice of Women's Autobiographical Writings* (Chapel Hill: The University of North Carolina Press, 1988).

13. Dominick LaCapra, *Writing History, Writing Trauma* (Baltimore: The Johns Hopkins University Press, 2001) 90.

14. It has been in particular Cathy Caruth who has articulated the unique link between trauma and language, trauma and literature in such a way to cause a whole new generation of scholars to become interested in Holocaust literature: ". . . trauma seems to be much more than a pathology, or the simple illness of a wounded psyche: it is always *the story* of a wound that cries out, that addresses us in the attempt to tell us of a reality or truth that is not otherwise available" (emphasis added). Caruth, *Unclaimed Experience: Trauma, Narrative, and History* (Baltimore: The Johns Hopkins University Press, 1996) 4. See also her introductory essay in *Trauma: Explorations in Memory*, ed. Cathy Caruth (Baltimore: The Johns Hopkins University Press, 1995). In turn, many literary scholars of poststructuralist bend have become interested in trauma literature through Caruth's assertion that in our encounter with trauma "we can begin to recognize the possibility of a history that is no longer straightforwardly referential" (Caruth, *Unclaimed* 11). Although her work has come under heavy criticism lately for putting too much emphasis on analyzing what this story means for "us," the readers, scholars, rather than for the survivors (a critique which I share), and for implying that the stories of survivors can only truly be understood by those who interpret it, rather than by the survivors themselves (more on this later in this chapter), her nonclinical language on trauma has made the subject more accessible to many.

15. These terms refer to slightly different processes. *The American Heritage Dictionary* 2nd College edition (Boston: Houghton Mifflin Company, 1985) defines to reify as "to regard or treat (an abstraction) as if it had concrete or material existence" (1042). To objectify can mean either "to present (something) as an object; externalize . . . to make objective" or "to rationalize" (857). Both processes apply here.

16. Kenneth Jacobson, *Embattled Selves: An Investigation into the Nature of Identity Through Oral Histories of Holocaust Survivors* (New York: The Atlantic Monthly Press, 1994) 8.

17. Sander L. Gilman, *The Jew's Body* (New York: Routledge, 1991) 1. As "no one who identifies, either positively or negatively, with the label 'Jew' is immune from the power of [societal] stereotypes" (3).

18. Moving descriptions of the results of this discrimination and isolation can be found in Margarete Limberg and Hubert Rübsaat, eds. *Sie durften nicht mehr Deutsche sein: Jüdischer Alltag in Selbstzeugnissen 1933–1938* (Frankfurt: Campus Verlag, 1990), a collection of essays written for a 1938 contest of German refugees in the United States. An example: "Das Ende war die Isolierung. Es gibt keine Isolierung, die nicht zu guter Letzt das Absterben des Isolierten zur Folge hatte" (172). "The end was isolation. There is no isolation that does not in the end lead to the dying off of the isolated [person]." My translation. The essays also show a deep conflict over identity and loyalty to the German homeland.

19. Central to the conceptual problems of Freudian psychoanalysis in dealing with Holocaust survivors is that it considers trauma as caused by internal childhood conflict, stemming in particular from anxieties and fantasies connected to sexuality.

20. Bruno Bettelheim's work in particular did much damage to the image of survivors, as he focused on their "narcissistic regression," and suggested that many underwent a process of infantilization during their imprisonment. Bettelheim based his work on his personal

observations during a brief concentration camp stay before 1939 whereby he concluded that those who were strong, autonomous, and self-sufficient could resist the impact of the Nazi humiliation, and survive with their psyche intact. In contrast, he asserted that those who suffered from lasting after-effects must have been psychically weak before they entered the camps. Bettelheim's work has been discredited since the 1980s, but his views have been quite influential. Bruno Bettelheim, *The Informed Heart* (Glencoe, IL: Free Press, 1960). For a discussion of the influence of Bettelheim on the field of Holocaust studies in the United States, see Kalí Tal, *Worlds of Hurt: Reading the Literatures of Trauma* (New York: Cambridge University Press, 1996), chapter 2.

21. William G. Niederland was the first to coin the term "survivor syndrome" in 1968 for a group of symptoms commonly found among survivors. A "survivor's syndrome" is characterized by anxiety, chronic depressive states, disturbances of cognition and memory, a tendency to isolate and withdraw, and many psychosomatic complaints. Niederland, "Clinical Observations on the 'Survivor Syndrome': Symposium on Psychic Traumatization through Social Catastrophe," *International Journal of Psychoanalysis* 49 (1968) 313–315. Since the 1980s, it is recognized that this syndrome is part of a larger phenomenon of PTSD, Post-Traumatic Stress Disorder. See also Caruth, *Trauma* 3–12.

22. To give an indication of the volume of this scholarship: in 1995 a bibliography was compiled that counted 2,461 citations of literature written between 1945 and 1995 on the medical and psychological consequences of the Holocaust on survivors and their children. Robert Krell and Marc Sherman, eds., *Medical and Psychological Effects of Concentration Camps on Holocaust Survivors*, Vol. 4, *Genocide: A Critical Bibliographic Review* (New Brunswick: Transaction Publishers, 1997). Today, several hundred more books would have to be added to update this list.

23. Jack Terry, "The Damaging Effects of the 'Survivor Syndrome,'" *Psychoanalytic Reflections on the Holocaust: Selected Essays*, ed. Steven A. Luel and Paul Marcus (New York: Holocaust Awareness Institute, Center for Judaic Studies University of Denver, KTAV Publishing House Inc., 1984) 139.

24. Translation in: Grete Weil, *My Sister, My Antigone*, trans. Krishna Winston (New York: Avon Books, 1984) 146. The original reads: "Wir sind nicht mehr das, was wir noch vor kurzem waren. Zumindest in den Augen der anderen. Aber es ist ausgeschlossen, sich in den Augen der anderen zu verändern, ohne daß im eigenen Sein etwas passiert." Grete Weil, *Meine Schwester Antigone* (Frankfurt/Main: Fischer Taschen Buch Verlag, 1982) 111. Ruth Klüger expresses a similar sentiment (through her own free translation of a poem by W.B. Yeats): "How in the name of Heaven can he escape / That defiling and disfigured shape / The mirror of malicious eyes / Casts upon his eyes until at last / He thinks that shape must be his shape?" Ruth Klüger, *Still Alive: A Holocaust Girlhood Remembered* (New York: The Feminist Press, 2001) 47. In the German original, the similarities with Weil's statement (above) are quite striking: "Man sieht sich im Spiegel boshafter Augen, und man entgeht dem Bild nicht, denn die Verzerrung fällt zurück auf die eigenen Augen, bis man ihr glaubt und sich selbst für verunstaltet hält." Klüger, *weiter leben: Eine Jugend* (Göttingen: Wallstein Verlag, 1992) 46–47.

25. Klüger, *Still Alive* 192.

26. For an insightful reading of Diner, see Jack Zipes, "The Negative German-Jewish Symbiosis," *Insiders and Outsiders: Jewish and Gentile Culture in Germany and Austria*, C.G. Dagmar Lorenz and Gabriele Weinnberger (Detroit: Wayne State University Press, 1994) 144–154.

27. Gilles Deleuze and Felix Guattari, *Kafka: Toward a Minor Literature*, trans. Dana Polan (Minneapolis: University of Minnesota Press, 1986) 66–67.

28. Sander Gilman, "Jewish Writing in Its German and Jewish Contexts: Two Jewish Writers," *Jews in Today's German Culture* (Bloomington: Indiana University Press, 1995) 42.

29. Gershom Scholem, one of the most outspoken critics to represent this view, thus argued in 1962 that the famed dialogue between German and Jews never really had taken place: "I deny that there has ever been such a German-Jewish dialogue in any genuine sense whatsoever. . . . It takes two to have a dialogue . . . Nothing can be more misleading than to apply such a

concept to the discussions between Germans and Jews during the last 200 years. This dialogue died at its very start and never took place. Jews had instead only spoken to themselves, as the discussion they held with Germans was always based on 'self-denial.'" Jews could only speak to Germans as Germans, and not as Jews. Scholem, "Against the Myth of the German-Jewish Dialogue," *On Jews and Judaism in Crisis: Selected Essays*, ed. and trans. Werner J. Dannhauser (New York: Schocken Books, 1976) 61–62. See also his essay "Once More: The German Jewish Dialogue" in the same volume. Scholem, *On Jews and Judaism* 62. For a good overview of these different views on assimilation and German Jews see Michael Marrus, "European Jewry and the Politics of Assimilation: Assessment and Reassessment," *Journal of Modern History* 49 (1979) 89–109.

30. Michael Bernstein, *Foregone Conclusions: Against Apocalyptic History* (Berkeley: University of California Press, 1994) 16–17.

31. "Durch Auschwitz seien Deutschtum und Judentum für immer dissoziiert," Christoph Schulte, ed., *Deutschtum und Judentum: Ein Disput unter Juden in Deutschland* (Stuttgart: Philipp Reclam jun., 1993) 7.

32. Bernstein suggests that in practicing "backshadowing," one uses the knowledge of the outcome of a series of events ". . . to judge the participants in those events as though they should have known what was to come" (16). These kinds of analyses are perhaps even more common today, as we move further away in time from the historical events that might explain the particular circumstances to us. In light of what later occurred at Auschwitz, "muß jener alte Diskurs um Deutschtum und Judentum tragisch, wenn nicht absurd erscheinen," Schulte suggests (8). "Every old discourse on Germanness and Judaism must seem tragic, if not absurd." My translation. This changes our assessment: "Sollten vor der Zeit des Nationalsozialismus deutscher und jüdischer Geist noch vermählt werden, werden sie danach um so radikaler geschieden. Hatte man zuvor nach Indizien gesucht, warum Deutschtum und Judentum füreinander bestimmt seien, sucht man danach oft nur noch die Vorzeichen der Katastrophe" (Schulte, *Deutschtum* 8). "If before the time of National Socialism one sought to unite the German and the Jewish spirit afterwards, they were all the more radically separated from each other. If one had earlier looked for indications of why Germans and Jews were meant for each other, afterwards one searched often only for the forebodings of the catastrophe." My translation. An example of the kind of troubling conclusions this can lead to can be seen in John Dippel, *Bound upon a Wheel of Fire: Why so Many German Jews made the Tragic Decision to Remain in Nazi Germany* (New York: Harper Collins, 1996), in which the tragedy of the German-Jewish persecution is seen as historically inevitable, and therefore in its logical extreme preventable through emigration. Jews who were caught in Nazi nets were de facto themselves responsible for their deadly fate, Dippel seems to argue.

33. Only a few German historians have noted this. See Trude Mauer, "Die Juden der Weimarer Republik," *Zerbrochene Geschichte: Leben und Selbstverständnis der Juden in Deutschland*, ed. Dirk Blasius and Dan Diner (Frankfurt: Fischer, 1991) and Reinhard Rurüp, "Jüdische Geschichte in Deutschland: Von der Emanzipation bis zur nationalsozialistischen Gewaltherrschaft," *Zerbrochene Geschichte*, ed. Blasius and Diner.

34. For what one is, or how one sees oneself, or how one is seen by others "is produced and reproduced against a complex of social, cultural, technological, and economic conditions." David Theo Goldberg and Michael Krausz, "Introduction: The Culture of Identity," *Jewish Identity*, ed. David Theo Goldberg and Michael Krausz (Philadelphia: Temple University Press, 1993) 1.

35. Shulamith Volkov, "The Dynamics of Dissimilation: Ostjuden and German Jews," *The Jewish Response to German Culture: From the Enlightenment to the Second World War*, ed. Jehuda Reinharz and Walter Schatzberg (Hanover, NH: University Press of New England, 1985).

36. As Marion Kaplan points out, the definition of assimilation (merger with host culture, loss of own culture) does not fit a historical reality in which there was a real desire to preserve Jewishness, for this definition does not allow for what we would now call ethnic pluralism.

Marion Kaplan, "Tradition and Transition—The Acculturation, Assimilation, and Integration of Jews in Imperial Germany—A Gender Analysis," *Leo Baeck Institute Year Book* (London: Secker and Warburg, 1982) 4–7.

37. This movement started in the early eighteenth century in Germany in response to the Enlightenment, and suggested a reorientation from Talmud and *halacha* (Jewish law) to the Bible, Hebrew language, and secular academic learning. The goal was initially to integrate formerly isolated Talmudic Jews into secular Enlightenment culture, and later, when secularization had become widespread, to integrate a more modern form of Judaism into the secular life of the Jew (e.g., by the mid-nineteenth century, as knowledge of Hebrew was waning among Germans, many Jewish religious organizations switched to the exclusive use of German). For an in-depth analysis of the development of *Haskalah*, see David Sorkin, *The Transformation of German Jewry 1780–1840* (Oxford: Oxford University Press, 1987), chapters 2 and 3.

38. That is, "Aus jüdischen Familien wurden deutsche Familien jüdischer Religion und mit gewissen jüdischen Traditionen." Rurüp, *Judische Geschichte in Deustchland* 88. "Out of Jewish families became German families of Jewish faith with certain Jewish traditions." My translation. The transition of these terms of self-definition suggests a new emphasis on national rather than religious or ethnic identity as it proposed a parallel identity (and comparable legal status) with Germans of Protestant, or Catholic Faith. A reversal of this term would later take place again under the Nazis: "Eine . . . Verwandlung deutscher Staatsbürger jüdischen Glaubens in Deutsche Juden." "A . . . transformation of German citizens of Jewish faith into German Jews." My translation. Dan Diner "Die Katastrophe vor der Katastrophe: Auswanderung ohne Einwanderung," *Zerbrochene Geschichte*, ed. Blasius and Diner, 148.

39. Marion Kaplan, *The Making of the Jewish Middle Class: Women, Family, and Identity in Imperial Germany* (New York: Oxford University Press, 1991) viii.

40. Paula E. Hyman, *Gender and Assimilation in Modern Jewish History: The Roles and Representations of Women* (Seattle: University of Washington Press, 1995) 18–19. Kaplan, "Ritual waned more slowly among Jewish women . . . they experienced less dissonance between religious practice and their daily routines than men. Their private world was more traditional than modern . . . for many, the year followed the pattern of religious festivals." Kaplan, *The Making* 77.

41. Kaplan, *The Making* 3.

42. Sorkin, *The Transformation* 38.

43. George Mosse suggests that Jews specifically were attracted to *Bildung* because "the age into which a minority is emancipated will to a large extent determine the priorities of its self-identification, not only at the time of emancipation itself but into the future as well." Mosse, "Jewish Emancipation: Between Bildung and Respectability," *The Jewish Response to German Culture*, ed. Reinharz and Schatzberg 1. Through *Bildung*, Jews searched for a common ground with other Germans that would transcend a history in which they did not have a part. What emerged, however, was the formation of a Jewish "subculture." Sorkin, *The Transformation* 2–9.

44. Kaplan, *The Making* 234.

45. About 176,000, or 90% of Austria's Jews lived in Vienna in 1938.

46. Steven Beller, *Vienna and the Jews, 1867–1938: A Cultural History* (Cambridge: Cambridge University Press, 1989) 152.

47. Marsha Rozenblitt, *The Jews in Vienna, 1867–1914: Assimilation and Identity* (Albany: SUNY Press, 1983) 3. Ethnic pride was arguably stronger in Vienna than elsewhere, as Vienna had a much higher and constant influx of traditional Jews from Hungary and Galicia than German cities (240).

48. Austria in many respects mirrored the development of the Enlightenment and Emancipation in Germany (legal Emancipation for Jews was in fact granted earlier in Austria than in Germany). Furthermore, formerly a part of the Holy Roman Empire of the Germans over

which the Habsburgs ruled for centuries, Austria was in many respects still a German state by the nineteenth century, even though cessation from Germany had taken place in 1866. See Gerhard Botz, "The Jews of Vienna from the Anschluß to the Holocaust," *Eine zerstörte Kultur: Jüdisches Leben und Antisemitismus im Wien seit dem 19. Jahrhundert*, ed. Gerhard Botz, Ivar Oxaal, and Michael Pollak (Obermayer: Druck und Verlag, 1990) 185–204.

49. Shulamit Magnus, "'Out of the Ghetto': Integrating the Study of Jewish Women into the Study of 'The Jews,'" *Judaism* 39.1 (1990) 28.

50. In the traditional versions of Jewish cultural history, most women are "treated as passive appendages of male actors . . . Presuming that the experiences of women and men were essentially identical, historians spoke explicitly of men but implied that women were included in the category of man." Paula Hyman, "Gender and Jewish History," *Tikkun* 3.1 (1988) 35.

51. An extended version of the following argument can be found in Pascale Bos, "Women and the Holocaust: Analyzing Gender Difference," *Experience and Expression: Women, the Nazis and the Holocaust*, ed. Elizabeth Baer and Myrna Goldenberg (Detroit: Wayne State University Press, 2003) 23–50.

52. See Hyman, *Gender and Assimilation*, Kaplan, *The Making*.

53. George Mosse, *German Jews beyond Judaism* (Bloomington: Indiana University Press, 1985), Donald L. Niewyk, *The Jews in Weimar Germany* (Baton Rouge: Louisiana State University Press, 1980), and Sorkin.

54. Hyman, *Gender and Assimilation* 20.

55. Kaplan, *The Making* viii.

56. See for instance the work of Myrna Goldenberg, "Lessons Learned from Gentle Heroism: Women's Holocaust Narratives," *Annals of the American Academy of Political and Social Science* 548 (1996) 78–93. "Testimony, Narrative, and Nightmare: The Experiences of Jewish Women in the Holocaust," *Active Voices: Women in Jewish Culture*, ed. Maurie Sacks (Urbana: University of Illinois Press, 1995) 94–106. Or that of Joan Ringelheim, "The Unethical and the Unspeakable: Women and the Holocaust," *Simon Wiesenthal Center Annual* 1 (1984) 69–87. "Women and the Holocaust: A Reconsideration of Research," *Signs* 10.4 (1985): 741–761.

57. One of the few analyses that also suggests this kind of an interpretation of gender difference can be found in Sara Horowitz, "Memory and Testimony of Women Survivors of Nazi Genocide," *Women of the Word: Jewish Women and Jewish Writing*, ed. Judith R. Baskin (Detroit: Wayne University Press, 1996) 258–282, and Karen Remmler, "Gender Identities and the Remembrance of the Holocaust," *Women in German Yearbook* 10 (1994) 167–187.

58. See Elizabeth Loftus et al., "Who Remembers What? Gender Differences in Memory," *Michigan Quarterly Review* 26.1 (1987) 64–85. This research suggests that males and females do not differ in overall memory ability, but that motivation and training (i.e., socialization) significantly affects the content of what is remembered. Because men and women tend to believe that there are in fact very distinct sex differences in memory, this belief affects later recall as it creates a "memory preference." Loftus et al. conclude that "differences in the unverified memories that men and women elicit when asked to generate a memory are more indicative of their memory preferences than their memory ability" (76).

59. Weil is now included in Andreas B. Kilcher, ed., *Metzler's Lexikon der deutsch-jüdischen Literatur* (Stuttgart: J.B. Metzler, 2000), and in Hans J. Schütz, *Eure Sprache ist auch meine: Eine deutsch-jüdische Literaturgeschichte* (Zürich: Pendo, 2000).

60. For a critical analysis of this absence, see Ernst Loewy, "Zur Paradigmenwechsel in der Exilliteraturforschung" *Exilforschung* 9 (1991) 208–219.

61. Alan Mintz, "Two Models in the Study of Holocaust Representation," *Popular Culture and the Shaping of Holocaust Memory in America* (Seattle: University of Washington Press, 2001) 38–on. Mintz distinguishes the "exceptionalist model" from a second model, a "constructivist" one that instead "stresses the cultural lens through which the Holocaust is perceived" (39). American scholars have focused either on the centrality of the Holocaust for the modern

Jewish experience, or for its moral implications for Western civilization as a whole. See, for instance, Lawrence Langer, *The Holocaust and the Literary Imagination* (New Haven: Yale University Press, 1975) and Alvin Rosenfeld, *A Double Dying: Reflections on Holocaust Literature* (Bloomington: Indiana University Press, 1980). These works discuss survivor literature without emphasis on the nationality of the author, or even the original language their work was written in, or the reception it received. David G. Roskies' *Against the Apocalypse: Responses to Catastrophe in Modern Jewish Culture* (Cambridge: Harvard University Press, 1984) instead focuses exclusively on Jewish authors whereby nationality matters less than the degree to which the author connects his or her work to a millennia-long history of Jewish destruction. Sidra DeKoven Ezrahi in her study, *By Words Alone: The Holocaust in Literature* (Chicago: University of Chicago Press, 1980) follows a somewhat similar principle.

62. Early examples are Günter Grimm and Hans-Peter Bayerdörfer, eds. *Im Zeichen Hiobs: Jüdische Schriftsteller und deutsche Literatur im 20. Jahrhundert* (Königstein: Athenäum, 1985), and Hans J. Schütz, *Juden in der deutschen Literatur: Eine deutsch-jüdische Literaturgeschichte im Überblick* (München: Piper, 1992). See for more recent work Stephan Braese, Holger Gehle, Doron Kiesel, and Hanno Loewy, eds. *Deutsche Nachkriegsliteratur und der Holocaust* (Frankfurt: Campus Verlag, 1998) and Stephan Braese, *Die andere Erinnerung: Jüdische Autoren in der westdeutschen Nachkriegsliteratur* (Berlin: Philo, 2001).

63. Work by among others, Sander Gilman, Anson Rabinbach, Jack Zipes, Dagmar Lorenz, Leslie Adelson, and Leslie Morris.

64. For instance, *Germanic Review* devoted an entire issue to "Women in Exile" not until 1987, and *Exilforschung's* first volume focusing on women authors in exile was published only in 1993. This suggests that a broader interest in the topic (among male as well as female scholars and a general audience) is only of fairly recent date.

65. This exclusion can be seen in many collections: Grimm contains seventeen essays on specific authors, but only two of those essays deal with female writers. See also Klara Pomeranz Carmely, *Das Identitätsproblem jüdischer Autoren im deutschen Sprachraum: Von der Jahrhundertwende bis zu Hitler* (Königstein: Scriptor, 1981), or the work of Marcel Reich-Ranicki. If female authors are discussed in the work of German language scholars at all, they tend to be the same few figures: Nelly Sachs, Elske Lasker-Schüler, Anna Seghers, and Gertrud Kolmar. Dagmar C.G. Lorenz is the only scholar who consistently discusses female authors along with male authors and who allots these authors an equal measure of attention. See in particular *Verfolgung bis zum Massenmord: Holocaust-Diskurse in deutscher Sprache aus der Sicht der Verfolgten* (New York: Peter Lang, 1992) and *Keepers of the Motherland: German Texts by Jewish Women Writers* (Lincoln: University of Nebraska Press, 1997), which focuses on women exclusively. Lorenz, however, lives and teaches in the U.S.

66. "In its crassest form, this mode of [feminist] reception equated the victimization of women in patriarchal societies with that experienced by Jews under National Socialism. . . . In contrast, literature written by Jewish women—whether survivors of the Holocaust or members of subsequent generations—were largely ignored by many German feminists and literary critics." Leslie A. Adelson, "1971 'Ein Sommer in der Woche der Itke K. by American born author Jeanette Lander is published," *Yale Companion*, ed. Gilman and Zipes 749. Susannah Heschel suggests that this inability of German feminists to look at the past critically is in part caused by the difficulty of facing and assessing the role their mother's generation had played during the Hitler years. For if they face the past by arguing that German women were powerless, they have to admit that almost all women failed to resist Nazism, and that some even actively collaborated with the Nazis. Susannah Heschel, "Configurations of Patriarchy, Judaism, and Nazism in German Feminist Thought," *Gender and Judaism: The Transformation of Tradition*, ed. Tamar M. Rudavsky (New York: New York University Press, 1995) 137.

67. Thus, a recent anthology such as *Facing Fascism and Confronting the Past*, while containing good essays on individual authors (considering both Jewish and non-Jewish women who

wrote "against" Fascism) does not contain any sustained analysis of the role of German-Jewish survivor authors within postwar German culture. Elke P. Frederiksen, and Martha Kaarsberg Wallach, eds. *Facing Fascism and Confronting the Past: German Women Writers from Weimar to the Present* (New York: State University of New York Press, 2000). Then again, in a text such as *Postwar Women's Writing in German*, edited by Chris Weedon, one finds some discussion of women's writing of the 1980s and 1990s, but no explicit discussion of Jewish women authors in this particular changing literary landscape. Chris Weedon, ed., *Postwar Women's Writing in German* (Providence: Berghahn Books, 1997). Finally, in Dagmar Lorenz's *Keepers of the Motherland*, an elaborate study of the lives and works of over forty German-Jewish women authors spanning more than three centuries, such an extensive selection of texts and authors is discussed that this leads to relatively brief sketches of each author's life and work, with no space for an in-depth analysis of individual works, or of a broader analysis of the context in which each of these works emerged. Furthermore, the work's structure as a broad literary history does not allow for a complex analysis of the issues of Holocaust representation.

68. A few essays exist on both authors' works, but no scholarly monographs have appeared in English with such a focus. One monograph appeared on Weil in German: Uwe Meyer's *"Neinsagen, die einzige unzerstörbare Freiheit": Das Werk der Schriftstellerin Grete Weil* (Frankfurt: Peter Lang, 1996). Based as it is on a dissertation, the study is long, repetitive, and not accessible to a broader audience. Another German dissertation which focuses in part on Weil's work is Carmen Giese's *Das Ich im literarischen Werk von Grete Weil und Klaus Mann: Zwei autobiographische Gesamtkonzepte* (Frankfurt/Main: Peter Lang, 1997). The recent Weil biography by Lisbeth Exner, *Land meiner Mörder, Land meiner Sprache: Die Schriftstellerin Grete Weil* (München: Monacensia/A1 Verlag, 1998) is useful for biographical details, but contains no literary analysis. Stephan Braese, *Die andere Erinnerung* contains several good chapters on Weil and other Jewish authors, but discusses only part of her oeuvre. A few scholars in the United States publish on Weil's work but only in (short) article form, and most write only on Weil's *Antigone* novel. See Moray Mc Gowan, "Myth, Memory, Testimony, Jewishness in Grete Weil's Meine Schwester Antigone," *European Memories of the Second World War*, ed. Helmut Peitsch, Charles Burdett, and Claire Gorrara (New York: Bergahn Books, 1999) 149–158; Michelle Mattson, "Classical Kinship and Personal Responsibility: Grete Wei's 'Meine Schwester Antigone'," *Seminar* 37.1 (Feb. 2001) 53–72 Miriam Fuchs; and Susanne Baackmann. Dagmar Lorenz, Leslie Adelson, and Laureen Nussbaum do discuss Weil's work in a broader context, but they do not discuss Weil's entire oeuvre. Quite a few German journalistic publications exist on Klüger, but remarkably little academic scholarship. Stephan Braese and Holger Gehle compiled a *Der Deutschunterricht* volume on the reception of her work in 1995, there is a school-edition interpretation of her work by Irene Leonard Heidelberger, *Ruth Klüger: weiter leben. Eine Jugend* (München: R. Oldenbourg, 1996), and Eva Lezzi's, *Zerstörte Kindheit: Literarische Autobiographien zur Shoah* (Köln: Böhlau Verlag, 2001) contains a chapter on Klüger. In the United States, Dagmar Lorenz has published an article on Klüger's *weiter leben*, Karein Goertz mentions her work in "Body, Trauma, and the Rituals of Memory: Charlotte Delbo and Ruth Klüger," *Shaping Losses: Cultural Memory and the Holocaust*, ed. Julia Epstein and Lori Hope Lefkovitz (Urbana: University of Illinois Press, 2001) 161–185, and Michael Rothberg's *Traumatic Realism: The Demands of Holocaust Representation* (Minneapolis: University of Minnesota Press, 2000) contains a chapter on her work.

69. Apart from the studies I have already mentioned, works such as (in order of date of publication): Maurice Blanchot, *The Writing of the Disaster*, trans. Ann Smock (Lincoln: University of Nebraska Press, 1986), Alice Yaeger Kaplan, *Reproductions of Banality: Fascism, Literature, and French Intellectual Life* (Minneapolis: University of Minnesota Press, 1986), Eric Santner, *Stranded Objects: Mourning, Memory, and Film in Postwar Germany* (Ithaca: Cornell University Press, 1990), Saul Friedländer, ed., *Probing the Limits of Representation: Nazism and the "Final*

Solution" (Cambridge, MA: Harvard University Press, 1992), Shoshana Felman and Dori Laub, *Testimony: Crises of Witnessing in Literature, Psychoanalysis, and History* (New York: Routledge, 1992), James Young, *The Texture of Memory: Holocaust Memorials and Meaning* (New Haven: Yale University Press, 1993), Geoffrey Hartman, ed., *Holocaust Remembrance: The Shapes of Memory* (Cambridge, MA: Basil Blackwell, 1994), Dominick LaCapra, *Representing the Holocaust: History, Theory, Trauma* (Ithaca: Cornell University Press, 1994), and *History and Memory after Auschwitz* (Ithaca: Cornell University Press, 1998), and *History in Transit: Experience, Identity, Critical Theory* (Ithaca: Cornell University Press, 2004), Marianne Hirsch, *Family Frames: Photography, Narrative, and Postmemory* (Cambridge: Harvard University Press, 1997), Ernst van Alphen, *Caught by History: Holocaust Effects in Contemporary Art, Literature, and Theory* (Stanford: Stanford University Press, 1997), Andrea Liss, *Trespassing through Shadows: Memory, Photography & the Holocaust* (Minneapolis: University of Minnesota Press, 1998), Barbie Zelizer, *Remembering to Forget: Holocaust Memory through the Camera's Eye* (Chicago: The University of Chicago Press, 1998), and Barbie Zelizer, ed., *Visual Culture and the Holocaust* (New Brunswick, NJ: Rutgers University Press, 2001), Vivian M. Petraka, *Spectacular Suffering: Theatre, Fascism, and the Holocaust* (Bloomington: Indiana University Press, 1999), Julia Epstein and Lori Hope Lefkovitz, eds., *Shaping Losses: Cultural Memory and the Holocaust* (Urbana: University of Illinois Press, 2001), Michael Bernard-Donals and Richard Glejzer, *Between Witness and Testimony: The Holocaust and the Limits of Representation* (Albany: State University of New York Press, 2001), Susan Gubar, *Poetry After Auschwitz: Remembering What One Never Knew* (Bloomington: Indiana University Press, 2003), and Amy Hungerford, *The Holocaust of Texts: Genocide, Literature, and Personification* (Chicago: The University of Chicago Press, 2003).

70. The body of analytical work on oral (video) testimony published in the past ten years by historians, psychologists, literary critics, and Holocaust scholars is remarkable, as is the proliferation of individual as well as institutional efforts to create videotaped records of the survivors who are still alive. For interesting recent work on oral Holocaust testimony see Felman and Laub, Caruth, Young, *Writing and Rewriting,* chapter 9. John Bornemann and Jeffrey Peck, *Sojourners: The Return of German Jews and the Question of Identity* (Lincoln: University of Nebraska Press, 1995), Geoffrey Hartman, "Learning from Survivors: Notes on the Video Archive at Yale," *Remembering for the Future: The Impact of the Holocaust on the Contemporary World*, ed. Yehuda Bauer et al. (Oxford: Pergamon Press, 1989), R. Ruth Linden, *Making Stories, Making Selves: Feminist Reflections on the Holocaust* (Columbus: Ohio State University Press, 1993), and Jacobson, *Embattled Selves.*

71. This anxiety over the loss of survivors, I believe, has been the central source of motivation (and funding) for these new forms of inquiry that focus on video testimony.

72. Lawrence Langer, *Holocaust Testimonies: The Ruins of Memory* (New Haven: Yale University Press, 1991) 46. This kind of reading of video testimony moves away from a detailed reading of the cultural construction of Holocaust memory, and focuses instead on the "immediacy" of the testimony. Langer's well-respected study argues that the literary narrative tends to transform reality more so than the oral narrative does, as "survivors who record their accounts unavoidably introduce some kind of teleology, inverting the incidents with a meaning" (40). Conversely, he asserts that oral testimony "is distinguished by the absence of literary mediation" (57). He defines this absence as follows: "Beyond dispute in oral testimony is that every word spoken falls directly from the lips of the witness. Not as much can be said for written testimony that is openly or silently edited" (210). Langer privileges these spoken "versions of survival, without literary echo" (46) as he naively assumes that there is no "mediating factor" involved in oral testimony. The fact that Langer overlooks the mediating function of the interviewer is particularly puzzling as there are several instances in his book in which he describes interviewers as interfering with the survivor's testimony through their comments, questions, and response (63–64, 158). For a critical analysis of Langer's work, see Gary Weissman, "Lawrence Langer and 'The Holocaust Experience,'" *Response: A Contemporary Jewish Review* 68 (1997/1998) 93.

73. Studies that focus on the medium of photography have made this point particularly clear: Hirsch (1997), Liss (1991 and 1998), Zelizer's (1998 and 2001) work, and Dora Apel, *Memory Effects: The Holocaust and the Art of Secondary Witnessing* (New Brunswick: Rutgers University Press, 2002).
74. This is also reflected in more self-conscious forms of testimony. Thus, Michael Rothberg argues that: "the need for a rethinking of realism is signaled by the emergence in the last decades of various new forms of testimonial and documentary art and cultural production" (9).
75. Caruth, *Unclaimed Experience* 11.
76. Caruth, *Trauma: Explorations in Memory* 5.
77. Hirsch, *Family Frames* 21–23. Hirsch refers specifically to the experience of those who have come to learn of the Holocaust *after* the events occurred, and I would count the work of most Holocaust scholars here as forms of "postmemory" work. See also "Projected Memory: Holocaust Photographs in Personal and Public Fantasy," *Acts of Memory: Cultural Recall in the Present*, ed. Mieke Bal, Jonathan Crewe, and Leo Spitzer (Hanover: University Press of New England, 1999) 2–23, and "Surviving Images: Holocaust Photographs and the Work of Postmemory," *The Yale Journal of Criticism* 14.1 (2001) 5–37.
78. Leys suggests that there is a wide diversity of opinion about the nature of trauma (something she clearly appreciates and would like to retain, including the contradictions and uncertainties), but that this diversity has been obscured "by the post-Vietnam effort to integrate the field" (6). She regrets that at this point the field is dominated by a notion of "nonnarrative" traumatic memory, that is, by the notion that traumatic events are encoded in the brain in a different way than ordinary memory. She argues that there is no proof for this neurobiological assertion (popularized by Bessel van der Kolk on whose work Caruth relies to build her case for psychic trauma), and that it leads to "dangerous" kinds of conclusions "among certain postmodern literary circles" (7). She criticizes that these theorists (she targets Caruth, Felman, and Laub here) on the one hand hold that the Holocaust has "precipitated, perhaps caused, an epistemological–ontological crisis of witnessing, a crisis manifested at the level of language itself" (168), but on the other hand suggest that the testimony of the survivor can succeed in reaching us, the listeners by passing on trauma, "horror itself" (168). In so doing, they collapse history into memory, and fail to distinguish between trauma experienced and trauma witnessed, making us all potentially "traumatized" by our encounter with the Holocaust, Leys argues. Leys believes that Caruth in particular dilutes and generalizes the notion of trauma too much: "in her account the experience (or nonexperience) of trauma is characterized as something that can be shared by victims and nonvictims alike, and the unbearable sufferings of the survivor as a pathos that can and must be appropriated by others" (305). Ruth Leys, *Trauma: A Genealogy* (Chicago: The University of Chicago Press, 2000).
79. I see this tendency more clearly in the work by Shoshana Felman and Dori Laub than in Caruth. As Tal, a particularly fierce critic of Felman and Laub points out: "Felman and Laub are entirely concerned with reenactment of the traumatic event in the psyches of those who 'encounter the real' " (53). In their work, Tal suggests, "the survivor's experience has been completely replaced by the experience of those who come in contact with the survivor's testimony—an appropriative gambit of stunning proportions. We are treated to a new traumatic phenomenon: 'the crisis of witnessing' " (53–54). The difference between the survivor's trauma and the effects it has on the listener or reader (which they also choose to describe as traumatic) disappears. Furthermore, the underlying assumption in their study is that survivors cannot bear witness to themselves, but are in need of interpreters (read: scholars, psychoanalysts) who can tell them what their stories really mean.
80. The ethical question remains of whether one should write Holocaust literature even if one found the language to do so, for as van Alphen suggests, the audience may derive aesthetic pleasure from reading these works, which in the case of the Holocaust is a problematic prospect (19–20). This particular dilemma is a central point of contention in van Alphen's study on Holocaust art.

81. Lorenz argues: "Nach 1945 stand der Mythos von der Unaussprechlichkeit des Holocausterlebnisses der Rezeption der Holocaustliteratur im Wege." "After 1945, the myth about the unspeakability of the Holocaust experience stood in the way of the reception of Holocaust literature." Lorenz, *Verfolgung* 4. My translation. Arguing on the basis of Adorno's statement that this literature could by definition not be written allowed scholars to dismiss all the work that was published as mediocre, or worse, as inappropriate. Adorno, however, did not argue that one could and should not write *at all* after Auschwitz, but pleaded for the rejection of the writing of a *certain kind* of lyrical prose after Auschwitz, namely, the "conservative continuation of pre-1933 poetic forms and themes that dominated poetic writing throughout the fascist years . . .," as he feared that by "affirming traditional poetics, such writing would be unable to overcome impotence in reacting to the devastations of fascism." Leonard Olschner, "1951 In his essay 'Kulurkritik und Gesellschaft,' Theodor W. Adorno states that it is barbaric to write poetry after Auschwitz," *Yale Companion*, ed. Gilman and Zipes 692. For a compelling reading of Adorno, see Rothberg, chapter 1 "After Adorno: Culture in the Wake of the Catastrophe" (25–58).
82. Central questions in these critical studies were: how to represent atrocity on a scale which prior to its occurrence was unimaginable; how to do justice to the magnitude of the events, the severity, cruelty, and the impact on the individual survivor as well as the individual Jewish communities in Europe; how to find the appropriate language; which kinds of representations are effective; which are insufficient, which are unacceptable?
83. Horowitz, *Voicing the Void: Muteness and Memory in Holocaust Friction* (Albany: State University of New York Press, 1997) 17.
84. I borrow this phrase from Young, *Writing* 23.
85. Young, *Writing*. See in particular the introductory chapter.
86. Lea Wernick Fridman, *Words and Witness: Narrative and Aesthetic Strategies in the Representation of the Holocaust* (Albany: State University of New York Press, 2000) 3–4.
87. Mintz, *Popular Culture* 54.
88. Mintz, *Popular Culture* 57. Mintz in fact argues that these narratives should be read as "inverted bildungsromans that recount the story of how the hero unlearns what culture has taught and learns the ways of death and survival of the new concentrationary 'planet'" (57). While I think this schema is too simplistic, Mintz's emphasis on the importance of the particularity of different cultural lenses of survivor authors is a useful corrective.

Chapter Two   The Jewish Return
to Germany

1. "In beiden Ländern stelle ich fest, dass ich mit Menschen, die nichts oder fast nichts mitgemacht haben, nicht zusammenleben könnte." Weil, *Leb ich denn wenn andere leben* (Zürich Köln: Benziger Verlag, 1980) 241. My translation.
2. "Ich hätte auch 45 in kein intaktes Land gehen können, das hätte mich rasend gemacht . . ." Weil as quoted in Laureen Nussbaum and Uwe Meyer, "Grete Weil: unbequem, zum Denken zwingend," *Exilforschung* 11 (1993) 159. My translation.
3. Weil, *Der Brautpreis* (Frankfurt am Main: Fischer Taschenbuch Verlag, 1991) 138. First published by Nagel & Kimche AG in Zürich and Frauenfeld, 1988. Translation comes from *The Bride Price*, trans. John Barrett (Boston: David R. Godine, 1991) 103. See also Weil as quoted in Nussbaum and Meyer: "Deutschland war ebenso kaputt wie ich selbst, und das war genau das Richtige für mich" (159). "Germany was just as damaged as I was, and that was exactly right for me." My translation.
4. Nussbaum and Meyer "Grete Weil" 159. My translation of: "Ob ich es mag oder nicht—und sehr oft mag ich es nicht— ich bin ein Deutsche." See also a very similar statement in Weil's writing in *Brautpreis*: "Immer wieder werde ich gefragt, warum ich nach Deutschland zurückging. Es ist mein Land, in dem meine Sprache gesprochen wird. Es bleibt mein Land,

ob ich es mag oder nicht. (Und sehr oft mag ich es nicht)" (165). "I was always asked again why I went back to Germany. It is my country, in which they speak my language. It remains my land, whether I like it or not." My translation.

5. "Ich will nach Hause, auch wenn ich weiß, dass alles, was ich früher geliebt habe, nicht mehr existiert. Ich will dorthin, wo ich hergekommen bin. Das Heimweh ist nicht kleiner, sondern größer geworden in all den Jahren." Weil, *Leb ich denn* 236. My translation.

6. "Um mich war Haß, den ich verstehen, den ich nicht teilen konnte. Manchmal schlug er auf mich zurück, wenn ich leise bekannte, daß ich nach Deutschland wollte. Verrückt, charakterlos, vergeßlich, das alles bekam ich zu hören." Meyer, *Neinsagen* 141. "Around me was hate, that I could understand, but not share. Sometimes it was directed at me when I softly confessed that I wanted to go to Germany. [I was] Crazy, without character, forgetful, all these things I came to hear." My translation.

7. "Trotz dieser Erkenntnis [of her Jewishness] ist es mir versagt geblieben, das Volkshafte des Judentums für mich zu akzeptieren." Weil in letter (August 1947) to German-Jewish author Margarete Susman, reprinted in *Lebe ich denn* 251. "Despite this realization it has been impossible for me to accept the [notion of] Jewish peoplehood for myself." My translation.

8. "Ich habe die Heimat Deutschland verloren und keine andere dafür gefunden." Letter to Susman, reprinted in *Lebe ich denn* 252. My translation.

9. This relationship is also one of the—rarely mentioned—other reasons for Weil's early return to Germany. In the 1947 letter to Susman Weil mentions this relationship as a prominent justification for her return. *Leb ich denn* 254.

10. A "sogenannte gute Erziehung." "A so-called good education." Grete Weil, *Meine Schwester Antigone* (Frankfurt am Main: Fischer Taschenbuch Verlag, 1982) 6–7. First published by Benziger Verlag in Zürich and Köln in 1980. The page numbers of quotations from this work correspond to those from the Fischer edition. Grete Weil, *My Sister, My Antigone*, trans. Krishna Winston (New York: Avon Books, 1984). I quote from the English edition when possible, but when the translation is lacking, I provide my own translation of the German text.

11. Some parts of this chapter (the discussion of Weil's background and the discussion of two of her early novels) have appeared in short form in Bos, "Return to Germany" 206–208.

12. Sorkin, *The Transformation* 38.

13. "Unter den Deutschen kann ich leben. Sie sprechen meine Sprache, haben die gleichen Dichter, die gleiche notwendige oder unnotwendige Bildung." Weil, *Generationen* (Frankfurt am Main: Fischer Taschenbuch Verlag, 1985) 72. "I can live among the Germans. They speak my language, have the same poets, the same necessary or unnecessary upbringing/cultivation." My translation.

14. For instance, Weil's family celebrated Christmas. It was a family gathering with lots of food and a tree, but decidedly without any Christian practice. Weil, *Generationen* 58.

15. Weil, *My Sister* 146.

16. Weil, *Antigone* 112. See also *Brautpreis* 10. This lack of a connection to Judaism as a *religious practice*—even a domestic form of it—seems to contradict Kaplan and Hyman's research, mentioned earlier, which suggests that generally speaking, women were less assimilated than men. I return to this point later.

17. Weil, *My Sister* 147.

18. Weil, *My Sister* 147.

19. "Ich will schreiben, deutsch schreiben, in einer anderen Sprache ist es mir unmöglich, und dazu brauche ich eine Umgebung, in der die Menschen deutsch sprechen." Weil, *Leb ich denn* 236. My translation.

20. "Da zu sein und vielleicht Verschüttetes auszugraben ist kein Verrat an den Toten sondern der tastende Versuch, ihr geliebtes und geheiligtes Leben nicht ganz verwehen zu lassen, solange man selber dauert." Weil in letter to Susman, as quoted by Meyer, *Neinsagen* 164. This part of the letter is not reprinted in Weil's 1998 autobiography. My translation.

21. Weil never tried to have this manuscript published, even as she became successful in the 1980s, as she felt that it was too dated. The text was published posthumously in 1999, after

her death in May of that year. See Grete Weil, *Erlebnis einer Reise: Drei Begegnungen* (Zürich: Nagel & Kimche, 1999).

22. ". . . die acht Jahre des Untergangs, in denen uns fast alles, was zu uns gehört, abhanden kommt. Land, Sprache, Sicherheit und schließlich die eigene Identität." Weil, *Antigone* 111. My translation.

23. Weil, *My Sister* 147.

24. For English sources on the history of the Netherlands under Nazi occupation, see J.C.H. Blom, "The Persecution of the Jews in the Netherlands in a Comparative International Perspective," *Dutch Jewish History*. Proceedings of the Fourth Symposium on the History of the Jews in the Netherlands, Vol. II, ed. Jozeph Michman (Assen: Van Gorcum, 1989) 273–289, Gerhard Hirschfeld, *Nazi Rule and Dutch Collaboration: The Netherlands Under German Occupation 1940–1945*, trans. Louise Willmot (Oxford: Berg, 1988), Louis de Jong, *The Netherlands and Nazi Germany. The Erasmus Lectures 1988* (Cambridge: Harvard University Press, 1990), Judith Miller, *One, by One, by One: Facing the Holocaust* (New York: Simon and Schuster, 1990), chapter on the Netherlands, Bob Moore, *Victims and Survivors: The Nazi Persecution of the Jews in the Netherlands 1940–1945* (London: Arnold, 1997), and of course, one of the earliest and most influential works: Jacques Presser, *The Destruction of the Dutch Jews*, trans. Arnold Pomerans (New York: E.P. Dutton & Co., 1969).

25. See Moore, *Victims and Survivors* 2. His numbers are based on Gerard Hirschfeld "Niederlande" in Wolfgang Benz, ed. *Dimension des Völkermords: Die Zahl der jüdischen Opfer des Nationalsozialismus* (Munich: R. Oldenbourg Verlag, 1991) 165.

26. Note on translation: while "*Grenze*" means literally "border," figuratively it also means "limit," a double meaning the title clearly hints at.

27. Weil, *Der Weg zur Grenze* (Unpublished manuscript, 1944) 3. Citation taken from Braese, *Die andere Erinnerung* 109. My translation.

28. *Weihnachtslegende 1943* was published without Weil's consent in 1945 as part of a postwar anthology of "resistance writing" in Amsterdam, *Das gefesselte Theater: Het tooneel in boeien* (Amsterdam: Hollandgruppe "Freies Deutschland," 1945). It was not available until recently, when Weil reprinted it in her last publication, at the end of her autobiography *Leb ich denn* from 1998, 195–227. *Der Weg* was never published, according to her biographer because Weil did not deem it good enough. Exner, *Land Meiner* 58.

29. Grete Weil, *Ans Ende der Welt* (Frankfurt am Main: Fischer Taschenbuch Verlag, 1987). First published by Verlag Volk und Welt in East Berlin in 1949. The original German reads: " 'Na ja, Jüdin sind sie ja auch, Fräulein,' meinte er einlenkend. 'Für die Dauer des Krieges'. . . . 'Und danach sind Sie es vielleicht nicht mehr?' 'Danach bin ich wieder Mensch.' 'Sie haben leicht reden, Fräulein, hier auf Ihrem guten Posten. Wenn der Jüdische Rat erst alle anderen Juden nach Polen geschickt hat, besteht für seine Mitglieder immerhin die Chance, jene glücklichen Zeiten, in denen man nur Mensch sein darf, zu erleben. Für uns gewöhnliche Sterbliche sind die Aussichten bedeutend ungünstiger' " (13). My translation.

30. Weil, *My Sister* 84.

31. Weil had to return illegally, because she no longer possessed a German passport, deprived as she was of her German citizenship: "Staatenlos bin ich, seit die Deutschen uns im September 1941 die Staatsbürgerschaft aberkannt haben." Weil, *Generationen* 88.

32. Albert Ehrenstein, a Jewish exile author, took her work to several German publishers and sent it out to foreign publishers and friends. See Meyer, *Neinsagen* 26–27, 144.

33. See Meyer, *Neinsagen* 146.

34. See Meyer, *Neinsagen* 145. Not only were the East German reviewers impressed with the theme and the tone of the book, several reviewers foresaw a successful future for Weil as an author, a hope that was dashed in the next few decades as literary acclaim eluded her in West Germany.

35. Weil: "Zwei Dichter, ein Schriftsteller sprachen für mich, doch sonst blieb alles stumm." "Two poets and one novelist spoke out for me, otherwise everything remained silent." My

translation. Weil refers here to a 1950 review by critic and poet Oda Schaeffer in the American publication *Neue Zeitung* in München, a review by the author Albert Ehrenstein (who had helped her to get the book published) in 1949 in the German language *Aufbau*, published in New York, and a review by the author Martin Gregor Dellin. See Meyer, *Neinsagen* 144.

36. Interview with Adriaan van Dis, "Grete Weil: Nee zeggen is de enige onverwoestbare vrijheid," *NRC Handelsblad* November 12, 1982, Cultureel Supplement: 3. My translation.

37. In her 1998 autobiography, Weil would write: "Heute, wo sie längst in Westdeutschland erschienen ist, weiß ich, dass es eigentlich ein Skandal war, dass niemand im Westen sie wollte. Doch noch ahne ich nichts von den Schwierigkeiten, denen ich viele Jahre lang begegnen werde, weil Literatur über dieses Thema unerwünscht ist" *Leb ich denn* 239. "Today, now that it has long since been published in West Germany, I know that it was actually scandalous that nobody in the West wanted it. But I did not yet know anything about the difficulties that I would come to face for many years because literature about this topic is undesirable." My translation.

38. As Laureen Nussbaum and Uwe Meyer suggest, it was "durchaus kennzeichend für die politisch-gesellschaftliche Lage im Nachkriegs-deutschland, daß Grete Weil in Westdeutschland vergeblich nach einem Verleger für diese Novelle suchte" (160). It was "quite characteristic for the political and social situation in postwar Germany that Grete Weil searched in vain for a publisher for her novel in West Germany." My translation.

39. See Werner Bergmann, Rainer Erb, and Albert Lichtblau, ed., *Schwieriges Erbe: Der Umgang mit Nationalsozialismus und Antisemitismus in Österreich, der DDR und der Bundesrepublik Deutschland* (Frankfurt/Main: Campus Verlag, 1995), and Agnes Blänsdorf's essay in this volume, "Die Einordnung der NS-Zeit in das Bild der eigenen Geschichte: Österreich, die DDR und die Bundesrepublik Deutschland im Vergleich," ed. Bergmann, et al. 18–45.

40. Jeffrey Herf, *Divided Memory: The Nazi Past in the Two Germanys* (Cambridge, MA: Harvard University Press, 1997).

41. It came to function as the "negativer Vergleichsmaßstab für die demokratische Ordnung." The "negative standard of comparison for the democratic order." My translation. Bergman et al., "Einleitung: Die Aufarbeitung der NS-Vergangenheit im Vergleich, Österreich, die DDR und die Bundesrepublik Deutschland," *Schwieriges Erbe* 16.

42. Andrei S. Markovits, Beth Simone Noveck, and Carolyn Höfig, "Jews in German Society," *The Cambridge Companion to Modern German Culture*, ed. Eva Kolinsky and Wilfried van der Will (Cambridge: Cambridge University Press, 1998) 97.

43. Ernestine Schlant, *The Language of Silence: West German Literature and the Holocaust* (New York: Routledge, 1999) 38.

44. "Dem eigentümlichen Konsens, daß die neue deutsche Demokratie nur auf den Weg käme, wenn ihre Bürger aus der Haftung für die monströsen Verbrechen der NS-Zeit befreit würden, wurde seinerzeit nur von den Kommunisten und manchen linken Sozialdemokraten widersprochen." Helmut Dubiel, *Niemand ist frei von der Geschichte: Die nationalsozialistische Herrschaft in den Debatten des Deutschen Bundestages* (München: Carl Hanser Verlag, 1999) 68. "At that time only communists and a few left-wing social democrats protested against the strange consensus that the new German democracy could only get on the right track if its citizens were acquitted of the monstrous crimes of the Nazi period." My translation.

45. ". . . die Deutschen hätten bereits zur westlichen Allianz gehört als sie Hitlers Kampf gegen Rußland unterstützten." Dubiel, *Niemand* 75. My translation.

46. Juliane Wetzel, "Trauma und Tabu: Jüdisches Leben in Deutschland nach dem Holocaust," *Ende des Dritten Reiches-Ende des Zweiten Weltkriegs: Eine perspektivistische Rückschau*, ed. Hans-Erich Volkmann (München: Piper, 1995) 440.

47. "Die Hitler-Barbarei hat das deutsche Volk durch die Ausrottung von sechs Millionen jüdischer Menschen entehrt." As quoted in Dubiel, *Niemand* 44. My translation.

48. This is what Wetzel calls the "Phänomen eines Antisemitismus wegen Auschwitz" (440).
49. Wolfgang Benz, "The Persecution and Extermination of the Jews in the German Consciousness," *Why Germany? National Socialist Anti-Semitism and the European Context*, ed. John Milfull (Providence: Berg, 1993) 94.
50. Benz, "The Persecution" 94. Many Germans questioned the necessity of war trials. Jewish witnesses were seen as "animated by a spirit of vengeance" and as suspect, since they came "for the most part from Israel or from socialist-bloc countries." Jean-Paul Bier, "The Holocaust and West-Germany: Strategies of Oblivion 1947–1979," *New German Critique* 19 (1980) 13.
51. Frank Stern, *The Whitewashing of the Yellow Badge: Antisemitism and Philosemitism in Germany*, trans. William Templer (Oxford: Pergamon Press, 1992) 349. See also Frank Stern, "German-Jewish Relations in the Postwar Period: The Ambiguities of Antisemitic and Philosemitic Discourse," *Jews, Germans, Memory: Reconstructions of Jewish Life in Germany*, ed. Y. Michal Bodemann (Ann Arbor: The University of Michigan Press, 1996) 77–98.
52. Most Germans did not feel that they owed the Jews even that much, however. Opinion polls of the period show that reparation payments were not a popular measure: only 11% supported financial restitution. Stern, *Whitewashing* 382.
53. Micha Brumlik, "The Situation of Jews in Today's Germany," Bodemann, *Jews, Germans, Memory* 8. Bodemann argues that this tight cooperation between the state and the Jewish leadership "reproduced the immobility and authoritarianism of the Adenauer era within the Jewish community." Bodemann as paraphrased by Brumlik, "The Situation" 9.
54. Markovits, "Jews in German Society" 98.
55. The assumption was that this new Jewish community would soon die out. Marion Kaplan, "What is 'Religion' among Jews in Contemporary Germany?" *Reemerging Jewish Culture in Germany: Life and Literature Since 1989*, ed. Sander L. Gilman and Karen Remmler (New York: New York University Press, 1994) 77–78.
56. Dagmar Lorenz argues: "Kein deutschsprachiges Land erwog ernstlich eine deutsch-jüdische Koexistenz. Die westdeutschen und österreichischen Medien und Politiker verwiesen auf Israel als legitimes Territorium der Juden. In der DDR hatte das Judentum im Sozialismus und die Diskussion des Holocaust in der des kommunistischen Widerstands, aufzugeben." Lorenz, *Verfolgung* 6. "No German speaking country seriously considered a German-Jewish coexistence. The West German and Austrian media and politicians referred to Israel as the legitimate territory of the Jews. In the GDR, Jewish culture was supposed to be absorbed by socialism and the discussion about the Holocaust was supposed to be absorbed by the discourse about the communist resistance." My translation.
57. Alfred Döblin returned to Germany as an officer of the French army soon after the end of the war. Other returnees: Rose Ausländer, Stefan Heym, Hans Habe, Friedrich Wolf, Anna Seghers, Stephan Hermlin, Arnold Zweig, Hans Mayer, Ernst Bloch. Some stayed only for a brief period before departing again and settling elsewhere: Wolfgang Hildesheimer, Jean Améry, Peter Weiss, Hermann Kesten, Carl Zuckmayer. Often, the returnees were politically left-leaning idealists who hoped to play a role in the rebuilding of a new democratic German state.
58. This literature presented viewpoints most Germans were not ready to face, and which challenged the now commonly held position that Germans themselves were victims.
59. Helmut Peitsch, "German Literature in 1945: Liberation for a New Beginning?" *The Culture of Reconstruction: European Thought and Film, 1945–1959*, ed. Nicholas Hewitt (New York: St. Martin's Press, 1989). Thomas Mann is usually seen as representing the argument of the exiles in this debate, as he claimed (while writing from the United States) that all literature published in Germany between 1933 and 1945 was worthless. In open letters between Frank Thiess and Thomas Mann in *Münchener Zeitung* in August 1945, entitled "Die Innere Emigration." Peitsch, "German Literature" 176–178.
60. The fact that most exiles had had no choice but to flee (otherwise they would have been persecuted as Jews or socialists) was not mentioned in this discussion.

61. The prevalent literary trope or theme of postwar German literature was thus not *Kahlschlag* as was suggested up to the 1960s, but a return to "the same aesthetic categories as the German-right wing intelligentsia had used to view the dangers of Fascism," namely the so-called "threat to traditional German values of the 'spiritual condition of the age' . . . [and] 'the endangered German spirit.'" Keith Bullivant, "Continuity or Change? Aspects of West German Writing after 1945," ed. Hewitt, *The Culture of Reconstruction* 193. These authors who represented *innere Emigration* argued that their literature had always remained autonomous and anti-Nazi. What lacked was any analysis of how their values (Christianity, or bourgeois humanism) had contributed to the Nazi turmoil. Peitsch, "German Literature" 177.

62. Much more poetry was published in the period 1945–1949 than prose, and this poetry was often escapist and did not deal with the recent past.

63. Bullivant, "Continuity or Change" 191. The image of a literary (and in extension, a moral) "clean slate" nevertheless found great resonance in the imagination of West German authors and their audience because it functioned to underplay the very real similarities and continuities between the Nazi era and the early postwar years, similarities that were abundantly clear to both (former) Nazi sympathizers and to those who had formerly been politically or racially persecuted.

64. For instance, authors such as Ilse Aichinger, Bruno Apitz, Paul Celan, Peter Weiss, Hilde Domin, Nelly Sachs, Ilse Blumenthal-Weiss, Lotte Paepcke, Jurek Becker, and Jakov Lind who published their first literary works only after the war.

65. Precisely because it was so ahistorical and apolitical this approach may have thrived.

66. Braese, *Die andere Erinnerung* 18–19.

67. As Marcel Reich-Ranicki, a preeminent Jewish critic of German literature, argues: "Es geht einfach darum, dass die Beschäftigung mit dem Werk der einst vertriebenen Schriftsteller die Auseinandersetzung mit der jüngsten deutschen Vergangenheit und—vor allem—mit der deutschen Gegenwart impliziert. Zu dieser Auseinandersetzung war man in der Bundesrepublik nicht bereit." "The issue is simply that an engagement with the work of once expelled authors implies a confrontation with the recent German past, and especially with the German present. One was not willing to have this confrontation in the Federal Republic." My translation. Marcel Reich-Ranicki, "Immer noch im Exil," *Literarisches Leben in Deutschland: Kommentare und Pamphlete*, ed. Marcel Reich-Ranicki (München: R. Piper Verlag, 1965) 264.

68. Braese, *Die andere Erinnerung* 29–30.

69. Feuchtwanger, Weil, and Nelly Sachs published their first postwar works in the *SbZ* or in the DDR. Alfred Döblin published in the DDR as well, while living in France.

70. For an interesting analysis of the cultural policies in the immediate postwar years in the different occupied zones of Berlin, see Wolfgang Schivelbusch, *In a Cold Crater: Cultural and Intellectual Life in Berlin, 1945–1948*, trans. Kelly Barry (Berkeley: University of California Press, 1998) 27–38.

71. Bullivant, "Continuity or Change" 200.

72. Weil in interview with van Dis. "Ik heb de wederopbouw-generatie verschrikkelijk gevonden" 3. My translation.

73. "[Er] besaß . . . einen großen Freundeskreis, der bald auch der meine wurde. Ich war integriert, fühlte mich nicht 'fremd im eigenen Land' und hatte es so ungleich leichter als die meisten anderen Remigranten" Weil in Exner, *Land Meiner* 73. "He had a large circle of friends that soon became mine, too. I was integrated and did not feel like a 'stranger in my own country,' and in this way it was considerably easier for me than for most other re-emigrants." My translation.

74. *Boulevard Solitude: Lyrisches Drama in sieben Bildern* (Mainz: B. Schott's Söhne, 1951; Mainz, 1951) Text by Grete Weil, scenario Walter Jockisch, music Hans Werner Henze. *Die Witwe von Esephus* Text by Grete Weil, music Wolfgang Fortner (Mainz: B. Schott's Söhne, n.y.), performed in 1952.

75. Exner, *Land Meiner* 76.

76. *Das Tagebuch der Anne Frank* had been published as a Fischer Taschenbuch in 1955. The play, a translation of the American adaptation by Francis Goodrich and Albert Hackett, was performed for the first time in Germany in 1956 and had an unprecedented opening on seven stages at the same time, in both West and East Germany. The play and its film version (shown in Germany in 1959) were a great success, and in turn, the diary became widely read. See Hanno Loewy, "Das gerettete Kind: Die 'Universalisierung' der Anne Frank," *Deutsche Nachkriegsliteratur*, ed. Braese et al., 19–41. On the inside cover of the Weil reprint, there is twice an explicit reference made to Anne Frank: "Als literarisches Dokument gehört diese Erzählung. . . . an die Seite von Anne Franks Tagebuch" and "Grete Weil [tauchte unter] in unmittelbarer Nähe von Anne Franks Versteck," suggesting the publisher's explicit attempt to gain interest for Weil's work by connecting to the success of Anne Frank's diary. As Leslie Adelson points out: "This type of marketing highlights the trope of victimized innocence, as if to say—as late as 1989—that Germans are willing to read only those Holocaust stories that mimic Anne Frank's diary!" Adelson, "1971 'Ein Sommer' " 751.

77. See Grete Weil, *Last Trolley from Beethovenstraat*, trans. John Barrett (Boston: David R. Godine, 1992) 12. Translation of *Tramhalte Beethovenstraat* (Frankfurt am Main: Fischer Taschenbuch Verlag, 1983). First published by Limes Verlag in Wiesbaden in 1963. Andreas returns in Amsterdam to a familiar photo studio. Upon seeing baby photos displayed in its window, he remarks that the (Jewish) babies who had been in the photos in 1942 "would be more than twenty now." This dates Andreas's comment to around 1962.

78. Weil's fragmentary style in this work in which she moves back and forth between the past of the 1940s and the present of the 1960s underscores, as Leslie Adelson argues, "the tormented quest for solutions that neither she nor her protagonist ever finds." Adelson, "1971 'Ein Sommer' " 751.

79. See, e.g., Nussbaum and Meyer who see the use of a German protagonist exclusively in this light: "Mit der Darstellung des Werdegangs eines nichtjüdischen, unpolitischen Intellektuellen, der erst allmählich zu weitreichenden kritischen Einsichten gelangt, hoffte sie das deutsche Lesepublikum der frühen sechziger Jahre zu erreichen und ihm endlich die Augen zu öffnen für die Verbrechen, die im Namen des deutschen Volkes begangen wurden" (160–161). "By describing the life of a non-Jewish and apolitical intellectual, who only later came to far-reaching critical conclusions, she hoped to reach the German reading audience of the early sixties and to finally open their eyes to the crimes that were committed in the name of the German people." My translation.

80. For instance, Andreas is neither perceived as a hero nor as a Nazi, but rather as typical of what most Germans of that particular class and education were like in the 1930s and 1940s: not pro-Hitler, but relatively unconcerned about the Nazis' antisemitic vitriol, focused on advancing their own careers, and deliberately attempting not to notice too much.

81. See also Braese, *Die andere Erinnerung* 156–157.

82. ". . . was im "Weg zur Grenze" zum eigensten Monikas gehörte. . . . ist in "Tramhalte Beethovenstraat" Bestandteil der Erfahrungen eines Deutschen. . . . in der Andreas-Figur [sind] beide Figuren aus dem "Weg zur Grenze," die flüchtende Jüdin Monika Merton und der deutsche Schriftsteller Andreas von Cornides aufgegangen. . . . die Situation des Dialoges ist aufgehoben." Braese, *Die andere Erinnerung* 155. ". . . what was in *Weg zur Grenze* part of Monika. . . . has become a part of the experiences of a German in *Tramhalte Beethovenstraat*. . . . in the character of Andreas the Jewish refugee Monika Merton and the German author Andreas von Cornides are combined . . . the dialogic situation is dissolved." My translation.

83. Braese, *Die andere Erinnerung* 157–158.

84. There were no reviews of the reprint of *Ans Ende* at all. See Braese, *Die andere Erinnerung* 158, footnote 70.

85. Braese, *Die andere Erinnerung* 158.

86. For an elaborate discussion of the reception of Weil's *Tramhalte*, see Braese, *Die andere Erinnerung* 158–167.

87. In contrast, in the Netherlands, *Tramhalte* did receive a positive response, as would all of Weil's later works. This prompted a German critic to remark in 1991 that Weil had in fact now become "the most read German (female) author" in the Netherlands. Alexander von Bormann as quoted in Nussbaum and Meyer, "Grete Weil" 168. My translation. In order to fully understand the contrast in the reception of Weil's work in the two countries, one would have to take into account the very different legacy of the war in Germany and the Netherlands, and the way in which these countries have chosen (were able to choose) to memorialize the past. Even though Weil suggests that many Dutch citizens' behavior toward the Jews during the war was less than admirable, as "victim of the Nazis," the Dutch had less difficulty than Germans in accepting the literature of a German Jew in the Netherlands who was hunted down by the Nazi invader.

88. This was important as very little about Nazism had been taught in German schools up to this point: "Nazism was regarded as an accident, a combination of the weaknesses of modern democracy and their exploitation by the unique, demonic genius of Hitler. . . . The enormities of Nazism's crimes were admitted, and denounced, but they were attributed mainly to Hitler himself." Richard J. Evans, *In Hitler's Shadow: West German Historians and the Attempt to Escape from the Nazi Past* (New York: Pantheon Books, 1989) 11–12.

89. For a thorough analysis of the impact of these trials in Germany, see the interesting recent collection of documents and essays compiled in, *Auschwitz-Prozeß 4 Ks 2/63 Frankfurt am Main*, ed. Fritz Bauer Institut (Köln: Snoeck, 2004).

90. Micha Brumlik has argued that: "Mit dem Auschwitz-Prozeß begann die eigentliche Phase öffentlicher 'Aufarbeitung der Vergangenheit.' Das massenhafter Mord als ein Verbrechen und nicht nur als Nebenfolge des grausamen Krieges an der Ostfront zu betrachten sei, war ein Gedanke, der vielen Deutschen damals noch fremd war." "With the Auschwitz-trial began the actual public phase of the 'working through of the past.' The fact that mass-scale murder could be seen as a crime, and not merely as side-effect of the horrible war at the Eastern front, was a notion that at that time was still new for many Germans." Brumlik suggests that the German justice system was in fact ahead of the curve in prosecuting war criminals, as the general population would not come to see the necessity to acknowledge and deal with the Nazi legacy until another fifteen years later. My translation. Micha Brumlik, "Zum Geleit: Ein Appell an die Politik," *Auschwitz-Prozeß 4 Ks 2/63 Frankfurt am Main*, ed. Fritz Bauer Institut (Köln: Snoeck, 2004) 48.

91. Schlant, *The Language of Silence* 53.

92. Günter Grass's *Die Blechtrommel* (1959), Heinrich Böll, *Billiard um halb zehn* (1959), *Ansichten eines Clowns* (1963), Martin Walser, *Halbzeit* (1960), Uwe Johnson, *Mutmaßungen über Jakob* (1959).

93. See Jack Zipes, "Documentary Drama in Germany: Mending the Circuit," *The Germanic Review* (January 1967) 50. Zipes discusses three new works of that period, Rolf Hochhuth's *Der Stellvertreter* that deals with the ambivalent behavior of Pope Pius XII during World War II; Peter Weiss's *Die Ermittlung* that was based on the Frankfurt Auschwitz trial (1963–1965); and Heinar Kipphardt's *In der Sache J. Robert Oppenheimer* that deals with the FBI's inquiry against Oppenheimer.

94. Schlant, *The Language of Silence* 53–54.

95. ". . . der Aktualisierung der Holocaust-Thematik durch den Eichmann-Prozeß." Lorenz, *Verfolgung* 167. My translation.

96. Citations stem from Weil, *Happy, sagte der Onkel* (Frankfurt am Main: Fischer Taschenbuch Verlag, 1982). First published by Limes Verlag in Wiesbaden in 1968. Translations to English are mine.

97. "Man denkt, hier ist gut sein, vielleicht brächte man es, umgeben von den Keep-smiling Leuten so weit, ein Weltbild zu haben, die Russen sind böse, die Amerikaner gut, die Neger

nur bedingt entwicklungsfähig, Besitzlosen ist mit Spenden zu helfen, und Menschen sind menschlich." My translation.

98. See for an excellent article on this intellectual climate that also discusses the contrast that the publication of Weil's *Happy* represents: Stephan Braese, "Grete Weil's America: A Self-Encounter at the Moment of the Anti-Authoritarian Revolt," *Germanic Review* 75.2 (Spring 2000) 132–149.

99. "Wenn ich ein Neger in den Staaten wäre, würde ich lieber in der Wüste wohnen als in den Städten. Selbst auf die Gefahr hin, daß hier die Chance zur Flucht sehr gering war . . . Das wußte ich, von Flucht verstand ich etwas, das hatte ich gelernt, fünf Jahre Flucht und Verstecken, lange genug, um ein Experte zu werden" (19). My translation.

100. "Jeder ist freundlich zu jedem" . . . "Nachbar hilft Nachbarn, Reich hilft Arm . . ." 31–32. My translation.

101. "Vieles ist besser geworden, doch kann man die Negerfrage von heute auf morgen nicht lösen. Die Neger sind faul und dumm. . . . Es ware am besten, man würde die Neger nach Afrika zurückschicken . . . Amerika den Amerikanern" (32). My translation.

102. "Aber Unglücke gleichen sich nur von außen . . . Ihr Schmerz und meiner, zwei Kontinente, zwei Zeiten . . ." (49). My translation.

103. "Eine Jüdin, eine Mörderin unsres Herrn. Hinaus aus meiner Wohnung" (57). My translation.

104. The title cannot be properly translated, however, as in German it has a double meaning: "B sagen" also sounds like the verb "besagen" that translates as: "to mean," "to signify." See for the translator's note (footnote 26) in Braese, "Grete Weil's America" 148.

105. "Warum hat man ihnen das angetan? Immer das gleiche, von Urbeginn an, nur die Manier verändert sich. Man lernt nicht aus" (75). My translation.

106. "Männerschädel, Frauenschädel, nicht mehr zu unterscheiden, im Tod sind sie gleich, Indianer, Neger, Zigeuner, Juden, immer dasselbe, zu allen Zeiten, zeitenlos, Ende im Massengrab . . ." (79). My translation.

107. ". . . wenn ich Sie so sehe . . . möchte ich wetten, daß Sie sich nicht nur abgefunden haben, sondern im großen und ganzen recht einverstanden sind mit dieser Welt, die sich zwar für Sie gebessert hat, aber für den größten Teil der Menschen immer gleich schlecht ist. Sie protestieren gegen das, was Sie nicht mögen, gegen Atombomben, Vietnamkrieg und Apartheid. . . . Doch von der jungen Frau, die aus Verzweifelung die Welt in Brand stecken wollte, ist nichts mehr da" (103). My translation.

108. "Unsere Vergangenheit ist keine, mit der sich leben läßt, und da wir leben, kann sie nicht existent gewesen sein" (106). My translation.

109. "B sagen, B sagen . . . Meinungen haben, Meinungen äußern. . . . Stets angewandt, weiterentwickelt, doch nie zu Meisterschaft gebracht. . . . Die Stunde der Wahrheit, und die Wahrheit ferner denn je. Wer könnte Ihnen die Wahrheit sagen? Was ist Ihre Wahrheit?" (106–107). My translation.

110. Historians have convincingly shown in the past few years that economic recovery after 1945 was so widespread and common in the Western world that it was neither uniquely German nor a "miracle." See for instance Hanna Schissler, "Introduction: Writing About 1950s West Germany," *The Miracle Years: A Cultural History of West Germany, 1949–1968*, ed. Schissler (Princeton: Princeton University Press, 2001) 3.

111. Richard Mc Cormick describes the development of the West German student movement as moving roughly through three phases: the politics of the first phase (1966 to 1968) were "based largely on the ideal of personal refusal: each committed individual would refuse to cooperate with a system seen as authoritarian and immoral" (32). The second phase (1968 into the early 1970s) is often called the "organized phase" (or "dogmatic" phase): "This was the period of splintering Marxist-Leninist groups . . . each of which asserted it held the true line on Marxist-Leninism. 'Subjectivity' was suspect, replaced by an inflexible party line based on supposedly 'objective' analysis of material conditions" (33). The third phase

(early 1970s on) was dominated by spontaneous actions by the antidogmatic *"Spontis."* These phases also overlap, and it was the great diversity in the student movement's means and goals that are evident from the different phases which weakened any impact the movement might have had, Mc Cormick suggests. Richard W. Mc Cormick, *Politics of the Self: Feminism and the Postmodern in West German Literature and Film* (Princeton: Princeton University Press, 1991).

112. Although this decree was aimed at leftist students, it affected their professors, as well as the student's future careers as teachers.

113. Dubiel, *Niemand* 123.

114. Robert Holub, "1965 The premiere of Peter Weiss's 'The Investigation: Oratorio in Eleven Songs,' a drama written from the documentation of the Frankfurt Auschwitz trial, is staged," *Yale Companion*, ed. Gilman and Zipes, *Yale Companion* 729.

115. This same pattern can be detected in the new progressive literature and theater of the 1960s, as here, too, the leftist political rhetoric of the time led the discussion of the Nazi past only to be used as a springboard for an analysis of the perceived problems of the present, averting a true confrontation with the past.

116. Schlant, *The Language of Silence* 54.

117. Schlant, *The Language of Silence* 54–55.

118. Andreas Huyssen, "The Politics of Identification: 'Holocaust' and the West German Drama," *After the Great Divide* (Bloomington: Indiana University Press, 1986) 95.

119. Lorenz, *Verfolgung* 30.

120. Jeffrey Herf, "The 'Holocaust' Reception in West Germany: Right, Center and Left" *New German Critique* 19 (1980) 31. Herf argues that three factors specifically hindered a more serious discussion of antisemitism within the New Left: first, the Jewish dialogue with the New Left was limited due to the small size of the community, second, "Marxist analysis of fascism did not place the Final Solution or anti-Semitism at the center of attention," and finally, the New Left was critical of philosemitism, as it was promulgated by the same Springer press that vilified the New Left (43–44).

121. Eric Santner, *Stranded Objects: Mourning, Memory, and Film in Postwar Germany* (Ithaca: Cornell University Press, 1990) 37.

122. Braese, "Grete Weil's America" 14. The word in brackets is mine.

123. Nussbaum and Meyer: "Als das Buch 1968 erschien, konnte man mit der darin praktizierten Schonungslosigkeit offenbar wenig anfangen, hatte man doch in der Bundesrepublik gerade erst begonnen, sich mit der nationalsozialistischen Vergangenheit auseinanderzusetzen" (161). My translation.

Chapter Three   Mythical Interventions

1. Dubiel: ". . . das System der liberalen Demokratie Westdeutschlands [war] nur eine Fassade, hinter der sich die Koninuität eines nach wie vor faschistischen Systems verbarg" (147). My translation.

2. The term "Hitler's children," *"Hitler's Enkel"* is now commonly used to denote the conflict between the political right and left over the legacy of the generation of '68. See, for instance, the title of a recent essay collection that deals with the subject: Hans-Jürgen Wirth, ed., *Hitlers Enkel—Oder Kinder der Demokratie? Die 68-er Generation, die RAF and die Fischer-Debatte* (Gießen: Psychosozial-Verlag, 2001).

3. Dubiel, *Niemand* 149.

4. Dubiel: "Es war ein Symbolischer Bürgerkrieg, in dem unerbittlich über die politischen Konsequenzen gestritten wurde, die sich aus der Erbschaft des Nationalsozialismus für die Gegenwart der Bundesrepublik ergaben," *Niemand* 148. My translation.

5. Some parts of this chapter have appeared in shorter form in Bos, "Return to Germany" 209–219.

6. George Steiner speaks of 1978 and 1979 as the years of "Antigone-fever" in Germany. "At least three major new productions modulating on Sophocles, Hölderlin, and Brecht, are mounted in Germany." The cultural reverberations of this figure were particularly strong at this moment: "Over and over again, western moral and political consciousness has lived . . . Antigone anno jetzt, 'Antigone year-now.'" George Steiner, *Antigones* (Oxford: Clarendon Press, 1984) 108. This "fever" was related to the tendency to see present-day terrorism in light of this myth, something Weil does as well. Both Meyer and Braese interpret Weil's success in light of this Antigone "*Welle.*" Meyer, *Neinsagen* 35–36, Braese, *Die andere Erinnerung* 545.

7. The text is "semiautobiographical" because even though it has strong autobiographical components, it also contains fictional elements. Furthermore, *Antigone* is explicitly billed as *Roman* (novel).

8. Susanne Baackmann suggests that: "in various ways, antiquity has always been an important reference point for German culture. Hölderlin's 1804 translation of Sophocles's drama . . . firmly anchored the Antigone story in the German imagination, eventually elevating it to a 'master narrative' of humanism." Susanne Baackmann, "The Battle with Memory: Grete Weil's My Sister Antigone," *Conquering Women: Women and War in the German Cultural Imagination*, ed. Hillary Collier Sy-Quia and Susanne Baackmann (Berkeley: University of California Press, 2000) 109.

9. This interpretation of the Antigone figure as a resistance fighter was not unique, but explicitly refers back to several other authors (Brecht, Langgässer) who in the immediate aftermath of the war (and Hochhuth in 1963), had portrayed Antigone as a figure of German resistance against the Nazis in their respective Sophocles' adaptations. Uwe Meyer, "'O Antigone . . . stehe mir bei' Zur Antigone-Rezeption im Werk von Grete Weil," *Zeitschrift für Literaturwissenschaft und Linguistik* 104 (1996) 150–151.

10. Weil, *Antigone* 17. My translation, as I do not like Krishna Winston's translation here. German original: "Ich möchte ein Buch schreiben über ein Mädchen, das sich von mir nicht schreiben lassen will, meinen Eigensinn an ihrem Eigensinn messen, sehen wer zum Schluß die Oberhand behält" (17).

11. Ensslin was one of the most notorious members of the *Rote Armee Fraktion*, involved in terrorist actions from the late 1960s into the 1970s.

12. See both Heinrich Weinstock's Sophocles translation (Sophocles, *Die Tragödien*, trans. Heinrich Weinstock (Stuttgart: Kröner Verlag, 1962), as well as those of Friedrich Hölderlin (Hölderlin, *Die Trauerspiele des Sophocles* (1804; Frankfurt am Main: Stroemfeld/Roter Stern, 1986)), and the interpretation of Gustav Schwab (Schwab, *Griekse mythen en sagen*, trans. J.K. van den Brink (Utrecht: Het Spectrum, 1956)). All these versions are mentioned explicitly in Weil's *Antigone* as sources on which the narrator bases her Antigone character.

13. In a later novel Weil makes this link explicit herself. Weil, *Generationen* 129.

14. Weil revealed in an interview that this particular scene refers to her being present in June 1943 at the Jewish Council when Hauptscharführer Aus der Fünten had 6,000 Jews deported from Holland. Van Dis, "Grete Weil" 3.

15. Adelson suggests that: "the complicated structure of the novel reveals that this Holocaust survivor cannot be Antigone, whose presence in the narrative nonetheless legitimizes the story that the survivor has to tell." Adelson, "1971 'Ein sommer'" 751.

16. Weil, and as her first and second husband all held doctorates in German or were working on them.

17. For a thorough discussion of the reception of *Antigone* in Germany, see Braese, *Die andere Erinnerung* 549–557.

18. See Bos, "Return to Germany" 209–219.

19. Anton Kaes, "1979 The American television series 'Holocaust' is shown in West Germany," *Yale Companion* ed. Gilman and Zipes 787.

20. Saul Friedländer, *Memory, History, and the Extermination of the Jews of Europe* (Bloomington: Indiana University Press, 1993) 7.
21. The only reviewer who does read the work as a commentary on present-day Germany, Robert Schirndig, still neglects to point to how politically controversial this kind of text is, in which Antigone and Gudrun Ensslin are compared (in a positive vain), and in which terrorists are described as lost souls, not as the major criminals the German state considers them to be. See Braese, *Die andere Erinnerung* 553.
22. "Das kam alles viel zu spät" Weil in Exner, *Land meiner* 97.
23. "Für mich ist das ein Symptom dafür, wie wenig man wirklich bereit ist, sich ehrlich mit der eigenen Geschichte auseinanderzusetzen" Weil as quoted in Braese, *Die andere Erinnerung* 560. My translation.
24. For a more elaborate discussion of *Generationen* and its reception, see Pascale R. Bos, "Homoeroticism and the Liberated Woman as Tropes of Subversion: Grete Weil's Literary Provocations," *German Quarterly* 78.1 (Winter 2005) 70–87.
25. In the German original: "Wie durch Schweigen Leben erstickt wird," "Sehnsucht nach Bindung," "Oft wollte ich weglaufen, nie habe ich es getan," "Orientierungslos," "Eskalation."
26. Weil, *Generationen* 22. Original reads: ". . . einer neuer Mensch werden in einer neuen Umgebung." My translation.
27. Weil, *Generationen* 34. Original reads: ". . . auch der Marxismus[ist] bei ihr nichts ist als ein vager Traum. Eine Sehnsucht, irgendwo dazuzugehören." My translation.
28. "Ich verstehe sie nicht, kann den Abgrund zwischen den Generationen nicht überspringen." Weil, *Generationen* 117. My translation.
29. Weil, *Generationen* 116. Original reads: "Ich bin abgestoßen, weil es mir vor Menschen graut, die unter einem Kommando stehen. Die hier geraten auf Befehl in Ekstase, erinnern mich an Reichsparteitage. . . . Wollt ihr die totale Hingabe? Mit verklärten Augen, lachend: Ja. Orangenes Gewoge, geborgtes Glück der Lebenswachen." My translation. Note here the mirroring of Goebbel's infamous rhetorical question in the Berliner Sportpalast: "Wollt ihr den totalen Krieg?"
30. Weil, *Generationen* 140. Original reads: "Du bist für sie ein Fall geworden."
31. Weil, *Generationen* 118. "1968 a short phase of revival . . . but just as quickly as it came, the firework goes up in smoke, and nothing is left." My translation of: "1968 eine kurze Phase des Auflebens. . . . Aber ebenso schnell, wie es entstanden ist, verpufft das Feuerwerk, und nichts bleibt übrig."
32. Weil suggests in an interview that even though the novel is "very strongly autobiographical" (Giese, *Das Ich im* 211), the figure of Hanna had been based on a man ". . . But Moni is real, she is still in Poona. . . . Our triangulated relationship on which I wrote. . . . was really as problematic as I depicted it there" (Giese, *Das Ich im* 217). My translation. The relationship described in *Generationen* as a double lesbian one turned out to have been a conscious literary choice for Weil: "I changed it [in the story], because that way it fit better" (Giese, *Das Ich im* 217). My translation. This choice elucidates how much of a deliberate women-centered project this book is, as the narrator muses over precisely the fact that their love triangle is so different without men, and that she is elated to find a new world in which women put each other first, connect, organize, reads women's literature, and so forth. Weil, *Generationen* 45. See also Bos, "Homoeroticism and the Liberated Woman" 78.
33. Weil, *Generationen* 12. Original reads: "Ich habe Angst, belogen zu werden. Und Angst, die Wahrheit zu hören. Oder Antworten zu bekommen, wie: Hitler ist schuld: am Krieg, an der Ausrottung der Juden, der Teilung unseres Landes. Hitler allein." My translation.
34. For a more in-depth discussion of why the text was received with less enthusiasm than *Antigone*, see Bos, "Homoeroticism and the Liberated Woman" 70–87.
35. A "stabiles historisches Selbstbewußtsein." Dubiel, *Niemand* 200. My translation.
36. Bitburg in particular, as not only *Wehrmacht* soldiers turned out to be buried at this cemetery, but SS soldiers as well, creating a massive international outcry, backpedaling by the Reagan

administration, changes of plans, and ultimately a highly controversial visit. In a speech, Reagan justified his visit to the Bitburg cemetery with an interesting example of ahistorical conflation: "those young men are victims of Nazism also. . . . They were victims, just as surely as the victims in the concentration camps." Evans, *In Hitler's Shadow* 16. For elaborate documentation on this controversy, see: Ilya Levkov, ed., *Bitburg and Beyond: Encounters in American, German and Jewish History* (New York: Shapolsky Publishers, 1987) and Geoffrey Hartman, ed., *Bitburg in Moral and Political Perspective* (Bloomington: Indiana University Press, 1986).

37. Jürgen Habermas, "Eine Art Schadensabwicklung: die apologetischen Tendenzen in der deutschen Geschichtsschreibung," *Die Zeit* (July 11, 1986). He responded to a lecture by Ernst Nolte published in *Frankfurter Allgemeine Zeitung* of June 6, 1986. Nolte, a conservative historian, argued that the crimes and the horror of the National Socialist past needed to be put into context. Nolte's article contained two controversial arguments that would be repeated in the ensuing discussion: one, that Hitler's deed was not unique, and in fact a "copy" of atrocities committed by Stalin, and that Hitler may have been justified in doing what he did for defensive reasons. The second work Habermas reacted to is Andreas Hillgruber's *Zweierlei Untergang: Die Zerschlagung des Deutschen Reiches und das Ende des europäischen Judentums* (1986). This book combines two essays, one on the expulsion of the Germans from Eastern Europe at the end of the war, and a second on the Nazi extermination of the Jews in Europe. Hillgruber discusses both events (genocide and the destruction of the Third Reich), in the larger context of mass resettlement of European populations. This analysis implied that Germany's downfall was not caused by Hitler alone, but also by the Allies. In the course of his argument, Hillgruber defends the German Army holding out as long as it did on the Eastern front (which indirectly caused tens of thousands of additional deaths, as the concentration camps could not be liberated).

38. Charles S. Maier, *The Unmasterable Past: History, Holocaust, and German National Identity* (Cambridge: Harvard University Press, 1988) 2.

39. Maier, *The Unmasterable Past* 1.

40. Eva Kolinsky and Wilfried van der Will, "In Search of German Culture: an Introduction," *Cambridge Companion*, ed. Kolinsky and van der Will (Cambridge: Cambridge University Press, 1998) 11.

41. Mc Cormick, *Politics of the Self* 25.

42. Mc Cormick indeed argues that the "political protest movement" in West Germany dissolved in large part "because of the failure to resolve the personal/political split adequately" (23).

43. Verena Stefan's *Häutungen* has been particularly influential, as has been the work of Christa Wolf, Anna Waltraud Mitgutsch, Luise Pusch, Brigitte Schwaiger, and Julia(n) Schutting.

44. Brumlik, "The Situation" 11.

45. Gilman and Zipes, "Introduction," *Yale Companion* xxvi.

46. Jack Zipes, "The Contemporary Fascination for Things Jewish: Toward a Minor Jewish Culture," *Reemerging Culture in Germany*, ed. Gilman and Remmler 17.

47. Gilman and Zipes, "Introduction," *Yale Companion* xxvi.

48. Zipes, "The Contemporary Fascination" 19.

49. Important instigator of this literature was a collection of interviews with German Jews published by Henryk M. Broder and Michel Lang, ed., *Fremd im eigenen Land: Juden in der Bundesrepublik* (Frankfurt/Main: Fischer Taschenbuch Verlag, 1979). This was the first text collection of German-Jewish autobiographical writings. More would follow in the 1980s, see e.g., Peter Sichrovsky, ed., *Wir wissen nicht was morgen wird, wir wissen wohl was gestern war: Junge Juden in Deutschland und Österreich* (Köln: Kiepenheuer & Witsch, 1985).

50. Authors whose work first appeared during this period are Barbara Honigmann, Esther Dischereit, Rafael Seligmann, Maxim Biller. Important as well is the social-historical and critical work of Michael Wolffsohn, Dan Diner, Ralph Giordano, and Micha Brumlik.

51. Particularly important in this regard have been Lea Fleischmann's *Dies ist nicht mein Land: Eine Jüdin verläßt die Bundesrepublik* (Hamburg: Hofman und Kampe, 1980), published

after the author had left for Israel, for, as she suggested, Germany was "unlive-able" for Jews, and Broder's *Fremd*.

52. Anke Manschot, "Ook ik heb last gehad van een Assepoestercomplex: gesprek met de Duits-joodse schrijfster Grete Weil," *Vrij Nederland Boekenbijlage* (April 13, 1985) 8. "I know of no books written by men which reach the level of Bachmann or Christa Wolf." My translation. She consciously opted to adopt the openness and directness about issues both personal and political found in these works in her own writing, a development not commonly seen in literature written by women of her generation.

53. "Das David-Thema [in *Der Brautpreis*] ermöglichte Weil die Auseinandersetzung mit dem Judentum als autonomer Kultur und Grundpfeiler des Abendlandes. Sie weist in dieser Kultur dieselbe Brutalität nach wie zuvor im Griechenland Antigones, dieselbe Unterdrückung der Schwächeren, besonders Frauen." Lorenz, *Verfolgung* 262. "The David-theme enabled Weil to critically discuss Judaism as an autonomous culture and as a pillar of the occident. She points in this culture to the same brutality as earlier in Antigone's Greece, the same oppression of the weak, in particular women." My translation.

54. *Tanakh: A New Translation of the Holy Scriptures According to the Hebrew Text* (Philadelphia: The Jewish Publication Society, 1985).

55. Judith Romney Wegner, *Chattel or Person? The Status of Women in the Mishnah* (New York: Oxford University Press, 1988) 13. "A daughter is . . . perceived as the property of the father; he collects bride-price from the man who marries her or from one who seduces or rapes her whether or not the violator marries the girl. The bride-price compensated for the loss of the daughter's virginity, treated as the father's economic asset" (13). Wegner also explains that "a girl or woman who may have become espoused to a given man cannot marry another until the first man divorces her . . . a girl or a woman who mistakenly consummates marriage with one man when she is promised to another counts as an adulteress, and her children will be illegitimate . . . worse still, she cultically pollutes the man who has intercourse with her" (29).

56. David marries his second and third wives Abigail and Achinoam, and later marries Maacah, Haggith, Abital, and Eglah (Samuel II, 1.25, 26). Jewish men, up to this point in time at least, were allowed by Jewish law to have more than one wife at any given moment, as is evident from David's multiple marriages. This suggests, as Wegner argues, that: "The polygynous system of the Mishnah involves a pervasive double standard. Though a man has the *exclusive* right to his wife's sexuality, the wife's right to the husband's sexual function is never *exclusive*. She cannot legally preclude her husband from taking additional wives or having sexual relations with unmarried women. By contrast, she can neither have more than one husband nor indulge in sexual relations with other men" (220–221).

57. In fact, the only way in which Michal stands out in the Jewish tradition is that "she is the only woman in the Hebrew Bible whose love for a man is recorded." That is, nowhere else is the love of a woman for a man described from the woman's perspective, except for in *The Song of Songs*, but here the character does not have a name. Joseph Telushkin, *Biblical Literacy: The Most Important People, Events, and Ideas of the Hebrew Bible* (New York: William Morrow and Company, 1997) 212.

58. Jewish feminist scholars since the 1970s have analyzed the role of Jewish women in ancient and in modern religious practice, the status of Jewish women in ancient Israel, as well as in the *Tanach* and in Rabbinic commentary. See among others, Elizabeth Koltun, ed., *The Jewish Woman: New Perspectives* (New York: Schocken Books, 1976), Susannah Heschel, ed., *On Being a Jewish Feminist* (New York: Schocken Press, 1983), Rachel Biale, *Women and Jewish Law: An Exploration of Women's Issues in Halakhic Sources* (New York: Schocken, 1984), Carol Meyers, *Discovering Eve: Ancient Israelite Women in Context* (New York: Oxford University Press, 1988), Judith Plaskow, *Standing Again at Sinai: Judaism from a Feminist Perspective* (San Francisco: Harper, 1990) and Wegner, *Chattel or Person*.

59. This makes it tempting to trace not only the identity transformation of the three different narrators' on the basis of passages from all three novels, but that of Weil as well. This is not my goal, however.

60. The German original conveys more strongly the emotional connotation see note 24, page 98.
61. Where I quote from the published English translation of *Brautpreis* in the following passages, I mark this by using title of the English translation, *Brideprice* in parenthesis.
62. The English translation does not do full justice to this quote, I therefore added my own alternative translation for its ending between brackets.
63. Adelson, "1971 'Ein Sommer' " 751.
64. Smith, *Subjectivity* 63.
65. This makes the process extra difficult, but significant "Die Selbstdarstellung oder auch nur die Fähigkeit, 'ich' zu sagen, scheint für die überlebenden lebenswichtig gerade wegen der Hindernisse, die sie als ehemalige Naziverfolgte, die in der deutschen Sprache über ihre Erlebnisse schreiben wollten, zu überwinden hatten." Lorenz, *Verfolgung* 155. "The self portait or even just the ability to say 'I,' seem to be of vital importance for the survivors, precisely because of the obstacles that they had to overcome as former victims of Nazi persecution who wanted to write in the German language about their experiences." My translation.
66. Kaplan, *The Making of* 77–84. Hyman, *Gender and Assimilation* 18–22.
67. Dagmar Lorenz notes this as she suggests that in writing on her double marginalization as a German and as a Jew, Weil managed to create for herself "a new intellectual and emotional position." Lorenz, *Verfolgung* 262. My translation.
68. Uwe Meyer suggests that within the context of the Holocaust, the term "Spätfolgen" in German has taken on clear connotations of belated, or latent psychological consequences, or of "after-effects," which refers more specifically to the "survivor's syndrome." Meyer, *Neinsagen* 84–85. (In the United States the term PTSD, Post-Traumatic Stress Disorder, tends to be more commonly used.) The stories within this collection all deal specifically with survivors and how they confront everyday life and culture as continual after-effects of their Nazi persecution. "Alles um mich herum ist Spätfolge, weil die Hitler-Zeit so tiefe Spuren hinterlassen hat, daß keiner, der damals lebte und wahrscheinlich auch nur eine Handvoll der später Geborenen sich ihr entziehen kann." Weil, "Und Ich? Zeugin des Schmerzes," *Spätfolgen* 101. "Everything around me is after-effects, because the Hitler era has left such deep traces that no one who was alive then, and probably just a handful of those born after, can pull themselves away from it." My translation.

Chapter Four   Creating Address

1. For a set of excellent essays on German identity since reunification see Konrad H. Jarausch, ed., *After Unity: Reconfiguring German Identities* (Providence: Berghahn Books, 1997). On German identity more broadly see Siobhan Kattago, *Ambiguous Memory: The Nazi Past and German National Identity* (Westport, CT: Praeger Publishers, 2001).
2. Meyer, *Neinsagen* 100. My translation.
3. For instance, the new constitution no longer contains a clause that holds Germany responsible for Auschwitz. The new unified Germany in which "the Germans are once again masters" seems less interested in appeasing its Jewish population. Bodemann, "How can one" 37–38.
4. It was believed that the German language had been polluted with Nazi jargon and Nazi euphemisms to such a degree that one could not use it without unwillingly recalling the Nazi-rhetoric of the twelve preceding years. Even many exile writers who, due to their early emigration, had not suffered incarceration in concentration camps, and who often retained their connection to the German language while away from Germany or Austria, came to consider the use of the German language problematic after 1945.
5. Klüger submitted the work to the editors at Suhrkamp who were not interested, stating that they had already published "enough" Holocaust memoirs. She finally placed the work with a small and relatively obscure publisher, Wallstein Verlag.
6. In 1993, Klüger was awarded the Johann-Jacob-Christoph von Grimmelshausen Preis, the Rausirer Literatur Preis, and the Niedersachsen Preis, in 1994 she was awarded the Heirich Heine Preis, and in 1999 the Thomas Mann Preis.

7. Marcel Reich-Ranicki mentioned in his literary magazine *Das literarische Quartett* on ZDF television, on January 14, 1993, that *weiter leben* counted "zum Besten, was in diesen letzten zwei, drei, vier Jahren in deutscher Sprache erschienen ist." As quoted in Braese and Gehle, "Von 'deutschen Freuden'" 76. It belongs "to the best [books] that have been published in the last two, three, four years in the German language." My translation.

8. In his early study *A Double Dying*, Alvin Rosenfeld writes, a bit cynically, that this kind of a "pattern" in Holocaust literature is so predictable that the "'Holocaust Novel' may now be seen as an available subgenre of contemporary fiction, to be written by anyone who is on to and can master the 'formula'" (172). Little did he realize how right he would prove to be, if one considers Binjamin Wilkomirski's pseudo-memoir *Fragments* from 1995 as an example of fiction that mastered the "formula" exceedingly well.

9. Examples of such literature are Gerda Klein's and Judith Magyar Isaacson's memoirs, for instance. While Elie Wiesel's *Night*, arguably the genre's most well-known text does not have a clear happy ending, in other respects it confirms to this model as well. Mintz indeed argues that *Night*, published in the U.S. in 1960 was in part responsible for foregrounding this model. Wiesel's writing was "influential . . . because it early on established a norm for what a Holocaust memoir should be" (73). I personally suspect that Primo Levi's *Survival in Auschwitz*, first published in Italian in 1947 and translated to English in 1959 may have been the first to set this pattern for much European survivor literature, perhaps influencing Wiesel as well.

10. Klüger considered calling her work *Zeitschaften*, as a variation on *Ortschaften*, in response to both Peter Weiss' essay "Meine Ortschaft" and Jean Améry's autobiographical narrative on his camp experiences, entitled "Örtlichkeiten," and which is structured, just as her narrative, semi-chronologically and through the use of place names. Klüger's title also corresponds to Améry's last work before his suicide: *Weiterleben aber wie?* Her text seems in part an answer to Améry's question: she did not commit suicide; this is her story of continuing to live.

11. That is, 116 versus 90 pages.

12. The audience is perhaps not so much imagined as already responded to, as Klüger added this commentary in after having colleagues in Göttingen read earlier drafts of the manuscript. She included their questions and tried to answer them within the text itself, anticipating other German readers' questions. This kind of a narrative reads as a constant intervention on Klüger's part, which, at times, makes the text seem either rather defensive or aggressive.

13. As Kaplan points out, this was an all too common pattern for Jewish women and girls: while men fled or went into exile, they stayed behind and were deported in far greater numbers than men. Kaplan, *Between Dignity and Despair: Jewish Life in Nazi Germany* (New York: Oxford University Press, 1998).

14. Klüger, *Still Alive* 52. The quotes in this chapter all stem from this English edition of *weiter leben*, translated by Klüger herself, unless noted differently.

15. In the English edition, she quotes a poem of W.B. Yeats here see note 24, page 98. Klüger's paraphrasing of this poem in the German editions shows much more clearly the parallel with Weil's notion of becoming objectified.

16. This passage is absent from Klüger's English translation, this is my translation of: "Ich habe Theresienstadt irgendwie geliebt, und die neunzehn oder zwanzig Monate, die ich dort verbrachte, haben ein soziales Wesen aus mir gemacht" (102).

17. This passage is absent from Klüger's English translation. "Wer nur erlebt, reim- und gedankenlos, ist in Gefahr, den Verstand zu verlieren . . . Ich hab den Verstand nicht verloren, ich hab Reime gemacht" (127). My translation.

18. When decades later her son tells the story of his mother's escape to the children in his American school, they do not believe him, as they cannot imagine that three women liberated themselves: "Your dad, o.k. But not your mother" (215).

19. This passage is absent from Klüger's English translation. My translation: "Der war beheimatet in Deutschland, verwurzelt in einer bestimmten deutschen Landschaft und wurde für mich der Inbegriff des Deutschen" (211–212).

20. By this I do not mean to suggest that Klüger plays self-consciously with the problematic referentiality of language, and so forth. In fact, she seems to have no patience for discussions of this kind within Holocaust studies, and does not waste a single word on it, even though she does otherwise engage with the field, both implicitly and explicitly.

21. My translation of the second half of the sentence in German is a bit different: "when now that the gas chambers are no longer threatening me I hint at the happy end of a postwar world that I share with you?" (139).

22. Braese and Gehle, "Von 'deutschen Freunden'" 76–83.

23. Walser, "Ruth Klüger zur Begrüßung," *Das Kulturjournal Bayerischer Rundfunk* (radio broadcast) presented by Peter Hamm, September 27, 1992. Reprinted in Braese and Gehle, "Von 'deutsch Freunden'" 84–85. My translation.

24. Irene Leonard Heidelberger, Ruth Klüger 88. My translation.

25. Braese and Gehle, "Das deutsche Dialog-Bemühen umgeht das Problem jüdischer Existenz nach Auschwitz . . . der von Klüger intendierte Dialog [ist] zum deutschen Selbstgespräch geworden" (80). They suggest that the analyses from Martin Walser and Andreas Isenschmidt and almost all other reviews read the book this way (80–83).

26. This passage is absent from Klüger's English translation, this is my translation.

27. This passage is absent from Klüger's English translation, this is my translation of: "Die ersten Bücher, die damals niemand lesen wollte, aber gerade die sind es, die unser Denken seither verändert haben, so daß ich heute nicht von den Lagern erzählen kann, als wäre ich die erste, als hätte niemand davon erzählt, als wüßte nicht jeder, der das hier liest, schon so viel darüber, daß er meint, es sei mehr als genug, und als wäre dies alles nicht schon ausgebeutet worden, politisch, ästhetisch und auch als Kitsch" (79).

28. This passage is absent from Klüger's English translation. This is my paraphrasing of "Für wen schreib ich das hier eigentlich? Also bestimmt schreib ich es nicht für Juden, denn das täte ich gewiß nicht in einer Sprache, die . . . heute nur noch sehr wenige Juden gut beherrschen . . ." and my translation of: "Ich schreibe es für die, die finden, daß ich eine Fremdheit ausstrahle, die unüberwindlich ist? Anders gesagt, ich schreib es für Deutsche" (141).

29. The additions tend to be passages in which Klüger elaborates on German and Austrian historical or cultural notions that an American audience may not necessarily know about, and occasionally commentary is inserted on how the German edition was responded to after its publication, and it adds some information about Klüger's life in the decade that has passed since finishing up *weiter leben*. Conversely, some references are added to the translation that speak more to the American situation (e.g., the Vietnam war, and race discrimination in the U.S. context). The cuts take a similar pattern: many passages that cannot be easily understood by an American audience (such as particular German and Austrian cultural and literary references) are taken out. Furthermore, Klüger cut out many of her own poems (composed during and after her life in the camps), as she felt they were untranslatable, and instead added some that she wrote in English.

30. Klüger in *Still Alive*: "What you have been reading is neither a translation nor a new book: it's another version, a parallel book, if you will, for my children and my American students" (210).

31. This passage is absent from Klüger's English translation, this is my translation of: "Erinnerung verbindet uns, Erinnerung trennt uns" (218).

32. My translation of: "Jetz hab ich euch mundtot gemacht, das war nicht die Absicht. Eine Wand ist immer zwischen den Generationen, hier aber Stacheldraht, alter, rostiger Stacheldraht" (72). This passage can be found in *Still Alive*, but here Klüger's translation reads quite differently: "because if I had, it would have effectively shut up the rest of the company. They would have been bothered, troubled, sympathetic, and thoroughly uncomfortable" (93).

33. Klüger thus sees no problem with the use of the word "Holocaust," however imprecise and problematic its connotations may be, as it is useful in conversation with Germans who were not there. Before this word was used in Germany, the events existed as "Ereignis, aber nicht diesen Ausdruck und daher auch nicht den Begriff . . . Solang es nur irgendein Wort

gibt, das sich ohne Unschweife und Nebensätze gebrauchen läßt" (233). As there was no word for it, communication about it was still that much more difficult.

34. This declaration, however, also held the Austrians in part responsible for the events that took place after the Anschluß. The part of the Moscow declaration dealing with Austria's responsibility nevertheless quickly disappeared from Austria's *Staatsvertrag* of 1955, and just the clause on victimization remained.

35. Ruth Beckermann, *Unzugehörig: Österreicher und Juden nach 1945 (Vienna: Loecker Verlag, 1989)*, and Bruce F. Pauley, *From Prejudice to Persecution: A History of Austrian Antisemitism* (Chapel Hill: The University of North Carolina Press, 1992) 96.

36. In 1948, an Austrian "*Verband der Rückstellungsbetroffenen*" which lobbied to have confiscated Jewish property not be returned to the Jewish owners or heirs was founded. Helga Embacher, "Die innenpolitische Partizipation der Israelitischen Kultusgemeinde in Österreich," *Schwieriges Erbe* ed. Bergman et al. 326.

37. Beckermann, *Unzugehörig* 23.

38. Pauley, *From Prejudice* 305. What the polls show is that 75% of Austrians privately express at least some antisemitic views, about 20 to 25% hold fairly antisemitic views, and about 7 to 10% are extremely antisemitic.

39. "Jüdische Existenz in Österreich nach 1945 ist mit einer Fülle von Identitätsproblemen verbunden." Ruth Beckermann, "Illusionen und Kompromisse: zur Identität der Wiener Juden nach 1945," *Eine zerstörte Kultur: Jüdisches Leben und Antisemitismus im Wien seit dem 19. Jahrhundert*, ed. Gerhard Botz, Ivar Oxaal, and Michael Pollak (Obermayer: Druck und Verlag, 1990) 358. My translation.

40. Since 1986, a number of new and important historical studies dealing with Austria during the Nazi period have been published in Austria as well. See Emmerich Talos, Ernst Hanisch, and Wolfgang Neugebauer, ed., *NS-Herrschaft in Österreich 1938–1945* (Vienna: Verlag für Gesellschaftskritik, 1988) and Anton Pelinka and Erika Weinzierl, ed., *Das große Tabu* (Vienna: Verlag der Österreichischen Staatsdruckerei, 1987). For a critical analysis of this past in Austrian (autobiographical) literature, see Jacqueline Vansant, "Challenging Austria's Victim Status: National Socialism and Austrian Personal Narrative," *The German Quarterly* 67.1 (1994) 38–57.

41. This particular passage is absent from Klüger's English translation, this is my translation of: "Heute habe ich keine Freunde, keine Verwandten mehr in Österreich, höchstens daß sich hie und da ein Kollege oder ein entfernter Bekannter dort aufhält. Nur die Literatur dieses Landes . . . redet mich intimer an als andere Bücher . . ." (65).

42. This passage is absent from Klüger's English translation, this is my translation of: "Mir ist die Stadt weder fremd noch vertraut, was wiederum umgekehrt bedeutet, daß sie mir beides ist . . ." (67).

43. "Ich glaubte fest, obwohl die Männer es unbegreiflicherweise bestritten, daß Frauen lebensfähiger als Männer sind. Aber auch weniger wertvoll; daß unsere Toten männlich waren, bedeutete demzufolge, daß die wertvolleren in der Familie nicht mehr lebten" (237).

44. She also argues that the image of women camp guards as more brutal than men is a myth. She argues instead that they were in fact considerably less violent than men (145–146).

45. This passage is absent from Klüger's English translation, this is my translation of: "Die Kriege gehören den Männern, selbst als Kriegsopfer gehören sie ihnen" (190).

46. Her adopted sister Ditha gets told after the war that "das KZ [könne] keine bleibende Beteutung für sie gehabt haben . . . weil sie älter als sechs gewesen sei." To this nonsense, Klüger responds: "Laut dieser Logik, sage ich ungerührt, haben die KZs niemanden psychologischen Schaden zugefügt, da Kinder unter sechs kaum eine Überlebenschance hatten" (239). "The concentration camp cannot have had any lasting meaning [effects] for her . . . because she was older than six. . . . According to this logic, I say unmoved, the camps have caused no one psychological harm, as children under six barely had a chance to survive." My translation.

47. This passage is absent from Klüger's English translation, this is my translation of: "Aber ging es überhaupt um die Wahrheit oder um gezielte Kränkung?" (239).

48. My translation of: "Nur loskommen von diesen Gesprächen, die mich vernichten. Er zerstört das, was 'ich' in mir sagt" (244).

49. "Das Wort Auschwitz hat heute eine Ausstrahlung, wenn auch eine negative, so daß es das Denken über eine Person weitgehend bestimmt, wenn man weiß, daß die dort gewesen ist. Auch von mir melden die Leute, die etwas Wichtiges über mich aussagen wollen, ich sei in Auschwitz gewesen. Aber so einfach ist das nicht, denn was immer ihr denken mögt, ich komm nicht von Auschwitz her, ich stamm aus Wien. . . . Auschwitz war nur ein gräßlicher Zufall" (138). "The word Auschwitz has such an aura today, even if it is a negative one, that it determines one's thoughts about a person if one knows that they have been there. People who want to say something of importance about me will mention that I was in Auschwitz. But it is not that simple, for whatever you may think, I am not from Auschwitz, I am from Vienna . . . Auschwitz was just a horrible accident." My translation.

Chapter Five   Belated Interventions

1. It grew from 40,000 in 1990 to 60,000 by 1992. Sergio Dellapergola, "An Overview of the Demographic Trends of European Jewry," *Jewish Identities in the New Europe*, ed. Jonathan Webber (London: Littman Library of Jewish Civilization, 1994) 64–65. Dellapergola discusses the difficulty of finding reliable data, however, since one deals within most Jewish communities with both a "core" and an "enlarged" Jewish community, the latter is often not counted in more strict population counts. This "enlarged" community is nevertheless important for my study.

2. By the 1980s, about 30,000 Jews lived in the Federal Republic. These numbers change drastically with the fall of the Soviet Union and the influx of Russian-Jewish émigrés, about 11,000 between 1970 and 1993. If one includes converts to Judaism and those with at least two Jewish grandparents who do not identify as Jewish, the total runs about 50,000–70,000 Jews. Y. Michal Bodemann, "A Reemergence of German Jewry?" *Reemerging Jewish Culture in Germany*, ed. Gilman and Remmler 49. Over the past decade with Russian-Jewish emigrants numbering about 50,000 in total, this number has grown still larger, to close to 95,000 Jews.

3. Lorenz, "The Case of" 240.

4. Sander L. Gilman, "Jewish Writers in Contemporary Germany: The Dead Author Speaks," *Inscribing the Other* (Lincoln: University of Nebraska Press, 1991) 249–278.

5. Zipes too, notes that when the "Jewish contribution" to German culture of the postwar years was discussed "most of the attention in the public sphere was paid to dead Jews. . . . émigrés, outsiders, or exceptions." Zipes, "The Contemporary Fascination" 18.

6. Brumlik, "The Situation" 10.

7. Gilman and Zipes, "Introduction," *Yale Companion* xxiii.

WORKS CITED

Adelson, Leslie A. "1971 'Ein Sommer in der Woche der Itke K.' by American born author Jeanette Lander is published." Gilman and Zipes, *Yale Companion* 749–758.

Alphen, Ernst van. *Caught by History: Holocaust Effects in Contemporary Art, Literature, and Theory.* Stanford: Stanford University Press, 1997.

The American Heritage Dictionary. 2nd College ed. Boston: Houghton Mifflin Company, 1985.

Améry, Jean. *At the Mind's Limits: Contemplations by a Survivor on Auschwitz and Its Realities.* Trans. Sidney Rosenfeld and Stella P. Rosenfeld. New York: Schocken, 1990.

Apel, Dora. *Memory Effects: The Holocaust and the Art of Secondary Witnessing.* New Brunswick, NJ: Rutgers University Press, 2002.

Baackmann, Susanne. "The Battle with Memory: Grete Weil's My Sister Antigone." *Conquering Women: Women and War in the German Cultural Imagination.* Ed. Hillary Collier Sy-Quia and Susanne Baackmann. Berkeley: University of California Press, 2000. 91–110.

———. "Configurations of Myth, Memory, and Mourning in Grete Weil's 'Meine Schwester Antigone.'" *German Quarterly* 73.3 (Summer 2000): 269–287.

Bal, Mieke, Jonathan Crewe, and Leo Spitzer, eds., *Acts of Memory: Cultural Recall in the Present.* Hanover, NH: University Press of New England, 1999.

Beckermann, Ruth. *Unzugehörig: Österreicher und Juden nach 1945.* Vienna: Loecker Verlag, 1989.

———. "Illusionen und Kompromisse: zur Identität der Wiener Juden nach 1945." *Eine zerstörte Kultur: Jüdisches Leben und Antisemitismus im Wien seit dem 19. Jahrhundert.* Ed. Gerhard Botz, Ivar Oxaal, and Michael Pollak. Obermayer: Druck und Verlag, 1990. 357–364.

Beller, Steven. *Vienna and the Jews, 1867–1938: A Cultural History.* Cambridge: Cambridge University Press, 1989.

Benstock, Shari. *The Private Self: Theory and Practice of Women's Autobiographical Writings.* Chapel Hill: The University of North Carolina Press, 1988.

Benz, Wolfgang. "The Persecution and Extermination of the Jews in the German Consciousness." Trans. Joe O'Donnell and John Milfull. *Why Germany? National Socialist Anti-Semitism and the European Context.* Ed. John Milfull. Providence: Berg, 1993. 91–104.

Bergmann, Werner, Rainer Erb, and Albert Lichtblau, eds., *Schwieriges Erbe: Der Umgang mit Nationalsozialismus und Antisemitismus in Österreich, der DDR und der Bundesrepublik Deutschland.* Frankfurt/Main: Campus Verlag, 1995.

Bernard-Donals, Michael and Richard Glejzer. *Between Witness and Testimony: The Holocaust and the Limits of Representation.* Albany: State University of New York Press, 2001.

Bernstein, Michael Andre. *Foregone Conclusions: Against Apocalyptic History.* Berkeley: University of California Press, 1994.

Bettelheim, Bruno. *The Informed Heart.* Glencoe, IL: Free Press, 1960.

Biale, Rachel. *Women and Jewish Law: An Exploration of Women's Issues in Halakhic Sources.* New York: Schocken, 1984.

Bier, Jean-Paul. "The Holocaust and West-Germany: Strategies of Oblivion 1947–1979." Trans. Michael Allinder. *New German Critique* 19 (1980): 9–29.

Blanchot, Maurice. *The Writing of the Disaster.* Trans. Ann Smock. Lincoln: University of Nebraska Press, 1986.

Blänsdorf, Agnes. "Die Einordnung der NS-Zeit in das Bild der eigenen Geschichte: Österreich, die DDR und die Bundesrepublik Deutschland im Vergleich." Bergmann et al., *Schwieriges Erbe* 18–45.

Blasius, Dirk and Dan Diner, eds., *Zerbrochene Geschichte: Leben und Selbstverständnis der Juden in Deutschland*. Frankfurt: Fischer, 1991.

Blom, J.C.H. "The Persecution of the Jews in the Netherlands in a Comparative International Perspective." *Dutch Jewish History*. Proceedings of the Fourth Symposium on the History of the Jews in the Netherlands. December 7–10 Tel Aviv-Jerusalem, 1986. Vol II. Ed. Jozeph Michman. Assen: Van Gorcum, 1989. 273–289.

Bodemann, Y. Michal. "A Reemergence of German Jewry?" Gilman and Remmler, *Reemerging Jewish Culture in Germany* 46–61.

———. " 'How Can One Stand to Live Here as a Jew . . .': Paradoxes of Jewish Existence in Germany." Bodemann, *Jews, Germans, Memory* 19–46.

———. ed., *Jews, Germans, Memory: Reconstructions of Jewish Life in Germany*. Ann Arbor: The University of Michigan Press, 1996.

Bornemann, John and Jeffrey M. Peck. *Sojourners: The Return of German Jews and the Question of Identity*. Lincoln: University of Nebraska Press, 1995.

Bos, Pascale. "Homoeroticism and the Liberated Woman as Tropes of Subversion: Grete Weil's Literary Provocations." *German Quarterly* 78.1 (Winter 2005): 70–87.

———. "Return to Germany: German-Jewish Authors Seeking Address." *Changing German/Jewish Symbiosis* Zipes and Morris, eds. 203–232.

———. "Women and the Holocaust: Analyzing Gender Difference." *Experience and Expression: Women, the Nazis, and the Holocaust*. Ed. Elizabeth Baer and Myrna Goldenberg. Detroit, MI: Wayne State University Press, 2002. 23–50.

Botz, Gerhard. "The Jews of Vienna from the Anschluß to the Holocaust." Oxaal, Pollak, and Botz, *Eine zerstörte Kultur* 185–204.

Braese, Stephan and Holger Gehle. "Von 'deutschen Freunden:' Ruth Klüger's 'weiter leben. Eine Jugend' in der deutschen Rezeption." *Der Deutschunterricht* 47.6 (1995): 76–87.

Braese, Stephan, Holger Gehle, Doron Kiesel, and Hanno Loewy, eds., *Deutsche Nachkriegsliteratur und der Holocaust*. Frankfurt: Campus Verlag, 1998.

Braese, Stephan. "Grete Weil's America: A Self-Encounter at the Moment of the Anti-Authoritarian Revolt." *Germanic Review* 75.2 (2000): 132–149.

Braese, Stephan. *Die andere Erinnerung: Jüdische Autoren in der westdeutschen Nachkriegsliteratur*. Berlin: Philo, 2001.

Braun, R.E. Trans., *Sophocles Antigone*. London: Oxford University Press, 1974.

Broder, Henryk M. and Michel Lang, eds., *Fremd im eigenen Land: Juden in der Bundesrepublik*. Frankfurt/Main: Fischer Taschenbuch Verlag, 1979.

Brumlik, Micha, Doron Kiesel, Cilly Kugelmann, and Julius H. Schoeps. *Jüdisches Leben in Deutschland seit 1945*. Frankfurt: Jüdischer Verlag bei Athenäum, 1986.

Brumlik, Micha. "The Situation of the Jews in Today's Germany." Bodemann, *Jews, Germans, Memory* 1–16.

———. "Zum Geleit: Ein Appell an die Politik." *Auschwitz-Prozeß 4 Ks 2/63 Frankfurt am Main*. Ed. Fritz Bauer Institut. Köln: Snoeck, 2004. 48–51.

Bullivant, Keith. "Continuity or Change? Aspects of West German Writing after 1945." Hewitt, *Culture of Reconstruction* 191–207.

Caruth, Cathy, ed., *Trauma: Explorations in Memory*. Baltimore: Johns Hopkins University Press, 1995.

———. *Unclaimed Experience: Trauma, Narrative, and History*. Baltimore: Johns Hopkins University Press, 1996.

Dellapergola, Sergio. "An Overview of the Demographic Trends of European Jewry." *Jewish Identities in the New Europe*. Ed. Jonathan Webber. London: Littman Library of Jewish Civilization, 1994.

Deleuze, Gilles and Felix Guattari. *Kafka: Toward a Minor Literature*. Trans. Dana Polan Minneapolis: University of Minnesota Press, 1986.

Diner, Dan. "Negative Symbiose: Deutsche und Juden nach Auschwitz." Brumlik, Kiesel, Kugelmann, and Schoeps, *Jüdisches Leben* 243–257.

Dippel, John V.H. *Bound Upon a Wheel of Fire: Why so Many German Jews made the Tragic Decision to Remain in Nazi Germany*. New York: HarperCollins, 1996.

Dis, Adriaan van. "Nee zeggen is de enige onverwoestbare vrijheid." *NRC Handelsblad* 12 November 1982, Cultureel Supplement: 3.

Dubiel, Helmut. *Niemand ist frei von der Geschichte: Die nationalsozialistische Herrschaft in den Debatten des Deutschen Bundestages*. München: Carl Hanser Verlag, 1999.

Epstein, Julia and Lori Hope Lefkovitz, eds., *Shaping Losses: Cultural Memory and the Holocaust*. Urbana: University of Illinois Press, 2001.

Evans, Richard J. *In Hitler's Shadow: West German Historians and the Attempt to Escape from the Nazi Past*. New York: Pantheon Books, 1989.

Exner, Lisbeth. *Land meiner Mörder, Land meiner Sprache: Die Schriftstellerin Grete Weil*. München: Monacensia/A1 Verlag, 1998.

Ezrahi, Sidra DeKoven. *By Words Alone: The Holocaust in Literature*. Chicago: University of Chicago Press, 1980.

Felman, Shoshana and Dori Laub. *Testimony: Crises of Witnessing in Literature, Psychoanalysis, and History*. New York: Routledge, 1992.

Fleischmann, Lea. *Dies ist nicht mein Land: Eine Jüdin verläßt die Bundesrepublik*. Hamburg: Hofman und Kampe, 1980.

Frederiksen, Elke P. and Martha Kaarsberg Wallach, eds., *Facing Fascism and Confronting the Past: German Women Writers from Weimar to the Present*. New York: State University of New York Press, 2000.

Fridman, Lea Wernick. *Words and Witness: Narrative and Aesthetic Strategies in the Representation of the Holocaust*. Albany: State University of New York Press, 2000.

Friedländer, Saul. *Memory, History, and the Extermination of the Jews of Europe*. Bloomington: Indiana University Press, 1993.

———, ed., *Probing the Limits of Representation: Nazism and the "Final Solution."* Cambridge, MA: Harvard University Press, 1992.

Fritz Bauer Institut. *Auschwitz-Prozeß 4 Ks 2/63 Frankfurt am Main*. Köln: Snoeck, 2004.

Fuchs, Miriam. "Recalling the Past and Rescuing the Self: Autobiographical Slippage in Grete Weil's *The Bride Price: A Novel*." *Shofar* 17.2 (1999): 73–83.

Giese, Carmen. *Das Ich im literarischen Werk von Grete Weil und Klaus Mann: Zwei auto-biographische Gesamtkonzepte*. Frankfurt/Main: Peter Lang, 1997.

Gilman, Sander L. "Jewish Writers in Contemporary Germany: The Dead Author Speaks." Ed. Sander L. Gilman. *Inscribing the Other*. Lincoln: University of Nebraska Press, 1991. 249–278.

———. *The Jew's Body*. New York: Routledge, 1991.

———. *Jews in Today's German Culture*. Bloomington: Indiana University Press, 1995.

Gilman, Sander L. and Karen Remmler, eds., *Reemerging Jewish Culture in Germany: Life and Literature Since 1989*. New York: New York University Press, 1994.

Gilman, Sander L. and Jack Zipes. *Yale Companion to Jewish Writing and Thought in German Culture, 1096–1996*. New Haven: Yale University Press, 1997.

Goertz, Karein K. "Body, Trauma, and the Rituals of Memory: Charlotte Delbo and Ruth Klüger." *Shaping Losses: Cultural Memory and the Holocaust*. Ed. Julia Epstein and Lori Hope Lefkovitz. Urbana: University of Illinois Press, 2001. 161–185.

Goldberg, David Theo and Michael Krausz. "Introduction: The Culture of Identity." *Jewish Identity*. Ed. David Theo Goldberg and Michael Krausz. Philadelphia: Temple University Press, 1993.

Goldenberg, Myrna. "Lessons Learned from Gentle Heroism: Women's Holocaust Narratives." *Annals of the American Academy of Political and Social Science* 548 (1996): 78–93.

Goldenberg, Myrna. "Testimony, Narrative, and Nightmare: The Experiences of Jewish Women in the Holocaust." *Active Voices: Women in Jewish Culture*. Ed. Maurie Sacks. Urbana: University of Illinois Press, 1995. 94–106.

Grimm, Günter E. and Hans-Peter Bayerdörfer, eds., *Im Zeichen Hiobs: Jüdische Schriftsteller und deutsche Literatur im 20. Jahrhundert*. Königstein: Athenäum, 1985.

Gubar, Susan. *Poetry after Auschwitz: Remembering What One Never Knew*. Bloomington: Indiana University Press, 2003.

Habermas, Jürgen. "Eine Art Schadensabwicklung: die apologetischen Tendenzen in der deutschen Geschichtsschreibung." *Die Zeit* (July 11, 1986).

Hartman, Geoffrey, ed., *Bitburg in Moral and Political Perspective*. Bloomington: Indiana University Press, 1986.

———. ed., *Holocaust Remembrance: The Shapes of Memory*. Cambridge, MA: Basil Blackwell, 1994.

———. "Learning from Survivors: Notes on the Video Archive at Yale." Bauer, *Remembering for the Future* 1713–1717.

Heidelberger, Irene Leonard. *Ruth Klüger: weiter leben. Eine Jugend*. Oldenbourg Interpretationen, Band 81. München: R. Oldenbourg, 1996.

Herf, Jeffrey. *Divided Memory: The Nazi Past in the Two Germanys*. Cambridge, MA: Harvard University Press, 1997.

———. "The 'Holocaust' Reception in West Germany: Right, Center and Left." *New German Critique* 19 (1980): 30–52.

Heschel, Susannah. "Configurations of Patriarchy, Judaism, and Nazism in German Feminist Thought." *Gender and Judaism: The Transformation of Tradition*. Ed. Tamar M. Rudavsky. New York: New York University Press, 1995. 135–154.

———. *On Being a Jewish Feminist*. New York: Schocken, 1983.

Hewitt, Nicholas, ed., *The Culture of Reconstruction: European Literature, Thought and Film, 1945–1950*. New York: St. Martin's Press, 1989.

Hillgruber, Andreas. *Zweierlei Untergang: Die Zerschlagung des Deutschen Reiches und das Ende des europäischen Judentums*. Berlin: W.J. Siedler, 1986.

Hirsch, Marianne. *Family Frames: Photography, Narrative, and Postmemory*. Cambridge, MA: Harvard University Press, 1997.

———. "Projected Memory: Holocaust Photographs in Personal and Public Fantasy." *Acts of Memory: Cultural Recall in the Present*. Ed. Mieke Bal, Jonathan Crewe, and Leo Spitzer. Hanover, NH: University Press of New England, 1999. 2–23.

———. "Surviving Images: Holocaust Photographs and the Work of Postmemory." *The Yale Journal of Criticism* 14.1 (2001): 5–37.

Hirschfeld, Gerhard. *Nazi Rule and Dutch Collaboration: The Netherlands Under German Occupation 1940–1945*. Trans. Louise Willmot. Oxford: Berg, 1988.

———. "Niederlande." *Dimension des Völkermords: Die Zahl der jüdischen Opfer des Nationalsozialismus*. Ed. Wolfgang Benz. München: R. Oldenbourg Verlag, 1991.

Hölderlin, Friedrich. *Die Trauerspiele des Sophocles*. 1804; Frankfurt am Main: Stroemfeld/Roter Stern, 1986.

Holub, Robert. "1965 the Premiere of Peter Weiss's 'The Investigation: Oratorio in Eleven Songs,' a Drama Written from the Documentation of the Frankfurt Auschwitz Trial, is Staged." Gilman and Zipes, *Yale Companion* 729–735.

Horowitz, Sara R. "Memory and Testimony of Women Survivors of Nazi Genocide." *Women of the Word: Jewish Women and Jewish Writing*. Ed. Judith R. Baskin. Detroit, MI: Wayne State University Press, 1996. 258–282.

———. *Voicing the Void: Muteness and Memory in Holocaust Fiction*. Albany: State University of New York Press, 1997.

Hungerford, Amy. *The Holocaust of Texts: Genocide, Literature, and Personification*. Chicago: The University of Chicago Press, 2003.

Huyssen, Andreas. *After the Great Divide*. Bloomington: Indiana University Press, 1986.

Hyman, Paula E. *Gender and Assimilation in Modern Jewish History: The Roles and Representations of Women*. Seattle: University of Washington Press, 1995.

―――. "Gender and Jewish History." *Tikkun* 3.1 (1988): 35–38.

Jacobson, Kenneth. *Embattled Selves: An Investigation into the Nature of Identity Through Oral Histories of Holocaust Survivors*. New York: The Atlantic Monthly Press, 1994.

Jarausch, Konrad H. ed., *After Unity: Reconfiguring German Identities*. Providence: Berghahn Books, 1997.

Jong, Louis de. *The Netherlands and Nazi Germany*. The Erasmus Lectures 1988. Cambridge, MA: Harvard University Press, 1990.

Kaes, Anton. "1979 The American television series 'Holocaust' is shown in West Germany." Gilman and Zipes, *Yale Companion* 783–789.

Kaplan, Marion A. *Between Dignity and Despair: Jewish Life in Nazi Germany*. New York: Oxford University Press, 1998.

―――. *The Making of the Jewish Middle Class: Women, Family, and Identity in Imperial Germany*. Oxford: Oxford University Press, 1991.

―――. "Tradition and Transition—The Acculturation, Assimilation, and Integration of Jews in Imperial Germany—A Gender Analysis." *Leo Baeck Institute Year Book*. London: Secker and Warburg, 1982. 3–35.

―――. "What is 'Religion' among Jews in Contemporary Germany?" Gilman and Remmler, *Reemerging Jewish Culture in Germany* 77–112.

Kaplan, Alice Yaeger. *Reproductions of Banality: Fascism, Literature, and French Intellectual Life*. Minneapolis: University of Minnesota Press, 1986.

Kattago, Siobhan. *Ambiguous Memory: The Nazi Past and German National Identity*. Westport, CT: Praeger Publishers, 2001.

Kilcher, Andreas B., ed., *Metzler's Lexikon der deutsch-jüdischen Literatur*. Stuttgart: J.B. Metzler, 2000.

Klüger, Ruth. *Still Alive: A Holocaust Girlhood Remembered*. New York: The Feminist Press, 2001.

―――. *weiter leben. Eine Jugend*. Göttingen: Wallstein Verlag, 1992.

Kolinsky, Eva and Wilfried van der Will. "In Search of German Culture: An Introduction." The *Cambridge Companion to Modern German Culture*. Cambridge: Cambridge University Press, 1998. 1–19.

Koltun, Elizabeth, ed., *The Jewish Woman: New Perspectives*. New York: Schocken, 1976.

Krell, Robert and Marc Sherman, eds., "Medical and Psychological Effects of Concentration Camps on Holocaust Survivors." *Genocide: A Critical Bibliographic Review*. Vol. 4. New Brunswick: Transaction Publishers, 1997.

LaCapra, Dominick. *History and Memory after Auschwitz*. Ithaca: Cornell University Press, 1998.

―――. *History in Transit: Experience, Identity, Critical Theory*. Ithaca: Cornell University Press, 2004.

―――. *Representing the Holocaust: History, Theory, Trauma*. Ithaca: Cornell University Press, 1994.

―――. *Writing History, Writing Trauma*. Baltimore: The Johns Hopkins University Press, 2001.

Langer, Lawrence. *The Age of Atrocity: Death in Modern Literature*. Boston: Beacon, 1978.

―――. *The Holocaust and the Literary Imagination*. New Haven: Yale University Press, 1975.

―――. *Holocaust Testimonies: The Ruins of Memory*. New Haven: Yale University Press, 1991.

Levkov, Ilya, ed., *Bitburg and Beyond: Encounters in American, German, and Jewish History*. New York: Shapolsky Publishers, 1987.

Leys, Ruth. *Trauma: A Genealogy*. Chicago: The University of Chicago Press, 2000.

Lezzi, Eva. *Zerstörte Kindheit: Literarische Autobiographien zur Shoah*. Köln: Böhlau Verlag, 2001.

Limberg, Margarete and Hubert Rübsaat, eds., *Sie durften nicht mehr Deutsche sein: Jüdischer Alltag in Selbstzeugnissen 1933–1938*. Frankfurt: Campus Verlag, 1990.

Linden, R. Ruth. *Making Stories, Making Selves: Feminist Reflections on the Holocaust*. Columbus: Ohio State University Press, 1993.

Liss, Andrea. *Trespassing through Shadows: Memory, Photography & the Holocaust*. Minneapolis: University of Minnesota Press, 1998.

Loewy, Ernst. "Zur Paradigmenwechsel in der Exilliteraturforschung." *Exilforschung* 9 (1991): 208–219.

Loftus, Elizabeth et al. "Who Remembers What? Gender Differences in Memory." *Michigan Quarterly Review* 26.1 (1987): 64–85.

Lorenz, Dagmar C.G. "The Case of Jacob Littner: Authors, Publishers, and Jewish History in Unified Germany." Lorenz and Weinberger, *Insiders and Outsiders* 235–250.

———. *Keepers of the Motherland: German Texts by Jewish Women Writers*. Lincoln: University of Nebraska Press, 1997.

———. "Memory and Criticism: Ruth Klüger's 'weiter leben.'" *Women in German Yearbook* 9 (1993): 207–223.

———. *Verfolgung bis zum Massenmord: Holocaust-Diskurse in deutscher Sprache aus der Sicht der Verfolgten*. New York: Peter Lang, 1992.

Lorenz, Dagmar C.G. and Gabriele Weinberger. *Insiders and Outsiders: Jewish and Gentile Culture in Germany and Austria*. Detroit: Wayne State University Press, 1994.

Magnus, Shulamith. " 'Out of the Ghetto': Integrating the Study of Jewish Women into the Study of 'The Jews.'" *Judaism* 39.1 (1990): 28–36.

Maier, Charles S. *The Unmasterable Past: History, Holocaust, and German National Identity*. Cambridge, MA: Harvard University Press, 1988.

Manschot, Anke. "Ook ik heb last gehad van een Assepoestercomplex: gesprek met de Duits-joodse schrijfster Grete Weil." *Vrij Nederland Boekenbijlage* (April 13, 1985): 8–10.

Markovits, Andrei S., Beth Simone Noveck, and Carolyn Höfig. "Jews in German Society." *The Cambridge Companion to Modern German Culture*. Ed. Eva Kolinsky and Wilfried van der Will. Cambridge: Cambridge University Press, 1998. 86–109.

Marrus, Michael. "European Jewry and the Politics of Assimilation: Assessment and Reassessment." *Journal of Modern History* 49 (1977): 89–109.

Mattson, Michelle "Classical Kinship and Personal Responsibility: Grete Wei's 'Meine Schwester Antigone.'" *seminar* 37.1 (February 2001): 53–72.

Mauer, Trude. "Die Juden der Weimarer Republik." Blasius and Diner, *Zerbrochene Geschichte* 102–120.

Mc Cormick, Richard W. *Politics of the Self: Feminism and the Postmodern in West German Literature and Film*. Princeton: Princeton University Press, 1991.

Mc Gowan, Moray. "Myth, Memory, Testimony, Jewishness in Grete Weil's Meine Schwester Antigone." *European Memories of the Second World War*. Ed. Helmut Peitsch, Charles Burdett, and Claire Gorrara. New York: Berghahn Books, 1999. 149–158.

Meyer, Uwe. *"Neinsagen, die einzige unzerstörbare Freiheit": Das Werk der Schriftstellerin Grete Weil*. Frankfurt: Peter Lang, 1996.

———. " 'O Antigone . . . stehe mir bei' Zur Antigone-Rezeption im Werk von Grete Weil." *Zeitschrift für Literaturwissenschaft und Linguistik* 104 (1996): 150–151.

Meyers, Carol. *Discovering Eve: Ancient Israelite Women in Context*. New York: Oxford University Press, 1988.

Miller, Judith. *One, by One, by One: Facing the Holocaust*. New York: Simon and Schuster, 1990.

Mintz, Alan. *Popular Culture and the Shaping of Holocaust Memory in America*. Seattle: University of Washington Press, 2001.

Moore, Bob. *Victims and Survivors: The Nazi Persecution of the Jews in the Netherlands 1940–1945*. London: Arnold, 1997.

Mosse, George. *German Jews Beyond Judaism*. Bloomington: Indiana University Press, 1985.

———. "Jewish Emancipation: Between Bildung and Respectability." Reinharz and Schatzberg, *Jewish Response* 1–16.

Niederland, William G. "Clinical Observations on the 'Survivor Syndrome': Symposium on Psychic Traumatization through Social Catastrophe." *International Journal of Psychoanalysis* 49 (1968): 313–315.

Niewyk, Donald L. *The Jews in Weimar Germany*. Baton Rouge: Louisiana State University Press, 1980.

Nussbaum, Laureen and Uwe Meyer. "Grete Weil, unbequem, zum Denken zwingend." *Exilforschung: Ein Internationales Jahrbuch.* Band 11 "Frauen und Exil: Zwischen Anpassung und Selbstbehauptung." Ed. Krohn et al. München: edition text + kritik, 1993. 156–170.

Olschner, Leonard. "1951 In his essay 'Kulturkritik und Gesellschaft,' Theodor W. Adorno states that it is barbaric to write poetry after Auschwitz." Gilman and Zipes, *Yale Companion* 691–696.

Pauley, Bruce F. *From Prejudice to Persecution: A History of Austrian Antisemitism.* Chapel Hill: The University of North Carolina Press, 1992.

Peitsch, Helmut. "German Literature in 1945: Liberation for a New Beginning?" Hewitt, *Culture of Reconstruction* 172–190.

Pelinka, Anton and Erika Weinsierl, eds., *Das große Tabu.* Vienna: Verlag der Österreichischen Staatsdruckerei, 1987.

Petraka, Vivian M. *Spectacular Suffering: Theatre, Fascism, and the Holocaust.* Bloomington, Indiana University Press, 1999.

Pinto, Diana. "The New Jewish Europe: Challenges and Responsibilities." *European Judaism* 3.1 61 (1998): 3–15.

Plaskow, Judith. *Standing Again at Sinai: Judaism from a Feminist Perspective.* San Francisco: Harper, 1990.

Pomeranz Carmely, Klara. *Das Identitätsproblem jüdischer Autoren im deutschen Sprachraum: Von der Jahrhundertwende bis zu Hitler.* Königstein: Scriptor, 1981.

Presser, Jacques. *The Destruction of the Dutch Jews.* Trans. Arnold Pomerans. New York: E.P. Dutton & Co., 1969.

Rabinbach, Anson. "Introduction: Reflections on Germans and Jews since Auschwitz." Rabinbach and Zipes, *Germans and Jews since the Holocaust* 3–24.

Reich-Ranicki, Marcel. "Immer noch im Exil." *Literarisches Leben in Deutschland: Kommentare und Pamphlete.* Ed. Marcel Reich-Ranicki. München: Piper, 1965. 262–269.

———. Introduction. "Ruth Klüger: weiter leben." *Das literarische Quartett.* Zweites Deutsches Fernsehen. January 1993.

———. *Über Ruhestörer: Juden in der deutschen Literatur.* München: Piper, 1973.

Reinharz, Jehuda and Walter Schatzberg, eds., *The Jewish Response to German Culture: From the Enlightenment to the Second World War.* Hanover, NH: University Press of New England, 1985.

Remmler, Karen. "Gender Identities and the Remembrance of the Holocaust." *Women in German Yearbook* 10 (1994): 167–187.

Ringelheim, Joan. "The Unethical and the Unspeakable: Women and the Holocaust." *Simon Wiesenthal Center Annual* 1 (1984): 69–87.

Ringelheim, Joan. "Women and the Holocaust: A Reconsideration of Research." *Signs* 10.4 (1985): 741–761.

Rosenfeld, Alvin. *A Double Dying: Reflections on Holocaust Literature.* Bloomington: Indiana University Press, 1980.

Roskies, David G. *Against the Apocalypse: Responses to Catastrophe in Modern Jewish Culture.* Cambridge, MA: Harvard University Press, 1984.

Rothberg, Michael. *Traumatic Realism: The Demands of Holocaust Representation.* Minneapolis: University of Minnesota Press, 2000.

Rozenblitt, Marsha. *The Jews of Vienna, 1867–1914: Assimilation and Identity.* Albany: State University of New York Press, 1983.

Rürup, Reinhard. "Jüdische Geschichte in Deutschland: Von der Emanzipation bis zur nationalsozialistischer Gewaltherrschaft." Blasius and Diner, *Zerbrochene Geschichte* 79–101.

Santner Eric. *Stranded Objects: Mourning, Memory, and Film in Postwar Germany.* Ithaca: Cornell University Press, 1990.

Schissler, Hanna, ed., *The Miracle Years: A Cultural History of West Germany, 1949–1968.* Princeton: Princeton University Press, 2001.

Schivelbusch, Wolfgang. *In a Cold Crater: Cultural and Intellectual Life in Berlin. 1945–1948.* Trans. Kelly Barry. Berkeley: University of California Press, 1998.

Schlant, Ernestine. *The Language of Silence: West German Literature and the Holocaust*. New York: Routledge, 1999.

Schoeps, Julius. *Leiden an Deutschland: Vom antisemitischen Wahn und der Last der Erinnerung*. München: Piper, 1990.

Scholem, Gershom. *On Jews and Judaism in Crisis: Selected Essays*. Ed. Werner J. Dannhauser. New York: Schocken, 1976.

Schulte, Christoph, ed., *Deutschtum und Judentum: Ein Disput unter Juden in Deutschland*. Stuttgart: Philipp Reclam jun., 1993.

Schütz, Hans J. *"Eure Sprache ist auch meine:" Eine deutsch-jüdische Literaturgeschichte*. Zürich: Pendo, 2000.

———. *Juden in der deutschen Literatur: Eine deutsch-jüdische Literaturgeschichte im Überblick*. München: Piper, 1992.

Schwab, Gustav. *Griekse mythen en sagen*. Trans. J.K. van den Brink. Utrecht: Het Spectrum, 1956.

Sichrovsky, Peter, ed., *Wir wissen nicht was morgen wird, wir wissen wohl was gestern war: Junge Juden in Deutschland und Österreich*. Köln: Kiepenheuer & Witsch, 1985.

Smith, Sidonie. *Subjectivity, Identity, and the Body: Women's Autobiographical Practices in the Twentieth Century*. Bloomington: Indiana University Press, 1993.

Sophocles. *Die Tragödien*. Trans. Heinrich Weinstock. Stuttgart: Kröner Verlag, 1962.

Sorkin, David. *The Transformation of German Jewry 1780–1840*. Oxford: Oxford University Press, 1987.

Spörk, Ingrid. "1992 Robert Schindel's Novel 'Gebürtig' continues the development of Jewish writing in Austria after the Shoah." Gilman and Zipes, *Yale Companion* 827–832.

Steiner, George. *Antigones*. Oxford: Clarendon Press, 1984.

Stern, Frank. "German-Jewish Relations in the Postwar Period: The Ambiguities of Antisemitic and Philosemitic Discourse." Ed. Bodemann, *Jews, Germans, Memory* 77–98.

———. *The Whitewashing of the Yellow Badge: Antisemitism and Philosemitism in Postwar Germany*. Trans. William Templer. Oxford: Pergamon Press, 1992.

Tal, Kalí, *Worlds of Hurt: Reading the Literatures of Trauma*. New York: Cambridge University Press, 1996.

Talos, Emmerich, Ernst Hanisch, and Wolfgang Neugebauer, eds., *NS-Herrschaft in Österreich 1938–1945*. Vienna: Verlag für Gesellschaftskritik, 1988.

Tanakh: A New Translation of The Holy Scriptures According to the Traditional Hebrew Text. Philadelphia: The Jewish Publication Society, 1985.

Telushkin, Joseph. *Biblical Literacy: The Most Important People, Events, and Ideas of the Hebrew Bible*. New York: William Morrow and Company, 1997.

Terry, Jack. "The Damaging Effects of the 'Survivor Syndrome.'" *Psychoanalytic Reflections on the Holocaust: Selected Essays*. Ed. Steven A. Luel and Paul Marcus. New York: Holocaust Awareness Institute, Center for Judaic Studies University of Denver, KTAV Publishing House, 1984. 134–149.

Vansant, Jacqueline. "Challenging Austria's Victim Status: National Socialism and Austrian Personal Narrative." *The German Quarterly* 67.1 (1994): 38–57.

Volkov, Shulamit. "The Dynamics of Dissimilation: Ostjuden and German Jews." Reinharz and Schatzberg, *Jewish Response* 95–211.

Weedon, Chris, ed., *Postwar Women's Writing in German*. Providence: Berghahn Books, 1997.

Wegner, Judith Romney. *Chattel or Person? The Status of Women in the Mishnah*. New York: Oxford University Press, 1988.

Weil, Grete. *Ans Ende der Welt*. Berlin: Verlag Volk und Welt, 1949. Frankfurt am Main: Fischer Taschenbuch Verlag, 1987.

———. *Boulevard Solitude: Lyrisches Drama in Sieben Bildern*. Music Hans Werner Henze, text Grete Weil. Mainz: B. Schott's Söhne, 1951.

———. *Der Brautpreis*. Zürich: Nagel & Kimche, 1988. Frankfurt am Main: Fischer Taschenbuchverlag, 1991.

———. *The Brideprice*. Trans. John Barrett. Boston: David R. Godine Publishers, 1991.

———. *Erlebnis einer Reise: Drei Begegnungen*. Zürich: Nagel & Kimche, 1999.

———. *Generationen*. Zürich, Köln: Benziger Verlag, 1983. Frankfurt am Main: Fischer Taschenbuchverlag, 1985.

———. *Happy, sagte der Onkel*. Wiesbaden: Limes Verlag, 1968. Frankfurt am Main: Fischer Taschenbuchverlag, 1982.

———. *Last Trolley from Beethovenstraat*. Trans. John Barrett. Boston: David R Godine Publishers, 1992.

———. *Leb ich denn, wenn andere leben*. Zürich: Nagel & Kimche, 1998.

———. *Meine Schwester Antigone*. Zürich, Köln: Benziger Verlag, 1980. Frankfurt am Main: Fischer Taschenbuch Verlag, 1982.

———. *My Sister, My Antigone*. Trans. Krishna Winston. New York: Avon Books, 1984.

———. *Spätfolgen: Erzählungen*. Zürich: Nagel & Kimche, 1992.

———. *Tramhalte Beethovenstraat*. Wiesbaden: Limes Verlag, 1963. Frankfurt am Main: Fischer Taschenbuch Verlag, 1983.

———. *Der Weg zur Grenze*. Unpublished manuscript. 1944.

———. "Weihnachtslegende 1943." *Das gefesselte Theater: Het tooneel in boeien*. Amsterdam: Hollandgruppe "Freies Deutschland," 1945.

———. *Die Witwe von Ephesus*. Music Wolfgang Fortner, text Grete Weil. Mainz: B. Schott's Söhne, 1952.

Weissman, Gary. "Lawrence Langer and 'The Holocaust Experience.'" *Response: A Contemporary Jewish Review* 68 (1997/1998): 78–97.

Wetzel, Juliane. "Trauma und Tabu: Jüdisches Leben in Deutschland nach dem Holocaust." *Ende des Dritten Reiches-Ende des Zweiten Weltkriegs: Eine perspektivistische Rückschau*. Ed. Hans-Erich Volkmann. München: Piper, 1995. 419–456.

Wirth, Hans-Jürgen, ed., *Hitlers Enkel—Oder Kinder der Demokratie? Die 68-er Generation, die RAF und die Fischer-Debatte*. Gießen: Psychosozial-Verlag, 2001.

Young, James. *The Texture of Memory: Holocaust Memorials and Meaning*. New Haven: Yale University Press, 1993.

———. *Writing and Rewriting the Holocaust: Narrative and the Consequences of Interpretation*. Bloomington: University of Indiana Press, 1988.

Zelizer, Barbie. *Remembering to Forget: Holocaust Memory through the Camera's Eye*. Chicago: The University of Chicago Press, 1998.

———, ed., *Visual Culture and the Holocaust*. New Brunswick, NJ: Rutgers University Press, 2001.

Zipes, Jack. "The Contemporary Fascination for Things Jewish: Toward a Minor Jewish Culture." Gilman and Remmler, *Reemerging Culture in Germany* 15–45.

———. "Documentary Drama in Germany: Mending the Circuit." *The Germanic Review* (January 1967): 51–62.

———. "The Negative German-Jewish Symbiosis." Lorenz, *Insiders and Outsiders* 144–154.

Zipes, Jack and Leslie Morris, eds., *The Changing German/Jewish Symbiosis, 1945–2000*. New York: Palgrave/St. Martin's Press, 2002.

INDEX